Change .com

Cyclops/Surge Duet
A Dixie Reapers Bad Boys Romance
Harley Wylde

Cyclops/Surge Duet
A Dixie Reapers Bad Boys Romance
Harley Wylde

All rights reserved.
Copyright ©2023 Harley Wylde

ISBN: 978-1-60521-857-1

Publisher:
Changeling Press LLC
315 N. Centre St.
Martinsburg, WV 25404
ChangelingPress.com

Printed in the U.S.A.

Editor: Crystal Easu
Cover Artist: Bryan Keller

The individual stories in this anthology have been previously released in E-Book format.

Table of Contents

Cyclops (Reckless Kings MC 5)
Harley Wylde

Leigha -- To say my dad is overprotective is too mild a description. Add in all my honorary uncles in the Dixie Reapers MC and going on dates is next to impossible. So when Lyssa invites me to visit her at the Reckless Kings in Tennessee, I jump at the chance. Maybe I can finally experience life a little. I know my family goes after bad men, the kind who hurt women and kids. I never counted on becoming a victim myself. The biker who comes to my rescue is... scary. Hot. And all alpha. He's exactly what I need!

Cyclops -- My stint in the military left me a parting gift. Scar tissue that not only left me blind in that eye, but makes the damn thing look spooky as fuck. I'm used to people staring. Mostly. Then my brothers had to stick me with the road name Cyclops. They're not funny, even if they think they are. Uncle Sam may no longer find me fit for duty, but it doesn't mean I'm useless. When I hear a scream, I don't hesitate. Thought I was saving a girl. Turns out she's a woman -- and one I shouldn't touch. The daughter of a Dixie Reaper, she's her daddy's little angel... and damn if I'm not tempted to lure her to the dark side and get her a little dirty.

Prologue

Leigha

"Foster, if you don't back off, I'm going to make sure you never have children." I gave him a shove. "Haven't you heard of personal space?"

I loved Foster. Like a brother. Even though we had different dads, we'd grown up together at the Dixie Reapers' compound. Bull, Foster's dad, might as well have been my uncle. Growing up in a motorcycle club meant I had a large extended family.

"Oh, he's heard about it. But he wants to be all up in yours," Owen said, giving me a wink. Rocky's oldest was certainly one of my favorites. Although, I wouldn't have minded if he wanted to lend more of a hand, getting Foster under control.

"I mean it. I don't think about any of you that way. It would be like kissing my brother, and I can assure you I have no desire to kiss Logan." I pushed again. If Dad came by right now... He might be called Preacher, but I knew he'd lay out Foster in a heartbeat.

Shoving Foster was like trying to move a damn mountain. Even though he was only twenty-one, about to be twenty-two, he'd already gotten his dad's height and overall build. And from what I'd heard, Bull had earned his name for both his size and his temperament. My dad said he was a bull in a china shop. Swing first, ask questions later.

"Damn." Owen winced. "Foster, that's worse than being friend-zoned. Time to throw in the towel."

"It was time the moment I said I wasn't interested... years ago." I folded my arms and glared. "Didn't I hear something about your mom and dad meeting because a bunch of guys tried to take advantage of her?"

Foster held up his hands and took a few steps away from me. "Whoa! I'm not anything like those assholes."

"Did I tell you no?" I asked. He couldn't be that dense, could he? Then again...

"Well, I mean, I wasn't trying to do anything but get you to kiss me, and maybe go on a date." His brow furrowed. "It's not the same thing."

My eyebrows lifted as his dad stepped up behind him, grabbed his neck, and hauled him off the floor. His booted feet dangled two inches above the wooden planks. "Foster, do we need to have another chat? Or perhaps you'd like to discuss it with your mother?"

"But, Dad..."

Bull gave him a shake before dropping him. "You wanted to prospect for the club, and I let you. Don't make me regret it. When a woman says no, you back the fuck off. If you can't understand that, then clearly I've raised you wrong."

"Thank you, Uncle Bull."

He gave me a wink. "Anytime, Leigha. Besides, your daddy might have been a minister in another life, but he wouldn't hesitate to gut anyone who messed with you. I like my son upright and breathing."

Torch stepped onto the clubhouse porch and passed a phone to me. I stared at it a moment before I realized it was his cell, and Lyssa's name was on the screen. I squealed and darted down the steps.

"Tell me everything," I said.

"You act like we don't talk all the time," she said.

"I know, but... the babies! We don't have any around here. Everyone's growing up. Our youngest is in kindergarten now. No one's having any more kids."

Lyssa laughed. "You sound like you have baby fever, and you're only twenty. I'm surprised you haven't roped someone into marrying you and giving you a family."

I sat in the grass, stretching out my legs and crossing my ankles. "Kind of hard to do when I can't even go on a date. Everyone watches me like a hawk. The only guy who'd even attempt to date me is Foster, and I keep telling him no. I don't want anyone at the club. Not even Viking, even though I know all my friends drool over him. The guys here are all family. You know?"

Lyssa hesitated a moment. I wasn't sure if it was a good pause or a bad one.

"All too well," she said. "What if you came to visit me here? I don't know about happily ever after, but I bet we can find someone to take you on a few dates. You could get a little experience under your belt to better prepare you. And by experience, I don't mean jump into bed with anyone. I don't need your dad, or mine, tracking me down for corrupting you. There are some decent guys around town."

"No one at the Reckless Kings who might be interested?" I asked. I might not want anyone at the Dixie Reapers, but I had a hard time picturing myself with a guy who wasn't a biker. Family dinners would be weird if I dated someone from town. Like a tax accountant or lawyer.

"Except for the Prospects, everyone here is a decade older than you, or more."

She seemed to forget her husband was much older than she was. My parents weren't exactly close in age either. In fact, I couldn't think of a single Dixie Reaper who'd settled down with someone who wasn't at least eight years younger. Most had a bigger gap than that between them, and every couple was blissfully in love.

"You know as well as I do that age is just a number, Lyssa. I don't care about that. But I want a guy who will treat me right, listen when I say no, and look at me the way I catch my dad watching my mom. Like I'm the only woman on earth."

"Pack a bag. I'll call and talk to your mom, smooth things over. You know she's the only one who could convince your dad to let you come here. Will you be okay driving that far on your own?"

"I'm not a baby," I pointed out.

"I know, Leigha. Sorry. I guess being a mom has rewired my brain. Beast says I even try to mother the Prospects. It's not intentional."

"I forgive you." I smiled. "Especially if you help me go on a few dates. And let me get some baby time in."

"Consider it done. I'll call your mom now. Tell my dad I had to go because the kids were screaming."

She ended the call, and I carried the cell phone back to Torch. He glanced at the screen before shoving the phone into his pocket.

"The kids were fussing," I said. He gave a nod and went back into the clubhouse.

I watched him a moment, wondering if anyone else noticed the slight hitch when he walked. Torch wasn't exactly getting any younger. I didn't know for certain how old he was, but I knew he had to be in his late sixties or early seventies. What would happen when he had to step down as President? I wasn't sure I was ready for that. I didn't think any of us were.

"I need to run home," I said, giving Bull a hug. "Thanks again for helping me."

"Anytime." He patted my back. "Next time Owen stands around like a dumbass, kick him in the balls. He should have been able to control Foster, since the idiot can't do it himself."

I smiled and hurried to my car. I needed to pack and get on the road, preferably before my dad came up with a reason for me to stay home.

I should have moved faster.

Chapter One

Leigha
One Month Later

I knew the Reckless Kings' compound was nearby. Instead of going straight there, like I'd promised, I took a slight detour through the nearest town. It seemed harmless enough. Sightseeing never hurt anyone, right? I pulled to a stop outside a line of shops and got out.

"Stretching my legs," I mumbled, thinking of what excuse I'd give Lyssa for being late. My phone rang again. I saw my dad's name and ignored the call. At twenty, I was old enough to leave town without my father's permission. He didn't seem to understand that, though. He'd called me no less than fifteen times in the last two hours.

The incoming text notification sounded, and I unlocked the screen. *Mom.* Could have been worse. At least Dad hadn't opted to berate me through messages instead of during a call or in person. *Your dad is pissed. You shouldn't have snuck out while we weren't home.*

I wondered if she realized how that sounded. Yes, I still lived at home. Not by choice, but necessity. I hesitated to respond but didn't want her to worry. If I didn't answer, she'd panic and think I was lying dead in a ditch. Then Dad would leave the house and track me down. This was my chance at a little freedom. *I didn't sneak out. I'm twenty years old, Mom. I'll be fine.*

After I sent the text, I shoved my phone into my pocket and browsed the shops on the main strip. I found the cutest café and bookshop. A calico cat in the window lured me inside.

"Aren't you pretty?" I cooed and gave the kitty a scratch behind the ear. She purred and rubbed her cheek against my hand. It made me wish I could have a cat. My dad would throw a fit if I brought one home.

Walking away from the cute bundle of fluff, I perused the shelves. In less than ten minutes, I'd picked up three books. As I reached for a fourth, I pulled my hand back. Books were my kryptonite. I'd never bought just one.

Knowing I needed to watch my spending, I checked out, got a coffee to go, and went back to my car. Lyssa might have promised me a few dates with some locals, but I knew it wasn't a guarantee. If I couldn't have an actual boyfriend, at least I'd have new ones in my books. The shirtless cowboy cover looked especially intriguing.

I set the sack down and reached into my pocket for my keys. If my dad had watched me walk out, unprepared to get into my vehicle, I'd have never heard the end of it. He constantly worried someone would snatch me and I'd disappear. I couldn't blame him. The club had seen a lot of darkness and helped save women who'd fallen prey to human traffickers.

I'd just pulled my keys free when I felt someone behind me. The heat of their body pressed into mine and I froze. How had I not heard anyone approaching? All the training I'd received flew out the window. My hand shook as the man caged me between his arms. He leaned in closer, the smell of beer and cigarettes making me cringe.

"Pretty little thing like you shouldn't be out here all alone."

Bluff your way out of this, Leigha. I licked my lips and tried to relax my body. "What makes you think I'm alone?"

"Saw you pull up. I don't see a man with you. Unless you prefer women?" He put his lips near my ear and bit down hard enough I yelped. "That it? Maybe you just need a good, hard fucking to change your mind. Prove to you cock is better."

No, no, no. This couldn't be happening. My heart raced and I couldn't stop my hands from trembling. "I like men." I took a breath and held it for a moment. "When one gets here, let me know."

"You bitch!" He spun me around, making me drop my coffee and my keys. He pressed his forearm against my throat. "Think I'm not a man? Guess I need to prove otherwise."

"Danny, there's too many people," another guy said. I glanced his way and realized he'd be no help. The look in his eyes said he didn't care for what his friend wanted to do to me, but he was too chicken to make him stop.

"Then we'll take her somewhere else." He yanked me away from the car, his hand bruising my arm as he dragged me toward an alley. I struggled and fought, hoping someone would see us. If they did, they pretended otherwise. He shoved me against the brick building and started tearing at my clothes.

He ripped my shirt down the middle and started working on unfastening my jeans. "Help! Someone..."

His fist connected with my stomach before he slapped me across the face. I gasped and coughed. "Shut up. You keep fighting, it's going to be even worse."

"Never." I spat in his face. "I'll never let you touch me."

He shoved my jeans down my hips and tried ripping my panties. I kicked at him, stomped on his feet, and clawed at his face. I did everything I could to break free. It only pissed him off more.

I refused to let this piece of filth take my

virginity. Reaching up, I jammed my thumbs into his
eyes and pushed as hard as I could. He screamed and
backed up. I didn't relent and clung to him like a
barnacle. I wanted his eyes to pop, to make him suffer
and remember this moment the next time he tried to
hurt a woman. He'd gotten the drop on me, and I'd
frozen like a damn deer in the headlights. But down
deep, I was my father's daughter, and while I might
not wear a patch, I was part of the Dixie Reapers by
blood. No way I'd let this asshole win.

"I'm *not* a damsel you can bully and terrify. I'll
kill you before I let you rape me." He knocked me to
the ground. Before I could stand, someone entered the
alley.

I eyed him, tensing as I wondered if he was here
to help, or to join my would-be rapist. Then I noticed
the leather cut over his shoulders, and his attire. Biker.
Relief flooded me. If he was part of a club, he'd likely
be from the Reckless Kings. And if he wasn't, my
chances were still good he might help me. Even the
weekend riders seemed to have a certain code they
followed.

The new man went after Danny. I saw the back
of his cut and smiled. *Reckless Kings MC.* Since he was
one of Beast's men, I knew he wouldn't hurt me. He
threw punches at the guy's face and torso, not holding
back. While he whaled on the asshole, I pulled up my
jeans. My shirt was a lost cause. Even trying to tie it
didn't help, so I let it fall to the ground. The worrier
who'd tried to tell his friend not to hurt me had fled
down the alley.

Danny fell to the ground, and the biker nailed
him in the ribs with the toe of his boot, then kneeled
down beside him. "If I ever see you put your hands on
a woman again, I will cut them off. Then I'll remove

your tongue. Your eyes. Your ears. And finally, I'll cut off your dick and shove it down your throat. Assuming I can find something that small without a magnifying glass. Understood?"

Danny groaned and nodded. The biker stood and kicked him in the face, knocking him out cold. When he turned to face me, I scanned his cut. *Cyclops*. I would have asked why he had that name, but the guy wore an eye patch over his left eye. There had to be a story there, and I'd love to hear it. "Thank you," I said.

He nodded and shrugged out of his cut. Reaching behind his neck, he pulled his shirt off and handed it to me. "Better cover up. Did I get here in time?"

"Yeah. He got close, but..." I pressed my lips together as I put on his shirt. A spicy scent made me want to lift the material to my nose and inhale, but I figured the guy might find that creepy. And weird.

My phone started chiming non-stop. The tone told me it was Logan, which meant my twin had sensed my fear. It had happened one other time when we were learning to drive. Except in reverse. Logan had taken Dad's bike out without permission and wrecked it. I'd sensed his fear and pain the moment it happened. I'd need to text him back before he freaked out. Well, more than he already had.

He slipped his cut back over his shoulders and I tried not to stare at his broad chest, or the fact his abs were well-defined. I definitely didn't eye the happy trail and imagine what he'd look like with his pants unzipped. Reaching up, I made sure I wasn't drooling. On the plus side, the incident with the fucker on the ground hadn't soured me toward men.

"Come on, kitten. I'll walk you to your car. Make sure you get inside safely."

I walked over to him and wrapped my fingers around his bicep. He reached up and covered my hand with his before leading me out of the alley. I pointed to my car and noticed he scanned his surroundings as we made our way over to it. I could feel the coiled tension in him and wondered if he'd gotten that way from being with the Reckless Kings, or if he'd been in the military. His behavior reminded me of all the men back home I called family, especially the ones who'd served our country.

He helped me gather my things, and I was thankful no one had stolen my purse and wallet. I didn't even remember dropping them. I eyed the empty coffee cup forlornly and picked it up. After I tossed it into the trash, Cyclops reached out to take my hand.

"Why don't we sit a minute? You have to be a bit shaken after that."

I'd thought I'd been doing an admirable job of hiding it. Apparently, I hadn't. I wondered if he knew who I was. Had Lyssa told anyone about my visit? I didn't know if I'd be staying at her house or elsewhere. She'd just said to pack and head up to Tennessee, and that's exactly what I'd done.

"You don't mind babysitting me?" I asked. "And your shirt... They won't let you inside without one."

He smiled, and my knees went weak. The man was beyond sexy. A hero. Smelled incredible. Rode a bike. I couldn't think of anything *not* to like about him. Although, Lyssa hadn't sounded too keen on the idea of me hooking up with one of the Reckless Kings. Which meant this mouthwatering man was likely off-limits.

He held the door to the café open for me, and I stepped through. I'd expected someone to demand he find a shirt or leave. Instead, they eyed his cut and didn't say a word. I wasn't sure how to feel about their reaction. Did it mean they feared the Reckless Kings? Or respected them?

The calico came to greet me, and I kneeled down to pet her. She placed her paw on my thigh and I couldn't resist. I lifted her into my arms and stood, nuzzling her soft fur and wishing I could take her home.

"Have a thing for cats?" Cyclops asked.

"I've always wanted one."

"Why don't you get a table and sit with her? Tell me what you had to drink before, and I'll order you a new one."

"Medium roast coffee." He stared and waited. "That's it. Just a medium roast coffee."

"Huh." He scratched at his beard. "Don't know many women who get plain coffee. I think the two of us are going to be friends."

"I'm Leigha," I said, holding my hand out to him, the one not holding the cat.

"Cyclops." His fingers closed around mine and I held back a sigh. Why couldn't I find a guy like him to date? His touch lingered. He seemed reluctant to pull away. Did he feel the same spark I did? "I'll get our coffees, then we can talk awhile. I don't want you driving until all the shakes are gone."

I nodded and found a seat. The cat seemed content to let me hold her, so I got in all the cuddles I could. It wouldn't be long before I'd have to put her down. Getting my own place looked better and better. I could have a pet. And my parents wouldn't constantly hover.

Cyclops stood in line, and I admired him. He folded his arms, feet braced apart, and eyed the menu.

Since he'd said he was getting two coffees, I wasn't sure why he needed to study it so hard. A coffee order didn't seem complicated enough for that much scrutiny. Unless it had to do with his vision. The line moved slowly. I didn't mind. Being here with him, and the cat, was exactly what I needed. I could feel the calm settling over me. Too bad I couldn't take them both home with me.

The man in the alley had nearly raped me. No matter how hard I smiled, I wasn't doing okay. Not even a little. I knew my father had gone up against men like that before. Still, it never occurred to me I could be a victim. The club had trained me to take care of myself. But the first time someone attacked me, I forgot everything I'd learned. If my father ever found out... Nope. I wouldn't even go there.

I couldn't tell Lyssa either. If she knew, she'd probably lock me away.

My phone started blowing up again. More texts from Logan. *I'm fine. I'm on a date!*

I saw the little dots and knew he would reply in a moment. *I felt your fear.*

Shit. I needed to think fast. *Misunderstanding. Someone startled me and I jumped to conclusions.*

More dots. *I don't believe you, but I'll let it go. For now.*

I had a reprieve, even if it would be short.

Every time I so much as blinked, I saw that man's hateful face as he'd yanked my pants down. The trembling in my hands increased, and I held the cat a little tighter. She didn't seem to mind. Maybe she understood how much I needed this right now.

Cyclops returned with our drinks, and I noticed a sack in his hand. He set it on the table in front of me. "Thought you might need something to eat. It's a plain bagel, and I got both cream cheese and avocado. Wasn't sure which you'd like."

"Thank you." I smiled up at him. "That was thoughtful. I'm feeling a little better. I still can't believe I..."

He sat and reached over, placing his hand on mine. "You're sure I got there in time?"

I nodded. "Yeah. It was stupid. I know better than to go to my car without having my keys already in my hand. Then he came up behind me, and I blanked on everything I learned about defending myself."

If I kept saying I was doing all right, maybe it would be true. Fake it 'til you make it, or something like that. I couldn't let anyone see how rattled I felt. A biker's daughter needed to be tough. I felt more like a marshmallow at the moment.

"Who taught you self-defense?" he asked, taking a sip of his coffee.

"My dad and his... brothers." I eyed him, wondering if he'd figured out yet who I was. So far, it seemed Lyssa hadn't told the Reckless Kings about my visit. I was certain Beast knew, but did anyone else?

"Do you need to call them? I can wait with you if you'd prefer for one of them to take you home."

I cocked my head to the side. "I'm a little old to ask Daddy to come pick me up. Besides, they don't live here. I came to visit a friend."

His fingers caressed my hand before he pulled away. "Boyfriend?"

I shook my head. "No. But you know her."

"Is that right? How do you figure I know this friend of yours? Town might be small, but it's not *that* small."

"Because she's your President's old lady. I came

to see Lyssa."

His eyebrows rose. "So when you say your dad and his brothers, either you met Lyssa at college, or you mean the Dixie Reapers taught you self-defense. I'm betting on option two. Which one is your dad?"

"Preacher."

"Thought his kids were all younger." He drank more of his coffee and leaned back in his seat. He crossed his booted feet beside my chair.

"I'm an adult, if that's what you're asking."

"Good to know." He smiled. "Eat your bagel, and you can follow me back to the compound. Unless you want to ride on the back of my bike? I could ask a Prospect to come get your car."

"You'd let me ride with you?" I asked.

He gave me a sexy smirk before taking another swallow of coffee. "I'd love nothing more."

I'd read novels where the heroine felt butterflies when she met the hero. I now understood. It felt like a dozen butterflies were swooping around inside my stomach. I drank my coffee and ate my bagel, not once taking my gaze off Cyclops. It felt a little surreal. Why did a man like him want anything to do with me?

* * *

Cyclops

The moment she said her daddy was Preacher, I should have backed the hell off. From what I knew of the man, he had a protective streak ten miles wide when it came to his kids. Especially his daughters. Something told me she'd be keeping what happened a secret, not only from her dad but from Lyssa too. She'd fought hard, even if the asshole had knocked her down. If I'd been a moment later, I worried he'd have succeeded.

She smiled brightly and did her best to show the world it hadn't bothered her. Unless you were looking hard enough to see the tinge of fear still in her eyes or notice the way her hands shook now and then. What happened would haunt her for a while. When she went to bed tonight, she'd relive those moments. There wasn't a damn thing I could do about it either. If she screamed out during a nightmare, anyone nearby would hear her. Then her secret would be out. Unless she'd had some other trauma I didn't know about or scared easily from horror movies. But the girl who'd fought back in the alley didn't seem like the kind to scare easily.

I eyed the cat, now curled up asleep at her feet. Anyone could see how much she loved the little creature. If Leigha lived here, I'd see about buying the cat for her. I didn't know if it was up for adoption or belonged to the owner of the café. But I'd learned most things had a price. The question was more about how much you were willing to pay.

"You visiting for a specific reason?" I asked.

"I needed a break. I love my family, but they can be overbearing. Not to mention it's hard to date with my dad and all the Dixie Reapers scaring everyone off."

Well, now. Wasn't that interesting? "You came up here looking for a date?"

"Yes. Although, I wouldn't be averse to finding a boyfriend. I wouldn't mind moving up this way if I could find a job and support myself." She looked down at her coffee and nibbled on her lower lip. The way she twirled the cup belied her anxiety and hesitation over whatever was on her mind. I waited her out, hoping she'd be open and honest with me. Whatever she had to say, I wouldn't think less of her. "I asked Lyssa about anyone available in your club. She seemed to think no one would be interested."

I tensed and forced myself not to move. I wanted to lean closer and assure her that was the furthest thing from the truth. Hell, I'd love nothing more than to take her home with me, and I had a feeling a few of my brothers would be more than slightly interested. Even knowing if I messed around with her, it would mean claiming her as mine, I still wanted her.

"Not sure why she'd think that," I said.

She took a breath and let it out slowly before lifting her gaze to mine again. "Would you be willing to go on a date with me? Or am I not your type?"

"You mean brave, beautiful, and sweet? Can't say that I know any guy who'd walk away from a woman like that. So, yeah. You're my type, and I'd do far more than date you." Her cheeks turned pink, and I smiled as I took another swallow of my coffee. I loved seeing that blush. She reeked of innocence, and if she'd had trouble going on dates at home, I'd bet good money she was still a virgin.

And now my dick was hard as granite, just thinking about being her first. Her only. I cleared my throat and decided it would be best to steer the conversation in another direction.

"If Lyssa said none of us would be interested, maybe she doesn't want you paired up with a Reckless King. Might want to talk to her before this goes any further." I paused. "Although this is kind of a date right now, isn't it?"

"You want this to be a date?" she asked, her voice so soft I nearly missed what she said.

"Guess that depends, kitten. Do *you* want it to be one?"

She nodded. "I'd like that."

"Then this is our first date." I settled into the chair more. "You said you're an adult. Exactly how badly am I robbing the cradle right now?"

She smiled. "I'm twenty."

I took another swallow of coffee and realized I'd drained the cup. I needed another one, maybe with a splash of something extra. Like rum. "I'm eighteen years older than you."

She pressed her lips together, but I saw a sparkle in her eyes. Hell. I had a feeling she was about to poke fun of my age. And I'd let her. Anything to see her smile right now.

"That makes you about the same age as my mother," she said. "And my dad is a lot older than her. In fact, that makes the gap between us pretty close to the age difference between them. So if you're worried my dad will be pissed, he can't say much. Not without being a hypocrite."

"Good to know." It still left me wondering why Lyssa hadn't wanted the sweetheart across from me to date anyone with the Reckless Kings. Of course, we seldom dated. We either hooked up for a casual fuck, or we outright claimed a woman. Had she only been trying to spare Leigha from getting treated like a club whore? She had to know none of us would do something like that -- not with Preacher's daughter.

She looked around the little café and sighed. "It's time to go, isn't it?"

"We can get another cup of coffee, if you'd prefer to sit awhile longer."

"You'd be okay with that?" she asked.

I uncrossed my ankles and leaned in closer. "Why wouldn't I want to spend more time with you?"

She glanced away. "It's not something I'm used to. Except with Foster. He's had a hard time taking no for an answer, but Bull straightened him out."

"Foster?" I asked, hoping the jealousy I felt didn't bleed into my voice.

"He's Bull's son. I have no idea why he's been so insistent. I've told him no countless times. It wasn't until Bull lifted him off the floor and shook him like a rag doll he got the hint." She smiled faintly. "And he threatened to not let him prospect for the club if he didn't learn to back off when a woman isn't interested."

"I'm buying Bull a drink next time I see him," I said. I didn't care if Foster was Bull's son. If he'd pushed Leigha for more than she was willing to give, then he needed his teeth knocked down his damn throat.

"I don't think he'd have actually hurt me." She twisted the cup in her hands. "He seemed offended when I compared him to the men our clubs take down. He said he'd just wanted a date. It never occurred to him me saying no repeatedly and him cornering me meant he'd crossed a line."

"No offense to Bull's kid, but he's a fucking idiot," I said.

"I won't disagree with you." She held her cup out to me. "If you were serious about staying longer, I'd love another cup."

I reached for it, my fingers touching hers. "I'd be happy to get you another. Or you could follow me to the compound, and I can brew a pot at my house. Unless you'd be uncomfortable. We're still strangers, so I'd understand if you prefer a public setting."

"How far do you live from Beast's house? Once Lyssa sees my car, she'll know I'm there."

"Other side of the compound, opposite direction." I stood with both our cups. "Tell you what.

I'll get us a refill here, and after you've let Lyssa know you're in town, we can plan our next date. Maybe you can come over for dinner tomorrow."

I could tell she enjoyed spending time with me, and hell if I didn't want to know more about her. But I also didn't want her getting into trouble. If Lyssa expected her today, then it meant Beast did too. Last thing I needed was the Pres breathing down my neck because I'd waylaid his old lady's friend.

Not to mention, with her being a Dixie Reaper by birth, I needed to do this the right way. Beast might have claimed Lyssa with no one's prior approval, but he had more clout as the President of the Reckless Kings. I might be a patched member, but that was it. I didn't hold an officer's position, and I wasn't sure her dad would think I was anywhere near good enough for her.

I ordered our refills, then carried them back to the table. I noticed the cat had wandered off and found a patch of sunlight. It sprawled on the floor. I stepped over and set our cups down on the table. Leigha had her phone out, and I saw Lyssa's name light up on the screen, right before the Allman Brothers' *Midnight Rider* started playing. I shook my head. Leigha kept surprising me. In good ways.

"Better answer or she'll freak out," I said.

She picked up the phone and accepted the call. "Hey, Lyssa."

I watched her facial expressions, sliding her coffee closer to her. She mouthed a *thank you* before taking a swallow.

"I'm fine. I swear I'm not dead in a ditch." She rolled her eyes. "Did my mom call? Because that's something she'd say."

Her gaze cut to me, and I wondered what the

Pres' old lady was saying to her. She made a few mmm-hmms and even nodded, like Lyssa could see her through the phone call. Her eyes went wide, and she glanced out the windows.

"You don't have to send anyone to get me. I'll be there in a little while." She pressed her lips together, and I saw panic flash in her eyes. "I'm having some coffee, Lyssa. It was a long drive, and my parents were blowing up my phone."

Her cheeks went bright pink, and I settled into my chair more. I didn't know what brought that blush to her cheeks, but I damn sure wanted to find out.

"You know why! I don't care what sob story my mother gave you. I refuse to be under house arrest because my dad realized I was serious about wanting to date. It's not the nineteen twenties. He can't lock me up and throw away the key simply because he doesn't want me to grow up. And don't you enable him! I told you I was coming to visit, and I am."

The blush deepened, and she looked ready to sink through the floor in embarrassment. Pulling out my phone, I lent her a hand. I looked through my contacts and found Beast's name, then pressed the button to open a text message.

Pres, call off Lyssa. Her friend is safe. I'm watching over her.

I saw the little dots and knew I'd get a response in a moment. Watching Leigha, I saw the curious look she cast my way. Made me wonder if Beast already said something to his woman. My phone chimed with his reply.

Keep her safe. She's Preacher's oldest daughter, and he's not taking this well.

Shit. *Need to talk when I get back.*

I saw the dots appear, then stop. They showed

up again, only to stop once more. Then my damn phone rang. He didn't even bother with a hello.

"What the fuck does that mean?" he asked when the call connected.

"It means I'm intrigued. But your woman told her none of us would be interested. I'd like to know more about that before I make another move."

"You're serious?" Beast asked. "Do you know anything about her family?"

"They're Dixie Reapers." Leigha's gaze lifted to mine, and I winked at her, letting her know everything was fine.

"Preacher lost his first wife in a car accident. Swore he'd never love again until he met Saint's twin sister. Leigha has a twin, Logan, and they're Preacher's first kids. He's protective as fuck over his family. Not sure anyone will ever be good enough for his girls. He's pissed because she snuck out while they were gone. Even though I can't blame her. They've got a tight leash on Leigha, and she's ready to break free and start her life."

"Good to know," I murmured. "You have a problem with this?"

"With you claiming her? Or toying with her? Because those are two different things," Beast said.

"The first one."

"Nope. I'd gladly welcome her into the family. But if you're going to do something, you might want to make it fast. Something tells me her daddy will be on our doorstep in the next forty-eight hours."

"So much for taking things slow," I said.

"When you know, you know." Beast sighed. "I'll stall him as long as I can, but he's coming here one way or another."

"Tell your woman Leigha is fine. I'd like to take

her to my place."

"I'll make sure Lyssa stands down," Beast said. "That all we needed to discuss?"

"No, but I'm not saying anything else over the phone. I'll text you later. It's something I want to keep between the two of us for now."

"All right. Just keep an eye on her, Cyclops. No pun intended. Anything happens to Leigha, and all our asses are on the line," Beast said, then I heard the call disconnect.

I had a feeling he was going to hit the roof when I told him what happened. As much as I didn't want to break my word to Leigha, someone needed to know about the asshole who tried to rape her. For one, the fact I kicked the shit out of him could blow back on the club. Second, if she went into town, she'd need protection. Cockroaches like that one would come back for more. The moment he saw her alone somewhere, he'd try again. Or do much worse.

I'd rather risk her ire than her life.

Only hoped she'd see it that way too.

Chapter Two

Leigha

Having Lyssa worry about me enough to call was both nice and embarrassing. I doubted the hunky biker across from me had people check up on him if he ran a little late. It made me feel like a child instead of a grown woman out on a date, which was precisely why I'd left home. Yes, something bad happened, but it could have been worse. If Lyssa or my parents ever found out, I'd never be able to leave the house again.

I tried not to eavesdrop on Cyclops' conversation but hearing the words *Dixie Reapers* piqued my interest. I wondered who had called him. My money was on Beast, but how had he known we were together? Unless... I'd noticed him texting. Had he told his President he'd found me in town? I didn't know how to feel about that.

By the time he ended his call, and I hung up with Lyssa, I felt nervous. Would he still want to spend time with me? It had to be less hassle dating someone closer to his age. I doubted a woman in her thirties, or even in her late twenties, had family and friends calling to ask where she was all the time. Or worse, trying to keep her home.

"Beast knows you're here with me," Cyclops said. "I told him I'd take you to my place when we left. That's, of course, if you want to go there. Or I can lead the way to Beast's house. Entirely up to you."

"I'm curious about something," I said. He motioned for me to continue. "You've seen how everyone treats me. Lyssa's call is the least of it. I'm twenty and they act like I'm a teenager. There's no freedom for me at home, and it looks like it will be the same here. I'd thought Lyssa would be enough of a buffer I could live a little, even if it was only for a few days."

"You plan on going home that soon?" he asked.

"I don't know." I looked down at my coffee for a moment, gathering my thoughts. "I wanted a taste of freedom, the chance to be myself without worrying I'd have a bodyguard breathing down my neck, or half the club trying to scare off men. I haven't even been here a day and my family keeps texting and calling. Lyssa is checking up on me, and I just..."

"Feel caged?" he asked.

I nodded. "Exactly. It's like I'm a prisoner. How am I supposed to figure out who I am if no one will let me do anything? I get it. My dad lost his first wife long before he met Mom. Add in all the darkness he's seen as part of the Dixie Reapers, and now he's terrified something will happen to us. But living in constant fear isn't living at all."

He smiled. "Seems like you have it figured out. Mostly. Beast thinks your dad will show up in the next day or so. I'm not sure how much freedom you'll have when that happens."

Naturally. I should have known better. The moment my dad found out where I'd gone, he'd probably started planning to come collect me, like a wayward child or pet. If I went back home with him, I'd die a virgin. There was no way he'd let me out of his sight anytime soon. I loved him. More than my next breath. But being Preacher's daughter had a downside. It meant being smothered with worry and affection. My mom loved how protective my dad was, and I could understand. Being his daughter, it was different.

"Why did you want me to go to your house? If my dad is on his way, I'll be going back home soon. He won't let me stay."

Cyclops folded his arms and studied me. "I think there are a few things for us to discuss. This café isn't the right place for that type of conversation."

The butterflies returned, flapping around my stomach. "Something we can't talk about here?"

He glanced around before meeting my gaze again. "I guess we could, but I wouldn't recommend it. Do you trust me?"

I nodded. He'd saved me, and even if he hadn't, since he belonged to the Reckless Kings, that was good enough for me. I knew Beast didn't keep traitors around, or evil men. Since he'd spoken to Beast, and the President was aware we were at the café together, it had to mean Beast trusted him.

"Then follow me to the compound. We'll go straight to my house and discuss your options. Beast knows where to find you, and he'll hold Lyssa back. But, kitten, it's not a horrible thing to have people love you so much they worry. I know it seems like the end of the world, and I'd imagine it's more than a little frustrating, but your parents only want to keep you safe. Nothing wrong with that."

"I know. It's overwhelming and tiresome, but I understand why they do it. Doesn't make it any more tolerable." I smiled. "Lead the way. I'd love to hear those options."

He stood and held out his hand. I took it, letting him help me up. On the way to my car, instead of paying attention to my surroundings, I admittedly stared at Cyclops' ass. Then again, if anyone tried to fuck with me right now, they'd have a pissed-off biker to deal with. He'd already proven he could protect me -- more importantly, that he *would*.

He led me to my car and waited for me to get in and start the engine. I watched as he walked farther down the street to his bike. When he drove past my parking space and stopped, I backed out and followed him to the Reckless Kings' compound. I'd never been before, and their clubhouse looked amazing. The entire compound screamed wealth, and I tried not to think about how they'd earned that money.

We pulled through the gates, and I caught the curious glance from the Prospect we passed. I stuck close to Cyclops and stopped on the street in front of his house. He parked in the garage. Far enough to the side I could easily fit my car in there too. I hesitated only a moment before doing exactly that, then shut off my engine.

Was I really doing this? Whatever *this* was. I didn't think I'd imagined the connection between us at the café. It made me both eager and terrified to hear what he had to say. He rapped his knuckles against my window, and I took a breath, then let it out. Grabbing my purse, I got out of the car. Cyclops reached down to take my hand and led me into his house.

The outside looked more like a log cabin with a red metal roof. Inside, it was breathtaking. The walls were the same timber used outside. His kitchen wasn't large and opened to the living room. An island in the center had a cooktop on one side and the other had barstools lined up. Clearly, it doubled as his table. Natural wood and black appliances gave the space a warm feel. I looked out into the living room and nearly gasped at the vaulted ceiling. A stone fireplace ran up the center of the room. On the backside, he had a small table with two chairs. A deck of cards sat on top. In front of the fireplace sat a leather sofa that looked inviting. I wanted to curl up there on a cold winter night.

"Your home is incredible," I said.

He smiled. "Thanks. When it was time for my house to be built, Beast asked what I liked. I told him I'd always wanted a cabin, gave him the specifics, and he made it happen."

I gave in to temptation and sat on the sofa, kicking off my shoes and curling my legs under me. Cyclops took the spot next to me, putting his arm along the back of the cushions. I felt a tug on my hair and glanced his way.

"I'm sure you get asked a lot, and it's rude as hell, but I have to know... The eye patch. Why do you wear it?" I asked.

"Served in the Army. Got a little too close to an IED that went off. Shrapnel hit my eye. Left me not only blind -- the scar tissue makes my eye look creepy as fuck. Scares children, and quite a few adults. It's easier to keep it covered," he said. He tugged his cut open, and I stared. "Got a few scars down that side of my torso too."

I wasn't sure how I'd missed those before. He'd been without a shirt all this time, and I'd drooled over his wide chest more than once. It seemed the attack had left me more rattled than I'd realized. Those scars weren't something I'd have ever missed before.

"May I see?" I asked. He paused a moment before removing the eye patch. The iris of his eye had turned milky and I could see why some would find it off-putting. To me, the patch was far worse. I reached out and ran my fingers along his cheek under the blind eye. "It doesn't make you less attractive. I'll agree it lends a certain air of danger. Personally, it doesn't bother me. In fact, I'd rather see all of your face than have you wear the eye patch."

He sucked in a breath and let it out, his body relaxing. I hadn't even realized he'd been so tense. It made me wonder how many people had told him to cover his eye. Then I wanted to hunt them all down and punch them in the nose for being assholes.

"I guess that's going to make our talk a little easier," he said.

"It has to do with your eye?"

He snorted. "No, but the fact it doesn't scare you, or make you want to gag, is a bonus. It might surprise you the things I've heard since it happened."

"People are idiots. Your blindness doesn't change who you are as a person. You came to my rescue today without knowing who I was. Which means you'd have done the same for any woman you heard in trouble. To me, that makes you a hero."

He shook his head. "Not a hero, kitten. Just in the right place at the right time."

"We'll have to agree to disagree. What did you want to discuss that you couldn't say in the café?"

He wound my hair around his fingers, and I fought the urge to lean into his touch. Other than Foster's annoying habit of cornering me, this was the most attention I'd ever had from a guy who seemed interested in me romantically.

"I talked to Beast about what you wanted. To date someone without your family breathing down your neck or trying to ruin any relationship you tried to build. He said there were only two paths. A casual hook-up or…"

"Or what?" I asked.

"Or claiming you. He asked me which I intended, and warned if it was a hook-up, your dad would probably bury me in an unmarked grave." He grinned. "Well, not in those exact words, but I got the gist of it."

My heart raced. Was he asking what I thought he

was? I'd heard the stories. I knew the Dixie Reapers fell fast and hard for their women. Especially Venom. I'd never thought it would happen to me. But what if. I was wrong? What if he meant he'd wanted something casual and only wanted to see where I stood on the matter?

Now I felt nervous. I ran my hands up and down my thighs and tried not to fidget too much.

"I can see the wheels turning," he said. "Something tells me you're jumping to the wrong conclusion. If you're wondering, I told Beast I was hoping you'd agree to be mine."

"After one coffee date?" I asked.

"Kitten, the moment I saw you in that alley, I wanted to toss you over my shoulder and bring you home. I only tried taking things slow for your benefit. Now we have your dad's imminent arrival, and that changes things. I no longer have a few days to a week to convince you we'd be good together."

"Well... I can't exactly agree to spend the rest of my life with someone I've never even kissed. What if you don't like the way I kiss? Or you could be one of those guys who's all tongue and slobbers all over me."

He smirked. "Only one way to find out. I'm game if you are."

I leaned in closer and tipped my face up to him. Cyclops tugged me closer, and his lips brushed mine. The spark I felt had me gasping. He took advantage and slipped his tongue between my lips. I moaned and reached out, gripping his cut in my hand. He kissed me soft and slow, taking his time. My toes curled and heat pooled in my belly. His beard felt soft against my skin.

Cyclops released me, but I didn't move away. If anything, I wanted to crawl into his lap. One kiss and I was hooked. I need more. Craved it. The man was a divine kisser. Sure, I had little to compare it to, but I'd never thought a kiss could have me ready to tear off my clothes and offer myself up to someone. I'd been wrong.

"You want to claim me?" I asked.

He nodded. "I do. Never wanted to keep a woman before."

"You've likely guessed it already, but I haven't been with anyone."

"I know. You have no idea how much it turns me on, knowing I'd be your first. Your only."

I licked my lips and leaned in to kiss him. I crawled into his lap, straddling him, and placed my hands on his cheeks. Cyclops banded an arm around my back and tugged me even closer. I felt the hard ridge of his cock press against me and couldn't help but grind against him a little. He nipped my lip and pulled back.

"Slow down, kitten. After today, I'm not about to rush you into anything."

I stilled and stared at him. "Because of the man in the alley?"

"Yeah. You might think you're okay right now, but that's going to come back to haunt you later. When you close your eyes tonight, I have a feeling you'll have a nightmare or two. Wish like hell I could do something about it."

Did I dare? I ran my fingers through his beard, then down over his chest. I traced the stitching on his cut before holding his gaze. "You can. You could replace those memories with something better. The scariest part was knowing he'd take my virginity. If he had, I don't know that I'd have ever wanted sex for the rest of my life. But he didn't. And now I need something to think about. I want to feel your hands on me. See the way you look at me when I take off my clothes. Then when I go to sleep, it will be you I see and not him."

"Sounds like you have it all figured out," he said.

"Not even close, but it's a start."

"You sure?" He held me a little tighter. "Once we go down that path, there's no going back. I take your innocence, and you're mine. Not just for right now, but for the rest of our lives. Or I guess the rest of mine. You're definitely going to outlive me."

"Then I guess we need to cram a lifetime into whatever years we have together. Does that mean you'll do it?"

He cupped my cheek. "Yeah, kitten. I'll be the one to take your virginity. To keep you. When your dad gets here, he's going to lose his shit. You prepared for that?"

"No. Not even a little." I smiled. "But I want this. Want *you*."

He kissed me again, a short kiss. "When we're done, I need to call Beast. Technically, the club needs to vote on you being my old lady. But I'd rather demand those fuckers let me keep you. It's always fun to light a match and see which one of my brothers will go off like a stick of dynamite."

"Then lead the way. I'm all yours."

He cupped my ass in his hands and stood. I wrapped my legs around his waist and Cyclops carried me up a staircase I hadn't noticed. A small balcony overlooked the living room, and I realized it was one enormous space. His bedroom. A king-size bed took up most of one wall. Large windows overlooked the backyard and beyond. He tossed me onto the bed and picked up a remote off the bedside table. With the press of a button, shades lowered over the windows, blocking us from view, yet they were sheer enough to let in some light.

Cyclops removed his cut, and I knew we'd reached the point of no return.

I smiled, knowing this was exactly what I wanted. What I needed. The sexy biker was about to be all mine.

* * *

Cyclops

I couldn't remember ever being with a virgin before. Not even when I'd been a teenager. It scared the fuck out of me. I might ruin this for her. I was man enough to admit it. Inside my own head anyway. Didn't stop my cock from being rock hard and ready to go. The thought of being her one and only made me want to beat my chest like Tarzan. Which led my thoughts down a decidedly not as pleasant path. There were things she needed to know.

"Before this goes further, I want you to know I'm clean. When I'm sexually active, I get tested every month, even though I've never fucked a woman without protection. Haven't been with anyone since my last test, which was three months ago."

She leaned up on her elbows. "You've been celibate for three months? Three *entire* months? You poor baby."

I shook my head. "Brat."

Might not seem like long to her, but when easy pussy could be had whenever I wanted? Three months was a lifetime. It was only by choice I hadn't fucked anyone. Now that I'd found Leigha, I was thankful I'd abstained. If I'd known the feisty woman would cross my path, I'd have gone even longer without sex.

"Do you know what it's like to live in a house full of your siblings and your parents within earshot? I can't even masturbate in my house. Not even in the shower, because the second I try, my sister will need to pee and come bursting through the door. Nothing can kill desire and need faster than my eighteen-year-old sister peeing two feet away from me. Well, maybe my mother walking in would be worse."

"Are you saying you've never gotten yourself off?" I asked.

"Still want me?"

I noticed her fingers tightened on the bedding. Did she really think that would deter me? It made me want to watch her come even more. Knowing I'd be the first one to make it happen, to give her that pleasure, was a feeling unlike any I'd felt before.

I noted the way her eyes tracked the scars on my body. "Maybe I should ask you that. The IED might have blinded me in one eye, and didn't remove any limbs, but it left some other damage behind. The scars I showed you in the living room, the ones you see now, aren't all of it. There's more down my hip and thigh."

She got up on her knees and reached out, tracing her fingers over the old scars. They'd faded a little, but I didn't think they'd ever go away. The doctor had said plastic surgery was an option for removing them. I'd laughed in his face. Men like me didn't get plastic surgery. Not unless it was a necessity, and these scars weren't bad enough for something like that. They didn't hurt. I just knew some women found them ugly.

"They're badges of courage," she said. "You earned these defending our country. How could you think I'd find them anything but remarkable?"

Damn. I'd known from the beginning she was different from any woman I'd ever met. And yet she kept proving it to me.

"Had a few complaints since I've been back. Not everyone finds them sexy."

She reached up and placed her hand on my cheek. "I like everything about you, Cyclops. The more I learn, the more I want to get to know you. You can't scare me off."

"Tucker." I took her hand and kissed her palm. "Call me Tucker."

"Make me yours, Tucker."

I studied her for a moment, making certain it was what she wanted. She hadn't had a chance to really live her life yet. With her overprotective family and a club at her back, she'd not been able to experience much. It made me a selfish bastard to tie her to me this way.

"I'm making you a promise here and now." I shifted closer. "There's so much you haven't seen or done, things made impossible by your parents and the Dixie Reapers. We'll explore this world together, try as many things as you want, and I swear we'll go on a date at least once a week. I don't want you to wake up one day and feel like I trapped you in a different cage from the one you're in already."

Her gaze softened. "I'd never think that, Tucker, but thank you."

I kissed her, my hands cupping her cheeks. I didn't know that I'd ever deserve someone as sweet as Leigha, but I'd damn sure try. Any man would be lucky to claim her, and she'd chosen me.

"Too many clothes," she murmured against my lips. "I want to feel you against me."

I backed up a step and unfastened my belt and jeans. My gaze stayed locked on her as she pulled off the shirt I'd given her earlier, then shimmied out of her jeans. Her bra and panties were black lace and looked sexy as hell on her. I shoved my jeans down my thighs, only to realize I still had on my boots. She bit her lip, but I heard her snicker when she saw my predicament.

I toed off one boot, then the other before stepping out of my jeans and pulling off my socks. The laughter died and her eyes darkened. She reached behind her and unhooked her bra, tossing it aside. Leigha ran her fingers along the scars on my thigh. Her touch made my cock harden even more, leaving me throbbing and aching to be inside her.

Leigha slowly lowered my boxer briefs. My heart hammered, and I hoped like hell the size of my cock didn't disappoint her. While I was slightly larger than average, I was still far from what I considered big. I heard her gasp and saw the look of wonder on her face.

"You're pierced?" she asked.

"It's a reverse Prince Albert. Makes using condoms a little trickier, but sex feels better for both myself and my partner." My fingers twitched as I fought the urge to reach out and touch her. "If you don't like it, I can take it out."

She ran her fingertip over the head of my cock and brushed both beads of the piercing. My cock jerked in response and pre-cum gathered on the tip. Leigha wrapped her hand around my shaft and gave it a stroke. I couldn't stifle my groan. Nothing had ever felt as amazing as her touch. Maybe it was because she was mine.

"Ever touched a man's cock before?" I asked, my voice raspier than usual.

"No, but I've seen one. Accidentally."

"How does that work?" I asked.

She smiled up at me. "One Prospect dared another to streak through the compound. I was fifteen and far too curious. All the old ladies received a call, so they'd know to keep the kids away from the windows. I peeked anyway."

Leigha pushed my underwear the rest of the way off, and I stepped out of them. As much as it killed me to hold back, I let her set the pace. She explored my body, her touch sending tingles down my spine. I noticed her nipples getting harder by the moment. Slowly, so she had time to back away, I cupped one of her breasts and rubbed my thumb across the hard peak.

She trembled and froze. Immediately, I dropped my hand. Had I just triggered a flashback to what happened in the alley? I didn't know if I should hold her or keep still.

"Leigha, talk to me. We aren't going to do anything you don't want. If this is too much right now, say the word and I'll get dressed."

She shook her head. "It's not that."

"Then what?"

Her cheeks turned pink. "You barely touched me and I... Um..."

"You what, kitten?"

"My panties are wet," she nearly whispered.

I bit the inside of my cheek so I wouldn't smile. Deciding to risk it and make a move, I pressed her back against the mattress and eased her panties down her thighs. She'd soaked them, but what surprised me was the fact she'd either shaved or waxed. Her pussy glistened and her little clit peeked out.

She tensed a moment, then closed her eyes and took a breath. As she let it out, her thighs parted more. The amount of trust she'd given me was humbling. I ran my palms up her thighs and spread her pussy open with my thumbs. Leigha bent her knees, placing her feet flat on the bed.

"You're beautiful. There's so much I want to do, but I know this is your first time. After what happened, I'm worried I'll move too fast or do something that scares you."

"Touch me, Tucker. Please."

I ran my finger down her slit, brushing against her clit. She cried out, and her hips bucked. I repeated the motion once. Twice. On the third time, my sweet little kitten came. Seeing her release soak the bed was the hottest fucking thing ever. Leaning over her, I took one of her nipples into my mouth. I sucked on the bud, letting my teeth lightly scrape her flesh.

Leigha dug her fingers into my hair, holding me tighter to her breast. I growled and worked a finger inside her tight pussy. Rubbing her clit, I made her come again, wanting her relaxed and slick. I pulled back, untangling her fingers from my hair, and stretched out on the bed on my back. Reaching for her, I pulled her across me. She straddled my hips, her hands splayed on my chest.

"Rub yourself against my cock, pretty girl. I want you to come again."

She shook her head. "I don't think I can. I already came twice."

I smiled and folded my hands behind my head. "Kitten, you're a woman. You can come a lot more than twice. Use that pretty pussy to get my cock nice and wet. Then I'll give you what you want."

Her motions were unsure, and a bit jerky as she rubbed against me. I gripped her hip and guided her, making sure she hit the piercing in my cock on the next stroke. Her eyes went wide, and she whimpered. Leigha leaned forward a little, giving me more of her weight as she rode me. When she cried out, coating me in her release, I rolled us so that she lay beneath me.

Notching my cock against the entrance of her pussy, I pushed inside. My muscles locked tight as I fought to move slowly. I wanted to give her time to adjust, to make sure she enjoyed every moment. Finally, I sank all the way inside her. She felt like fucking heaven! Her pussy squeezed me, and I damn near came.

"You ready?" I asked.

She nodded. "More than. It doesn't even hurt."

Thank Christ! I braced my weight with one hand and reached between us with the other. As I thrust into her, I worked her clit. The swollen bud was slippery, and it didn't take much to get her off. As she came a fourth time, I grabbed hold of her hip and drove into her, pounding her pussy as I chased my own orgasm.

I couldn't hold back my shout as I filled her up, my cum spurting inside her. I kept pumping my hips until every drop had been wrung from me. My cock twitched inside her. Panting for breath, I looked down at the beautiful woman spread out beneath me. She gave me a sated smile and I couldn't help but kiss her.

"Mine," I said, giving her bottom lip a nip. "All mine."

"Just so we're clear, I'm not on birth control," she said. "Probably should have mentioned that before."

I ran my beard along her collarbone and over the side of her neck. "Good. No one will dare take you from me if I get you pregnant."

"Do all men think alike? I swear it's like you find the woman you want, then do your best to knock her up."

I smiled at her. "Harder for you to run away if you're swollen with my kid. Besides, I'm not getting any younger. If you want a family, we should probably work on that."

"If I didn't want one?" she asked.

My stomach tightened. I hoped like hell she was teasing me. It never occurred to me she wouldn't want kids. While I'd thought I'd never find the right woman and settle down, it didn't mean I hadn't hoped I'd have kids someday.

She reached up and cupped my cheek. "Relax, Tucker. I want children. I was only giving you a hard time. I have a twin and two other siblings. I'll give you as many kids as you want. I'm not scared of having a big family."

I brushed my lips against hers. "I'll take as many as you feel like having. You might be mine, Leigha, but it means I'm yours too. We're in this together."

She lifted her hips, and my cock started to harden again. I hadn't been able to go again that fast in almost a decade. What the hell was this woman doing to me? And why the fuck hadn't I met her before now?

Chapter Three

Leigha

Cyclops had worn me out. My pussy ached, but in a good way. Even my hips and thighs were a bit sore. After round two, he'd run a bath for me and let me soak for a while. Then he'd claimed me all over again. He'd fallen asleep shortly after, his arm over my waist. I ran my fingers through his hair. It hung past his shoulders and the dark blond strands reminded me of a lion's mane.

He seemed peaceful as he slept. The ink on his back beckoned me to trace each line, but I didn't want to wake him. Besides the Reckless Kings colors, he had a script font that said *This We'll Defend*. I didn't know what it meant. He also had a tattered American flag on his shoulder that draped partway down his back and upper arm.

I studied his face and realized he'd woken and was watching me.

"What does this mean?" I asked, running my finger over the script on his back.

"It's the Army motto," he said. "Got medically discharged because of my eye, so I didn't get to serve my full term. It's a reminder that the Army might have been done with me, but I wasn't finished serving my country. Try to make a difference when and where I can."

"Like rushing into alleys to rescue damsels in distress?" I asked.

"You're a fighter, kitten. Wouldn't call you a damsel."

"It's getting late. Is your kitchen well-stocked? I could make dinner for us."

He squeezed my hip. "You don't have to cook for

us tonight. I can have something delivered. Once things are settled with my club and your parents, we'll go out to celebrate. It's not every day I claim an old lady."

"I should hope not." I snuggled closer. "Do you need to speak with Beast?"

"Told him to come by tonight. I guess we should order some pizzas. That way, there's enough for the three of us, and whoever shows up from your family."

"You're certain about this? About me?" I asked.

"Wouldn't have taken your innocence if I weren't. You're stuck with me now, kitten. Until the day I die, you're mine."

I toyed with the ends of his hair. "How official do you want to make it?"

"What did you have in mind?"

"You said you'd make your club accept me as your old lady. But would you marry me?"

He smiled. "Yeah, I'd marry you. That what you want?"

"My dad can fuss all he wants. If we're married, he won't even try to take me from you. What about your club? Would they accept me if we were married?"

He sighed. "Unfortunately, no. Forge tried that with Whisper and pissed Beast the fuck off. Not sure I want on the Pres' bad side. Give me one second."

He leaned over the side of the bed and yanked his jeans off the floor. Cyclops pulled a cell phone from the pocket and unlocked the screen. He turned over, leaning against the headboard, as he opened up a text message to Beast.

I'm claiming Leigha.

I moved closer, leaning against his side. Cyclops lifted his arm and held me close, letting me see the phone screen. I couldn't remember my dad even letting my mother read his texts. Although, it was possible he did it when the rest of us weren't around.

I saw dots pop up and then Beast's reply. *You are? Let me check… No, my patch still says President. Why the fuck do you think you're special and don't need a vote?*

I winced. "I don't think he's happy about your decision."

"He'll be fine with it. I think it's my delivery that made him mad. No worries, kitten. He won't make you leave."

Cyclops started typing again. *She's mine, Beast. The club can vote if they want, but it doesn't change anything. I want to marry her. Already did my best to put a baby in her.*

The phone rang. He answered, putting it on speaker.

"Pres, Leigha is here with me and can hear everything you say. So be nice." He smirked.

"Fucker. Why do you insist on putting me in this position? Forge pulls that shit, marrying Whisper before bringing her home, and now what? You think you'll give it a shot too?" Beast demanded.

"Her family is coming for her," Cyclops said. "You know it as well as I do. If I marry her, they can't try to take her from me. But I didn't want to do that without talking to you first."

Beast sighed. "Leigha, I'll have to make an example of him in Church later. It's nothing against you, and I'm not going to keep him from marrying you if that's what he wants. Just warning you ahead of time. If I don't, then the club will do whatever the fuck they want and not worry about consequences."

"I understand," I said.

"Welcome to the Reckless Kings," Beast said. "I'm not telling Lyssa. If your dad loses his shit, I want her to be able to deny she had any knowledge of what's happening."

"I'll keep Lyssa out of it," I promised.

"Fine. Do I need to get Shield to marry the two of you?" Beast asked.

"Will that get your club in trouble?" I asked. "I don't want to cause problems between the Reckless Kings and Dixie Reapers. I know with Lyssa being Torch's daughter, and Cowboy's daughter being with Ranger, you already have a family connection. But if my dad is mad enough, he could try to start something."

"I'll call Torch," Beast said. "I'll text and let the two of you know what's going on in a little while. Your dad will be here within the hour. If not sooner."

"Then work fast, Pres." Cyclops kissed my temple. "Because I'm not letting her go. I refuse to fight her dad, but he's not taking her from me."

"I'm on it. Congratulations, Cyclops. You too, Leigha."

The call dropped, and Cyclops tossed his phone aside. "Guess we should shower and dress."

"My things are still in my car."

"You can put on one of my shirts until I bring your bag in."

I pulled away from him and glared. "Do you really want my dad walking in and finding me in your shirt with no panties on? Because that will not go over well."

He smiled. "All right. I'll get your bag. Go start the shower and I'll join you in a minute."

I watched him get out of bed, admiring his body as he bent down to grab his jeans. He pulled them up, leaving them open, and walked out. I went into the bathroom and started the shower. The glass enclosure looked like heaven. Stone walls kept the cabin's natural feel. Dual showerheads and a bench made me eager to get in there. At home, I'd shared a bathroom with my siblings. Just a tub/shower combo. Nothing special.

Once the water had warmed, I stepped under the spray. I'd just soaked my hair when Cyclops joined me. He'd already removed his jeans before entering the bathroom. When he stepped into the shower, I immediately reached for him.

"Your bag is on the bed." He placed his hands on my cheeks and kissed me, soft and slow. "You need more clothes."

"I can get someone to ship my stuff to me, or bring it during a visit," I said.

He shook his head. "No need. I'll buy you whatever you want."

"I'm not with you for your money. You know that, right? All I need is you, Tucker."

"And that right there is why I want to spoil you a little. Other women might have demanded I take them shopping or give them access to my accounts the moment I said I was claiming them. Not once have you brought up money. You don't even know what I do for the club."

"Thought club business wasn't *my* business. At least, that's how it is at home."

He ran his nose down mine. "This is different. It's my job, and one you probably won't like. I can ask Beast to move me elsewhere."

"Why?"

"Because I work at the strip joint the club owns. I've never touched the dancers, and don't plan to start now. But I know most women wouldn't be too happy having their man around naked women every day."

I bit my lip and tried not to laugh. "Tucker, you

go to the clubhouse, don't you?"

"Well, yeah. I enjoy having a few beers with my brothers."

"And there are club whores there, right?" He nodded, his eyes narrowing. "So what's the difference? Why am I going to demand you get another job because of the dancers, when you can just head down the street to the clubhouse and see naked women? Except those will put their hands on you. The dancers probably have better boundaries."

"Damn," he mumbled. "Now I see the draw in claiming a woman who's been part of this club or another. You already know the score and aren't shocked by any of it."

"Did you want me to be?"

"No. You're perfect as you are. And all mine." He grinned and kissed me again. "I can't wait to see what life has in store for us."

"Hopefully, a lot of laughter, happy memories, and…" I stopped myself before I said the L word. We were still strangers. Did I hope he might love me one day? Of course. But I'd also seen plenty of guys like him run the moment a woman said that word. I wasn't risking it.

"And what?"

"Nothing. Or rather, everything. I want it all." *Nice save, Leigha!*

"I'll give you the world. It's all yours. Name it and I'll make it happen."

I wrapped my arms around his waist. "Careful. Don't make broad promises like that. It's only setting yourself, and us, up for failure. Besides, I don't need or want the entire world."

"You're unlike anyone I've ever known," he said. "In a good way."

"We should hurry. Beast said my dad would be here in an hour or less. And since the water is cooling down, I think we've been in here longer than we realize."

"Do I get to wash you?" he asked.

So not fair. I wanted to say yes more than anything. The logical side of my brain told me it was a bad idea. Something other than washing would end up happening, then we'd be even later getting out of the shower. The last thing we needed was my dad storming this house and finding me and Tucker together. Naked. In the shower. Possibly with his cock inside me.

"Next time," I promised. "When we aren't about to fight my dad and possibly your club just so we can stay together. Besides, if there's even a chance he's here already, keeping him waiting is a bad idea."

"All right, kitten. Raincheck." He nuzzled me once more before taking a step back. "We'll wash, get out, and order food. I'll call Beast and let him know it's safe for your dad to stop by."

"Just promise you won't take a swing at him. He can be infuriating, but he's not as young as he thinks he is."

"You said he's older than your mom, and I'm closer to her age. When you say there's a big gap between them..." Cyclops winced. "He's still going to kick my ass. No matter how we look at it, I'm over a decade older than you."

"He's a little over fifty," I said. "So he still has more than a decade on you. But Mom... she's close to your age."

"Damn. Make me feel old, why don't you?" He griped, but the wink he gave me told me he'd only been joking. "Guess you'll have to make me feel young again once we're alone."

I paused. "Exactly how often do you have sex? You said you'd gone three months without. Is this just a build-up you need to purge from your system? Or do I need to invest in ice packs? Because my pussy is sore as hell, but if you wanted to go again, I'd readily agree. I'd pay for it later, but I'd agree just the same."

He sobered and held out his hand. I went to him, letting him hold me once more. "Leigha, never let me do something that will cause you pain. It doesn't matter if my dick is hard. I'll live. But the thought of hurting you? It fucking guts me."

"It's a good kind of pain. Promise."

He kissed me and my toes curled. The man was potent. I hadn't lied. No matter how sore I was, I'd gladly let him take me again and again. It seemed in just a few hours, I'd become addicted to his touch. I wondered what it would be like a year from now, or a decade. I couldn't wait to find out!

* * *

Cyclops

A right hook came at my face and I ducked, throwing up my arm to deflect the blow. "I'm not going to fight back."

"Good," Preacher snarled as he swung once more. "Then stand still so I can beat the hell out of you. Why the fuck is my daughter in your house? Did you touch her?"

I swallowed, not ready to admit I'd done far more than that. I'd been her first and only. Thankfully, I wasn't getting a hard-on thinking about her. I didn't think it would go over well with her dad. "She's mine," I said.

Wrong fucking answer. He let out a roar and

launched himself at me, knocking us both to the floor. He got in a blow against my ribs and another on my jaw. I deflected the next hit and tossed him off me.

"Would you stop? I'm not breaking my word to Leigha. I promised I wouldn't hit you."

He staggered to his feet and froze. "What?"

Pinching the bridge of my nose, I wondered how I'd feel in his place. Probably pissed as fuck. I didn't fault him for wanting to tear me in two. All I'd said earlier was I *wouldn't* hit him. I hadn't told him why.

"I get it, Preacher. She's your little girl. Doesn't matter she's a grown adult and can make her own choices. You want to keep her safe forever, hold the monsters at bay. But I'm not going to hurt her any more than you'd hurt her mom."

His shoulders sagged. "Shit. You're claiming her, aren't you?"

I nodded. "Marrying her too."

He worked his jaw back and forth, his hands clenched at his sides. I braced in case he decided to punch me again. Thankfully, Leigha hadn't come out yet. I didn't know if she was hiding, or just hadn't finished getting ready. The moment I'd stepped out of the shower, I'd heard someone pounding on the door. Instead of waiting for her, I'd answered the door, knowing damn well it was likely her dad standing on the other side.

"Are you the reason she left home?" he asked.

I could have lied. Made it seem like we knew each other longer. But I wouldn't do that. I didn't want to start my relationship with Leigha by lying to her dad. I had no doubt it would come back to bite me in the ass later. But I also wouldn't tell him the entire truth of how we met. I'd leave it to Leigha.

"No. She came here hoping to find the freedom

to go on some dates without someone watching over her shoulder. We met outside a café in town. I didn't realize who she was at first, only knew she was the most beautiful woman I'd ever seen." I smiled. "I know we're moving fast. Not once have I ever been tempted to keep a woman. Until now. She accepts me, flaws and all."

Preacher's gaze went to my fucked-up eye and over the scars on my chest. I hadn't had time to do more than pull on my underwear and jeans before letting him in the house. I typically kept myself covered. My brothers didn't give a shit about my scars, or my eye, but the women were another matter. I either got pitying looks, or they were disgusted.

"Military?" he asked. "Or did you get that on a mission for your club?"

"Looking for a reason to haul her out of here?"

He shrugged. "Maybe. Can you blame me?"

I shook my head. "To answer your question, I was in the military. Got this and the scary-looking eye courtesy of an IED. I usually wear an eye patch when I'm outside the house, but your daughter says she prefers me without it."

He smiled. "That's my Leigha. Accepting of everyone. Probably got all pissed someone made you feel like you needed to hide your true self."

"Something like that."

"She's the first daughter to leave the nest. Her brother moved into the clubhouse and asked to prospect for the club. No one's voted either way yet, but Torch said let him have a room, so he'd feel a little independent. Maybe if I'd let Leigha live a little, she wouldn't have felt the need to come all the way here to go on a date." He ran a hand down his face. "I admit I hold on a little tight."

"She told me you lost your first wife."

"Yeah. Long-ass time ago, but I guess I still harbor this fear I'll blink and my kids and woman will be gone. You know Saint is her uncle, right? He came with me, along with Savior. Left them at the clubhouse. I wasn't sure what I was walking into."

"Beast know you're here?" I asked.

"I didn't call before pulling up if that's what you mean, but I'm sure someone has notified him by now. He knew I was on my way. That's as much courtesy as I gave him, so I'm sure he's ready to tear me in two."

"Call Saint and Savior. They're welcome to stop by. Grab some beers from the fridge while I get Leigha. And a shirt. I'd already planned to order some pizzas."

"Is she..." He put his hand over his mouth a moment. "Is Leigha okay?"

"She's fine." I hesitated. It was up to Leigha to tell him what happened, but I felt like he needed to know. There was a chance the asshole would pop up again, wanting revenge. Should have killed the fucker. If I hadn't worried how she would react, I would have. Now that I knew Leigha was born into the Dixie Reapers, I'd have done things different.

"But she wasn't?" he asked.

"It's her story to tell."

"Guess I can respect that. As long as you let me handle my daughter the way I see fit?"

I folded my arms. "I'll stay out of it, up to a point. She's your daughter, but she's soon to be my wife."

"Fair enough."

I walked back to the bedroom, where Leigha sat on the edge of the bed only halfway dressed. I shut the door and went to crouch in front of her. Taking her hands in mine, I kissed them.

"You all right?" I asked.

"I heard my dad hitting you. I wanted to rush out there, but I didn't think you'd be happy if I interfered. So I've been sitting here waiting on you to come back."

"Naked?" I asked, eyeing her exposed breasts. She'd put on leggings and nothing else.

"If I'm not dressed, I'm not leaving the room."

My lips twitched but I refused to laugh. I had a feeling she wouldn't appreciate it. She seemed so serious. Although, I had to admit I was grateful she hadn't come out to confront her dad while we were fighting. Neither of us would ever hurt her on purpose, but if she'd gotten in the way, one of us could have accidentally hit her.

"I guess that makes sense. Get dressed. Your dad and I have worked out our issues. He's getting a beer and I'm going to order some pizzas. Your uncle Saint is on his way over, and so is Savior."

She stared at the floor, refusing to meet my gaze. I could see the worry etched on her features. I'd thought she'd be excited to spend time with her dad and uncle. Even though she'd dreaded him showing up, she had to know Preacher loved her.

"You're going to make me tell them what happened, aren't you?"

I reached up to cup her cheek. "Honey, I'm not going to force you to, but I think you should."

I stood and picked up her bra where she'd tossed it farther up the bed. Handing it to her, I dug through her bag and pulled out a shirt. Once she'd dressed, I put on a tee and led her into the living room.

Preacher was no longer alone, and each man had a beer in his hand. I grabbed one, and a soda for Leigha, before joining them. Since I ordered out a lot, I had all the local places on my phone for quick access. I didn't know what everyone liked, but I had a feeling it would be more than just the five of us soon enough, so I ordered enough to feed a small army and a variety of toppings.

"Any idea where the three of you are staying?" I asked.

"Beast offered the guest house," Saint said. "We accepted."

"I'm sure you'd prefer us not staying under your roof." Preacher took a swallow of his beer. "But I plan to visit with my daughter before heading back."

Leigha reached over and took her dad's hand. "I'll come visit, Daddy. It's not like I moved all the way to California. Besides, Lyssa and Danica are here too. You can come whenever Torch and Cowboy visit. Or anytime you want."

"Think we're going to need more guest housing," I said.

Preacher smirked. "Well, if your club would stop stealing all our daughters, it wouldn't be an issue. At this point, I think the Dixie Reapers just need a chapter down the street from your clubhouse."

"It would make it a lot easier to steal all your daughters." He flipped me off and I laughed. "Joking! Sort of. Leigha said her sister is eighteen. Only five of us have old ladies. Better lock up your eligible daughters if you don't want them poached."

Leigha glared at me. "You make me sound like livestock."

"Keep talking." Preacher leaned back and relaxed. "At this rate, she'll be begging me to take her home."

"You're not taking her anywhere," I said.

Leigha rolled her eyes and got up, heading for

the kitchen. "The two of you can stop fighting over me. If I'm not livestock, I'm damn sure not a bone either."

Saint shook his head. "No one going to address the elephant in the room? Clearly there's something Leigha doesn't want us to know. That girl is deflecting like she's done every time she's tried to be secretive. And you two are playing into her hands. She's keeping all of us going so she doesn't have to say anything."

"Not my story to tell," I said.

"So she is hiding something," Saint said. "I knew it."

Leigha peeked in from the kitchen. "It's no big deal. I know you'll blow it out of proportion. I'd rather just keep it to myself."

Preacher eyed me. "Is that true? It's nothing huge?"

I ran my hand over my beard. "Could have some blowback. I need to discuss it with Beast."

"Leigha, get in here," Preacher said. "You're going to tell me exactly how you met Cyclops, and don't leave a damn thing out."

Leigha groaned and I heard a banging sound. If I had to guess, it was her head against the wall. A knock sounded at the door, and I went to answer, hoping it was the food. We needed an ice breaker, and I couldn't think of anything better than pizza.

I yanked open the door and froze. Nope. Not the food.

"Pres. Wasn't expecting you."

Beast pushed past me and entered the house. "I see you're still standing."

"We've come to an understanding," Preacher said. "And I'm sorry for not calling before I arrived. I tend to have tunnel vision when it comes to my kids."

"Since I have a daughter, I get it. Not to mention

what happened when Torch arrived after I claimed Lyssa. But if anyone asks, I came in pissed and let you have it."

Preacher gave a nod.

"Now, let's talk about the trouble your woman got into," Beast said, shoving his hands into his pockets. "Read your text on my way here. That lowlife could be a problem. Should have fucking ended him, especially after what he did."

"No!" Leigha screamed out the word and ran into the living room. "Not another word."

Beast arched an eyebrow. "Last time I checked, I'm the President of this club. If I want to discuss something, I will. And unless Cyclops married you, then you're a guest here. Nothing has gone to a vote."

"Beast," I said, not wanting him to hurt Leigha's feelings, or piss off Preacher.

"Did you marry her?" he asked.

"Haven't exactly had time."

"They don't know," Leigha said. "And now that you've said I'm not part of your club, my dad will make me leave."

Preacher eyed me and I shook my head. No way would I let him take her away from me. Didn't matter if my club had voted yet or not. As he said, my brothers had a tendency to pick Dixie Reaper daughters. I didn't see anyone voting against me.

"Then I think you need to tell them," Beast said. "When you're done, we'll discuss the options."

I went to Leigha and put my arm around her shoulders, tugging her against me. I felt her tremble and knew the last thing she wanted to do was tell her dad about the attack in the alley. Beast had shit timing, but I couldn't disagree Preacher needed to hear what happened.

"Come on, kitten. Get it over with."

She sighed and nodded. As the story spilled out of her, I saw fury flash in the eyes of each Dixie Reaper. And the moment Preacher's gaze met mine, I knew none of them were leaving until we'd buried that fucker six feet under.

Chapter Four

Leigha

Shame filled me after I told my dad and uncles what happened. Savior might not be blood, but he was family just the same. I couldn't even look my dad in the eye. Cyclops had held me the entire time, and only released me long enough to answer the door when the pizzas arrived. Everyone had a slice, including me, but I'd lost my appetite. I nibbled mine and hoped no one noticed.

"What do you know about this asshole?" Dad asked.

"Local lowlife," Cyclops answered. "Deals drugs for someone higher up. His boss also pimps out girls."

"You mean women," I mumbled.

"No, kitten, I don't. We've tried putting him out of business multiple times. The rat runs off for several months, then comes back with a new stable. Almost had him last time. Beast planned to put him in the ground. Fucker escaped at the last second."

I swallowed hard. "Girls. He's dealing in children?"

"Found out last week he was back in town," Beast said. "I've had Shield gathering intel on him. Trying to find any patterns to his routine, or where he's hiding the girls."

"I want in on this," Dad said.

"Us too," said Uncle Saint.

"Why did you let him live?" I asked. "You had him. Instead of leaving him knocked out in the alley, you could have killed him."

Cyclops ran his hand up and down my thigh. "Didn't know who you were at the time. He had attacked you. If I'd gutted him like I wanted, it could have scared you more. If I'd realized I was dealing with a Reaper's daughter, I wouldn't have hesitated. Still wouldn't have taken down the big guy, but it would have put a small chink in his armor."

"So what happens now?" I asked. "Or is it club business and I need to leave the room?"

Beast and Cyclops shared a look. The President of the Reckless Kings turned his gaze to me, and I fought the urge to squirm. I knew Lyssa was head over heels for him, but the guy was a little scary to me.

"I'll call Church tomorrow and we can come up with a plan then. For now, I think it's best for you to visit with your family." Beast looked away and the tension drained from me. He gave me a wink when no one else was looking. I wasn't sure what to make of it.

"I'll walk you out, Pres," Cyclops said as he stood. The two men went to the front door, leaving me alone with my dad and uncles.

"Were you ever going to tell us?" Uncle Saint asked.

"No." I bit my bottom lip. "I know all of you worry, especially Dad. I thought if he knew what happened, he'd never let me stay here. And things would be worse at home for Lara. I had to leave home when no one was around. Do you know how embarrassing it is to be my age and never have gone on a date? And you're doing the same thing to Lara."

My dad ran his hands up and down his face and sighed heavily. "I know. I'm sorry, Leigha. I never intended to make you feel caged. I only wanted you to be safe. If you'd dated someone from inside the club..."

I held up a hand. "Is that why Foster kept coming on so strong? Did you put him up to it?"

Dad growled and his eyes narrowed. "What?

That fucker has been sniffing around you?"

"Only since I was fifteen," I muttered. "Don't worry. Uncle Bull handled it."

"What do you suggest I do with Lara?" Dad asked. "What do you wish I'd done differently with you?"

"Allowed me a little freedom? I couldn't date because someone from the club scared off all the guys. At the very least, arrange a date for her with someone you trust. She doesn't have to know you set it up. Let her live a little, Dad."

"Or we could just arrange for her to be claimed by someone," Uncle Saint said.

I noticed Savior frowning and wondered about his thoughts on the matter. He glanced at my dad and Uncle Saint before training his gaze on me. His expression blanked when he realized I was watching him. I knew Savior was in his early fifties now. To my knowledge, he'd never seriously dated anyone, and hadn't once asked to claim a woman. I found it sad. He had so much to offer.

And that's when an idea formed. One I hoped would work in both my sister's favor and in Savior's. Assuming he agreed to it.

"There's someone Lara has a crush on." Every man in the room turned toward me, giving me their undivided attention. Even Cyclops had returned. "You know him."

"Who?" Dad asked.

"Griffin. Gwen and Lance's oldest," I said.

"No." Dad shook his head. "Absolutely not."

"He's a good guy," I argued. "Besides, you didn't hear the rest of my idea. You can set it up. A coffee date at the new café."

"How is that beneficial? We don't own anyone

- 63 -

there," Uncle Saint said.

"Because the new barista has been eyeing Uncle Savior. He can just happen to be there, enjoying some coffee, maybe flirting a little, so it doesn't seem like he's there to spy, but he can keep an eye on Lara and Griffin."

Savior stared at me in disbelief. "The barista who looks like she's closer to your age than mine?"

"She's actually older than me. She's almost thirty. And she has a kid," I said.

Savior leaned back in his seat. "Son or daughter?"

"A daughter. One who could really use a hero." I watched him and got a nod. "The daughter is ten and has been having trouble at school. Mostly from kids teasing her because they live on the poor side of town, and she doesn't have a dad."

Savior frowned, as did my dad and Uncle Saint. I knew none of them would like hearing that little tidbit. I wondered what it would take to pair up all the single Dixie Reapers with moms who had kids in desperate need of a father figure in their lives. To my knowledge, no one had ever tried before.

"Fine. I'll chat up the barista and see where things go." Savior ran a hand over his hair. "What makes you think she'll agree to a date with me? If she's under thirty, I'm old enough to be her dad."

"Because I've seen her watching you. Trust me. You make the first move, and the rest will fall into place," I said.

"You finished matchmaking?" my dad asked, a smile on his lips.

"Yeah. For now."

He shook his head. "Girl, focus all that attention on the Reckless Kings. This is your home now. Don't get me wrong. You're welcome to visit anytime you want. We'll always be your family, but with Cyclops claiming you, your loyalty now lies with him and his club."

We finished the pizzas and watched a movie. Cyclops got along well with my family, now that my dad wasn't trying to kill him. In fact, the two were acting like old friends. I watched the men in my life, happy they got along. Even Saint and Savior seemed at ease.

My phone buzzed in my pocket, and I checked it. I almost didn't read the message from Lyssa. I wasn't sure if Beast had told her what happened to me or not. Plus, she'd acted like none of the Reckless Kings would want anything to do with me. Clearly that wasn't true, and it left me wondering if she didn't want me to live here. She hadn't been upset over Danica or Hayley moving here. Not that I knew of.

I relented and read the message.

Want to hang out with the old ladies during Church tomorrow?

It seemed Beast had already told her the plan. While I knew Hayley, Lyssa, and Danica, I hadn't met Forge's woman.

I'd like that.

I put my phone back in my pocket and enjoyed the rest of my visit with my family. Soon enough, they left for the guest house, leaving me alone with Cyclops. My first night at my new home. Even though he'd already taken my virginity, I felt unsettled knowing we'd share a bed tonight.

Cyclops locked the house and held out his hand. "Come on, kitten. You've had a long day."

"Does that mean no sex?" I asked.

He smiled. "Not tonight. I think you need to

sleep more than anything."

"What if I hog the covers? Or kick you out of the bed?" I asked.

"Guess I'll have to hold you close, so neither of those happens. Nervous?"

I nodded. "Is that silly?"

"No, it's not. You've never lived with anyone but your family. All this is brand new to you. Let's get ready for bed, then we'll cuddle for a bit. If you start feeling anxious, let me know and we'll talk about it."

I leaned up to kiss him. "You're so sweet and understanding. How did I ever get lucky enough to find a guy like you?"

"Think I'm the lucky one, kitten."

He led me to the bedroom, and as promised, all he did was hold me while I fell asleep. I knew the Dixie Reapers were different from other men. It never occurred to me I'd find someone just as wonderful so far from home. Coming to see Lyssa was the best decision I'd ever made. Even if I'd known that man would attack me, if it would have ended with Cyclops claiming me, I'd go through it all over again. Although, I'd hopefully be more prepared and hold my own a bit better.

I hadn't thought I'd ever go on a date, much less have a boyfriend. And now I had a biker of my very own.

* * *

Cyclops

My brothers stared at me as I stood at the front of the table by Beast. To say I'd shocked them was an understatement.

"You're claiming Preacher's daughter?" Brick asked. "And he's okay with it?"

"He wasn't at first."

A knock sounded at the doors, and I knew it was the Dixie Reapers. I'd hoped to have this part of Church over with before they arrived. Looked like I wouldn't get my wish. Beast called out for them to enter, and Preacher, Saint, and Savior walked in, letting the doors close behind them.

"Cyclops was just asking for our vote to claim your girl, Preacher," Brick said.

What the fuck? Was the asshole trying to stir shit up? I glared at him and the bastard just grinned. "You're a shithead."

Brick flipped me off but kept smiling.

"He has my blessing," Preacher said. "He already saved her from being raped and possibly killed. She seems to like him, so I won't stand in the way. If they want to be together, I'm all right with it."

"Raped?" Brick's gaze narrowed. "What the fuck is going on?"

Beast filled them in on what happened with Leigha, and how I'd left the bastard alive since I hadn't realized who she was. I still wanted to kick my own ass over that one. But like I'd said last night, taking out the man who'd hurt her wouldn't stop the prostitution of underage girls. We needed to go higher up for that.

"You mean to tell me that shit Matteo is back in town?" Brick asked.

"Why are we just now hearing about it?" Forge frowned. "Some of us have families here. You can't keep that shit a secret, Pres. It's not right."

"I wanted more information before I let everyone in on it. Cyclops knew, as well as Shield and Hawk. Forge, I know you're the Sergeant-at-Arms, but with a pregnant wife and a son under your roof, I had a feeling you'd swing first and ask questions later."

Beast sighed. "I'm sorry I didn't tell you. All of you. Now everyone knows and we can work on taking out those assholes before more girls are hurt. This time, we don't let him leave this town alive. If he escapes, we track him down and bury him."

"Can we vote on Leigha being mine?" I asked, trying to draw their attention back to the first topic of conversation.

"Everyone who votes for Leigha to be Cyclops' old lady, raise your hand," Beast said. Every hand at the table went up, and so did the hands of the Dixie Reapers. The Pres slammed his fist onto the table. "It's unanimous. Congratulations, Cyclops. You have an old lady. I'll put in the request for her property cut."

"She the reason you aren't wearing the eye patch?" Wrangler asked. "Not that I think you need it. Just curious."

"Leigha got pissed I was wearing it when my eye isn't missing. Something about people accepting me as I am." I shrugged a shoulder. "If it freaks everyone out, I can wear it again."

"You won't," Preacher said from behind me. "If you do, it will hurt Leigha. Or worse, she'll go after the person who made you feel it was necessary. Then you'll have a bigger issue on your hands."

"She's feisty?" Wrangler asked. "I like her already."

"She fought back against the guy trying to rape her. Gave him hell before I got there." I still hated she'd been in that position. If we'd taken out Matteo and his crew, it would have never happened. Then again, if I hadn't heard her struggling, there was a chance we wouldn't have ended up together.

"I'm going to need some volunteers to keep an eye on Matteo and his men. Shield, see what you can find on his current operation. We need as many details as we can get," Beast said.

"I know Wire would be happy to lend a hand," Preacher said. "Especially if you're going to deal with the man who hurt Leigha."

Beast nodded. "Appreciate it. Shield, reach out to Wire and Lavender. We'll take all the help we can get. Forge, I'll need your help to assess any intel so we can come up with a strategy for taking these fuckers down. Permanently. I don't want Matteo on the run and showing his ugly-ass face back in our town at a later date. The fucker is going down. All of them are."

"And the girls?" Forge asked. "You know they'll never be the same. Hell, some may never recover at all."

"I'll call Charming. They've dealt with human trafficking lately where kids were involved. They may have some people in place who could get those kids the help they need, either get them home to their families, or find new ones for them." Beast looked around the room. "Everyone will receive an assignment in the upcoming days."

"Put us to work," Saint said. "We want a part in this. Leigha might be Cyclops' now, but she's our family."

Beast nodded. "I'll take whatever help you want to give. And if more of your brothers, or men from other clubs, want to give us some assistance, we'll figure out where to put everyone. I might want these men buried, but I don't want to risk our families to do it. We need to make sure the women and children are protected at all times."

"When do we get to meet Leigha?" Brick asked. "As Cyclops' official old lady. I know some of us have met her before, but this is different."

"We'll have a formal meet and greet when this is behind us," Beast said. "Cyclops, spend time with her until we have a concrete plan in place. I know the two of you need a chance to bond. Take it before all hell breaks loose."

"Thanks, Pres." I'd promised Leigha some dates. I'd have to figure out how to do that safely. If we went into town, I'd have to take some brothers with me. No way I'd put her in danger. Which mean getting creative around the compound.

"Church is dismissed," Beast said. "Everyone grab a beer. We'll get to work in an hour. You need to fuck? Find a club whore. Need a drink, you know where the bar is. Anything else, you're on your own."

"Thanks, Pres, but I think I'd rather fuck my woman," Hawk said. "Hayley would have issue with me being balls-deep in a club whore, and honestly, they aren't appealing these days."

Beast snorted. "You know damn well what I meant. I wasn't about to tell Forge to go fuck his woman when her dad is sitting right here with us, same for Cyclops."

Preacher narrowed his gaze at me. He might have given his blessing, but I didn't know a dad out there who wanted to think about his daughter getting fucked. They knew it happened, especially when the grandbabies came along. They just didn't want to consider it wasn't a stork that dropped the kids off. And I knew I'd be the same whenever I had a daughter.

If I had one.

It was possible we could have only sons. Although, part of me wanted a little girl who looked just like her mom. Then I'd gut every fucker who looked at her too long.

We all filed out of Church. I headed for the clubhouse doors when Beast stopped me.

"Might as well have a drink. Your woman is with the old ladies. I doubt they're finished having their fun. Everyone went to my house, so you can follow me home in a bit."

I eyed the door, wanting to go straight to Leigha, but I understood why he wanted me to stay. It was important for her to feel like she was part of the Reckless Kings. Since Lyssa had made it sound like none of us would want Leigha, I knew they needed this time together. For one, I hoped my woman found out why Lyssa had lied to her. As beautiful as Leigha was, there wasn't a snowball's chance in hell one of us wouldn't have gladly claimed her. Hell, even if I'd met her here at the compound, I'd have still wanted her. Might have moved slower, though.

"I promised Leigha I'd take her on some dates," I said as I got a beer and took the seat next to Beast. "She didn't get to date back home. Not sure how I'm doing that until all this is settled, but I want to keep my word. Told her we'd go on at least one date a week."

"That a forever kind of thing?" Beast asked.

"Yeah. I think it will be good for us. I've heard of couples having a date night, but I never really understood it. Until my coffee date with Leigha. I want more dates like that one."

Preacher came up beside me. "Don't overthink it. Leigha doesn't need or want fancy."

"I'm not sure we know each other well enough for me to adequately plan a date around the compound. We haven't even known each other a full day."

"Leigha likes movies and books. She likes simple things like fried chicken and biscuits. Or taking a walk in the moonlight." Preacher looked at me. "None of those things require you to leave the compound if that's your fear."

"Cats," I mumbled.

"What?" His brow furrowed. "Cats?"

I nodded. "There was a calico at the café inside the bookstore. It's where we had our date today. She loved that cat, said she'd always wanted one."

Beast held up a finger and pulled out his phone, making a call. He put it on speaker and I saw Doolittle's name on the screen.

"Hello," the man said as he answered. I heard what sounded like a small zoo in the background.

"Need a favor," Beast said. "I'll talk to Charming in a little while, but we're facing some shit here. I could use an extra hand or two."

"Okay. So why call me first?" Doolittle asked.

"Whoever he sends, I need them to bring something. A kitten or cat. Cyclops just claimed an old lady, and she's always wanted a feline. Knew you'd have one needing a home."

I smiled. I hadn't even considered calling Doolittle. Hell, the Devil's Fury weren't exactly right next door, but if Charming did send some help our way, it would be easy enough for someone to come in a truck or SUV instead of on a bike and bring a cat with them.

"I've got two litters of kittens right now who haven't been placed yet, and a fat black fluffball who looks evil as shit but is actually really sweet. His previous owner called him Lucifer," Doolittle said. "Just tell me which she'd prefer, and I'll have them ready to go."

"Is the cat housebroken?" I asked. "Lucifer. Is he going to tear the place up?"

"He uses a litter box, and his previous owner had him de-clawed, which I fucking hate. Do you know how a cat is declawed? You have to break their toes to remove the claws. It's fucking barbaric, and a service my practice doesn't offer. So no, he won't tear anything up. He's three years old, so he'll live a lot of years."

"We'll take him," I said.

Preacher shook his head. "Did she tell you why she couldn't have a cat before?"

I grinned at him. "Because you're allergic. Guess your visits to the house will be brief or you'd better load up on allergy meds first. No offense, Preacher, but you're not my priority. She is. If she wants a cat, she's getting one."

He grinned. "Good answer."

"I have some extra things I can send with Lucifer. Bowls, a small bag of the food he's been eating, a few toys. You won't be starting from scratch. But you'll need a litter box. I'll text you with the type of litter we've been using," Doolittle said. "He's a picky little shit when it comes to his litter. If you change it, he's not going to be happy."

"Got it. I'll send a Prospect for whatever we need. Just send me a list of stuff you recommend," I said. "And thanks, Doolittle. She's going to be excited."

My phone chimed and I checked it, smiling at the image. Doolittle was right. The cat looked evil as shit, but if he said it was a sweet one, I'd trust him. No one knew animals like he did. And I knew he'd never place an animal with someone who couldn't handle them. Lying about their disposition would be a disservice to the critter as well as the person adopting.

"I'm finishing my beer, then I'll call Charming," Beast said.

Hawk moved in closer. "Hey, you got anything

that might get along well with Cuddles?"

I shook my head. "What? A pet racoon isn't enough?"

Hawk shrugged. "I wouldn't mind something that will occupy both Cuddles and our kid. They get tired of each other."

"I think you mean Freya is annoying Cuddles as a way to pretend she doesn't have a little brother," I said. "That girl is upset you didn't give her a sister and you damn well know it."

Hawk flipped me off. "What about it, Doolittle? Got anything?"

"I think it would be better to bring Cuddles here and we can see if he bonds with anyone. I'd hate to send an animal all the way there only for the two of them to hate each other," Doolittle said. "I know your son is still a newborn, so you'll want to stay close to home a while longer. Whenever you're ready, bring the family for a visit."

"Thanks, Doolittle," Hawk said.

"Can I go get my woman yet?" I asked, glaring at Beast.

He shook his head. "Let me call Charming, then we'll go."

He finished his call with Doolittle and then drank his damn beer before he talked to Charming. And the fucker knew exactly how pissed I was getting. Asshole did it on purpose.

* * *

Leigha

I'd had a blast with the old ladies, although I felt some tension between me and Lyssa. I didn't know if I was imagining it or not. It didn't help that I kept thinking about her words before. Why had she felt no one here would want me?

Whisper hugged me as she gathered her kids. Little Dove was too cute for words!

"It will be nice having another woman around here," she said. "Don't be a stranger. You're welcome at our house anytime. Well, maybe not nap time. Anyone who wakes up the kids had better run fast because if I don't kill them Forge might."

I laughed. "I understand."

Once Whisper, Danica, and Hayley had left, I faced Lyssa and wondered if I should voice my concerns with her. She busied herself cleaning up and brewed a fresh pot of coffee. I figured it must be for Beast. Had Church ended? If so, how did she know? I hadn't seen her check her phone since I'd arrived, and no one had called.

"Can we talk a minute?" I asked, deciding to just dive in. The not knowing would make me crazy.

"Sure. Everything okay?" she asked.

"Maybe." I pulled out a kitchen chair and sat. "When you invited me here, you made a comment that's been bothering me."

Her eyebrows rose and she sat across from me. "Really?"

"Yeah. I asked about the men at this club, and you made it seem like no one would be interested in me. Then I met Cyclops." I traced a pattern on the table. "Lyssa, did you not want me here? Were you trying to make me look outside the Reckless Kings because you didn't want me to live at the same compound as you? I'm trying to understand, but I... I just don't. Am I..."

"Are you what?" she asked.

"Am I not good enough?" I lifted my gaze to meet hers, trying to hold back my tears. "Was that it?"

She sighed and rubbed her forehead. "Each of us has given something back either to the club or our men, if not both. We're meant to be here. Beast needed someone strong who wouldn't take anyone's shit. As the daughter of the Dixie Reapers President, I fit the bill. Not to mention, he's sexy as hell.

"Then there's Danica. She's so damn horse crazy, I wasn't sure she'd ever find a guy, unless it was another cowboy. Then she met Ranger and they clicked. Who knew he'd grown up on a horse farm? They're perfect for one another.

"Whisper grew up here. She's known most of these men all her life, and she was head over heels for Forge even when she was just a teenager. They were destined for one another."

I nodded, feeling worse by the minute. "And Hayley?"

"Hayley's dad is a cop, and while that doesn't make Beast and Hawk all that comfortable when he comes to visit, that connection to law enforcement has actually been a bonus a time or two."

"And me?" I asked.

"You..." She shook her head. "I have no idea how you fit in here, Leigha. I'm not trying to be mean or bitchy. With the exception of Whisper, you already had a connection to the old ladies here. But how do you fit with Cyclops? I don't even know how you two met. Beast hasn't said much."

I got up and poured myself a cup of coffee. Staring out her kitchen window, I tried to gather my thoughts. As much as I didn't want to tell Lyssa what happened to me, maybe she needed to hear it.

"I stopped at the bookstore in town, with the little café? The one on the square." She nodded and I continued. "I wasn't paying attention when I went back to my car. Didn't have my keys ready. Had no idea someone had come up behind me, until it was too late. He dragged me into an alley and ripped my shirt. He nearly raped me, no matter how hard I fought."

"Jesus," she muttered. "Why the fuck didn't anyone tell me?"

"I asked Cyclops not to say anything." I turned to face her. "He saved me. Heard me fighting against that man, and he came charging down the alley like an avenging angel. He didn't want me to drive while I was so shaken. Gave me his shirt, and we went back into the café for some coffee."

"And he decided to keep you?" she asked.

Her flat tone left me guessing at her thoughts and feelings. I didn't like feeling this distance between us. While we hadn't been close enough in age to be best friends growing up, I'd still always thought of Lyssa as family.

"We talked for a while. I told him why I was here, about my family, how I was friends with you. He gave me a sexy smirk that curled my toes and said he'd take me on another date. He was counting our coffee and conversation as a date. I felt all warm inside, and he... I don't know how to explain it."

I took a swallow of my coffee, then twisted the mug in circles, refusing to meet her gaze. The awkwardness I'd been feeling since I arrived at her house doubled. If I had a ride home, I'd have left already. Sadly, I hadn't driven myself. I started to stand, thinking the walk would do me some good, when I heard the door open and the heavy tread of booted feet before it shut again.

"Lyss?" Beast called out.

"We're in the kitchen," she yelled back.

Beast and Cyclops found us, my sexy biker

leaning down to kiss me sweetly. I smiled up at him, running my fingers through his beard. Just seeing him made me so damn happy, and it had nothing to do with the cold shoulder Lyssa had been giving me.

"What's going on?" Beast asked, his gaze narrowed on his woman.

"Nothing," Lyssa said.

Oh, hell no! She wasn't going to sweep this under the rug as no big deal. I held Cyclops' gaze and he gave me a slight nod.

"Actually, I was just asking Lyssa why she'd told me no one in your club would be interested in me," I said.

Beast folded his arms. "That's a great question, Leigha. Clearly, Cyclops is more than ready to make you his. I think he'd have fought the entire club if we'd voted against the two of you. So, Lyssa... why would you tell her no one would want her?"

"She's too soft," Lyssa said. "And what the hell does she have in common with Cyclops?"

"That's for us to worry about, not you," Cyclops said. "I've never known you to act this way. Is there a problem with Leigha being here? Or is something else going on?"

"Foster," she blurted out.

"Foster?" My brow furrowed. "What does he have to do with anything?"

"He's in love with you, Leigha, and you didn't even give him a chance! Would it have killed you to go on just one date with him? The two of you make more sense than you and Cyclops." Lyssa slouched in her chair. "My dad is going to kill me."

"I'm so confused," I said.

"You're not the only one," Beast said. "Start at the beginning, Lyssa, and this better be damn good."

"Fine," Lyssa mumbled. "We all know how Foster feels about Leigha. He's been chasing her since she was only fifteen or sixteen. I thought I'd invite her here, let her go on a few dates to gain some confidence, then send her home. Once she saw how awful men are in general, I thought she'd be happy to give him a chance."

"And the part about your dad?" Cyclops asked.

"There are now five old ladies at the Reckless Kings. Three are the daughters of Dixie Reapers and the fourth is related to the Chief of Police back home. Whisper is the only one who didn't come from my hometown. Dad made a comment about me stealing away all their daughters to hook up with the Reckless Kings. And now Leigha's with Cyclops," Lyssa said.

"My dad is fine with me being here," I said. "As for me and Cyclops... He makes me feel things I've never felt before, Lyssa. I've never thought of Foster in a romantic way, and I never will. I thought I made that clear."

Cyclops took my hand and helped me stand. "Come on, kitten. We're going home. Think the Pres has a few words to say to his woman."

Beast nodded. "The two of you need anything, let me know. Soon as I have her property cut, I'll get it to you."

Cyclops led me from the house and out to his bike. I climbed on behind him, wrapping my arms around his waist. I loved the wind in my hair, and riding with him. If only we could hit the open road for an hour or three...

He pulled into the driveway at home and into the garage. I reluctantly got off and went into the house. It seemed Church had gone well, since Beast said I would get a property cut. It meant I officially belonged to Cyclops, which thrilled me.

Cyclops came up behind me, placing his hands on my waist. I felt his beard against my neck as he breathed in my scent. Leaning back against him, I put my hands over his. He made me feel safe. Cherished. It was crazy since we were strangers. Then again, I knew my parents hooked up at a party, and Dad never stopped thinking about her.

"Want to go on another date?" Cyclops kissed my temple. "Thought we could pack a picnic and find somewhere quiet."

"That sounds perfect." And romantic. Something told me it wouldn't take long for me to fall head over heels for Cyclops.

Chapter Five

Cyclops

I couldn't remember ever putting a picnic together. I didn't have one of those hamper or basket things. Thankfully, I found a plain gift bag tucked in the back of my closet. I didn't even remember where it came from. It wouldn't hold anything heavy, but it was perfect for a few sandwiches, some chips, and two sodas. Next time, I'd plan better and have something delivered.

With a blanket thrown over my arm, and the bag in my hand, I led Leigha out of the house and farther down the road, going deeper into the compound. The houses thinned out until they were all behind us. When I knew we'd gone far enough for some privacy, I spread the blanket under a tree and stretched out next to where Leigha sat.

"It's so beautiful here," she said, taking everything in.

"You know, the house isn't just mine. It's yours too. We can make any changes you want. Or if you don't like it at all, I can ask Beast if we can build a new one. Maybe farther back this way."

She shook her head. "I like your house. Our house."

Her cheeks flushed, and I couldn't help but think she was too damn adorable. I took our food and drinks from the bag and set them out on the blanket. I should have packed paper towels or something, but I hadn't thought about it. I couldn't remember the last time I planned a date. Had I ever? Certainly not something like this.

"I have something to show you," I said, taking my phone out. I pulled up the picture of Lucifer and turned the screen to face her. "He's been abandoned and needs a new home. Told Doolittle we'd take him."

She gasped and reached for the phone, cradling it like it was the most precious thing in the world. "He's ours?"

I nodded. "The previous owner named him Lucifer because he looks evil. Doolittle swears he's a sweet boy. He's sending a few essentials with the cat, but we'll need to get a litter box, at the very least. He texted me the type of litter Lucifer likes. Maybe we can get one of those kitty condo things."

"No one's ever done something so sweet for me." She leaned in to kiss me. "Thank you, Tucker. He's adorable and I can't wait to meet him."

"I don't want you leaving the compound right now, Leigha. I know that seems unfair, but I won't put you at risk. We can pick something out online and I'll send a Prospect to pick it up. Same for anything else you want for the house, or groceries we might need."

"When do you go back to work?" She ate a chip and lifted her gaze to mine.

"Beast told me to take a few days off, get to know you better. Guess we're sort of on a honeymoon. If you can call it that, since we won't be leaving the compound."

She smiled. "A honeymoon?"

"We can do whatever you want, as long as we stay inside the gates. I thought we could go on another date tomorrow. Maybe a walk at night if the weather is nice?"

"I'd like that."

"You never mentioned anything about taking college classes. Were you not interested in going, or did Preacher have too tight a hold on you?" I asked.

"Some of it was my family. I also didn't know

what I wanted to do with my life. There didn't seem a point in taking classes with no direction of where I'd end up. Dad didn't like me being out of sight for too long. Which would have meant taking classes online."

"I won't hold you back, kitten. If you want to get a degree, we'll figure it out."

She shook her head. "Not right now. Maybe someday I'll change my mind. I've always wanted a family of my own, and a cat or two. Unless you want me to get a job? I can if it's important to you."

"No." I reached out and cupped her cheek. "You want to be at home? I'm fine with that. In fact, I like the idea of you being there waiting for me. The house isn't all that large. How big a family do you want?"

"At least four kids. Maybe more. Depends on if we're blessed with twins." She cocked her head to the side. "I haven't explored the house yet. How many bedrooms do we have?"

"In addition to ours? Two. Neither has furniture. They'd have to share the hall bathroom."

Her nose wrinkled, and I remembered what she said about life at home with her siblings. As much as I didn't want to think about our kids masturbating when they got older, I'd prefer they do that than have sex and possibly end up pregnant. Or in the case of sons, knock up some girl.

"We may need a bigger house," she admitted.

I picked up my phone from where she'd set it on the blanket and shot off a text to Beast. *My woman wants a big family. Need to build a new house.*

I saw the dots and knew I'd get a response soon enough. The phone chimed, and I smiled. *Pick a spot. Choose a style and get me the specifics.*

"Beast said to pick a spot," I told her.

"Could we build one here?" she asked.

"Probably not this exact location. He wouldn't want to cut down the trees. But in the clearing across the road would be fine. If you want trees in the yard, we'll plant some."

"We're really having a house built?" she asked.

"The sooner we tell him what we want, the faster it will get done. Think it takes six months or more to build one the size we'll need." I scanned the space across the street. "Unless Beast gets a pre-fab cabin. I honestly don't care. It might shave a month or two off the timeline."

"Do you know who designed the house we have now?" she asked.

I cleared my throat and glanced at her. "I did. I mean, I didn't draw up the plans. I hired an architect for that, but the overall way it looks was all me."

She moved in closer. "You didn't make it sound like you were so involved when I asked about the house before. You put so much into it, and you're willing to give it up?"

I placed my hand on the back of her neck before I kissed her. My lips lingered on hers for a moment. "Kitten, it's just a building. What makes it a home is the people inside it. You want a lot of kids, then I'm happy to have something else built. We can live in the house we have until it's ready. Doesn't matter if it's done in three months or two years."

"Then let's do it." She smiled. "But I want it to look a lot like the one we have now. At least on the inside. Although, I'm not sure I want our bedroom open to the rest of the house. A loft master is cool right now. When the kids get older?"

"Worried we'll scar them for life if they hear us having sex?"

Her cheeks turned pink. "Something like that."

"You can help me design it. Whatever you like about the house we have now, we can incorporate into the new one. But we can make some things different too."

She ate more of her food with a contemplative look on her face. I could tell she had questions for me and gave her time to sort them out in her head. She'd ask when she was ready. Until then, the silence was companionable. But the closer our picnic came to being over, the more I realized I liked being out here with her. Dating my sweet Leigha was proving to be one of my favorite pastimes. I hoped we had many more days like this one.

"You said you have a twin. Have you talked to them since you've been here?"

She shook her head. "Not really. I texted Logan to tell him I was all right, and I'd gone on a date. He sensed my fear in that alley. I had to say something to make him back off. There hasn't really been time since then to have a conversation with him. He wants to prospect for the Dixie Reapers, but Dad hasn't let him yet, even though he stays at the clubhouse."

"The two of you are close, right?"

She nodded. "Extremely."

I smiled, knowing what I was about to ask would piss her dad off more than he'd already been. "Invite him for a visit. I'll make sure there's a room at the clubhouse for him. Let him see what it's like here."

She leaned in closer. "Are you trying to steal my brother away too?"

"Maybe. Would you want your twin here?"

"More than you could ever know." She gave me a wistful smile. "That was the hardest part of agreeing to be yours. Don't get me wrong. I'll miss my parents and other siblings, but Logan is like an extension of me. Not being able to see him whenever I wanted would be torture. We'd figure it out."

"I don't think Beast would have an issue with him being here. I'll talk to him later, feel him out a bit. In the meantime, I wouldn't mind your brother coming up in a few days. I like the idea of him being around to help keep an eye on you when I'm not home."

"Then I'll call him when we get back home." She kissed my cheek. "Thank you, Tucker."

"Anything for my kitten." I winked at her, using my good eye on purpose. She giggled and shook her head at me. "Let's clean this up and head home. We need to check the contents of the kitchen anyway and place an order at the grocery. They have a curbside pickup option."

"All right." She looked across the road at where we'd build our house, a dreamy expression on her face. "I can't wait to start our lives together, Tucker. I know we technically have already, but building a house together, starting a family... it's more than I'd hoped for when I left home to drive up here."

"Fate brought us together, Leigha. And I meant what I said yesterday. You want to be more than my old lady, you want to get married, then I'll make it happen."

"Just ask Shield to do it," she said. "I don't need a ceremony. Although, I wouldn't mind a ring. Not a fancy one. A plain band is more than enough. I just wanted another way to show the world I belong to an incredible man like you."

"Then I'll see it's done." I tugged her closer again and kissed the hell out of her. "Come on, kitten. The sooner we order supplies, the faster I can get you out of those clothes. If this is our honeymoon, I'm making the most of it. With some luck, you'll be knocked up by tomorrow night."

"You mean if you didn't get me pregnant already?" She smiled. "They say practice makes perfect. Guess we'll have to try and try again until we know for sure."

I liked the way my woman thought. Sweet. Cute. Sexy. And she wanted the same things in life as me. Lyssa might have thought we had nothing in common, but she was dead wrong. If there was a perfect match for me, it was Leigha.

* * *

Leigha

Groceries were ordered, and so were kitty things. A Prospect named Iggy had picked them up and dropped them at the house for us. What I hadn't expected was the ring he'd delivered too. How Cyclops had bought it without me knowing was a mystery. Other than trips to the bathroom, we'd been joined at the hip since Church had let out.

I stared at the white gold band, with a rose gold design overlaid. To say it was stunning was an understatement. I'd never seen anything so beautiful. And he'd listened when I said I only wanted a band. Shield had worked his magic quickly, and we'd been married within an hour of getting home from our picnic. To some, it might seem unromantic. Having grown up with the Dixie Reapers, I knew the ceremony didn't matter. It was the life we'd build together that meant something. Everything else was window dressing.

Cyclops had put the kitty condo together already, and we'd found the perfect spot for it in the living room. The litter box went near the back door on a rubber mat. The cabinets and fridge were full to bursting, and I couldn't think of a single thing we'd need in the next few days. Which meant we'd be able to focus on each other. I couldn't wait!

I eyed Cyclops as he came back into the room after his phone call with Beast. "Well?"

"Call your brother. Beast said he's welcome to come visit, and even to stay if that's what he wants."

I let out a little *whoop* and quickly pulled up Logan's number on my phone. He answered immediately, which made me feel bad. He only did that if he'd been worrying about me.

"Finally! You ready to tell me the truth?" he asked.

"We can discuss it in person in three days."

"What the hell is in three days? You coming home then?"

I chewed my bottom lip. It seemed Dad hadn't called home, or if he had, he'd only told Mom that Cyclops had claimed me. My siblings didn't know I wasn't coming home. That wouldn't be a fun conversation.

"I'm already home. My new home."

The line was quiet for so long I looked at the screen to see if the call had dropped. "What the fuck is going on, Leigha?"

"So, I came to visit Lyssa at the Reckless Kings. I wanted a chance to go on some dates and live a little without everyone watching my every move."

"And what? You're just moving in with her? I doubt Beast is happy about it."

"Um, no. Actually…" I looked at Cyclops. He came closer and wrapped an arm around my waist, giving me his support. "I'm married."

I heard Logan spew a drink, and he started coughing. "Excuse me?"

"Married. I got married, and I'm staying here. Permanently."

"Who am I killing?"

I rolled my eyes. "Don't be dramatic, Logan. I'm married to Cyclops, and you aren't going to do anything. For one, he has Dad's blessing. And secondly... I'm happy. Thrilled. Don't ruin this for me, Logan. Please."

"Shit," he muttered.

"We're having a stay-at-home honeymoon, which is why I said we'd talk in person in three days. I want you to come here. Dad's here, along with Uncle Saint, and Savior. They're sharing the guest house Beast had built after he claimed Lyssa. He's already said you can have a room at the clubhouse."

"The clubhouse?" he asked.

"Well, you have a room at the one back home. I thought you might like to experience the clubhouse life here." I licked my lips and braced myself for his answer. "I'm sort of hoping you'll love it enough you'll want to stay. I don't want to be away from you, Logan, but this is my home now. I'll understand if you want to go back with Dad. I only ask that you give it a shot."

"Does Dad know?" he asked.

"No. He doesn't know I've called you, much less asked you to move here. You wanted to prospect for the club. I know Dad is holding you back for whatever reason. That won't happen here."

Cyclops took the phone from me. "Logan, it seems we're brothers now since I married your twin. Look, it's a lot to consider, and there's no rush. Leigha really wants you to come visit, and I could use your help. Stay for a few days. Stay for a week. A month. Whatever. If you don't like being here, no one will force you to stay. However, if you want to prospect for the club, I've already gotten it approved. The decision is yours."

He gave the phone back to me and I talked to Logan another few minutes before ending the call. The heated way Cyclops looked at me was enough of a clue we were heading to the bedroom. Not that I minded! Other than our first time together, we hadn't done more than kiss or hold hands.

"We have food. We're prepared for Lucifer to move in, and we have a few days without people interrupting us," I said. "Whatever shall we do with ourselves?"

He tugged me against his body. "I have a few ideas. But unless you want anyone walking past this window to witness all the things I want to do to you, I suggest we take this upstairs."

I leaned up and nipped his bottom lip. "Race you!"

I squealed as I broke free of him and ran to the stairs. Taking them two at a time, I hurried up to the loft, removing my clothes as I went. I heard his booted steps chasing after me, and my heart pounded in anticipation.

He growled as he tackled me to the bed, and I couldn't help but giggle. Between his heavy weight pressing me down, and the hair on his chest tickling my back, it was a little like being pounced on by a bear. My humor at the situation fled when I felt his hard cock prodding me. With a moan, I parted my thighs and tried to wiggle closer.

Cyclops gently bit my ear. "Something you want?"

"You damn well know what I need," I said.

He flexed his hips and rubbed his cock along the seam of my pussy, then pressed a little harder. I buried my face in the bedding as he stroked the head over my clit and an ache started building inside me. After what happened, I shouldn't be so turned on while he pinned me down, but I knew it was Cyclops on top of me. No one made me feel safer than him.

"Damn, kitten. You're getting so fucking wet." He flexed his hips again, and I lifted my ass, spreading my legs even more. He wasn't wrong. I could feel how slick I'd gotten. "You okay with this?"

"You holding me down?" I asked.

"Yeah."

"I actually like it." I turned my head to hold his gaze. "Being at your mercy is turning me on."

"We're going to explore that thought more later. Right now, I want inside you. Once my cum is leaking out of you, I'll try a few things. Need to figure out what you like in the bedroom."

I gasped as he sank into me, his cock filling me up. It burned as he stretched me but felt so amazing. The weight of his body settled something inside me as he pumped in and out of me. Every thrust of his hips made my nipples scrape against the sheets, just enough to make them harden even more. Cyclops shifted, placing a hand near my head and gripping my hip with the other. His strokes deepened and came faster.

No matter how incredible it felt to have him inside me, it wasn't enough to get me off. I wanted to come in the worst way, but my orgasm remained out of reach. Cyclops grunted as he lost his rhythm, slamming into me over and over, until I felt the heat of his release.

"You didn't come," he said, sounding disappointed, and a bit disgusted. "I'm an asshole."

"No, you aren't." At least I knew he wasn't mad at me, and only at himself.

He got off me and turned me onto my back. "Guess I need to make it up to you. Wait here."

Cyclops went into the bathroom, and I heard the shower running. When steam billowed out the door, I got up to investigate, and what I saw had my jaw dropping a little.

"What the hell is that?" I asked.

"Technically, it's an inflatable chair. But for the moment, it's going to be used in a different way. Come here."

I opened the shower door and stepped inside, closing my eyes as the water hit me. I could stand under the hot spray for hours, if it were possible. The new house needed a shower like this one, or a better one.

Cyclops made sure every inch of me was wet before he detached one of the showerheads. "They do that?"

He nodded. "Sit on the bench."

I looked at where he pointed and sat on the built-in seat near the inflatable chair. Cyclops adjusted the showerhead, then leaned in closer and kissed me. The nozzle sprayed across my nipples, the more concentrated stream sending a *zing* straight to my clit from my breasts. He rotated the spray, circling the peaks, until I wanted to beg him to let me come.

Cyclops lowered the showerhead, letting the water trail down my abdomen. He used his palm to spread my legs wide before hitting my clit with the spray. I jolted and squealed, my body tensing. He adjusted the setting, so the water pulsed, drawing out the sensations.

"Come for me, Leigha."

"So close," I murmured.

He drew back, taking the showerhead with him.

I watched as he turned the inflatable chair so that it faced the other bench, then he helped me to my feet. "Over it. Put your hands on the bench and let the chair brace your hips."

I got into position and felt him kick my feet wider apart. He arched his body over mine, bracing one hand on the bench. With the other, he wedged the showerhead through a slit I hadn't noticed in the inflatable chair. The water hit my clit in just the right spot.

"What do you want, Leigha? Want me to fuck you? Or do you want the water to make you come first?"

"Fuck me." I whimpered. "Please, Tucker!"

He thrust into me and I cried out. My grip on the bench tightened as he pounded into me. He did something to the showerhead that made the water pattern change and it sent me over the edge. I screamed I came so hard and felt the heat of his cum filling me up.

Cyclops pulled out and hooked the showerhead back into place before kicking the inflatable chair out of the way. I sagged to my knees, my legs unable to hold me. He lifted me and sat on the bench with me straddling his thighs. My eyes widened when I saw his cock was still hard and erect.

"How? I mean…" I blinked, and he laughed.

"You're the sexiest woman I've ever seen, Leigha. I don't think getting hard will be an issue."

I gripped his shaft and lowered myself onto him. The laughter died on his lips and his gaze heated. I rode him, my movements awkward since I was still new to all this. Cyclops leaned forward and took one of my nipples into his mouth. As he sucked and licked, I felt his fingers toying with the crack of my ass. He pressed one against that forbidden place, massaging gently, and my cheeks burned in embarrassment when I realized how good it felt.

The tip of his finger sank into me, and it nearly made me come. Something wild came unleashed inside me as I rode him harder. The scrape of his beard on my breasts, and that finger slowly thrusting in and out of my ass, had me digging my nails into his shoulders as I chased another orgasm.

When I came again, my body trembled, and my thighs shook. He worked his finger in deeper as I felt his cock pulse inside me. I didn't think I could have another orgasm, but he proved me wrong. As I screamed out his name, he banded an arm around my waist and thrust up into me, not stopping until he'd filled me up with his cum.

"What just happened?" I asked, feeling dazed.

"I think we discovered that my sweet little kitten likes a bit of kink with her sex." He grinned. "I'm placing another order, this time from a specialty shop. I'll give you until dinner to recover. After we eat, we're going to find out just how wild you really are."

I felt a flutter of excitement at his words and couldn't wait to see what he had planned. I might have been a virgin, but it didn't make me a prude. Whatever he'd be willing to try with me, I was all in.

Chapter Six

Cyclops

I'd never thought I'd have an old lady, much less a wife. Leigha slept soundly beside me in the bed, and yet, I found myself wide awake. She looked peaceful. Angelic. The way she curled so trustingly against me made my chest ache with an unfamiliar feeling. I wanted her to be happy here. Even though she visited, hoping to go on a few dates, moving here was another matter. Because she'd chosen to stay with me, she was giving up everything she knew.

I knew her family had made her feel overprotected and maybe even suffocated, but she loved them as much as they loved her. How long before she wanted to see her siblings or her parents? The Dixie Reapers might not be across the country, but it was a longer drive than heading into Nashville or even riding over to Chattanooga. I'd feel like an asshole if she wanted to visit her family and I had to say no. Having her drive so far on her own would leave me unsettled, especially after the way we met. It might be a while before I let her travel that far without me being by her side.

Great. Now I was a controlling asshole. Not something I'd ever aspired to become. But if anything happened to her... No, I wouldn't even think about it. How the hell had someone come to mean so much to me so fast? If I were honest with myself, I'd admit the moment she'd looked at me in that alley, I'd been hers.

"What am I going to do with you, kitten?" I ran my fingers through her hair.

Rolling to my back and pushing up so I could lean against the headboard, I reached for the notebook beside the table. I'd already started jotting down a few things to include in our new home. I wanted to expand the shower, add another showerhead, and have the bench take up the entire length of two walls. Now that I knew she was open to exploring sexually, I wanted more room to play.

Our bedroom was a decent size right now. She was right about needing a door and a way to keep the kids from being too nosy. I liked having a loft overlooking the lower level. I flipped the page and made a rough sketch. Instead of the bed being in that section, we could make it a sitting area with a wall separating it from the bedroom. I wanted enough room for the furniture we had already, plus I wanted to add a comfortable chair and a mirror. If my sexy woman liked the toys I'd ordered, I wouldn't mind expanding the collection, which would mean we'd need a locked chest as well.

I went back to my list and made a note of other things Leigha liked about our current home. Mostly, I wanted to keep the same design. But expand it. We'd need at least four bedrooms downstairs. Although she said she wanted a large family. What if she decided four kids weren't enough? I knew they could share a room, but it wasn't like Beast would tell me to keep it small.

I picked up my phone to text him. *Master bedroom and bathroom upstairs with sitting area. Five bedrooms and three baths downstairs. Problem with any of that?*

I hit send and went back to writing and sketching. The kitchen would need to be twice as big, and we'd need a formal dining area. Didn't mean we had to use a fancy table, but I wanted a space big enough for us, at least fix or six kids, and maybe even a few grandkids. Whatever house we built would be the one we kept until we died.

I looked up rustic dining sets and decided on a fourteen-foot table. I sent the link to myself, then noted the dimensions so I could make sure the dining room would be large enough. My phone chimed, and I bit my lip so I wouldn't laugh out loud at his reply.

Exactly how many kids are you having?

I quickly texted back. *As many as she wants. She said at least four.*

The phone rang, and I answered with a quick glance at Leigha to make sure the sound hadn't woken her. She still slept, and I relaxed.

"Hey, Pres," I mumbled.

"She sleeping?"

"Yeah, right next to me. Just making notes for the new house. Didn't want to go so big you told me there wasn't enough space, but she wants a big family and I want the same thing. But she made a comment about sharing rooms and bathrooms with her siblings, and how little privacy she always had. While some of the kids may have to share a room, and certainly a bathroom, I didn't want them to feel as closed in as she did."

"Where are you wanting it built?" he asked. I described the area, explaining why I'd chosen that spot. "I can't say we won't ever need more homes back that way, but yours will be the only one for a while. Possibly ever. Make the damn thing as big as you want, but you're chipping in on supplies. I'm sure one of the Prospects would love to have your current home whenever you move, but we have a few more who will hopefully patch in soon. Plus Leigha's brother, if he prospects for us."

"You really don't care if it's bigger than your place?" I asked. "I'm not even an officer in the club. I don't want anyone to think I'm trying to overstep."

"Cyclops, most of us don't want more than two or three kids. Hell, only five of us have women. You want enough kids to have your own baseball team, then make sure you have enough room for them. No one's going to give you shit about it. If they do, they can answer to me," he said.

"Thanks, Pres. I just want the house to be perfect. She likes this one, so I want something similar, just on a larger scale."

"Get me your notes and sketches whenever you have them ready. I'll get the same architect to draw up the plans and hire a crew. Might take a year, possibly more with the size house you want."

"We're fine living in this one for now," I said.

"Y'all need anything else? Got enough groceries? I know she didn't bring all her stuff with her. Leigha need more clothes or anything?"

"We're good. I'll order anything we need and have someone pick it up. Already got groceries, and we're ready for Lucifer whenever he gets here."

"Speaking of that…" Beast cleared his throat. "I spoke with Charming and Badger. They're both sending someone, and whoever the Devil's Fury sends will bring Lucifer. Should be here in two days. I told them not to rush since we're trying to give the two of you some bonding time."

"I appreciate it. She's so excited about the cat."

"Good. I've had a nice long talk with Lyssa. She's really sorry if she made Leigha feel like she wasn't wanted here. I guess her heart was in the right place, trying to get Leigha and Foster together, even if what she did was flat out wrong. I asked how she'd have liked it if someone meddled and said we didn't make sense together. Think it put it into perspective for her." He sighed. "I honestly think part of it is hormones."

"Wait. Is Lyssa pregnant again?" I asked.

"She hasn't told anyone, but yeah. She's only about eight weeks. With Mikhaila being so small, we'd hoped we were wrong. I love my girls, but they're exhausting."

"Congrats, Pres. You wanting a boy this time?"

He laughed. "I don't think I'm that lucky. Looks like I'm doomed to have all daughters. Good thing I'm well-armed."

"I don't care if we have all girls or all boys. The thought of having kids with Leigha... I can't even find the words to express how it makes me feel. I told her if we're lucky by the end of this short honeymoon, she'll be pregnant. If she's not already."

"Get back to staring at your woman, and don't tell me you weren't. I remember how those first days were. I'm glad the two of you found each other. I hope you have a lot of happy years together."

I smiled as I ended the call and set the phone aside. I faced Leigha and realized I'd woken her. The fact she was smiling at least meant she wasn't angry about it.

"I can't wait to have kids with you too," she said.

"Want to practice some more?" I asked.

She giggled and rolled toward me. "Is that all you think about? Sex?"

"When my sexy wife is lying next to me... naked? Of course. What the hell else would I think about?"

She traced hearts on my abdomen. "We could cuddle and watch a movie, since we're both awake. Maybe pop some popcorn. Make it a stay-at-home date?"

I kissed her forehead. "If that's what you want, that's what we'll do."

She went up on her knees and crawled across me. I groaned as she flashed her pussy and couldn't help but reach out and touch her. My fingers grazed her slit, making her freeze before she'd crawled off the bed.

Leigha turned her head and stared at me, her eyes dark and lips parted. I brushed her clit. Once. Twice. Her eyes slid shut, and she moaned. I teased her another moment before smacking her ass and giving her a nudge off the bed.

"Come on. You said you wanted a movie."

She sputtered and puffed up. "What? That was before you… you…"

I grinned and took her hand, leading her downstairs. While she found the popcorn in the cabinet, I washed my hands, then got out a large bowl. She popped our treat, and I gathered drinks and napkins. When it finished, I dumped the snack into the plastic bowl and carried it to the living room.

"Are we really going to sit on your leather couch naked?"

"Our couch," I corrected. "There's a blanket in the hall closet if you want to grab it. We'll put it down, but I rather like seeing you walk around without clothes. The doors are locked, so no one is going to surprise us by walking in unannounced."

"Fine."

I shook my head as she flounced out of the room, clearly still miffed I hadn't let her come. Little did she realize I had a plan. She'd said she wanted to watch a movie, but she hadn't said what kind. I queued up a soft porn I thought she might enjoy and started it when she walked into the room.

Leigha froze mid-step, her jaw dropped, and her eyes going wide as she stared at the TV. "What the hell did you put on?"

"Something I think we'll both enjoy." I pointed to the couch, and she hurried over, laying out the blanket before we sat. I took my usual spot, and she curled up next to me, with the popcorn bowl on my thigh for easy reach. "Ever watched porn before?"

"Of course not," she said, her brow furrowed. "Where would I have done that exactly? In the living room with my parents or younger siblings? Or maybe you thought I should have headed over to the clubhouse and watched it with the guys?"

I choked on the swallow of soda I'd just taken. "No."

"Well, don't ask stupid questions."

Jesus. Just the thought of her watching something like this in a room full of guys made me want to hit someone. I could only imagine Foster's reaction if she'd asked him to watch porn with her. I didn't know the guy, but I disliked him immensely. Anyone who craved Leigha the way I did was on my shit list. She was mine, and I hoped the Dixie Reapers made sure that little fucker knew it.

We only made it fifteen minutes into the film before Leigha started to squirm. I noticed her nipples were hard little points, and I'd be willing to bet her pussy was soaked. The woman on screen moaned as the man pounded into her. With her hands bound over her head, she couldn't get away from him. Not that she looked like she wanted to. Her thighs spread wider as he took her harder.

"Look like something you want to try?" I asked.

"Can we?"

"Kitten, we can do whatever you want in the bedroom. Within reason. We both have to consent to whatever we try, and I don't want either of us getting hurt. Aside from that, I'm open to trying just about anything once."

The couple on the screen changed positions, with the woman riding the man. Leigha tipped her head to the side. "Why is she facing the wrong way?"

"It's called reverse cowgirl," I said.

Moving the popcorn to the floor, I wiped my hands with the paper towels and motioned for her to come closer. My cock had been hard as granite since before the movie started. I helped position her and let Leigha set the pace. I placed my hands on her hips to help guide her.

"Keep watching the movie," I said.

She eased down onto my cock and started riding me slow and steady. I reached up and cupped her breasts, tweaking her nipples.

"Tucker!" She tipped her head back. "Oh, God! It feels…"

"Fucking amazing," I said.

"I need more. Please, Tucker. I can't… can't move… fast enough." She panted, and I felt her legs trembling.

"Want me to take over?" I asked. She nodded. I lifted her long enough to change positions. I flipped her so she faced the back of the couch and sank into her tight pussy. I gripped the couch frame with one hand and her hip with the other. "Hold on, kitten."

She pushed back against me. "Make me come, Tucker."

Slipping my hand from her hip down between her legs, I worked her clit as I thrust into her. Every stroke was harder than the last, until I worried we might break the couch. Her sweet cries were music to my ears. I fucked my beautiful wife until she came on my cock. She clenched down on my shaft, and it was enough to send me over the edge. I powered into her, filling her up with cum.

My heart pounded and sweat slicked my skin. I felt my dick twitch inside her, and I was loath to pull out. I loved being inside her.

"I think I like porn," she mumbled.

"Then let's watch another one. In our bedroom."

I groaned as I slipped out of her and watched our mingled release slide down her thighs. Lifting her into my arms, I carried her back upstairs, and made her come so many times she nearly lost her voice.

* * *

Leigha

I lay on my stomach, a pillow under my hips, and Cyclops curved over my back, his cock still buried inside me. I'd thought older men had trouble going multiple times, or at least I'd heard the younger guys back home tease the older generation about it. It seemed they'd been wrong because Cyclops had no trouble in that department.

"Do you plan to wake me up every morning like this?" I asked.

"Not a bad idea." He kissed my shoulder. "Want to stay in bed all day?"

"Is that your way of asking me to stay naked?" I smiled. I didn't mind, especially if it meant more orgasms. I was already addicted to Cyclops. The man was lethal. One touch and I wanted more.

"Kitten, if I thought you'd agree, I'd ask you to lie back with your legs spread so I could look at your pussy all day. I especially like it covered in my cum."

I sighed and closed my eyes, a feeling of contentment settling deep in my bones. "Think we've made a baby yet?"

"I don't know, honey. But I'm afraid if we keep going, you're not going to be able to sit for a while. Let's give your body a rest. Want a hot bath?"

I nodded. "That sounds nice."

"I'll get the tub going. While you soak, I'll make us something to eat. Any requests?"

"Waffles? Do we even have a waffle maker?"

"We don't, but I can get someone to pick up a waffle from the diner."

I reached out and laced our fingers together. "That's not necessary, but it's sweet of you to offer. Pancakes would hit the spot too. We can buy a waffle maker next time we're able to go shopping. I want to check them out in person to pick the one I like."

He leaned down and kissed me. "All right. Wait here a minute."

I watched him walk into the bathroom and wondered if all men looked that sexy when they didn't have clothes on. There wasn't a single thing I'd discovered about Cyclops that I didn't like. The thought of spending the rest of my life with him made me so incredibly happy.

When he came back out of the bathroom, I got up and met him halfway across the room. Wrapping my arms around his waist, I went up on tiptoe to kiss him. He tangled his fingers in my hair, deepening the kiss. My toes curled, and I sighed.

"Enjoy your bath. I'll keep the food warm until you come down." He trailed his nose down mine.

"Thank you. For everything."

He placed his palm against my cheek. "Kitten, I'm the one who should thank you. I didn't realize how empty my life was until I had that coffee with you. I know things are still new between us, but I will never regret making you mine. You're the best thing to ever happen to me."

My eyes misted with tears, and I kissed him once more before hurrying into the bathroom. I didn't know how he could be so damn sexy one second and endearing the next. I had the entire package with Cyclops. Badass biker, and big teddy bear. In some ways, he reminded me of my dad and Uncle Saint. Although, I doubted Cyclops had ever been a man of God, unlike my father.

I sank into the hot water and closed my eyes. He'd been right about me being sore. I felt swollen and puffy, maybe even bordering on raw. The water stung some but relaxed my muscles at the same time. I skimmed my hand over the water and tried to let my mind drift. I wondered if anyone would come with Logan or if he'd be alone. I should have asked him to bring some of my things. Maybe my mother would think to box up some stuff, or at least pack more of my favorite clothes.

When the water began to chill, I let it drain and got out, wrapping a large towel around me. I had to admit I felt better. Any tenderness had gone away. Since I didn't know what to expect downstairs, I pulled on a pair of panties and my pajamas. The tank and shorts didn't cover much, but at least I wouldn't walk into the kitchen naked.

I heard voices and crept closer, not wanting to disturb Cyclops if it was club business. Then I recognized my uncle's voice.

"He may cause problems," Uncle Saint said. "Just try not to kill the dumbass."

"As long as he respects that she's mine, we won't have an issue."

Who were they talking about? I poked my head around the doorway and Cyclops spotted me. He motioned me into the room. I stopped partway to hug my uncle before going to my husband. I still felt giddy inside when I realized he was mine in all ways.

"Everything okay?" I asked.

"Foster came with Logan," Uncle Saint said. "He brought the club truck, so your mom tossed more of your things into the back. I thought it would be best if I delivered them."

"It's all in the living room," Cyclops said. "You can put it away later. Right now, you need to eat. And put on more clothes."

My uncle rolled his eyes. "I helped change her diapers, and I'm her family. To me, she'll always be a little girl."

"I meant before Foster and Logan decide to drop by. I doubt they'll wait for her to come to them," Cyclops said.

"Good point." Uncle Saint ran a hand through his hair. "I'm heading over to the clubhouse. I'll try to wrangle the two of them long enough for you to eat and dress."

Cyclops pulled a plate out of the oven and set it on the table. The three pancakes made my mouth water as I took a seat. He set the butter and syrup out before retrieving his own place, then sat next to me.

"How are they still warm?" I asked, as the butter melted on top.

"I turned on the oven while I made the pancakes. Not enough to damage the plates, but it kept enough heat to keep our food warm."

I took a bite and nearly moaned. It was so good. "Keep feeding me like this and I'll get fat."

He glared. "The only way you're getting *fat* is if you're pregnant. Not that it matters. I don't care if you're the size you are now or weigh over two hundred pounds. You'll still be you."

I sighed and gave him a sappy smile. He said the sweetest things. "You're almost too good to be true."

"Would you prefer I be a dick? I'm sure I can come up with something that will have you calling me an asshole instead."

I shook my head. "No, thanks. I like you just the way you are."

"If you're finished eating, we should get ready. I believe our honeymoon is officially over. I know your brother will want to see you, and Beast is probably ready to put a plan into place to save those girls."

I nodded. "I'll hurry. It makes my stomach twist and turn, thinking about all the fun we've had together the last two days while those girls were being raped and abused."

He reached over to take my hand. "Hey, none of that. Beast needed time to get a plan together. Even if you and I hadn't taken the last two days to get better acquainted, those girls wouldn't be any closer to being rescued. None of this is your fault."

No matter what he said, it wouldn't ease my guilt. Having felt the fear of that man tearing at my clothes, I wondered if that's what they went through every day. Had they given up hope of anyone coming for them?

Hurrying upstairs, I changed into a pair of jeans and a plain navy tee. I hoped my Harley Davidson boots were in the box downstairs. I tugged on some socks and went downstairs to check. I found them at the bottom, under some of my favorite clothes, and quickly put them on.

Cyclops stepped into the room, already dressed and wearing his cut. His hair hung loosely around his shoulders, and my fingers itched to braid it. I hadn't been brave enough to ask if I could. I knew my dad kept his braided when it was longer. But not all men liked having their hair styled that way.

"Beast doesn't have your property cut yet, but it should be ready in another day or two. Everyone knows you're mine, except the club whores. Since I haven't been to the clubhouse other than for Church a few days ago, I haven't seen any of them. If they start shit, handle it however you see fit."

I wasn't sure how to take that. Did he want me to punch one of them if they started something? I wasn't like Venom's daughter, Farrah, or even Lyssa, for that matter. Would he be disappointed if I tried a nice approach first? After all, they were women like me, right? Surely they would see reason. I'd heard stories about club whores and knew some were pure trouble. It didn't mean they were all that way, though.

I took Cyclops' hand, and he led me out of the house and to his bike. I got on behind him, wrapping my arms around his waist. He eased it down the driveway, then pulled out onto the street. The small curvy lane winding through the compound didn't really give him a chance to open her up, but I enjoyed the ride just the same. I leaned into him and closed my eyes.

We arrived all too soon, and I spotted my brother's bike right away. I couldn't help but smile. It felt like forever since I'd seen Logan, and I'd missed him. Rushing inside, I scanned the interior of the clubhouse. The club whores were easy enough to spot, in their mostly naked state. I didn't know if they were still here from the previous night, or if they were starting their day early. I would have thought this behavior was more of a nighttime thing. Apparently not.

"Logan!" I scanned the room again, not seeing them. Then I heard my name. I looked up at the balcony and waved like an idiot at my twin brother. He shook his head, a smile on his lips, before he disappeared from view. I saw him a moment later, coming down the hallway that I assumed led to Church, and it seemed the stairs as well.

I threw myself into his arms and hugged him tight. "Damn, you'd think we'd been apart for months."

I gripped a handful of his artfully styled faux hawk and yanked, making him curse and drop me. Sticking my tongue out, I folded my arms and glared at him. Before I could say anything, two arms wrapped around me from behind and lifted me off the floor. By the scent, I knew it wasn't Cyclops. I tensed and looked over my shoulder, meeting Foster's gaze.

"Good to see you, Leigha. I don't get a hug like that?"

"No," I said with a bit of bite. "Put me down, Foster."

He frowned and set me on my feet. "No need to be so pissy."

"Fuck you, Foster. Nice didn't work. Your dad pulling you away from me also didn't sink into your thick head. I wasn't interested then, and I'm damn sure not now." I narrowed my gaze at him and took a step closer to my brother. Logan threw his arm around my shoulders and hugged me to his side.

"That better be your fucking twin," Cyclops muttered as he entered the clubhouse.

I smiled and held my hand out to him. "Of course, it is! Logan, meet Cyclops. My husband."

"Are you shitting me?" Foster asked. "I thought Logan made that shit up. You haven't even been gone a week and you're *married*? And to…"

I punched Foster in the arm. "Shut up."

Foster shook his head. "I don't get it. Why do you want him and not me?"

"Yes, I'm married." I stared at him, almost wishing he'd take a swing at Cyclops. Then I felt bad because I had no doubt my sexy hubby would knock him flat. I knew Foster's comment had to do with Cyclops' eye. My brother didn't seem to mind it. If he did, I couldn't tell.

"I take it this is Foster," Cyclops said, making his way to my side. He shook Logan's hand before facing the bane of my existence. "Keep away from my wife or we're going to have a problem."

Foster held up his hands. "I don't poach. If I'd realized Logan was serious about Leigha being married, I wouldn't have bothered tagging along. Then again, if I hadn't, neither one would have any of their shit. The truck came in handy. I'd thought she just wanted to stay for a while, change of scenery and all that."

I sighed. "Thank you for bringing my things, Foster. I appreciate it."

He nodded and looked around. "Yeah, well… I also wanted to make sure you were all right. You may not want to date me, but it doesn't mean I stopped caring. Maybe coming here wasn't the best idea, especially after you went to another state just to get away from me."

I wanted to reassure him that wasn't why I'd left. Except I didn't want to lie. He really had been part of it. Not *all* of the reason, but still.

Foster shoved his hands in his pockets. "So… the club pussy available to guests?"

"Well, that was fast," I mumbled. Cyclops gave a

nod, and I assumed Foster was free to hit up whatever club whore he wanted. "Go for it. Just remember, they may say no. It isn't necessarily their version of foreplay, so try to listen."

Foster grumbled under his breath as he walked off, but I hoped he took my words to heart. He was like a dog with a bone. Once he latched onto the idea of being with someone, he didn't let go. After being on the receiving end of that attention, I felt bad for any woman he set his sights on. I wondered if I should call Uncle Bull and have a chat with him. Clearly Foster still struggled with what was and wasn't acceptable behavior toward women.

I saw him chatting up two of the club whores and hoped one of them would find him charming enough to distract him a while.

A redhead came closer, folding her arms around her bare breasts as she approached. She glanced at me before quickly looking away, holding Cyclops' gaze. "You're married now?"

"I am," he said, lacing his fingers with mine. "This is my wife, Leigha, and that's her twin standing beside her. The club voted her in as my old lady, so she'll have a property cut soon. We going to have any issues?"

The woman shook her head. Her cheeks flushed as she held my gaze. "You got one of the good ones. But I guess you already know that."

"I do." I smiled. "He's more than I ever hoped for, and I keep thinking this must all be a dream. No way someone like him picked me. For whatever reason, he seems to like me."

She bit her lip and glanced away for a moment. When her gaze clashed with mine again, I saw acceptance there. I didn't know about the other club whores, but this one wouldn't try to cause any problems. I was certain of it.

"Welcome to the Reckless Kings," she said. "And congratulations on your marriage."

"Thank you. What's your name?"

She shook her head and backed up a step. I tugged on Cyclops' hand, hoping he'd get the message. For whatever reason, this woman felt like she couldn't talk to me. As long as she wasn't trying to steal my man, I didn't have any issue with her. Far be it from me to say who she could and couldn't sleep with. Her life was hers to do with as she pleased. Maybe she enjoyed being with all the bikers. They were certainly easy on the eyes.

"Her name is Sonja, and yes, I've been with her in the past, but not for a while," Cyclops said.

"It's nice to meet you, Sonja," I said.

She tipped her head to the side. "You're different. Like Whisper. She doesn't look down on us."

"You serve a purpose here. Will I be nice if someone puts their hands on Cyclops? Probably not. But until any of you gives me a reason to be a bitch, I don't see why I can't be civil."

Logan kissed the top of my head. "Proud of you, sis. Think your man is too."

"Leigha is amazing. I've thought so from the moment I met her," Cyclops said. "Now, why don't you get her to show you our home? I need to catch up with Beast and find out if he's calling Church anytime soon. I don't have an issue with her riding on your bike."

"Come on," I said, taking Logan's hand. "I think we've been dismissed."

Cyclops swatted my ass, making me squeak. I shot him a glare over my shoulder and went outside with Logan. I couldn't wait to show him our house and catch him up on everything he'd missed. Well, minus the hot sex. There were some things even twins didn't need to share.

Chapter Seven

Cyclops

I knocked on Beast's office door before stepping inside. He had papers spread out everywhere and looked like he needed a stiff drink. He didn't even glance up as I took a seat across from him. Scanning the documents, I realized they were a combination of files. Some of the girls Matteo had put into his stable, a few on his other business dealings, and one in particular that caught my attention. Reaching over, I lifted it off the desk to skim the contents.

"What the fuck is this?" I asked.

"Exactly what it looks like."

I held Beast's gaze. "The fucker put a hit out on me?"

"You injured one of his employees. Don't worry. No one within one hundred miles would touch that bounty. The second they realize you're a Reckless King, they'll back off."

"And the ones who decide it's worth the gamble?" I asked. "Jesus, Pres. How do I tell my woman she's not the only one in danger now? It's not like I can sit here, all locked up tight, while the club fights this battle."

"Technically, you could. We'll need a few brothers to stay behind and keep an eye on the old ladies and kids. No reason you couldn't be one of them." Beast looked away. "But I know you'd rather be out there in the thick of it. For you, this is personal. Even before you saw that paper."

"You weren't going to tell me, were you?" I asked.

"No." Beast rubbed his eyes. "I wasn't. I've been sitting here looking over all this shit and trying to find ways to convince you to stay behind. You're newly married, and I know the two of you are already trying to start a family."

"Pres, you didn't run and hide when Lyssa brought trouble to the gates. Ranger tackled Danica's problems head on. Hell, Forge has gone to battle more than once for Whisper, even if she was just a kid the first time. What makes you think I'd want to sit on my ass at home? Is it because of my eye? Do you think I'm a liability or something?"

"Of course not!" He growled and leaned back in his seat. "Look, Preacher has made it clear what he expects of this club regarding his daughter. You've been married to her for less than a week. I don't need to stir shit up with the Dixie Reapers. Pissing off Preacher, and possibly the others who came here, isn't the way to maintain the peace. My woman might be the daughter of their President, but it doesn't mean we get a free pass."

"I respect that you're in a precarious position, but I'm not sitting this one out. Leigha is mine to protect, and to avenge. Matteo's lackey planned to rape her. I can't let that slide, Beast. He needs to pay, and at my hands. I want that little shit's head."

"Fine, but you get to tell Preacher. Maybe if you explain why you're going, he'll settle down."

"So we have a plan?" I asked.

"We do. Church in fifteen. If you want a beer, get one now. I have a feeling we'll be in there for a while. Especially since I'm inviting the Dixie Reapers. Your wife's cat will be here any minute. That's the only holdup."

"Lucifer is on his way?" I asked.

Beast nodded. "Colorado, Romeo, and Ripper are coming. One of them is bringing a truck, along with your cat and whatever shit is coming with him. The Prospect on the gate has been instructed to send the truck directly to your house. Maybe the new furball will distract your wife while we hammer out the details of how all this will go down."

"Good. She's been excited about getting a cat. I only wish I could be there to see her face when she meets him. Hell, the cat will be half mine. I wouldn't mind getting to know him, but it can wait."

Beast pinched the bridge of his nose. "Jesus fucking Christ. Go home. I'll stall to give you a little more time. But haul your ass into Church as soon as you can."

I stood and went to the door, pausing. "Thanks, Pres. It means a lot to Leigha, and for now, this cat will be like our kid. It might not seem like it's a big deal, but it is. I appreciate you giving me the time to greet our new family member."

He waved me off, and I rushed out to my bike. I saw a truck and two motorcycles pull through the gate, and the truck veered off toward my house. Looked like Lucifer was here already. The truck parked in the center of the driveway, so I left my bike on the road in front of the house. Colorado got out of the truck and waved.

"Sorry. Do I need to move?" he asked.

"I can't stay long, but I wanted to be here when Lucifer joined the family. Mind if I carry him inside?"

Colorado opened the passenger side door. "Be my guest. He's been very vocal the last hour, so I'm sure he's eager to get out and stretch his legs."

"We have a little box set up, and a cat tree. We waited on anything else to see what Doolittle sent with him."

"A lot. Food, bowls, toys. He said you can keep

that kennel too. I have papers for you, showing he's up to date on his shots and when they had him neutered. His previous family kept detailed records. They blacked out their name and address but provided a copy of his medical history in case you need it."

I unbuckled the seatbelt Colorado had threaded through the kennel handle and lifted Lucifer from the truck. Carrying him inside, I found Leigha and Logan in the living room. "Kitten, our new baby is here."

She squealed and jumped up. Dashing over to me, she dropped to her knees to peer into the kennel. Sadly, my cock thought she should pay attention to him instead, and I started getting hard. Counting backward from ten, I tried to get myself under control. Unsuccessfully, if Logan's smirk was any indication. I flipped him off while Leigha focused on the cat.

"Lucifer, you're such a pretty kitty," Leigha said, cooing at the cat. "Let him out! I want to pet him."

I kneeled down and opened the kennel. Lucifer stuck his head out and gave a pitiful *meow*. Leigha scratched him behind the ear and sat on the floor.

"Thought you had Church," Logan said.

"I do. Beast let me come home to welcome Lucifer into the family. I can't stay but just a minute."

Colorado stepped into the house, carrying a bag of cat food and a bowl. "I'll get his other things. Thought you might convince him to eat something. Doolittle said he wouldn't eat this morning. I think he sensed another change was coming."

"Poor baby," Leigha said. "Let's show you to the litter box and get your food and water set up. Are you hungry?"

Meow.

Leigha reached into the kennel and pulled him out. The cat was larger than I'd expected. While a good bit of him was floof from the medium-length hair, Leigha grunted as she picked him up. I doubted she'd have done that if he were lightweight.

After taking the food and dish from Colorado, I followed them to the kitchen. I set the bag on the counter and filled one side of the bowl with water, then set it on the floor while Leigha showed Lucifer where to find his litter box. I poured a small amount of food into the other side of the dish, and he came running.

Meow. Meow.

"Talk all you want, Lucifer. Welcome to your new home," I said, bending down to pet him. He purred loudly as he gobbled up the food.

Colorado came into the kitchen with a small tote bag. "There are some cat toys in here, a laser pointer, and a blanket. Most of it is new stuff. A few pieces came from his previous home. It should help him settle in quicker, or so Doolittle said."

"Thanks," I said. I dug through the bag and pulled out a fake mouse, then dropped it onto the floor for Lucifer to find when he'd finished eating. "Kitten, I need to get to Church. See what Lucifer likes out of the things in this bag. It will give us an idea of what else we should buy for him."

"We'll be fine while you're gone," she said, not taking her eyes off the cat. "Thank you. For letting us give Lucifer a home."

I pulled her against me and tipped her chin up for a quick kiss. "Anything for you. I saw how much you loved that cat at the café. Knew then you needed one of your own."

"Hurry home. I don't want him to bond only with me."

"Make sure Logan has my number. If anything

happens and you can't get to a phone, I want to make sure he knows how to reach me."

She kissed me again. "You worry too much. We'll be okay. I don't plan to leave the house."

"Good. I'll be home as soon as I can. And Leigha?" I cupped her cheek. "You mean everything to me. Only death would keep me from your side, and I'm not sure even that would be enough to keep me away."

She hugged me tight, and I had to pry her loose so I could leave. I gave Logan a nod on my way out, then rode back to the clubhouse, hoping I hadn't just jinxed myself. I didn't know if Beast planned on us making a move today, or if we were just talking shit out. Either way, I'd wanted to say so much more to Leigha. Just not with an audience.

I hurried through the clubhouse and into Church. The room went silent as I took my seat, and I hoped I hadn't missed too much. Beast gave me a chin lift before he shuffled the papers in front of him.

"Now that Cyclops has joined us, let's get to the heart of things. As you all know, Matteo is back in town, and he's already got a new crew. He's also got a stable up and running, full of underage girls." He leaned back in his seat. "I think we can all agree that we can't allow this shit to happen in our town. Hell, it shouldn't be happening anywhere."

"Cut off one head and two grow back," Forge said. "Pedophiles and rapists are like a damn hydra. No matter how many we kill or send to prison, more seem to pop up. It's never ending."

"There's always going to be wicked people in the world," Brick said. "We could fight every bit of evil out there from now until the day we die, and we still wouldn't even the scales."

"Not just your club either," Preacher said. "We've taken out our fair share of bad guys, and more keep coming. The world gets uglier with each year that passes. All we can do is try to make a difference in whatever way we can and hope it's enough."

"How big of a fish is this Matteo?" Saint asked.

"He's been lurking around town for more than two decades," Beast said. "We've chased him off more than once. He always gets away and comes back a year or so later."

"We need more than one person keeping their eye on Matteo this time. Since we have extra help, we should be able to put that fucker in the ground," Forge said.

"Is there a plan?" I asked. "Or are we just running at him with everything we've got?"

"Matteo is being smart. He has his girls spread out across three locations. One on either side of town, and another out in the county. The only way to free them is to hit all of three at once. Otherwise, Matteo will get tipped off and he'll move the others." Hawk folded his arms. "Those girls are going to be traumatized. I'm not sure how they'll react to a bunch of bikers busting into the place. Be careful and remember they're victims."

"We're going to send five men to each building," Beast said. "I'll take the one on the east side. Brick, Copper, Colorado, and Ripper are with me. Forge is taking the house on the west side. Savior, Saint, Snake, and Nitro are with him. Hawk is taking the house in the county. Wrangler, Hatchet, Satyr, and Samson are with him. I want Romeo to stay and helped guard our families."

"Pres…" He held up a hand to stop me.

"Cyclops, I want you and Preacher to spend time

with Leigha and keep an eye on the compound. Prospero is in charge while the rest of the officers are gone. Shield will be here, but he's monitoring the situation on the computer with help from Wire and Wizard."

"The girls are going to need some things when they get here," Hawk said. "Hayley has already started getting some stuff together. Clothes in different sizes, shoes, and basic toiletries. We're clearing the clubhouse of all club whores. There's a bathroom downstairs the kids can use to clean up and change. I can't ask those women to stay gone too long. For some, this is their home. But I'm not sure how the children will react to them. They'll understand, and I'll only ask them to be gone a few hours. Overnight at the longest, in which case the club will pay for motel rooms."

"Danica and Lyssa are making a few platters of sandwiches of different types. The girls might be hungry once they realize they're safe," Ranger said. "I'm staying behind to keep our families safe."

"Fine. But the asshole who put his hands on Leigha is mine. If he's at any of those locations, bring him to me," I said.

Beast nodded, and I knew he'd make sure it happened.

"Those who are staying help the old ladies with anything they need, and make sure Matteo doesn't send anyone to the compound. Keep our families safe," Hawk said. "You're dismissed. The rest of us are going to discuss the logistics of how we're hitting those buildings, then we're moving out."

I stood, along with the others who would remain at the compound, and we filed out. I didn't like being left behind, but I understood Beast's reasoning. As long as I could assure Leigha she was safe, that the man who'd hurt her was buried in a shallow grave, then I'd rest easy tonight. Nothing else mattered.

* * *

Leigha

Lucifer had tired himself out, exploring the house and poking his nose into cabinets. He finally curled up in his cat tree and went to sleep. Logan sprawled on the couch watching some sci-fi flick he'd picked out, and I tidied up the place. Mostly to keep myself busy. I didn't know what was going on. Whisper called and mentioned something about the girls being brought here. When I'd asked how I could help, she'd assured me the others had everything in hand.

I hated not feeling like I was part of the club. Back home, someone would have assigned me a task. A way to help. Here, it felt like I was only visiting. Except for Logan, I was willing to bet every Dixie Reaper had been given a job to do. Even Foster. If he'd stayed behind, I hadn't seen him. Which meant he'd either gone with the men, was still at the clubhouse, or maybe he'd decided to go home. I wasn't about to ask.

"I think Lyssa hates me," I said.

Logan sat up. "What? Why the hell would you think that?"

"She didn't want me to be with one of the Reckless Kings. When I told her Cyclops was claiming me, she said we didn't have anything in common. She didn't know why we'd be together."

My brother shook his head. "Clearly, she's gone blind. I wasn't around him much, but I could see right away that man is crazy about you. Lyssa will come around. Maybe there's something else going on that has her stressed."

"I think she's pregnant," I said. "No one has outright said it to me, but it makes sense. She's never been the type to react based on emotions. I'm sure her hormones are out of whack, but she's never been a bitch to me before. I don't understand it."

"Did you ask why she was acting like she didn't want you here?"

"She gave me some bullshit excuse about how I belonged with a Dixie Reaper and she thought I should have accepted a date with Foster." I blew out a breath and looked around the room. There wasn't a single thing left to clean. "I don't like feeling like I don't belong here, Logan."

"Are you fucking kidding me?" I turned so fast I nearly tripped over my feet. Cyclops stood in the doorway, along with my father. Both looked pissed as hell. My husband stomped over to me and yanked me against his body. "You belong. You're mine, Leigha. I don't care what Lyssa thinks, or anyone else for that matter."

"I'll be back," my dad said, and I heard the front door slam shut. I winced, having a gut feeling he was about to go confront Lyssa.

"Whisper called," I said. "She mentioned something about the girls coming here. When I asked what I could do to help, she said they had it handled."

"I can promise Whisper doesn't have a mean bone in her body." Cyclops cupped my cheek. "She probably thought she was doing you a favor by not asking for your help. She's also right, though. From what Beast said, it sounds like the other ladies have everything handled."

"So I'm just useless?" I asked.

He growled and leaned in closer to kiss me. "Never. If it makes you feel better, I've been stuck on the sidelines too. I think the club is trying to give us more time together. You've only been mine a few days, and now hell is about to break loose around here. They're probably worried it will be too much of a strain on our new relationship."

"I'm not a delicate flower," I grumbled.

My brother snorted. "She's really not. If the three of us have nothing to do, I say we come up with something on our own."

I turned to face him. "Like what?"

"Any idea how old the girls are?" he asked.

I glanced up at Cyclops, but he shook his head. All I'd heard was they were underage, which could mean they were in high school or younger. I didn't know if someone would give us more information or not.

"I'm assuming someone is handling things like clothes and food?" Logan asked.

"Yes," Cyclops answered. "What did you have in mind?"

"Assuming any of them are younger, what about toys or coloring books? Even regular books might be nice. Something to let them escape from reality for a little while," Logan said.

"My brother is so smart, sweet, and thoughtful." I went over to hug him. "How are you still single?"

"Well, if I follow in everyone else's footsteps, it's because my perfect match is a toddler or hasn't been born yet." He arched an eyebrow at me before glancing at Cyclops and back again. I punched him in the arm.

"I take it back. He's an ass," I said.

"But he's not entirely wrong." Cyclops tugged me into his arms again. "And I like the idea of getting some books and other things to occupy the girls when they get here. I'll place an order and have it delivered to the gates. Or rather, we'll place one. The two of you pick out whatever you think they might like, then I'll finish the order."

He unlocked his phone and handed it to me. Logan and I sat on the couch and went through the app. We picked out both adult and children's coloring books, crayons, colored pencils, art pads with regular pencils, and a variety of young adult and juvenile fiction books. By the time we'd finished, the total had risen to over two hundred dollars.

"We got a little carried away," I said.

Cyclops looked at the total and handed the phone back. "There are three locations with girls. I don't know the exact number coming to the compound, but I'd assume at least eight. Let me see if I can find out any information on them from Shield."

"Could you put it on speaker?" I asked. "Or is this one of those club business things?"

"This is different." He called Shield, and I heard the phone ringing, which meant he'd done as I asked. When Shield answered, I could hear the strain in his voice.

"Is something wrong?" Shield asked instead of saying a simple *hello*.

"Not exactly. Logan and Leigha wanted to help, so we're gathering things that might distract the girls from their problems. Any idea how many and what ages?" Cyclops asked.

"You sure you want to hear this?" Shield asked, his voice dropping lower. I knew then whatever he'd found was bad.

"We need to know," I said. "Please, Shield."

"There's a boy who's only six years old. One who's nine, and another who's eleven. The girls are ten, twelve, fourteen, fifteen, and sixteen. But there are two who are fourteen, three who are fifteen, and two who are sixteen. So three boys and nine girls."

My stomach knotted and twisted. I felt bile rise in my throat. "How have they prostituted that many children right under the club's nose?"

Cyclops flinched, and I hated that I'd hurt him, but what I said was true. If they'd been aware of this Matteo person, and knew he trafficked children, how had they let him stay long enough to have so many children to abuse?

"We didn't think he had that many, or any so young," Shield said.

"It's no excuse!" I yelled. "Y'all knew about this man and what he could do. You spent too much time planning, and these children have been suffering. Are you going to look them in the eye and tell them they've lived through hell because none of you were ready to make a move?"

"Damn, Leigha," Logan muttered. "Dial it back some."

"You don't understand. You have no idea how scared they are, or what they feel when those men tear at their clothes, and..." I pressed my lips together and closed my eyes, trying not to think about the alley.

Logan tensed and straightened. "What the hell does that mean?"

"One of Matteo's men attacked your sister," Cyclops said. "It's how we met. She didn't want you to worry."

Logan stormed out of the house, and I heard him screaming outside. A tear slipped down my cheek and Cyclops kneeled in front of me. He cupped my face in his hands and pressed his forehead to mine.

"We'll help those children however we can," Shield said, reminding me he was still on the phone.

"They're going to need homes, unless they have families to return to," I said. "Where will they all stay while everything is sorted out?"

"I don't think Beast has thought that far ahead. They're out raiding the buildings now. But there's something to keep in mind. Once those kids are here, Matteo is going to be out for blood. It won't be safe to leave the compound, not for any of the women and children," Shield said.

I held Cyclops' gaze. He ended the call and watched me, waiting while I gathered my thoughts. I knew what I wanted -- no *needed* -- to do. I only hoped he'd be on board with it. After all, it was a decision that would affect us both.

"If one of the younger ones needs a home..." I couldn't even finish my sentence without my throat getting tight with unshed tears.

"Then we'll adopt them," he said. "Not the teenagers?"

"Too close to my age." I smiled. "We'll get odd looks as it is. But if you go out with me and our fifteen-year-old daughter, can you imagine how people will react?"

He grunted. "Good point. They'll think I'm like Matteo and starting a stable of children."

"We'll see if they have families who are missing them," I said.

Cyclops handed the phone back to me. "Get some toys too. I'll put a rush on the delivery so it's here within the hour. If we could leave the compound, I'd have just taken you shopping, but I won't risk you."

I bought things I thought the younger ones would like, as well as some picture books. By the time Cyclops paid for everything, we'd spent several hundred dollars. I only hoped it would help those poor children in some way.

"Are they going to the clubhouse when they arrive?" I asked. Cyclops nodded. "Can we meet them there?"

"Of course." He kissed me. "Get your shoes on. We'll head that way now so I can intercept the order when it arrives. I'll help carry everything in."

Logan came back inside, his face flushed and his eyes red. I could tell he'd been crying and felt awful. I hadn't wanted him to know for this very reason. Walking toward him, I hesitated only a moment before hugging him tight.

"It's not your fault, Logan. And I'm safe. Cyclops got there before that man could rape me. I fought as hard as I could, but the guy was stronger."

"I know, Leigha. I felt it. When you blew me off with some bullshit reason, I knew you were lying, but I didn't force you to tell me what happened. I should have. I'm so fucking sorry you went through that."

"You can't control what other people think and do, Logan. The world doesn't work that way. I survived, and now I'll help those children do the same thing."

"We're going to the clubhouse, so we'll be there when they arrive," Cyclops said. "Order should be here in thirty minutes. I put a rush on it."

"I'll help wherever I can," Logan said.

"I'm taking my car. I know you both have your motorcycles, but I..." My gaze clashed with Cyclops' and I knew he understood. If there was a chance we were bringing home a child tonight, I'd need my vehicle.

"We'll follow you there," Cyclops said.

I grabbed my keys and went out to my car, my heart pounding. I didn't know what condition the children would be in when they arrived, or how badly broken they would be mentally. Whatever they needed, I'd do what I could to see they healed and were safe. It hurt, knowing they'd been suffering when they should have years to still be innocent. Instead, the monsters of the world had snatched them.

"Never again," I muttered. I'd protect them with my last breath if that's what it took. I hoped the club made those men suffer, and I'd damn sure ask Wire and Lavender to try and track anyone who hurt the children. The clients needed to pay too.

Chapter Eight

Cyclops

I couldn't have been prouder of Leigha and her brother. I hoped like hell he stayed and prospected for the club. I'd be honored to have him at my side. And I knew my wife would feel better having her family nearby. Her dad and uncle would return to the Dixie Reapers soon. While Lyssa and Danica had come from there too, for whatever reason, they hadn't welcomed Leigha with open arms. To be fair, she hadn't seen Danica at all yet.

Some children were already at the clubhouse when we arrived. Leigha dove right in, trying to set them at ease. I loved watching her.

She kneeled in front of the six-year-old boy. He'd backed himself into a corner and curled up in a ball, trying to make himself as small as possible. My chest ached, and I rubbed at it. The people responsible for hurting all the kids would pay, even if I had to go after each of them myself.

So far, no one had found Danny, the asshole who'd tried to rape Leigha. Or if they had, they weren't saying a word to me about it. Matteo was also in the wind, but I doubted he'd left town. No, this time we'd hurt his business, and I'd heard some of his clients had died in the process of retrieving the kids. He'd come for us.

Leigha coaxed the little boy from the corner. He moved slowly, freezing after every inch. She remained patient, and soon, she held him in her arms. When she faced me, I saw the tears in her eyes. He clung to her, his fingers knotted in her hair. The little guy buried his face in her neck. I could see him trembling, and wished I knew how to calm him. I dug through the bags of things I'd had delivered and found a stuffed bear. Carrying it over to them, I kneeled down next to Leigha.

"What's his name?" I whispered.

"Tyler." She rubbed his back. "He won't say his last name."

I nodded and gave the bear to her. I doubted he'd accept it from me. She took it, giving me a grateful smile, and I went to find Shield. He'd set up in Church, trying to locate Matteo.

"Talk to me about the smallest boy," I said, pulling out a chair and sitting next to him.

"I've been trying to follow the trail, but it's not easy. Even Wire and Lavender haven't been able to unravel everything yet. Looks like Matteo took him in trade for a debt owed, but the person who gave the kid away wasn't his mother."

"His name is Tyler, but Leigha said he wouldn't tell her anything else."

"That's more than I have on him. No names. Just his age, where Matteo got him, and that the debt was canceled and considered paid in full. I found some dirt on the woman, but there's no record of her ever having a child. She could have stolen him for all I know."

"Have you run him through any programs to see if there's a missing person report on him?" I asked.

"Wire did. There's nothing. If anyone is missing that kid, they haven't gone to the police or FBI. I have no idea where he came from."

I leaned back in my chair and stared across the room a moment. Leigha clearly liked the boy, and he trusted her. I wasn't sure how he'd feel about me. If we could convince him he'd be safe with us, I had no problem taking him home. Something told me if we did, he'd never leave. Leigha would claim him as our kid, and I was fine with that.

"What aren't you saying?" Shield asked.

"Leigha is holding him. I think she'll want to take him home with us. Not sure how he feels about it, and if he does have family out there looking for him, I'd hate to deprive them of their kid."

Shield laced his hands behind his neck and tipped his head back. "Unofficially, no one's looking for him. I can't find a damn thing, and if Wire can't either... But until Beast tells me to throw in the towel, or that kid speaks up, I'll keep digging."

"He can stay at our house tonight, or for however long he's here," I said. "But if we have to give him up, it's going to break Leigha's heart. I can tell she's already getting attached, and she's only had the kid in her arms for a few minutes."

"Hey, you took one look at her and wanted to keep her, right? Maybe she feels the same about the boy," Shield said. "If Beast gives me permission, then I'll legally make that kid yours and Leigha's."

"I won't tell her that until I know for sure. I don't want to give her hope that he's ours, then hand him over to his actual parents."

He nodded. "All right. Want any other ones? I don't think any of these kids are going anywhere tonight."

"I'll check with Leigha. Depends on how much Tyler needs. I want to make sure he gets the attention and help he requires, even if that means we focus only on him for a little while."

"Well, if you leave with more than one, just make sure someone knows. I don't want to spend hours searching the compound for a kid that's safely tucked into bed at your place."

He pulled the laptop closer and got back to work,

which I took to mean our conversation was over. I stood and went back into the main part of the clubhouse. Leigha and Tyler were sitting at a table not far from where I'd left them. He had the bear clutched in one arm and used his other hand to color. I pulled out the chair across from them, and noticed the kid froze.

"Tyler, this is Cyclops. He's my husband," Leigha said. She kissed the kid's head. "He saved me, just like his brothers saved you tonight. I promise he'll never hurt you."

"She's right," I said. "I'd sooner cut off my hand than ever harm you. Do you remember your last name, Tyler?"

He shook his head and started coloring again. Leigha hugged him, and I knew there was no fucking way that kid wouldn't be ours. Because even if his parents showed up tomorrow, my wife wouldn't let the boy go. I saw it in the way she held him, the look in her eyes, and the determined set of her jaw. And maybe she wasn't wrong. Until we knew how Tyler had ended up with the person who traded him to Matteo, I wasn't handing him over to anyone. For all we knew, the parents sold him.

"Do you remember your mom?" I asked.

He turned and curled into Leigha. "Momma."

My gaze held hers, and I saw the resolve there. Yeah. This kid was ours now. No way my woman was letting him go. Not now, not ever.

"Tyler, if I'm your momma, then it means Cyclops is your daddy. Is that what you want? To live with us?" Leigha asked, her voice soft.

He nodded, casting me a shy glance. I had a feeling he'd have accepted anyone else in his life, as long as Leigha kept holding him. Couldn't blame the kid. He kept staring, and I wondered if it was my eye. I had to imagine to a kid it was especially scary looking.

I touched the corner of my bad eye. "I can't see out of this side. I know it looks weird. I was in the military and got hurt while fighting for our country."

The boy stared at me, and I wasn't sure if he understood anything I'd just said, other than the part about not seeing. Since I didn't know anything about his past or his upbringing, it was possible he had no idea what the military was. But it was a conversation for another day.

"All right. Then if anyone asks, we're your parents. End of story. You want to go home, Tyler? We can decorate your room tomorrow. Buy some toys. Anything you want." I reached out my hand, palm up, on top of the table and waited to see what he'd do. The little boy reached out and put his hand in mine. I closed my fingers around his, but it felt like he'd reached out and grabbed my heart. The moment he gave me his trust, he'd owned me, much like his mom. I looked at Leigha and saw she felt the same. "Let's take our son home."

She nodded.

The clubhouse doors opened and more of my brothers came in, a group of kids shuffling between them. The poor things looked terrified, and my brothers looked like they'd been to hell and back. As much as I wished I could have gone with them, I was glad I'd been here with Leigha. For one, I'd been able to keep her from feeling unwelcome by the Reckless Kings. And if I hadn't been here, we may not be taking Tyler home with us, or have been able to provide a bit of distraction for the children with toys and art supplies. Hell, I should have bought some games and puzzles.

I looked across the room and caught a Prospect's eye. He hurried over.

"You need something, Cyclops?" He glanced where my hand still held little Tyler's.

"Yeah. I'm going to give you some cash, and I want you to head to the nearest open store. Get at least four board games, two for younger kids and two for the others, as well as a few puzzles of different sizes. They need things to keep them occupied and stop their minds from going down dark paths." I released Tyler's hand long enough to get out my wallet and hand Kye roughly one hundred dollars. I knew games could be pricey, but hopefully he'd have enough for what I'd requested.

Tyler tensed, and I wondered if it was because Kye was standing too close. After all these kids had been through, a bunch of men in the room probably had them nervous. I looked around and noticed quite a few seemed terrified. With some luck, they'd settle down before the day was over, and realize they were finally free.

Prospero heard me and came closer, taking out his wallet. "I'll add to that. Maybe get some pudding cups too. All kids like that stuff, right?"

Two more brothers came over, adding to the fund. This was part of what I loved about my club. We banded together when times got hard, and we all enjoyed helping those in need. Especially when it came to women and children.

"I'll take one of the club trucks and get it taken care of now," Kye said. "And if we need beds for everyone, I'm willing to give up my room for however long they'd need it. I know Beast sent the girls into town and the club offered to pay for motel rooms. I'm not asking for money to pay for a place to stay, but I'm happy to sleep elsewhere until we get everyone situated."

"Appreciate it, Prospect," Beast said. I hadn't even heard him come in, nor had I seen him. Then I realized the last batch of children had arrived. "We'll figure everything out. It's going to be a long-ass night. Right now, the primary focus is getting them cleaned up and fed."

Shield came down the hallway with some papers in his hand. It looked like he'd stopped in Beast's office to use the printer, since I knew there wasn't one in Church. And he damn sure hadn't had those when I'd seen him earlier.

"I've got a list of kids who have families looking for them," he said, giving the papers to Beast. Then he looked from Leigha to me. "Tyler isn't the only kid we can't track. There's no record at all for the nine-year-old boy or the ten-year-old girl. Not so much as a name. Same for Tyler. If he hadn't told Leigha his name, we wouldn't know it. Other than what I mentioned previously..."

I nodded, knowing he didn't want to bring it up in front of the kid. So aside from him being given to Matteo to pay off a debt, this kid was a ghost. No one was searching for him, and there was no record of him anywhere.

"Where are the two kids who don't have anyone?" I asked.

"I'll get them," Beast said. "I know which two he means."

A moment later, the Pres came back with a boy not much larger than Tyler and a little girl who looked painfully thin. Both had shadows under their eyes, and nearly vacant gazes. As much as I wanted to focus only on Tyler, I couldn't leave these two without a home.

Leigha's eyes teared up and her lip trembled as she stared at them. "What are your names? I'm Leigha, this is Tyler, and the big man in front of you is my husband, Cyclops."

The girl blinked a few times and mumbled, "Don't have one."

I kneeled down, not wanting to scare her with my height and size. I made sure not to move too close and not to touch her. "You don't have a name?"

She shook her head. When she saw my eye, she froze a moment and stared. I told both kids the same thing I'd already said to Tyler. They took it in stride, but I could tell they had questions.

The boy staggered back a few steps, his eyes wide as he stared at me. My stomach knotted when I realized why he was so scared. I wanted to hit something, to tear the world to pieces, because everyone had failed these children. Monsters like Matteo shouldn't be able to grab them so easily, or have junkies use them in trade.

"Do you have a name?" I asked the boy. "Like my wife said, I'm Cyclops. My club thought the name was funny since I'm blind in one eye. But I guess it suits me well enough. We'd like to find your family. See that you both get home safely. Do you remember your parents? Where you lived? Anything?"

The girl swayed a moment, and I caught her before she toppled to the floor. Cradling her close, I hated I could feel her bones. Tears ran down her cheeks and she tried to hold back a sob.

"No parents," the boy said.

No parents. I eyed both kids and looked at Shield. "Did you check the foster system? Orphanages? Hospitals? These kids didn't just appear out of thin air as if by magic."

"There's nothing," Shield said. "Their faces aren't traceable in the system. Even if we took fingerprints, the chances we'd find anything are slim."

"Neither of you have a name?" Leigha asked, keeping her voice low.

"No," the boy said, inching closer to her. He watched Tyler, and I saw a flash of envy in his eyes when he glanced at Leigha before turning his face away.

The girl in my arms shook, but she didn't try to get away. I sat in a chair and held her on my lap, firm enough she wouldn't fall and loose enough she'd know I wasn't holding her captive.

"Would you like a name?" Leigha asked. "You could name yourself, or... if it's okay, Cyclops and I could give you a name."

He looked at Tyler again. "Can you name me?"

I heard Leigha audibly swallow as she nodded. "Of course, sweetheart. Since Cyclops' real name starts with a T, and Tyler's name starts with that letter too, why don't we call you... Do you like the name Tristan?"

His eyes lit up, and he smiled. "That's my name?"

"Yes. Your name is Tristan," she said and held out her hand. He went to her, letting her put her arm around him and hug him close.

"Do you want us to pick a name for you too?" I asked the girl in my arms.

She nodded and leaned a little closer to me, relaxing a little every minute that passed. It would take time before she realized she was safe now. We wouldn't let anyone hurt her ever again.

"Since my wife decided all the men in the family need T names, I guess that means you need an L name like her. What about Lacy?" She tucked herself tight against me and I hugged her harder. "If you don't like that one, we can come up with something else."

"She likes it," Tristan said, watching her. "You said family. Does that mean... Are we..."

I held Leigha's gaze, and she gave me a nod. I knew we were in over our heads with three abused kids, but neither of us could turn our backs on them. Especially knowing they had nowhere else to go. "Yeah, Tristan. The three of you are now part of our family. You said you didn't have parents, but you do. Me and Leigha."

Savior came over, one teenager following in his wake. He turned to look at her before walking up to Shield. "This one says she was in the foster system, and she refuses to go back. They placed her in a home with five other kids, and the dad kicked her out when she wouldn't allow him to prostitute her for drugs. It's how Matteo got her. The parents owed him a lot of money. So he took her as payment."

Shield flipped through his files and paused when he got to hers. I knew it had to be hers the way he looked from the picture to her and back, sorrow etched on his face. "The foster parents reported you as a runaway. Pia Thompson, right?"

She nodded and moved closer to Savior, reaching out to hold on to his cut. The fact he let her spoke volumes. He reached back and took her other hand. "Can you do the same type of stuff Wire does? Change her name? Erase her from the system and reinvent her as someone new?"

"Yes, to some of that, but honestly, Wire and Lavender are way better," Shield said. "What did you have in mind?"

"I need you to change her names to Ares Black."

He lifted his chin a notch. "And list me as her father."

Shield paused. "Are you?"

"In every way that counts." Savior pulled her from behind him and put his arm around her. She looked delicate, yet there was a fierceness in her eyes. They hadn't broken her. The ragged fingernails and bleeding nail beds told me she'd fought back. Bruises lined her arms, and she had one on her jaw.

"All right. Ares Black. Age fifteen. Do you want me to keep the birthday the same? I don't think altering it a few days would hurt anything if she wants a completely fresh start. June third could just as easily be May twenty-eighth, or June ninth." Shield watched them both, and I noticed they seemed to have a silent communication going already.

"May," Savior said. "Any day is fine. I want any necessary papers ready before I take her home. I'll also need a trailer for my bike. I'll ride back in the truck with her and Foster."

"I'll do what I can," Shield said. He turned back to me and Leigha. "Since your family will be remaining here, I'm going to handle Savior's stuff first. But I'll make sure all three kids have birth certificates, social security numbers, and we'll make sure they get their immunizations within the next week. After that, you can enroll them in school whenever you're ready."

I stood and set Lacy on her feet. "Y'all ready to go home?"

The kids nodded. I turned to Kye, who hadn't left just yet. "Can you come by the house before you go? I've got more cash there. The kids are going to need some basics to get them through tonight and tomorrow morning."

"The club will take care of it," Beast said. "Write down their sizes and what you need. I'll have it delivered to the house within the hour."

"Thanks, Pres." Shield gave me a piece of paper. I saw it was what little he'd found on Tyler. Flipping it over, I got a pen from someone else and then asked the kids what sizes they wore. We made a short list, and I handed it over before herding my new family out to Leigha's car.

"Just for today, Lacy gets to ride in the front seat. We'll look at bigger vehicles so all three of you can ride in back where it's safer." I helped buckle the kids in, kissed my wife, and followed behind the car. I hadn't thought to tell the kids about the cat. I hoped none of them were allergic.

* * *

Leigha

Lucifer adored the children, and they loved him too. I'd been worried as we'd driven home, but the cat had taken one look at the kids and acted like he was seeing his best friends for the first time in years. The club had given each child a package of underwear and a clean outfit, so we'd let them bathe and change. I'd had to help Tyler, but the other two could take care of themselves in the bathroom.

Cyclops found a cartoon for them to watch, and each child had stretched out on the floor with Lucifer lying longways in front of them. Each kid could pet him, and he looked to be in heaven from all the attention. Every little noise made the kids jump, and I knew it would be a while before they felt truly safe.

Cyclops sat next to me on the couch, but he drummed his fingers on his thigh. I could feel the tension in his body and wondered if it was because of our recent additions to the family or something else. As badly as I wanted to ask, I didn't dare with the children so close. They'd been through hell and deserved as normal a night as we could give them.

A knocked sounded at the door and Cyclops stood so fast I'd have missed it if I blinked. He let Kye inside, loaded down with shopping bags. I got up to help, knowing it was the items for the children. They stared, and I saw a spark of interest in their eyes. Taking the bags from Kye, I started separating things into three piles. One for Tyler, one for Tristan, and one for Lacy.

I motioned Lacy over first. She eyed the pile of clothes and toys but didn't reach for any of it.

"After we get your bedrooms set up, we can put the clothes away. Since you're our only daughter, you'll have to take the slightly smaller room since the boys will be sharing." I reached out and smoothed her hair from her face. "But one day soon, we'll have a great big house, and everyone will have their own rooms."

She reached slowly for the doll and picked it up. It had a frilly pink dress on, and a pacifier hung on a ribbon around its neck. Lacy ran her hands over the doll reverently, and I wondered if she'd ever had one before. If she hadn't had parents, and Shield couldn't find any record of her existing, it was possible she'd never had a chance to be a child. It broke my heart and I nearly started crying again.

"She's yours. All of these things are. The first bedroom is yours. Want to help me carry everything in there? You can set your toys out and we can talk about how you want the room to look. Your dad thinks the new house will be ready within a year, but that's still a way off. No reason we can't make your bedroom extra special until we move."

She took my hand and Cyclops came over,

gathering the rest of her things. He followed us down the hall and into her room. I flipped on the light and Lacy went to the bed. She trembled as she stared at it.

"Take the beds out of the rooms." I turned to face him. "I hate to send Kye back out, but if he could get a few sleeping bags, or maybe some cots, that would be better for tonight."

Tristan stood in the doorway, Tyler's hand clutched in his. "Could we all stay in the same room?"

I bit my lip so I wouldn't cry and nodded. "Of course, you can, sweetheart. Tell you what. We'll make this room the playroom. All the toys and crafts can go in here. We'll even get a table and chairs for the three of you to color or do puzzles. And for tonight, we'll get some temporary beds in the other room. We'll buy furniture as soon as I know it's safe to take you outside the gates."

"We can sleep in a bed like that," Tristan said. "As long as we're together."

"All right. I'll make sure the other room is ready when you want to go to sleep. We can still take the bed out of this one." Cyclops leaned into the hallway and called out for Kye, then told him to move to the bed out of the house. The children scattered when Kye entered the room. One day, they wouldn't react that way. Whatever it took, I'd help them heal and make sure they were confident and strong. Just like my parents had done for me.

My eyes widened as I stared at the kids. "Oh, my goodness! I completely forgot. Did you know you have an Uncle Logan and a grandpa? They're visiting right now, as well as my Uncle Saint. Would you like to have breakfast with them tomorrow?"

"A grandpa?" Lacy asked.

I nodded. "And a grandma, but she's not here

right now. They live in another state. My dad and uncle were visiting, otherwise they wouldn't be here either. But I'm hopeful my brother will decide to stay. How could he not when he has an awesome niece and two amazing nephews now?"

The kids smiled and relaxed a little. Baby steps. I wanted to rush out and get everything they could ever need or want, make this house look like they'd always been here. At the same time, I didn't want to overwhelm them. It was difficult to balance between wanting them to feel secure in their place with us and not giving them too much at once.

Kye stripped the bedding off the bed and carried the mattress out. While he was gone, Cyclops kneeled down in front of the kids. "It's been a long, rough day. If you could have anything in the world for dinner, what would it be?"

"Cake," Lacy said.

Tristan huffed. "You can't have cake for dinner."

"Maybe not for dinner, but we can have it for dessert," I said. "What else do you want? Tristan? Tyler? Any requests?"

"Chocolate milk," Tyler said.

I watched Tristan and saw the war he waged with himself. I just didn't understand it. Did he worry what he wanted cost too much?

I reached out and took his hand. "Honey, whatever you want, tell us and we'll try to get it. If you're worried about the cost, don't."

Cyclops groaned as he lowered himself the rest of the way to the floor, stretching one leg out and crooking the other. "Do you know what it means to be a parent?"

The kids shared a look, and the sadness I saw ate at me.

"Being your parents means it's our job to take care of you. That includes giving you healthy things to eat, making sure you have clothes and shoes that fit, giving you ways to occupy your time and learn new things." Cyclops stretched out his other leg, wincing as he rubbed his knee. "Next time I get on the floor, remind me I'm not twenty anymore."

I tugged on his beard. "Sure thing, old man."

He growled and scowled at me. I shrugged. He'd left himself open for that one. Our age difference bothered him at times, even though he tried to say it didn't. More than once, I'd caught him checking for gray hair. He didn't seem to realize women liked a silver fox.

"What your dad is trying to say, is that you can make any request you want. It doesn't mean you'll get it. For instance, cake for dinner. We can have it afterward, but it's not a healthy meal." I held Tristan's gaze. "And there's no price for the things you want or need. Well, maybe a small one. I do expect the three of you to pick up after yourselves. Put your clothes where they belong, keep your toys picked up. That sort of thing."

Kye came back in and started taking the bedframe apart. The kids watched and waited. Once he'd left the room again, the tension eased once more. I frowned, staring at the now empty doorway.

"Do the three of you know Kye?" I asked.

Tristan shook his head.

"He looks like Mr. Sanders," Lacy said, her voice nearly a whisper. "He liked hurting us."

Cyclops tensed, and I reached over to place my hand on his thigh. When Kye returned to the room, I knew one of us needed to ask.

"Kye, is your last name Sanders?"

He stopped and froze. "What?"

"Your last name. Is it Sanders?" I asked.

"No. But Sanders was my mother's maiden name." He glanced at the kids before looking at me. "How did you hear that name, and why did you associate it with me?"

Cyclops stood. "Outside. Now."

"Wait." I reached for his hand, making him stop. "The kids need to know they're safe. Let them hear what you have to say. Show them you're going to protect them."

Kye backed up, hands in the air. "Whoa, I'd never hurt those children!"

"Someone who looks like you and goes by Mr. Sanders has already harmed them," I said. "Any idea who they could mean? Do you have a relative who looks like you?"

Kye's face blanked for a moment, then filled with fury. "That son of a bitch! I'm going to kill him with my bare hands."

"Who?" I asked, standing and putting myself between him and the children.

"My cousin. Bradley Sanders. People often said we could have been twins. If those children are scared of me, and said I look like Mr. Sanders, then it has to be him. I didn't realize he was back in town." Kye clenched his fists. "If he's mixed up in all this, I want him. No one gets to end his miserable life except me."

"Find your cousin and maybe we'll find others who hurt the kids," Cyclops said. "We need to talk to with Beast."

"The kids and I will be fine. But maybe send their Uncle Logan over? And order pizzas for us?" I took Lacy's hand. "Cake will have to wait until tomorrow, sweetheart. But I promise we'll get whatever kind you want, even if I have to make it myself."

Tristan studied Cyclops and Kye. "You're going to kill the men who hurt us?"

Cyclops came closer and stared down at the children. "Any man or woman who has dared to touch you will answer to me or my club. We'll make them suffer, and I promise they will never hurt anyone else ever again."

Tristan threw himself at Cyclops, hugging him. "Thank you, Dad."

I saw the emotion on my big biker's face and knew that simple word had meant the world to him. Much like it had when Tyler had called me Momma. These kids might need us, but we needed them too.

"We'll be back," Cyclops said. "I'll tell Logan about the pizza and see what he can do about a cake. Maybe he can order from the place that sells brownies on their dessert menu. It's not quite the same, but it should do for tonight."

Cyclops looked at each child, then at me. "All of you stay inside and be safe. I'll return as quick as I can."

"We will. Be careful, Tucker."

He kissed me before walking out the door. It was only after he'd left; I realized I'd called him by his real name in front of Kye. Thankfully, neither he nor the Prospect said anything about it. I knew better. If he wanted to discuss it later, I'd apologize. He'd earned the name Cyclops, and I needed to use it around his club.

"Come on. Let's finish bringing the toys in here. When your Uncle Logan gets here, we'll watch a movie while he orders dinner."

I picked up Tyler, took Lacy's hand, and Tristan

led the way back into the living room. It didn't take long to get their things temporarily put away. And when their Uncle Logan arrived, the real fun started. I hoped Cyclops didn't get his feelings hurt when the kids didn't stop talking about my brother. The bond between the four of them happened in an instant. Even I felt a little jealous.

Chapter Nine

Cyclops

Finding out Kye's cousin had hurt my kids, made me want his blood. I understood why Kye wanted to be the one to handle him. Something told me it would help him earn his patch, so I'd have to stand back. Danny, on the other hand... that fucker was mine! No one had mentioned him, and I had to wonder if he'd slipped past them like Matteo, or if they hadn't wanted to pull me away from Leigha and the kids.

We entered the clubhouse and found most of the kids still gathered around the tables. The board games I'd asked Kye to purchase seemed to be a hit, as were the puzzles. Beast saw us and approached, his lips thinned.

"What the hell are you doing back here?" he asked.

"Found out something you need to hear. Not around little ears."

He nodded. "Let's go into Church. Do the others need to know about it too?"

"Yeah, Pres," Kye said, looking a little green.

I clapped him on the back, letting him know without words he had my support. Just because his cousin was a rotten apple, didn't mean he was too. We went into Church, with several others joining us. Not everyone was at the clubhouse, but I knew Beast would relay anything important, or call an official meeting.

"The kids feared Kye," I said, "and Leigha wanted to know why. They said he looked like a man who hurt them."

Kye cleared his throat. "I think it's my cousin.

We've often been told we could be twins. I didn't realize he was in town. He left a while back, and I haven't seen or heard from him since. Pres, I know I'm only a Prospect, but I feel like he's my responsibility. If we can find him, I want to be the one to take him out. I owe it to those kids."

Beast studied Kye a moment before scanning the brothers gathered around us. He nodded and patted Kye on the back. "He's yours. You want to go after him, tell me what you need."

"What about Danny?" I asked. "That fucker tried to rape Leigha. I want his blood."

"You'll have it," Beast said. "He's in the old barn. Figured he'd hold until tomorrow while you got your new family situated. But if it will make you sleep better tonight, go ahead and have at him."

"I need to look Leigha in the eye tonight and tell her the man who hurt her is no longer breathing," I said. "And the sooner I can say the same to my kids about Matteo, the better."

"With the exception of Matteo, and two of his known associates, we cleaned house. No one else is still breathing. Or won't be. Danny is the only one we took alive, and I know you'll send him to hell when you're ready." Beast folded his arms. "As for Matteo... Shield has been checking camera footage all over town. We can't find him. He could be long gone by now."

I shook my head. "No, Pres. He's here. We cleaned him out, killed his men. He'll want revenge, and he'll want those children back."

A knocked sounded at the door and Beast opened it. One of the girls stood on the other side. I hadn't met her, but she looked older than the girl Savior adopted.

"If you want Matteo, use me as bait." She licked

her lips and scanned each of our faces. "He only let the others touch me when I'd done something wrong. I was his favorite, and his own personal whore. If he sees me, or hears I'm out and about, he'll come get me."

"We're not using you to set a trap." Satyr frowned. "That would be suicide! One misstep and you're back under his control. No, Brenna. It's not happening."

Wait. What? How the fuck did he know her name? And why was he being so damn protective? I felt like I'd missed a shit ton of stuff when I'd gone home. Beast pinched the bridge of his nose, and the other men looked anywhere except at Satyr.

"Are you shitting me right now?" I asked. "Minnie threw herself at you and you treated her like shit, but a girl who's nowhere near old enough to be yours, and you're going all alpha protector over her?"

Satyr flipped me off. "Stay the fuck out of it, Cyclops."

"No. I won't. You use the women who come here. Treat them like they're expendable, and now you're mooning after an underage girl? Have you lost your fucking mind?" I demanded. "Pres, there's no damn way you're okay with this."

"I'm not, and he knows it. We've already had words." Beast sighed. "Brenna, if you want to help catch Matteo, I'm not going to say no. We'll do whatever it takes to bring him down and make sure all of you are safe."

"I'm not letting her go out there..." Satyr didn't get to finish his statement before Copper punched him hard enough he staggered back into the table. "What the fuck?"

"She's not yours, will *never* be yours. You even

- 151 -

think of looking at her, talking to her, much less touching her, and I will rip your fucking head off. Not like you're using it anyway," Copper said.

"What's going on?" I asked.

"Copper has offered Brenna a place to stay. She doesn't want to return to her family. Since she's been missing for seven years, her parents had her declared dead." Beast leaned against the wall. "I'm not going to force her out of here. If she wants to stay, she can. Copper isn't old enough to be her dad, but they can work it out later. Dad. Brother. Cousin. What the fuck ever. Long as she's safe and happy, I don't give a shit."

"How old are you?" I asked.

"Fifteen. I'll be sixteen next month." She went over to Copper and leaned against his side. He hugged her and glared at Satyr. "I know you think I'm only a kid, but I've lived through hell with Matteo. I got my period when I was eleven. He said it meant I was a woman."

I knew where the story was going and didn't want to hear it. He'd likely been grooming her before that. Knowing he'd used her for four years while she was just a kid sickened me. I hated men like Matteo. No, they weren't men. They hadn't earned that title.

"I'll take care of Danny, but if you need me to help with Matteo, just say the word, Pres."

Beast shook his head. "Go handle your business, then go home to your family. Those kids need you more than we do right now. Brenna will have plenty of protection. Except Satyr. You, my brother, are going on a trip."

"To where?" he demanded.

Beast smiled and the sight chilled me. I'd never seen that look on his face before. Wasn't sure I wanted to ever again.

"The Devil's Boneyard could use a hand with something. You've been there before. Remember Stripes?" Beast asked.

"What about him?" Satyr glowered. "Big Russian can't handle his own shit?"

"Oh, he wants to handle something all right," Beast muttered. "That big Russian found out he has family. Closer than he realized."

"Pres?" I asked, my brow furrowed as I tried to piece together what the hell he was saying.

"Stripes would like a few words with you about your treatment of his granddaughter. I'll leave it at that. The two of you can figure shit out on your own. And if he breaks some of your bones, maybe you'll have learned a valuable lesson and keep your eyes off Brenna. Because if Stripes doesn't get the point across, then I'll let Copper do his worst."

"You can't do this!" Satyr glared at all of us. "I'm your brother! A patched member of this club. You can't just..."

Beast moved lightning fast, his fist cracking against Satyr's jaw. "I can, and I will. You step one toe out of line, and it will mean your colors. I happen to know you've inked them into your body. When I say we'll remove your colors, I mean *all* of them. Think about it, Satyr. You want to screw around with the club whores, be my guest. They know the score. You knew damn well Minnie liked you, wanted more, and you toyed with her like a cat playing with a mouse. Now you're salivating over a teenager? Fuck no. I'm done with your sorry-ass bullshit. This club doesn't allow men like you inside our gates, so either find your damn balls, man the fuck up, or get gone."

"This club is going to shit since all of you started settling down. Now the rest of us have to be on a leash too?" Satyr asked.

"That's it." Beast grabbed Satyr's cut and yanked it off him. "Someone take his ass to the barn. We can deal with him and Danny at the same time. You're done here. Assuming you live through this, I don't want to see your face anywhere near this town ever again. Hell, leave the entire state."

Satyr struggled as two of our brothers dragged him out of Church. I wasn't sure what to think about it all, but I knew Beast was right. Satyr was getting worse and not better. We'd thought things were different, that he was learning and growing. Either he'd had us fooled, or something happened to make him revert to his old ways. If he was looking at Brenna like a potential hookup, then he needed to go. I knew Forge had known Whisper when she'd been younger, but he'd never once done anything disrespectful. Hell, he hadn't even touched her when she'd turned eighteen.

Beast sighed and faced Brenna, who'd gone pale. "I'm sorry, Brenna. You shouldn't have seen or heard any of that. I hope it doesn't change your mind about staying with Copper. He'll keep you safe, and he won't be biding his time for you to get older so he can get in your pants. He may not be a monk or a saint, but if he says you're his family, that's exactly how he'll treat you."

Brenna leaned into Copper even more. "I trust him."

Copper met my gaze. "I'm the one who freed her. I swore I'd let no one touch her again until she was ready. Next time, it will be her decision."

I nodded, grateful the girl had someone like Copper standing up for her. As for Satyr... I didn't look forward to what had to be done. He'd been my brother, and I'd trusted him. Now we had to cause him pain. He'd brought it on himself, but it didn't change how it made me feel.

"Someone get a message to Leigha. Let her know I'm going to be late, and I don't want the kids to see me when I first get there. I'll need to shower and change." Shield put his hand on my shoulder, and I knew he'd take care of it. "Let's get this over with."

Every brother would be called in for this one. The roar of our bikes filled the air as the entire club made their way to the old barn. None of us wanted to throw out a brother, but Satyr had gone too far. I didn't think anyone would question Beast's decision.

The barn came into view, and I parked off to the side. Walking inside, I saw Danny strung up from the center beam. His toes barely brushed the ground, and his hands were turning purple from the weight of his body pulling on his bound wrists.

Satyr kneeled on the floor, his hands on his thighs. They had already stripped him down to his underwear and he waited for what came next. His head hung, and his shoulders drooped. I didn't know if he'd survive or not. Hell, would he even want to?

Everyone circled Satyr, and I noticed Danny watching.

"Watch what we're going to do to someone we care about. Someone we've trusted. Then think about what kind of pain I'm going to inflict on a piece of shit rapist like you." I smiled when he paled.

Beast stared at Satyr a moment. "It's never a good day when one of our own betrays us. Satyr, I warned you to change your ways. We have given you multiple chances to become a better man. You ignored them all, then spit in our faces by lusting after an underage girl. Do you have anything to say?"

"Get it over with," he mumbled.

"You know what happens next," Beast said. He gave us all a nod.

I let Copper take the first shot. He hit Satyr so hard, a tooth flew out of his mouth as blood poured down his face. I took my shot, not holding back. I felt the bone of his cheek crunch. Each brother took a turn. When we'd finished, he wasn't recognizable. Beast motioned for us to hold Satyr down. I kneeled on one of his wrists. Copper took the other one. Two other brothers held his legs as we pinned him on his stomach.

Beast took out a large knife and cut the colors off Satyr's back. He screamed and cried until he passed out from the pain. We stood, leaving him on the dirty barn floor.

"If he's alive when we're done with Danny, dump his ass outside of town. Let the wildlife decide if he lives or dies," Beast said.

I faced Danny, who openly cried. I had no sympathy for the fucker. He deserved everything we gave him, and more. Someone had been kind enough to lay out a bunch of tools on the nearby table. I went over and perused the selection before picking up a hammer. Approaching Danny, I watched his face as I slammed it against his toes, breaking them one at a time.

He screamed and wailed, begging for his life.

"Did she beg you?" I asked. "Did my wife ask for mercy? What about the others?"

"What others?" he asked.

"She wasn't your first. Not someone like you. No, there have been more. Were they adults, or did you touch the children Matteo prostituted?" I asked.

"Oh, God." He moaned. "I paid like everyone else. I'm no different from them. You aren't torturing anyone else."

"Not today. But I will. Once I track them all down," I said. "Three of those kids are mine, and I will seek vengeance. Today is about my wife. You touched her. Ripped her clothes in an alley. Planned to rape her. I should have killed you then."

I slammed the hammer into his kneecap, and he squealed like a pig. Before tossing the hammer aside, I busted his other one. I took my time, making him bleed, and breaking as many of his bones as I could. He pissed himself multiple times.

Beast put his hand on my shoulder. "Brother, why don't you let us finish it? Go home to your family. Tell Leigha she's safe. We'll make sure he never hurts her, or anyone else, ever again. If he gives me the information I want, maybe I'll end his life quicker."

Danny started blubbering again. "I'll tell you anything you want. Just please stop."

"Find out who hurt the kids. I want them all to suffer," I said.

Beast nodded. "I will. Now go. You're needed elsewhere."

I went outside, breathed in the fresh air, and got on my bike. When I pulled up at home, I saw the living room light on. I hoped like hell the kids weren't watching for me. I had blood coating my skin and clothes. The last thing I wanted was to scare the hell out of them.

I cautiously opened the door and peered inside. Leigha greeted me with a sad smile.

"I told the kids to stay in their playroom for a little bit and come up with ideas of how they want it to look. I closed the door so you can get past them without terrifying anyone."

As much as I wanted to kiss her, I didn't dare

Harley Wylde   Cyclops/Surge Duet

right now. "I'll shower and change."

Logan stepped out of the living room, eyeing the blood on me. "I'll watch the kids. Both of you take your time."

He shook his head after I arched an eyebrow. I assumed Leigha would help me clean up. She went to the stairs, and I followed, going up to our room. She started the shower while I stripped out of my clothes, then I watched as she undressed too. I stepped under the spray and let it wash all the blood down the drain. By the time she joined me, the water ran clear.

Leigha reached for the shampoo and washed my hair, massaging my scalp with her fingers. Then she grabbed the conditioner. I'd never bothered with any in the past. Since she'd moved in, a few things were changing in my grooming routine. I hadn't told her yet, but I'd ordered some beard supplies. Her dad had mentioned a place that sold oils, beard balms, and beard wash. Figured it wouldn't hurt to try it. Maybe look less like a homeless mountain man.

She started soaping my body, and my cock stiffened. The moment her fingers wrapped around the hard length, I knew I wasn't getting out of the shower without fucking her. She finished cleaning me and I rinsed before reaching out and pulling her against me.

"Danny won't bother you again," I said. "And my brothers are going to find Matteo."

"Was all that blood from him?" she asked.

I shook my head. "No, kitten. I'm afraid not. We had to kick a brother out of the club. He wanted one of the girls, kept staring at her and acting like he owned her. Beast decided he'd had enough. Satyr had been in trouble before, so this wasn't out of the blue."

"I'm sorry," she said, reaching up to cup my cheek. "Need me to take your mind off it?"

I smiled. "And how do you plan to do that?"

She turned and walked over to the built-in bench, then leaned over, bracing her hands. Leigha parted her thighs, and I groaned. The woman wasn't playing fair. I went up behind her, placing my hands on her hips. Her skin felt like satin. Leaning over her, I kissed my way down her spine, then nipped one of her ass cheeks.

"Do you have any idea how much you turn me on?" I asked. "I'm the luckiest bastard in the world because I get to call you mine."

"You're also a dad now, which means we probably have another ten minutes before the kids decide to come out of their room." She looked at me over her shoulder. "Take me, Tucker. Make me yours. It doesn't have to be sweet or slow. I won't break."

I curved my body over hers and eased inside her. Her pussy clenched down when I was only halfway in, and I growled. I could feel my balls draw up and knew I wouldn't last. Slipping my hand between her legs, I worked her clit. It only took a few strokes before Leigha pressed back against me.

"Please, Tucker! Don't make me wait."

I started thrusting, my hips smacking against her ass as I pounded into her. She'd said she didn't need sweet or slow. I unleashed all the pain, anger, and fear I'd been feeling since I'd walked into the clubhouse earlier. She took it all and gave herself to me fully. I rubbed her clit faster, refusing to come before she did. When she cried out my name, her pussy gripping me tight, I pumped into her faster.

With a roar everyone could probably hear downstairs and outside, I came inside her. I panted for breath, and pressed a kiss to her shoulder, then her neck. "I love you, Leigha."

I felt her shaking and pulled back, worried I'd done something wrong. She stood and faced me, a smile on her lips before her laughter spilled out. "You just had to tell me that for the first time when your cock was inside me."

"What?" I stared and blinked, wondering if she was upset about it. Since she was laughing, I hoped that meant everything was all right between us.

"I love you too. You said you loved me for the first time after sex. I hope that isn't going to be the norm."

"Ummm…"

She pressed her lips to mine. "It's okay. Until this moment, I'd thought you were different from every man I know. You proved you are a typical guy. I bet there isn't a man out there who hasn't said those words right after he came -- at least once."

"I'll tell you many times, every day, for the rest of our lives."

She wrapped her arms round me, and I'd have gladly gone for round two, if I hadn't heard the kids yelling for us from downstairs.

"Time to go be parents," she said.

"Can't wait." And I really couldn't. I now had everything I never realized I needed, and I'd protect them with my life.

Epilogue

Cyclops
Two Months Later

I winced when I heard Leigha throwing up. She'd done it every morning, and even some afternoons, for the last three weeks. While I was beyond thrilled about the reason behind it, I wished the pregnancy was easier for her. The kids were excited about getting a brother or sister and were already helping us come up with a list of names. All boy names with a T and girl names with an L, of course.

I kneeled down next to the kids and made sure I had their attention.

"There's something I need to tell you, and it's important. I know you've each been through a lot, and you're still healing. I got some news today. Matteo and the two men who were hiding with him have not only been found, but they've been dealt with. Kye also found Mr. Sanders, and he won't be hurting you or anyone else ever again."

"Are they dead?" Tristan asked. "Did anyone get hurt going after them?"

"They're dead. The two men Beast sent after them, Wrangler and Snake, found them and made sure they suffered before they died. I know I shouldn't tell you things like that, but you haven't exactly lived normal lives up to this point. I don't want any of you looking over your shoulders, worrying that man will come for you. You're safe. Brenna wanted to help catch them, but Copper wouldn't let her. It's why it took longer. Wrangler, Snake, and Kye are all okay. It's over."

Lacy put her arms around me. "Thank you, Daddy."

"The three of you sit tight. I'm going to check on your mom."

They went back to watching the cartoon I'd put on for them, and I went down the hall to the bathroom. Leigha groaned and had her forehead pressed against the edge of the bathtub.

"If I get up, I'm going to puke again. But this floor is hard as shit. We need a thicker rug if I'm going to spend so much time down here."

I rolled my lips in and pressed down so I wouldn't utter what was dying to come out. *But I like it when you're on your knees.* Nope. Not saying it. I didn't have a death wish.

"Need something, kitten? Water? A cold, wet rag?"

She lifted her arms. "Carry me to the couch? Maybe if I don't walk, it won't be so bad."

I knew different. We'd tried it a million times before. Wouldn't matter. The little peanut inside her would still make her puke off and on all day. The doctor said the morning sickness would pass in another month. I hoped like hell he was right. I'd heard of women who were sick their entire pregnancy. If that happened, I didn't think Leigha would want that huge family she'd been talking about, and I wouldn't either. I hated seeing her so miserable.

I eased her onto the couch, then went to get the bucket for her. It grossed the kids out when she used it, but I didn't want her rushing to the bathroom and possibly falling. I kissed her forehead and smiled at the most beautiful woman I'd ever seen.

"I love you, Leigha."

"We love you, Daddy," Lacy said behind me.

I chuckled and turned to the kids. "I love the three of you, too. Very much. Let's let Momma rest for a bit. Why don't y'all go out back to play? Uncle Logan put a surprise out there for you."

They rushed from the room and Leigha held out her hand to me. "What did my brother buy now?"

"A sandbox. Small enough we can easily move it to the new house when it's ready. Still want six bedrooms?"

She smiled and nodded. "We'll need them."

My brow furrowed and I stared. "What do you mean? We have three kids, and a fourth on the way."

"Sorry, Papa Bear. We don't have *one* on the way. Remember the appointment you missed yesterday? And I told you I had news to share?"

I sank to my knees next to the couch. "Are you saying we're having twins?"

"Yep. Told you it was possible."

I placed my hand on her belly and leaned down to kiss her. Putting my face near her still-flat stomach, I had a brief talk with my children. I promised to keep them safe, to always love them, and make sure they would have happy lives.

And I'd do anything to keep that vow. Not just to the unborn twins in Leigha's stomach, but to Lacy, Tristan, and Tyler as well.

"Finding you in the alley that day was the best thing to ever happen to me," I said. "I know it was scary and traumatizing for you. If I could change the events, I would. But the one thing I will never wish away is meeting you. Leigha, you're the most amazing, kind, loving woman I've ever known. I'm so damn glad you're mine."

She ran her fingers through my hair. "I'm the lucky one."

"You're both lucky," Logan yelled out from the front entry. "Hopefully, you're both dressed too."

He walked into the room, and I glowered at him. "Don't you have your own place?"

He shrugged. "Why would I be there, when I know how much it annoys you to have me underfoot? Besides, we're family."

I smiled. "Yeah, we are. All right, Prospect. Come visit with your sister while I try to tire the kids out. Make yourself useful."

He flipped me off and I chuckled as I went to find my kids.

Life wasn't perfect. It was messy, sometimes bloody, and scary as fuck. But mine was as close to heaven as I'd ever get. Whatever it took, I'd make sure my wife and kids never regretted having me in their lives, because I damn sure wouldn't trade them for anything in the world.

Surge (Hades Abyss MC 8)
Harley Wylde

Colette's a sweet angel in need of saving, and like it or not, I have a hero complex. Marrying her seems like the right thing to do. Then my sometimes lover, Aidan, finds us together. The hurt in his eyes nearly guts me.

My club knows I'm bisexual. I've not hidden it from them. Doesn't mean I've flaunted it in their faces either. So when I decided to claim Aidan and Colette, I'm not sure how it's going to end. All I know is they both need me, and I need them too.

With human traffickers after Colette, a possible traitor in the club, and more chaos than I can handle, I do the only thing I can... I run with my new wife and husband. Once I figure out who wants Colette, I'll do whatever it takes to destroy them. Until then, I'll keep her safe, and Aidan too. Because they both mean more to me than I realized.

Prologue

Colette

I gripped Jacques' hand as we slipped through the alley. The dumpster at the other end usually had something somewhat edible. I'd never lived on the streets before, but Jacques kept me safe. Or as safe as he could. We'd been strangers until a few months ago.

Jacques approached the other end of the alley, tensing as he listened to booted steps draw closer. When no one passed by, he eased forward and peered into the dumpster. I gasped as a shadow drew closer and my hold on Jacques tightened. More than once we'd been cornered. It had taught us to be overly cautious. My heart pounded as I stared at the man coming toward us.

"If you're up for a party, you can stop by the Hades Abyss clubhouse. There should be food and drinks. No charge," the man said. As he came even closer, I saw he had on jeans, a T-shirt, and a black leather vest that said *Prospect* on it. "No strings attached. You're both welcome."

Clubhouse? Party? I didn't understand. Why would he invite homeless people to a party unless he had something nefarious planned? I didn't trust him. I edged a little behind Jacques, even though the man had barely spared me a glance. Something about him set me on edge.

"Where is the clubhouse?" Jacques asked, his accent thicker than usual. It was a sure sign he didn't trust this man either. I eyed the guy from around Jacques, prepared to run if this was a trap. Each time we moved to a new town, Jacques made sure to scout a safe place for us to meet up if we ever became separated. Would I need that space now?

"Edge of town. Just ask around. Anyone can point the way. Party usually starts close to sundown but come by anytime you want. I'm sure you've had some unsavory offers, living on the streets. That's not what this is. Ask around about us." He left as quickly as he'd arrived, and I leaned into Jacques.

He'd told us to check up on the Hades Abyss before going to the party. Did that mean it was a legitimate offer? Could we trust him? My stomach cramped painfully. It had been more than a day since I'd eaten, and the last meal had been a discarded sandwich I'd shared with Jacques.

"Food, Colette. We can eat something that didn't come from the trash," Jacques said.

"You trust him?"

"*Non*. But what other options do we have?"

I nodded, knowing he was right. We'd made it so far, and yet we still weren't safe. There were times I wondered if we'd ever live normal lives again. Even though I'd not known Jacques before coming to America, he'd been my lifeline the last few months. I knew he'd do what he could to keep me safe, just as he had every time someone had offered to help us.

"We survived this long," Jacques said, kissing my forehead. "We'll make it a while longer, Colette. You saw that man. Someone like that could protect you."

My breath caught and I hoped he didn't mean what I thought he did. Why would I need someone other than Jacques to protect me? We'd done okay so far. Maybe we were living on the streets, and I could admit I hadn't slept well in months. But still...

"What are you saying, Jacques?"

He tipped my chin up and gave me a sad smile. "It's time, *ma belle*. You knew we would part ways eventually. This is your chance."

"*Je ne comprends pas.*" What was he saying? Part ways? Did that mean he planned to leave me with the man who'd invited us to the party? A stranger? How did Jacques know I'd be safe with him?

"I've seen those bikers around town. That one isn't part of the club yet. You need to find someone who is, and they'll protect you."

"*Pourquoi?*"

"English, *ma belle.* You need to use your English more if you're going to have a chance. As to why… I've seen the ones who have women. They're considerate, caring, and shield them from harm. That's what you need. I can't keep you safe forever, and you know it." He sighed. "We've been in this town a few weeks now. I've been watching and waiting, hoping to find someone worthy to keep you safe. Those men are your best bet."

"You're giving me to them?" I asked softly. Was he no different from the men we'd escaped from? Had I been wrong all this time?

"*Non.* You're going to *choose* to stay with one. Make him want to keep you. It might mean putting on another show." He winced. "I hate doing that to you."

I knew there was more than one reason he disliked it. Jacques had made it clear from the beginning he preferred men. It was the main reason I'd trusted him so easily. He'd never once been interested in me sexually, even if we'd had to fake it sometimes.

"If it will ease your mind, I'll do it," I said. "But, Jacques, what's going to happen to you?"

"I have a contact farther north. I'll go there, but it's a hard trip and not safe for you."

I bit my lip. It hurt, knowing I'd been holding him back. He'd had a place to go and had stayed for me. How long? How many days or weeks had he suffered when he could have made a run for it? Why hadn't he said something sooner? I knew we'd been in this town longer than the others. Now I understood why. He'd been hoping one of those men would take me in.

"I'll do it," I agreed, and hoped I hadn't just made a big mistake. If the men with the Hades Abyss found out we were tricking them, were using them, I could only imagine the hell I'd have to pay. I hoped that day never came.

Chapter One

Surge

Another lame-ass party. It had been a while since I'd enjoyed myself at these things, and yet, here I was. I'd been checking out the crowd, but it was the same women who were always here. And none of the men were interested. They were all straight as fuck. Sometimes being bisexual just meant more frustration. I had the joyful experience of being disappointed not once, but twice. How the hell could I be in a room this full of people and not find one potential partner for the night?

Although, there was always one person I could turn to. I just hadn't called him lately. I knew Aidan wanted more than I was ready to give. My club knew I liked men and women, even if they didn't acknowledge it publicly. More than one brother had seen me with other men. No one had ever said anything. But moving a man into my house and claiming him like I would an old lady? Yeah, I didn't see that one going over well.

I looked across the room and saw Slider sipping a beer. We'd had a thing for a while. Now he was happily married, and only came to these events long enough for a drink or two with his brothers, then he went home to his wife. I didn't know if I had it in me to be like him and only be with a woman the rest of my life. Then again, I felt the same about only being with a man forever. I knew the Devil's Fury had a poly couple and wondered if the Hades Abyss would accept that type of relationship. Then again, I'd have to find both a man and a woman I wanted to hang onto forever. Probably not happening.

I drank more of my beer and pushed off from the

wall. Heading for the hallway, I'd check for wayward partygoers and then I'd head home. It never failed. Every party, someone ended up where they shouldn't. The clubhouse mostly contained rooms used by the Prospects these days. Didn't mean random people needed to be in there.

The sounds of moaning had me cursing under my breath. Fuckers! I stomped down the hall, not bothering to be quiet, as I approached the lit-up room toward the back. If I hadn't known where every Prospect currently was, I'd have thought one of them brought someone to their room. But no way that was the case this time. Pausing in the doorway, my heart nearly stopped beating. The couple on the bed were too beautiful for words.

The woman had her head tipped back, her long dark hair trailing down to her hips. The man behind her had fine bone structure, and light scruff along his jaw. His muscles were understated, yet I found him just as mesmerizing as the woman he fucked. His gaze met mine, and I saw interest flare in his eyes.

"Want to join us?" he asked, his accent thick. French? "Colette won't mind, will you, *ma belle*?"

She opened her eyes and looked at me. The gray depths nearly took me to my knees as she held out her hand to me. I stepped into the room, setting my beer aside. Were they serious? It had been a while since I'd shared a woman with a man.

His gaze skimmed over me, heating as I removed my cut and my shirt. It made me pause, wondering if he was like me, or if the woman was all for show. The way he'd looked at me that first time... I'd thought it had been over the idea of sharing his woman. What if I was wrong? I watched them a moment, studying every detail.

Had I walked into a trap? My pause didn't go unnoticed. The man pulled away from the woman, and I realized he might have been humping her, but there had been no penetration. His cock stood erect, and dry as hell. If he'd been inside her, that wouldn't be the case. But damn… I nearly licked my lips.

"The two of you aren't supposed to be in here," I said. "This part of the clubhouse is off-limits to guests. I should ask you to leave."

The woman on the bed tensed, her panicked gaze turning to the man. Colette is what he'd called her. It suited her. Delicate. Beautiful. Just like her.

"Jacques." She nibbled her lower lip, and as I stared at her, I noticed more things. I could see her ribs, and her face had a gauntness to it. These two hadn't come to party. They were junkies, or starving. What kind of trouble were they in? And why had they come here? How had they even heard about the clubhouse? With their accents, they clearly weren't local.

I pulled my shirt and cut back on, then folded my arms and stared at Jacques as he approached me. He glanced at the open doorway before facing me again.

"Don't ask Colette to leave. *S'il vous plaît*. She needs to be here," he said.

I didn't know what the hell he'd said when he wasn't speaking English, but the tone was still clear. These two needed help. I didn't know how they'd come to be here, but I couldn't force them out. Not knowing if they would be okay. Although, he'd only asked me to help the woman. I didn't know what to think.

"Start talking," I said.

Colette got off the bed and scrambled into her clothes. Her cheeks turned pink as she glanced at me.

She came closer and took Jacques' hand.

"A man invited us," he said. "He promised there would be food and drinks. Said we were both welcome. We can leave. We won't cause trouble."

"And this little display?" I asked, motioning to the bed. Her cheeks burned brighter, and she dropped her gaze. "Were you hoping to lure someone in and rob them?"

She gasped, and Jacques shook his head. "*Non.* We would never do such a thing. I only hoped Colette could eat something we didn't pull from a dumpster. Your party offered us something for now, but…"

If they'd been living on the streets, it would explain the malnourished look. At least for the woman. The man might be thin, but he didn't look like he'd missed as many meals. Had they only recently come together? Something felt off about the entire thing.

"It still doesn't explain the rest," I said.

"Beautiful, isn't she?" Jacques asked. He put Colette's hand in mine. "We always pay our way."

My stomach twisted at the implication. No fucking way. Nope. I wasn't about to use this pretty woman just because they'd come here to eat something.

"You're selling her to me for a meal?" I felt her tremble and knew my words had upset her. I hated doing that to her, but I needed to be clear on what was happening. For one, if that's what this motherfucker meant, I wanted to knock his teeth down his damn throat. I noticed he hadn't offered up himself as payment. No way he'd missed the way I'd checked him out. How long had he been whoring her out for food and shelter?

"Not selling her. Not exactly. You keep her for as long as you like, in exchange for a few sandwiches I can take on the road. Colette and I are parting ways."

I growled and advanced on him. Dropping her hand, I swung and hit the asshole right across his jaw. "You fucker! How dare you sell her!" I went to punch him again, but small hands grabbed at me. I looked down into Colette's pleading eyes.

"Don't hurt him."

"You're going to protect him after what he just said?" I asked.

She flinched and glanced at him before looking at me once more. "I'm holding him back. He has a place to go, but he's stayed because I would have slowed him down. I won't be any trouble. I'll do whatever you want. Anything!"

I closed my eyes, not liking what she implied. I couldn't toss her out. But the asshole who'd just bartered her for food was fair game. I didn't know why she cared about him, but I'd give him a few sandwiches like he'd requested, and send him on his way. Preferably with my boot print on his ass. Now I remembered why my cock hadn't gotten wet in a while. Aside from the random drunk hookup with Aidan, but the last time had been several months ago. Men were assholes and women were bitches. Except possibly for the angel holding onto me. She seemed more like a victim in all this.

"Fine. I'll give him some sandwiches, but we have to go to my house. All three of us."

Colette relaxed. "*Merci.*"

Now that word I knew. Even if I hadn't, the look she cast me would have made it clear enough. I didn't know why she was worried about the guy. He'd been an asshole to sell her out like that. He didn't deserve her affection.

"You're welcome, angel. As for Jacques…" I eyed

him. "Put your fucking clothes on and meet me out front."

I planned to find out more about this asshole before he left tonight. I wanted his full name. Where he'd come from. And anything else I could pry out of him. Then I'd do a thorough analysis of him and figure out what the fuck was going on. If he'd been using her, selling her, I'd put him in the ground. I didn't care how pretty he looked. There were some lines no one should cross. That was one of them.

I led Colette through the clubhouse and outside. I stopped next to my bike and got on, starting her up. Lifting my hand to Colette, I helped her onto the back. She put her arms around my waist, and I patted her hands.

"I'll go slow, but hold on tight." She nodded against my back and pressed closer. And fuck if I didn't enjoy it a little too much. My dick got painfully hard, and I shifted on the seat of my bike. Jacques came outside a moment later. I pointed in the direction of my house.

"Walk down this road and around the corner. Just put gray siding on my damn house. You can't miss it. You'll see the bike under the carport. I'm afraid you'll have to walk your ass there, unless you drove." He nodded. "We'll meet you there."

He said something in French to Colette that had her tensing. But her reply sounded an awful lot like goodbye. I hoped I was wrong. I needed answers from that man, but I was too fucking pissed to go slow enough for him to walk alongside us. If I didn't put some space between me and Jacques, my fist would try to go through his face again. Repeatedly.

I might have bought my ex-lover a mail-order bride from Russia, but this was different. Or it would have been if I'd had the full story behind Slider's wife. I'd known she was in trouble and needed help, but I hadn't realized exactly how awful her life had been. I wouldn't make that mistake again.

I zipped through the compound and pulled up my driveway and stopped under the carport. Turning off the bike, I patted Colette's thigh. "You can get off, sweetheart."

She stood on shaky legs as I swung my leg over the seat and led her inside. I flipped on lights as we went and took her straight to the kitchen.

"When did you last eat?" I asked.

"Not long before you found us," she said.

"Before that?" She fidgeted and wouldn't hold my gaze. I went to her, tipping her chin up, and forcing her to look at me. "I'm not going to hurt you, Colette. If you're hungry, just tell me. I'll be happy to give you some food. Whatever you need, all you have to do is ask."

"Nothing is ever free. What is it you want in return?" she asked.

Motherfucker! What the hell had she been through? She seemed young. No way she should be this cynical already. Shit. Was she even legal? Had I just brought a teenager to my house? If I had, Spider was going to rip me apart with his bare hands, unless I explained the situation really damn fast. And I wouldn't blame him.

"You're in charge, beautiful. I just want to make sure you have something nutritious. I'm not a monster, and I sure the fuck don't hurt women." She dropped her gaze and sighed softly. "Colette, I meant what I said. I just want to help you."

"Jacques was right," she murmured.

"About what?"

"He said I needed one of you to protect me, that he'd seen the men like you around town with their women, and he could tell they were cared for. He wanted that for me before he left town."

I leaned back against the counter and braced my hands on the edge. "He's not coming here, is he?"

She shook her head. "He said he was leaving and to do whatever was necessary to get you to keep me. He said you were a good man."

Right. A good man wouldn't have wanted to take him up on his offer to join the two of them. I hadn't stopped to even see if she truly wanted me there, or if she'd even wanted the man already with her. I'd only seen the two of them apparently having sex, and I'd wanted to be part of it. Being in this club, I'd helped enough women in trouble that I should have seen the signs. But no, I'd been thinking with my dick.

"I'd planned to get some answers from him. What's your full name, Colette?" She remained quiet, and I ran a hand through my hair. "Surge. It's what my club calls me. But when it's just the two of us, you can call me Cameron. Or Cam."

"Jacques isn't a bad man. He's done a lot to keep me safe. Please don't think poorly of him."

"Do you love him?" I asked.

Her eyes widened. "*Non.* We didn't know each other before all this happened. We've only been trying to survive. He could have left me behind."

Interesting. So they were running from something. The same thing? Or had their paths crossed as a mere coincidence? They both seemed to have come from France, or French immigrant parents. I'd met more than one person in my life who had the same accent as their parents, even if they'd lived here their entire lives.

"Then tell me your name. Is someone looking for you?"

She paled and swayed for a moment. I lunged forward to catch her before she fell. Yeah. Someone was after the pretty angel, and it terrified her. Whatever she was running from, I knew I couldn't toss her back onto the streets. I'd help her, because that's what the Hades Abyss did. Besides, I had to admit I felt protective of her, even if I didn't know why.

"Easy, Colette. Sit down and I'll get you some juice." I helped her into a chair, then pulled the orange juice from the fridge. I poured a small glass and instructed her to sip it. The color returned to her face a little at a time.

"Let's start slow," I said. "I'll make some dinner for us, and then I'll figure out sleeping arrangements. I don't have a guest room, but I don't feel right asking you to sleep on the couch, either."

"We've been sleeping on the street for a while. Even the floor inside your nice home is an improvement. Please, don't go to any trouble."

I leaned in and cupped her cheek. Her eyes dilated and her lips parted. Interesting. I didn't detect even a hint of fear in her. It seemed my attraction to her wasn't one-sided. I'd have thought after what she'd apparently suffered, she wouldn't be so trusting. Not this fast. Maybe Jacques had protected her as she'd claimed, and kept the worst of the darkness from touching her. If so, then it lessened my anger. Slightly.

"Colette, I'm sure you're grateful for Jacques, but that boy didn't take proper care of you. If he had, I wouldn't be calling him that. I'd consider him a man. Let me help you."

"All right," she whispered. "My name is Colette Fontaine, and I'm from Toulouse, France. Jacques came from the nearby town of Cahors. Men lured us from our homes, along with several others. Someone brought us here illegally."

So a group of people, most likely young women and men, had been smuggled into the country. Didn't take a genius to figure out why. Lots of powerful men in this country would pay top dollar for someone like her, or even for Jacques.

"And the others?" I asked. "Where are they?"

She pressed her lips together. "They sold the children. One man died. The others... I don't know. Jacques saw a chance to flee and took me with him."

Fucking hell. Hearing her confirm my suspicious made me both sick and furious. Human traffickers had abducted her and brought her to the US, which meant they'd most likely intended for her to be sold as a sex slave. Was she aware of what they'd planned? If not, it seemed Jacques had a clue. If they hadn't known one another previously, I couldn't think of another reason he'd have taken her with him. Not unless he'd been in love with her.

"You said you didn't love Jacques. Did he have feelings for you?" I asked.

Colette shook her head. "He preferred men. Although, there were times, like earlier, when we had to put on a show in order to eat."

I growled and took a breath so I wouldn't launch a chair across the room. My hands fisted, and I tried counting to ten to cool my temper. "It wasn't necessary, Colette. You'd been fed, and no one expected anything in return. Sure, whoever invited you probably hoped you'd be eager to spread your legs, but no one would have forced you to do anything."

"Jacques planned to leave," she said. "He wanted

to make sure someone would take care of me. I have nothing except my body to offer."

I put a hand over my eyes and wished I'd hit Jacques a little harder. "Sweetheart, you have plenty to offer besides sex. We may be strangers, but even I can tell you're the closest thing this dark world has to an angel. Men would happily spend time with you and not ask for you to sleep with them in return."

She gave me a skeptical look, and it made me wonder what her life had been like before she'd been abducted. Had men always treated her horribly? I knew I hadn't exactly been the nicest guy in the world. I'd broken hearts of both men and women, but I'd always been up front I only wanted a bit of fun. I couldn't control what other people hoped for.

"I'm not a gourmet cook, but I won't poison us either. Need to hit the store tomorrow. For now, the options are spaghetti, chicken breasts, or…" I went to the fridge and opened it, forgetting what else I'd bought. "Hamburger Helper."

"What's that?" she asked.

I turned to face her. "What? The Hamburger Helper? It's a meal in a box and you add meat, water, and sometimes milk. There are different types. I usually keep a few boxes stocked. Let me check what's in the cabinet."

I shut the fridge and opened the cabinet beside it. I moved two soup cans and a stack of Ramen noodles to get to the boxes behind them. Pulling out three, I showed her each as I told her what they were, not having any idea if she could read English.

"We have Tuna Helper, which I have canned tuna to go in that one. Or there's Cheeseburger Macaroni and Southwest Pasta. Ground beef goes in those last two, and I usually add a can of black beans to the Southwest Pasta."

She opened and closed her mouth, then stared at the boxes. Standing, she came closer and studied each one closer. She tapped the Cheeseburger Macaroni. "This one."

I nodded. "All right. I can do that. Have a seat while I make us something to eat. Why don't you tell me more about yourself while I cook?"

She seemed nervous as she went back to the table. And as I pulled out the ingredients I'd need, I noticed she hadn't uttered another word. It seemed the little angel didn't like talking about herself. Then again, I hadn't done enough to earn her trust yet. But I would. Somehow.

Chapter Two

Colette

He wanted to know about me? I'd never had a man ask me something like that. They all wanted one thing. Sex. Except this man... He was different. When he'd entered the room, my heart had raced, and I'd actually been excited to have him join us. I'd never wanted to have a man touch me before. I knew what I did with Jacques had been for survival. This had been different. Until Surge had taken a closer look at us. He'd stopped, and I knew he'd realized something was wrong.

What did I say? Did I tell him about my childhood? About losing my family? I'd wondered more than once if it had made me an easy target. Had those men known I didn't have anyone who would miss me? Then they'd had that horrid doctor examine me. I could still feel his fingers inside me and see the smirk on his face as he'd checked to see I was a virgin.

I didn't think he wanted me to tell him those things. Or maybe he did. I watched him cook and studied him. He'd turned his back toward me, so I took the time to admire him. The black leather vest remained over his shoulders, and the emblem on the back looked a bit scary. Hades Abyss MC. The name itself even sounded frightening.

He rubbed at his eyes and stopped what he was doing to walk across the kitchen. He pulled out an eyeglass case and put on a pair of wireframe glasses. I nearly moaned when I saw him wearing them. My favorite superhero had always been Superman, but I preferred him as Clark Kent with his glasses on. And now I found out Surge wore a pair?

Yes, I liked nerdy men. I hadn't expected this one

to check that particular box for me. The way he was built, and the fact he rode a motorcycle, had made me assume he was the typical tough guy. Mostly brawn. What if I was wrong? I'd already been contemplating ways to get him to let me stay. Now he intrigued me, and my staying was about more than my survival.

"Do you like to read?" I asked. "I always wanted a library. The movies where the heroine goes into a castle or large manor and finds a room filled with books were always my favorites."

Surge grinned at me over his shoulder. "I read, but probably not the types of books you'd approve of. I'll show you after dinner if you'd like."

What sort of reading material would I find offensive? Although he hadn't worded it that way. Did he mean he preferred children's books? Or maybe scary ones?

"My favorite is *The Count of Monte Cristo*," I said. "Do you have a favorite?"

"It's not a classic," he said. "Not in the same sense as the one you mentioned. But yes, I do have a favorite. Guess I might as well tell you. I like to read graphic novels. My favorite series is Swamp Thing."

Graphic novels. "Oh! Like *Mélusine*. I enjoyed reading that one."

He glanced at me over his shoulder again. "You read graphic novels?"

I nodded. "*Oui*. Not a lot, but I've enjoyed the ones I've found."

"Can you read English?" he asked.

"A little. But not enough words to read a story. Just enough not to traverse a city without getting lost."

"We'll have to fix that," he said. "I just need to cover this and let it cook about ten minutes, then we can eat."

He pulled down two glasses, added ice, then pulled a pitcher of lemonade from the refrigerator. The man kept surprising me. A biker who liked comic books and lemonade? Had I read him entirely wrong?

"Is there anything I can do to help?" I asked.

"Just sit and relax, Colette."

I sipped the lemonade he handed me and watched as he took down plates, put silverware on the table, and got a bag of shredded cheese from the refrigerator. By the time he'd fixed our plates and set them down, my stomach rumbled. I hadn't lied about eating at the clubhouse, but he'd also been correct when he assumed it had been a while since I'd had a decent meal.

Steam rose from my plate. The scent made my mouth water. Honestly, I'd have eaten anything he fixed. I'd learned how precious food was. Even before finding myself on the streets in America, I hadn't had an easy life. Those men had picked me for a reason.

"Tell me about living in Toulouse," he said as he took a bite of his dinner. I didn't know how he hadn't burned his tongue.

"There's not much to tell. It's expensive to live there. I shared a three-room flat with five other people. We weren't friends. I hardly spoke to them." I toyed with my fork. "I doubt they noticed I'd gone missing until rent was due. My job likely thought I'd quit without calling in. There's no one looking for me back home."

"What about your family?" he asked.

I shook my head. "Gone. They died several years ago. I lived with a foster family and several other children until I became an adult."

His eyebrows rose as his gaze skated over me. "And that was what? About two seconds ago? Sorry, but you seem young."

"And yet you were going to join me and Jacques in that bedroom."

He set his fork down. "I was. Until I took a closer look. Didn't take a genius to figure out something wasn't right with the situation. He do that to you often? Fuck you in the hopes someone would come along and pay to join in or to watch?"

I looked away. "When it was necessary."

"I should have castrated the fucker," he muttered before picking his fork up again. "How old are you, Colette?"

"Twenty-two. I think. I've lost track of the days. When they kidnapped me, I was going to have a birthday soon.

"When's your birthday?" he asked.

"April fifteenth."

He nodded. "Then you've already had a birthday this year."

Had so much time passed already? It didn't seem possible, and yet... I remembered coming into the country in New Orleans. I'd admired much of the city while we stayed there, once Jacques and I escaped, but we'd had to leave all too soon. We'd mostly traveled on foot but caught rides where we could. And we'd never stayed in one place for very long.

I ate my food and considered my situation. Surge seemed nice, and he hadn't asked me for anything, or tried to hurt me. Staying with him wouldn't be a hardship. The lack of any sort of request bothered me, except for him asking about my past. I'd learned at a much younger age people always wanted something. So what did Surge want from me?

I finished my meal and took my dishes to the sink. I'd rinsed them by the time he joined me at the counter. He showed me how to load and start the dishwasher, and I was grateful. It meant I could at least do this one small thing while I stayed here. Maybe I could clean the rest of the house to help pay for my keep.

"Would you like to take a shower?" Surge asked. "I don't have any women's clothing, but I could get one of my shirts for you to sleep in. I think you're close to Vasha's size. I'll ask Slider if his wife can spare an outfit or two until I can buy you a few things."

"It's too much," I protested.

He cupped my cheek. "No, Colette. It's not nearly enough. Come on. I'll show you where you can shower."

I followed him past a bathroom and two bedrooms. I paused outside the door to what seemed to be his room. Had we reached the time he'd want something more from me? I looked around the space and tried to calm my nerves.

"I'll have to get shampoo and soap for the other bathroom," he said as he set a towel out on the counter. "But take your time in here. I'll wait in the living room until you're finished. Shirts are in the top dresser drawer. Help yourself to whichever one looks comfortable."

So, he wasn't planning to shower with me or watch me bathe. He walked out, shutting the bedroom door behind him. Surge confused me. I'd never known there were men in the world like him. I kept waiting to see if something would change. If he was truly as nice as he seemed, I knew I had a different sort of danger to face. Losing my heart. It had been so very long since anyone had been kind to me. Yes, Jacques had rescued me when he'd escaped. But I'd quickly learned he hadn't done it entirely out of the good of his heart.

Having a woman along made it easier to earn food, shelter, or the chance to clean ourselves. Most men weren't interested in only Jacques.

At least he hadn't taken my virginity or let anyone else. He'd done me that kindness. I didn't know how far he needed to travel to reach his friend, but I hoped he made it safely. Neither of us were to blame for our situation. Jacques may have used me to get us farther down the road, but it was still better than what my captors had planned.

I started the shower and undressed, leaving my dirty clothes on the floor. Stepping under the hot spray, I sighed in complete bliss. I washed my hair twice before soaping my body. Even though Jacques hadn't done more than touch me during our little show, I always felt dirty afterward. I scrubbed my skin until it turned pink, then got out and dried off.

My belly full, and my body clean for the first time in days, sleep pulled at me. I glanced at the dresser but didn't think I had the energy to find a shirt. Instead, I crawled into the bed and stretched out on my back. Staring up at the ceiling, I wondered what would happen next. If Surge didn't plan to fuck me, why was he helping me?

The man confused me. And aroused me. Even now, my nipples were hard, and I felt an ache I didn't know how to satisfy. I cupped my breasts and pressed my thighs together. I wanted... needed... something. When Jacques came, I saw the look on his face. Even when the men had settled for fucking Jacques, they'd made me watch. Was that the feeling I yearned for? *La petite mort*.

I eased my hand between my legs and spread the lips of my pussy. My cheeks burned with embarrassment. I'd never touched myself like this. Not for pleasure. I stroked my clit lightly and moaned. It felt so good.

"Yes! Oh, God." I rubbed a little harder and felt my pussy getting slicker. Even though the pleasure kept building, it wasn't enough. I couldn't quite get there.

As I spread my legs more, I groaned. I teased my nipple with my other hand. Frustration welled inside me when nothing I did seemed to make me come.

"Colette, did you need…" I gasped and yanked my hand from between my legs. Too late. Surge had already seen what I'd been doing. "I, uh…"

"I-I'm sorry, I…" Pressing my lips together, I looked away, unable to hold his gaze.

Surge came closer, leaving the door open behind him. I felt the mattress dip and glanced at him. He crawled closer on his hands and knees until he hovered over me.

"Angel, were you trying to make yourself come?" I nodded. "Having trouble getting yourself off?"

"*Oui.* I've never… that is… I haven't…"

His brow furrowed. "You've never had an orgasm?"

I shook my head. He growled and mumbled something I didn't quite catch. It sounded like he said *inconsiderate assholes*, but I didn't understand what he meant.

"Do you want some help?" His gaze dropped to my breasts before flicking back up to my eyes. "Or you can tell me to get the fuck out and leave you alone. This isn't a condition of you being here. But if you want me to touch you, I will."

"I want it to be you," I said.

"When I first walked into that room and saw you

with Jacques, I got hard. You were the most beautiful woman I'd ever seen, but I need to be completely honest. I liked Jacques too. I'm bisexual, so I've been with men and women. Does that bother you?"

"*Non*. I don't care, Surge."

"Call me Cam," he said right before he kissed me. His tongue swept into my mouth and his body settled over mine. The weight of him felt right. I loved the way he pressed me into the mattress.

"Cam, you have on too many clothes."

He smiled and sat up long enough to quickly remove his clothing. He tossed everything onto a nearby chair. Reaching up, I ran my fingers over his tattoos. He had a dusting of hair over his pecs that trailed down his stomach. I'd always loved a man with hair on his chest. All my teenage crushes had been older celebrities. Men who actually looked like men and not little boys. Nothing against Jacques, but he'd never once made me crave sex. Not the way Surge did.

He still had on his glasses and reached up to remove them. I stopped him, wrapping my fingers around his wrist.

"Leave them. I think they're sexy."

He smiled and kissed me again. I felt breathless when he trailed his lips down my neck. He licked my nipple before sucking it into his mouth and I cried out, the foreign sensation too incredible for words. I muttered rapidly in French as I clung to him, begging him to never stop.

"Jesus, Colette. I can't remember wanting a woman more. I'm so fucking hard for you." His lips brushed against mine again. "Tell me I can have you."

"Take me, Cam. I want to feel everything. To experience my first orgasm with you."

His lips claimed mine again, and he groaned as

he shifted. I felt his cock brush against my pussy, and my heart raced. He reached between us and rubbed my clit. The hard, quick strokes got me off so fast it made my head spin. As I screamed out his name, he thrust hard and deep, tearing through my innocence. Tears pricked my eyes for a brief moment, but the pain was gone as quickly as it had come.

I hadn't thought to tell him I was a virgin. Would it make a difference?

"So fucking tight." He groaned. "So wet. God, Colette. I think I could fuck you for hours. Days. Hold on to me, angel."

I wrapped my arm around his shoulders and gripped his bicep with my other hand. He pounded into me, the bed slamming into the wall with every flex of his hips. The wood creaked and groaned, and as he shouted out his release, the heat of his cum filling me, the bed jolted right before the top portion crashed to the floor. The small headboard somehow remained upright.

Surge froze, his cock pulsing inside me.

"Holy shit. We just broke the bed."

I pressed my lips together but couldn't contain my giggles. I'd heard of such a thing happening, but I'd thought it was only in movies. He shifted his position, and the bed made another noise before the foot of it crashed to the floor too.

"Is it wrong I don't want to pull out and see how bad the damage is?" he asked. "Because I'm still hard and could easily fuck you again."

I couldn't contain my laughter and soon tears streaked my cheeks and my sides hurt. The heated look Surge gave me killed my laughter and my heart raced for a different reason. He kissed me again, then pulled his hips back, only to sink into me once more. He looked so intense. His thrusts were slow and deep, each one making my toes curl as hit just the right spot inside me.

"Cam, I... I've never... I didn't know..." I pressed my lips together. How could I tell him he was my first? I didn't think he could tell. His reaction when he realized he'd taken my innocence would determine if I could stay or not. I wouldn't remain with an angry man, even if the alternative was living on the streets alone.

"You're so fucking perfect, Colette. No one's ever made me feel this way. Is that what you were trying to say? That it's different with me?"

My throat tightened and felt like it was closing. If I said yes, I'd be lying. But if I said no...

"I don't have anyone or anything to compare it to," I whispered.

Surge froze, his body tensing. "Colette, are you telling me... Wait. No. Please tell me I fucking didn't just..."

He pulled out and sat back on his heels, staring down at his cock. I stared and saw the smear of blood on him, along with other fluids. My cheeks burned, and I turned my face away. Would he hate me now?

"Motherfucker," he muttered. "Did I hurt you? I wasn't exactly gentle."

I shook my head and continued to stare across the room. Surge lightly gripped my chin and made me turn back toward him.

"Colette, I'm so fucking sorry. If I'd known, I probably wouldn't have touched you. But even if I had, I'd have damn sure been gentler."

"It didn't hurt," I said.

"Doesn't make it right. You were clearly saving yourself for someone special, and I took your virginity carelessly."

"I wanted it to be you," I said. "Please don't be angry with me."

"Angry? With you?" I nodded, and he gave a humorless bark of laughter. "Jesus, you really are too sweet. Angel, I'm fucking pissed as hell, but not at you. I'm mad at myself. I made assumptions and could have seriously hurt you. As it is… I didn't stop to think about birth control. I took you bare."

Birth control. I'd never used any. I knew some girls who'd started taking birth control to regulate their periods, but I never had. Did that mean I might be pregnant? It took more than once, didn't it?

"I'm clean," Surge assured me. "You're positive I didn't hurt you?"

"I'm sure." I reached up and trailed my fingertips over his cheek. "I'm not sorry you were the one who took my virginity. Please don't be upset with yourself. I should have told you. I knew when you saw me with Jacques you'd think I had experience with men. It was deceitful for me to let you think I'd been with someone."

Surge curled his hand around mine and lifted my fingers, pressing a kiss to them. "Do you want a warm bath? It might keep you from being sore later."

The bed gave another groan and the bottom banged down on the floor, the footboard falling over. Surge cursed and glared at the broken furniture.

"Just hold me? *S'il te plaît.*"

"Does that mean please?" he asked, focusing on me again.

" *Oui.* I mean, yes. I'll try to do better about only speaking English."

He kissed me softly before stretching out on his side and tugging me against his chest. "Just be yourself, Colette. If you say something I don't understand, I'll ask what it means. You're French. It makes sense you'd speak that language. The fact you learned English is great, but don't feel like you can never speak your native tongue ever again."

I curled into him, a smile on my lips. Maybe Jacques had gone about things the wrong way, but he'd been right about the bikers. Or at least, about this one. Being with Surge made me feel safe. Cared for. I wondered what it would take for him to keep me forever instead of as a temporary houseguest. Because I wasn't sure I ever wanted to leave.

Chapter Three

Surge

How the hell could I have fucked up this bad? Not only had I gone off the assumption multiple men had screwed her, but I hadn't bothered to put on a condom or even ask her about birth control. I'd never, not once gone without protection. Not even when I fucked men. I'd always guarded my health, and that of my partners. Until Colette.

Yeah, she was gorgeous, and the sweetest thing I'd ever met. Didn't excuse my lack of brain cells right now. I hadn't even been drinking long enough to blame it on too many beers.

Walking in and seeing her pleasure herself had made me hard as granite. I'd had every intention of leaving her alone. Until then. If I'd been smart, I'd have backed out of the room and left the house. Gone for a ride. Hooked up with a club whore. Anything but stay in the bedroom and take her so damn hard we broke the bed.

The door crashed into the wall and I jolted, already reaching for the gun I kept in the bedside table drawer. One glance at the bedroom doorway and I froze.

"Aidan? What the hell are you doing here?" I asked, yanking the sheet up over Colette.

"Guess this explains why you haven't called lately. Thought you didn't bring lovers to your bed." He folded his arms and took in the destruction. "Jesus, Surge. You never fucked me that damn hard."

I heard a gasp and looked down at Colette. Her eyes were wide as she stared at me. Fuck. I'd mentioned being bisexual, but hadn't told her I'd been seeing a man recently. Since she'd been with Jacques and he'd clearly preferred men, I didn't think she'd have an issue with it. Still, there were better ways for her to find out.

"I'm sorry, Colette. I'd planned to tell you. I've been seeing Aidan off and on for a while, but I didn't think he'd show up unannounced."

"Damnit," Aidan muttered. "I didn't mean to out you like that. It's just... seeing you and her, I..."

"Are you two dating?" Colette asked.

"No," I said at the same time Aidan said, "Yes."

I glanced at him. "I told you I couldn't offer you something serious. And you didn't out me. I told her I was bisexual, but I hadn't mentioned you."

"That's bullshit and you know it," Aidan said, his face flushing as he ground his teeth together. "Admit you're ashamed of being with me. I'm not tough enough. Not cool enough for someone like you."

"Aidan."

He held up his hand. "Since when do you wear glasses?"

I cleared my throat. "Since about five years ago. I only wear them for reading or when I'm on the computer. Colette thought they were sexy, so I left them on."

"Colette. Right. Is she your girlfriend? You could have at least told me we were finished," Aidan said.

"I need to discuss that with her before I talk to you about it," I said. "As for us being finished, we weren't in a committed relationship. I never offered exclusivity to you, and I didn't expect it in return."

Colette reached up to cup my cheek, drawing my attention back to her. "If you need to go speak with him, it's all right. We made no promises to each other. You were helping me and nothing more. I don't expect forever from you."

"Angel, we need to talk. Whether or not you expect it from me, that's what you're going to get. I need to protect you, and since I lost my damn head, there's a chance you could be pregnant."

Aidan made a sound like someone had strangled him and he stumbled back into the wall. Shit. First, I fucked up with Colette, and now I was hurting Aidan. I'd never wanted that to happen, which is why I'd tried to keep my distance. I'd known he was getting too close, wanting more than I could offer.

"You're going to marry her, aren't you?" Aidan whispered.

"*Non*. I won't come between the two of you," Colette insisted.

Her words made me pause. *Between* the two of us. She'd been willing to let me and Jacques share her. I knew now it had been out of desperation, and Jacques' idea, but it made me wonder.

Leaning down to whisper in her ear, so I wouldn't get Aidan's hopes up, I asked, "Colette, would you be willing to be with me *and* Aidan? And don't agree hastily. I'm not talking about right now. I mean, for the long haul. A real relationship between the three of us."

"You'd be all right with that?" she asked.

"It would give you more protection. I can't be with you all the time. I like knowing you have someone else watching out for you." I'd thought I'd been quiet enough for the conversation to remain between me and Colette, until Aidan interrupted.

"Hold up," Aidan said, moving closer. "What kind of trouble is she in?"

"You heard that, huh?" I asked, sitting up. The sheet pooled at my waist, barely covering me. Aidan's gaze dipped and he swallowed hard before giving a nod. "Someone smuggled Colette into the country, with other men, women, and children. She escaped from them with the help of another captive. I don't know if they're searching for her, or even know where she is right now."

Aidan sat on the edge of the bed. "What did you ask her before all that?"

"I asked if she'd be willing to have a relationship with the both of us, and I hope she's open to you and me being intimate too. This is the only way I can think of to keep you in my life, Aidan. My club would never accept me claiming a man, but they might be okay with me claiming both of you."

"And you're okay with that?" Aidan asked Colette.

She nodded. "*Oui*. Although, I've not been with a man other than Surge. Well… That is…"

Her cheeks flushed, and I pulled her onto my lap, holding her close. "We never discussed exactly what you did to survive, and I don't need to know. You were a virgin. I saw the blood."

"Sometimes the men who watched, they would make Jacques…" Her cheeks turned a brighter crimson. "He'd hold me open when he took me, so they could see better."

My hold tightened on her. The fucker had taken her ass and used her. Sure, he'd kept her virginity intact, but there had to have been a way to avoid hurting her like that. Shit. I'd assumed she was clean once I'd realized she was a virgin.

"Colette, did he… use protection?" I asked.

Colette nodded, and I felt relieved. I knew condoms weren't foolproof, and we should all get tested together just to be safe. Still, I'd taken her without a condom. The damage had been done if he had given her something.

"Where is this asshole now?" Aidan asked, his fists clenched.

"Gone," I said. "He traded Colette for food, then didn't come to the house. I think he knew I wouldn't go easy on him. Said he had someone waiting for him."

"So what's the plan? You going to petition to club to make her your old lady? And what does that make me?" Aidan asked.

"How do you feel about prospecting?" I asked.

Aidan snorted. "You can't be serious. Me? Riding a motorcycle?"

"We'll figure it out." I kissed the top of Colette's head. "I need to forge some documents."

"For Colette?" Aidan asked. "You aren't going to just work your keyboard magic to marry her? You've done it for your club before."

"Yeah, and I don't want them asking another hacker to undo it. No, if I'm going to marry her, it's going to be the right way. Sort of. I was thinking of a same day license and a quick ceremony at the Justice of the Peace." I hugged Colette to me. "If you're all right with that? I know it isn't very romantic."

"Are you sure?" Colette asked. "I can still leave. You don't have to go to all this trouble."

Aidan chuckled. "She doesn't get it. Colette, if he says he's marrying you, it means you're already under his skin and he doesn't plan to ever let you go. He's just being nice by asking. It wouldn't take him long at all to hack into the government and create every file needed to show you're his wife."

Her eyes widened. "You can do that?"

"Yes. And I'm going to leave you with Aidan for now. I need to go into the office and work for a bit. You're going to need some documents showing you're here legally. I'll have to get a copy of your birth certificate from France." I frowned. I hadn't had to mess with international records like that. What if I couldn't do it?

"Just a thought... would it be easier to erase Colette in France and create everything new here? Birth certificate, social, and anything else she'd need?" Aidan asked. "Unless she has family back home?"

Colette shook her head. "There's no one. I don't even have friends who will miss me. It's why I think they chose me. Little chance someone would try to find me. How will we explain my accent?"

"I'll think of something," I said. "Get to know Aidan while I'm gone. And if things get... Um..."

Aidan smirked. "He's trying to say if you're up for it, he's fine with the two of us having sex. Jesus, Surge. Get a pretty woman in your bed and suddenly you get all tongue-tied and shit."

I flipped him off, but he only laughed.

"And just so the both of you know, I'm clean," Aidan said. "Only one I've been with for months is Surge, and I still got tested every month because I knew he sometimes hooked up with the women at the clubhouse. Or at least, the opportunity was there whether or not he took it."

"Way to make me feel like an asshole," I muttered as I slid out of bed. I walked over to the dresser and grabbed a pair of athletic shorts. I didn't miss the hungry look on Aidan's face before I covered up the goods.

"That wasn't my intention," Aidan said. "And you know it. I knew the lifestyle you led from the first day we met. Not once have I asked you to change. I only wanted to be a part of your life. Never wanted to be the *only* part of it."

"I know. I'm sorry." I sighed and ran my hand over my head. "I'm going to see what I can do to make it possible to marry Colette tomorrow."

"I'm still waiting," Aidan said.

I stared at him. I knew what he meant. He had never been to my house before. Somehow, he'd gotten into the compound and come right through my front door. I didn't know what he'd told the Prospect on the gate. Wasn't sure I wanted to.

"Doesn't matter."

"It's in the living room," Aidan said. "What I brought. The reason they let me in. You know, in case you wanted to see it."

I nodded and left the room, letting him and Colette get to know one another. As much as I wanted to get started on the stuff she'd need, the idea of Aidan bringing something was a lure I couldn't resist. I made my way to the living room and stared at the sculpture he'd placed along the wall between the TV and the window. The wild twists and curves wound their way toward the ceiling. Each textured a different way. Beautiful. Chaotic. And I couldn't seem to look away.

Damnit. He knew I'd wanted to commission a piece from him. The shithead had refused repeatedly. I hadn't seen this particular work in his studio the last time I'd been over there. Which meant he'd either been working on it in secret or had created it in the past month.

Knowing he'd been thinking of me, had put effort into something I wanted, while I'd been doing my best to avoid him, made me feel even worse about myself. Now he was here. In my house. Talking to my future wife. What the hell had I gotten myself into?

I went to my office and shut the door. Putting in my earbuds, I cranked some music. It always helped me focus. Didn't matter what was playing, but I preferred something with a heavy bass line. Logging into my computer, I got to work. First, I needed to hack into the vital records in France and erase Colette. After that, I'd have to locate any trace of her and remove every single file I found. I didn't know how long it would take, but I had all night. Aidan would keep Colette occupied, and by morning, we could head to the courthouse.

My fingers flew over the keys, each stroke faster than the one before as I found my groove. I'd thought it would be more difficult to access the records in France. I'd been working with Wire off and on, honing my skills. It looked like it had paid off. Within a few hours, Colette Fontaine had never existed. As much as I hated to take even her name from her, when I started creating the new files in our government's system, I gave her a new one. She remained Colette, but I changed her last name to Moreau.

My fingers were cramping by the time I'd finished, and I had a wicked headache. Stretching my back and cracking my neck, I went to the kitchen for a cold beer. It remained silent in the bedroom. As curious as I was, I made myself finish my drink before I went to check on Colette and Aidan.

It would piss my club off I went behind their backs. I only hoped I could reason with Fox. If anyone would understand why I felt the need to protect Colette, it would be him, and even Rocket. They both had claimed women who'd been badly abused. Which also meant they'd wonder why I hadn't just come to them in the first place. I didn't want to risk Fox offering to help Colette, giving her a reason to leave and start a new life elsewhere. Yeah. I was an asshole. A selfish one. I wanted her, and the fact she might be carrying my child only added to my need to tie her to me in every way possible.

I listened intently and still didn't hear anything coming from the bedroom. With some luck, they'd both gone to sleep. It was going to be a busy fucking day once the sun rose.

"Shit. She's going to need clothes." I'd never contacted Slider. Motherfucker. If I asked now, he'd want to know what was up. Then he'd be implicated if the club lost their shit over my marriage to Colette.

Fuck it. I needed those clothes.

I picked up the phone in the kitchen and called Slider, knowing he'd be pissed if I woke him. He answered almost immediately, which meant he didn't want Luka and Anya to wake up.

"Surge?" he asked, whispering into the phone. "Something wrong?"

"Um, kinda. I have a favor, but I need you to not ask questions. I don't want you getting tied up in my shit."

I heard the rustle of covers and realized he'd been in bed already. *Of course, he was. Dumbass. He's married with two kids.*

"What do you need?" he asked.

"I need a few of Vasha's things actually. A dress, shoes, and some underthings."

I heard the *snick* of his lighter and knew if his wife saw him lighting up, she'd tear him a new one. The bastard had supposedly quit.

"Tell me what sizes you need and I'll get some brand-new shit. Won't be fancy. Just from one of the twenty-four-hour stores. Text me the details. I'll go throw some clothes on."

"Won't Vasha wonder where you're going so late?" I asked.

"I'll tell her a brother needs help. You heading to bed? I can leave everything out front."

I looked down the hallway again. "Yeah. I think I'm going to crash. If you could just leave it in the living room? The door will be unlocked."

"On it. And, Surge, whatever the hell is going on, you know I have your back. I might have been pissed all those years ago when I found my wife in my bed, and realized what you'd done, but it was the best thing to ever happen to me. I owe you one."

"That's not what you said back then," I said, smiling at the memory. He'd been livid.

"Yeah, yeah. I'm heading in to get dressed. Text me."

I hung up and put the phone down on the counter.

Only one way to find out Colette's sizes. I'd have to check the things she'd had on. Creeping down the hall as quietly as I could, I opened the door. My chest ached and my throat grew tight when I saw Aidan curled around her. She faced away from him; her hand out like she'd been searching for me. I doubted that was the case. But it made me realize... this would be my life from now on. I'd get to come home to these two.

I picked her clothes up off the floor and noted the sizes, then sent the text to Slider. Once that was finished, I crawled into bed and put my arm over Colette, resting my palm on Aidan's hip. Neither of them stirred. Whatever had transpired after I'd left, they both seemed at peace right now.

I hoped it would last.

* * *

Aidan
Six Hours Earlier

Coming to Surge's house had been a gamble. I hadn't known what to expect when I got here. Although, I'd thought he might be pissed. In all the time we'd been together, not once had he ever invited me to his house. He'd wanted to keep a wall between us. I understood. Or tried to. Hell, my parents had thrown me out of my house at sixteen because they'd caught me with a boy. I'd couch surfed at a few friends' homes while I looked for a job and got emancipated.

So, knowing the guy I really liked didn't want me around long-term hurt like a bitch. I knew we were good together. But Surge didn't think his club would accept the two of us, so he'd hidden me away like a dirty secret. I'd hated it, even though I loved being with him.

Finding him in bed with a woman... I'd felt like I'd been kicked in the balls. Especially after seeing the way he'd wrecked the bed.

Colette watched me, waiting patiently. She didn't prod or try to fill the silence with idle chatter. I appreciated it more than she realized. Or perhaps the woman was just scared. I wouldn't blame her. It sounded like she'd been through hell, and now some strange man burst in on her while she was with Surge?

"Sorry for barging in," I said. "I hadn't realized he would be with someone. I had my suspicions, but..."

"I'm the one who should apologize," she said. "I didn't know he'd been seeing someone. I should have. Cam is so kind and heroic. The moment he recognized something was wrong, he stepped in to help. No one's ever done that for me before. Not without wanting something in return."

Cam. She calls him Cam, and he's never once given me permission to use his real name. I swallowed the knot in my throat. These two had gotten closer in a short time, and I'd been trying for what felt like forever. Was it wrong of me to stay here? They'd asked me to be part of their relationship, but I had to wonder if Surge would have ever reached out to me if I hadn't dropped by unannounced.

"You didn't do anything wrong, Colette. It's clear he's fond of you. He cares enough he wants to marry you. There are ways to protect you without going that far. Did he consider them?" She didn't say anything. "Of course, he didn't. Because he didn't want to."

"You think he really wants to marry me?" she asked.

"I can't blame him. You're beautiful and seem sweet. I bet he didn't stand a chance."

"I'm worried he'll regret his decision. I'm nothing special." She looked down at her hands, twisting her fingers together. "In France, I was alone. No family. No friends. When those men brought me here, I didn't know what to expect. Jacques escaped, and he took me with him. We lived on the streets, walking from New Orleans all the way here. We'd get rides when we could, but there was always a cost. It wasn't easy, but we managed. He was the closest thing I had to a friend, and…"

"He used you," I said. If I'd been the one on the run with her, I'd have found ways to provide for us.

"*Oui.* I think he did. I didn't realize it until now."

"I met Surge in town one day. I'd been getting coffee at the café, and he'd come in right before me. I'd been admiring him as we stood in line. Too scared to make a move on the sexy badass biker. Then the barista mixed up our drinks." I smiled, thinking of my first conversation with him. "We realized the mistake when we got outside and swapped drinks. Then we talked for a few minutes, and I found the courage to give him my number. Never thought he'd use it."

"But he did," she said.

"Yeah. A few days later, he called. Asked me to meet him at a bar outside of town. And that was the beginning of what I thought would be a great relationship. Until I realized he wanted to keep me hidden." It still bothered me. "I guess I should have been grateful to have any time with him. A guy like that pairing up with someone like me?"

She cupped my cheek, much like she had with Surge. Her smile was soft, and her eyes bright. I'd never met anyone like her before, and Surge probably hadn't either. I could see why he wanted her. Hell, I might sleep with the occasional woman, but I preferred men, and even I wanted to hold on to her.

"He's lucky to have you in his life," she said.

"Trust me when I say I'm the lucky one. He might look like he's all brawn and no brain, but he's one of the smartest people I know. There's not much he can't do with a computer. I'm an artist, so I can admit the outer package attracted me first. Then I got to know him."

"An artist?" she asked.

I nodded. "I sculpt. Mostly, I make small things I can carry with me to different craft fairs and such, and I have business cards in case people want something larger or custom-made. I don't get rich off my work, but I'm comfortable. I bought a place that allows me to have a studio for my art and a small apartment in back. It's just one big room with a small kitchen area, and a separate bathroom. Nothing fancy, but it's mine."

"I think you're more amazing than you realize."
When she leaned in, I didn't stop her. Her lips pressed
against mine.

I put my arms around her, drawing her closer. I
kept the kiss soft and sweet, like her. Even though
Surge had seemed okay if something happened
between me and Colette, I wasn't sure I wanted to
push that boundary yet. The man was marrying her
tomorrow. What if he changed his mind about me? Or
worse. What if Colette decided she couldn't be with
both of us? I had a feeling Surge would choose her
over me. If for no other reason than she needed him
more.

"We don't have to do anything, Colette. I'd be
content just holding you."

"You don't like women?" she asked.

"I do. I've been with several over the years."

She let the sheet fall and I couldn't help but stare
at her breasts. I couldn't remember ever seeing such a
perfect pair before. My hand seemed to lift of its own
volition and reached out to touch her. I cupped the soft
mound and stroked my thumb over her nipple. It
hardened and her breath caught. I watched as her eyes
darkened and she flicked her tongue out to wet her
lips.

"What do you want, Colette? Anything that
happens has to be your choice. I need the words, need
to hear you say what you need from me."

More than that, I needed to know she didn't feel
obligated to do this. As much as I wanted her, it had to
be her choice. I'd never taken anyone by force before,
and I wouldn't start now. If something happened
between us, and I found out later she'd felt like she had
no other option, it would destroy me. I wouldn't be
able to look at myself ever again. Not without seeing a

monster.

"Cam was my first. My only. I don't count Jacques since he only took my..." Her cheeks flushed. "He really did only like men. He told me he had to imagine I was a guy for him to even get hard. He always used a condom with me, and he never came."

"If we do this, I'll use one too. Surge didn't, which means if you're pregnant, it's his baby. I don't want to take that from him, make him wonder whose child it is."

She smiled. "The bed is already broken. You don't have to be gentle."

"Maybe I don't *have* to, but I want to." I stood and removed my clothes and shoes, pulling a condom from my wallet. I set it on the bedside table before I kneeled on the mattress. Colette stretched out and I pulled the sheet off her completely.

The woman really was a goddess, and I wasn't sure she even realized it. I bent her knees and spread her thighs. When Surge said he'd come inside her, he hadn't been lying. They must have gone at least twice with the amount of cum coating her pussy and thighs. Leaning down, I licked her pussy lips before flicking my tongue over her clit. Colette made a soft squeaking sound and her legs trembled.

I urged her calves over my shoulders and settled in. I used my tongue to clean every bit of cum off her, then worked my fingers inside her, curling them slightly as I pulled them back out. She moaned and tipped her head back. Every thrust pulled more of Surge's cum from her, and I lapped it up like honey. While I knew his taste intimately, this was different. His unique flavor had mingled with Colette's, and I wasn't sure I'd ever get enough.

I pumped my fingers in and out of her pussy

while I licked and nipped at her clit. It didn't take much to make her come, and the feel of her squeezing me was enough to make my dick hard. I wanted inside her, more than I'd ever wanted to fuck a woman before. I got up on my knees and reached for the condom, tearing open the package and rolling the latex down my cock.

"Are you sure?" I asked one last time.

"*Oui.* Make love to me, Aidan. Please."

There was no way I could refuse her request. I settled my hips between her thighs, bracing my weight over her. My cock wasn't as large as Surge's, and for a brief moment, I worried she'd compare the two of us and be disappointed. I dispelled the negative thoughts and slid inside her.

Colette was tight and hot. She clasped me perfectly, and I wasn't sure how long I'd last. It had been over a month since I'd been with Surge, and there hadn't been anyone else. I rubbed her clit with my thumb as I thrust into her. Long. Slow. I took my time building up the pleasure for both of us.

"Aidan," she said, my name a near whisper.

"Come for me, beautiful. Let me see how pretty you are when you find your pleasure."

She moaned again, and her pussy clenched down. I rocked into her, and the moment she came, it was enough to set off my own orgasm. I groaned and kept thrusting until every drop of cum had been wrung from my balls. My cock jerked inside her, and I wished we could stay like that for a while. I knew it wouldn't be long before I started to shrink and I'd fall out. And since there was a condom to deal with...

I pulled out, holding the condom just in case. Leaning down, I kissed her once more before I went to the bathroom. I tossed the used rubber into the trash and cleaned up. It took a moment to hunt down a washcloth. When I found them, I wet one with warm water and used it to clean Colette.

She hummed, her eyes closed, and I could tell she was seconds from falling asleep. I got into bed and curled my arm around her. She shifted and put her back to me. Reaching down, I pulled the sheet over us and shut my eyes. Sleep didn't come as quickly as I'd thought. The house remained quiet, and I knew Surge must still be working. If anyone could pull this off, it would be him.

I heard his office door open and his footsteps walk in the opposite direction. I wasn't sure if he just needed a break, or if he'd finished. Keeping my body relaxed wasn't easy, but I tried to feign sleep when he walked into the bedroom. I heard him rustling around and cracked my eye open enough to see him checking out Colette's clothes and shoes. I hadn't even thought about the fact she wouldn't have something to wear for the wedding. For that matter, if she'd been living on the streets, did she have any clothes at all, other than what she'd had on?

My heart broke for her, and everything she'd suffered. I didn't know how fate had managed to bring her to Surge, but I was glad. If anyone would keep her safe and take care of her, it would be him. He'd always had a hero complex, even if he wouldn't admit it. He tried to be tough and act aloof. I always saw through to the heart of gold he tried to hide.

And no matter what happened between me and him, I'd do my part to make sure Colette had what she needed. I wouldn't be much good in a fight and didn't know how to stop the men who'd brought her to this country, but I could give her my support and offer her whatever comfort I could. I'd be her friend. If she wanted more than friendship, I'd give it to her, gladly. I couldn't remember meeting someone so sweet and pure, so genuine. I hoped the darkness in the world never dimmed the bright light shining inside her.

When Surge got into bed and snuggled up to the front of Colette, I felt jealous for a moment. I hadn't left him room on this side of the bed, but some part of me had wanted to curl up with him. We never had. Not even at my place. It was always a quick round of sex, and then he'd find a reason to leave. All the signs had been there, showing me he would run first chance he had. I'd ignored them.

He settled his hand on my hip, and it felt like my heart would swell so big it would burst from my chest. I discreetly watched him and smiled when I heard the soft snore escape him. He'd worn himself out, between the sex with Colette and the work at his computer.

I pressed a kiss to Colette's shoulder and finally let sleep pull me under.

Chapter Four

Colette

I'd stopped dreaming of my wedding day a long time ago. Now, I would actually have one. It might not have been in a church or anywhere fancy, but that didn't matter. Somehow, Surge had managed to get me a dress and shoes, as well as a pretty bra and pair of panties. The bags he'd given me also held a few changes of clothes and more practical underthings, as well as two nightgowns. It was more than I'd owned in a while, and his kindness brought tears to my eyes. I held them back, refusing to cry on such a happy day.

"I didn't think about girly stuff for the bathroom," Surge said. "We can stop after we get married."

"You're shopping for shampoo after you tie the knot?" Aidan asked, giving him an *are you serious?* look.

"Food first," Surge said. "A nice place. Anywhere you want. I'm afraid you'll have to shower with my stuff again. I do have spare razors, though, so you can have one of your own."

Hot showers whenever I wanted. I could shave. Wash my hair. He'd even offered to run a bath for me last night. I'd been with Surge less than twenty-four hours, and already I felt like a pampered princess. I knew he didn't like Jacques, but if I ever saw that man again, I owed him a big thank-you. If he hadn't brought me to the clubhouse last night, hadn't insisted we invite a biker to join us in the bedroom, I might not have ever met Surge. And he was… wonderful. So was Aidan, but in a different way.

"What are you going to wear?" I asked.

"I have a dress shirt I can put on, and a nicer pair

of jeans. I'm afraid that's about all I own. If I'd had more time to plan this out, I'd have bought some dress pants or at least khakis."

"While the two of you get ready, I'm going to head home," Aidan said.

I bit my lip and glanced at Surge. He didn't seem happy with the news, but for whatever reason, he wasn't asking Aidan to join us. Had he not planned to include him in our wedding? He'd asked if I would consider a relationship with the two of them. I knew I could only marry one of the guys, but it didn't mean we shouldn't have Aidan come with us.

The tender way he'd made love to me last night still made my body hum. Where Surge had a commanding presence, Aidan had a calming effect on me. They were opposites in every way, and yet, they complemented one another.

To an outsider, I could imagine the way I'd attached myself to both men would look bad. People would call me a whore. I'd been alone for so long in France, then dragged to this country against my will and held captive. It changed the way I viewed the world and other people. I hadn't felt safe since waking up as nothing more than property to be sold. Being with Jacques had been one stressful day after another. Yes, I'd felt like he offered me some protection, but I'd still lived in fear. Would I starve to death? Would someone rape me? What would happen if the show Jacques put on for the men didn't appease them?

Then I met Surge and Aidan. With the two of them, I finally felt like someone genuinely cared. For a while, I'd thought Jacques did. Now I knew differently. Maybe it should have made me mistrust everyone I met, but looking in Surge's eyes, I knew he was different. Same for Aidan. Neither man was like anyone I'd met before.

They hadn't hurt me. I'd been vulnerable when Surge first found me with Jacques. He hadn't taken advantage. Aidan could have done the same. Forced himself on me. Instead, he'd been sweet and taken his time.

It didn't matter if other people accepted my decision to be with both men. As long as the two of them wanted me, I'd do what I could to make them happy. They didn't realize how much they'd saved me. Not only by getting me off the streets, but by giving me a family.

Aidan's gentle smile and soft touch warmed my heart. The way he cradled me against him as if I were the most precious thing in the world was something I'd never experienced before. And I could tell Surge was more than just fond of him. I was about to jump in with both feet, and I refused to look back or ever have regrets.

"You'll meet us there?" I asked.

His eyebrows lifted. "You want me to?"

Surge snorted. "Don't be an idiot. Of course, we want you there. I might only get to pick one spouse, legally, but it doesn't mean you're a lesser part of this relationship."

He stepped over to Aidan and put his hand on the back of the other man's neck. Surge pressed his forehead to Aidan's a moment, and whispered something I didn't catch, right before he kissed him. I smiled, watching the two of them. I could see how much Aidan adored Surge, and even though the biker tried to hide it, he cared for Aidan too.

"I'll change and be waiting on the courthouse steps," Aidan said. "Maybe we should take some pictures? They have that little garden off to the side.

The dogwoods and crepe myrtles were blooming the other day."

"I'd love that," I said. "We can ask someone to take a picture of all three of us, then we can frame it."

Surge hugged Aidan and mouthed a *thank you* to me.

He leaned back and cupped Aidan's face between his hands. "This isn't just my day with Colette. It's yours too. If I could, I'd marry both of you."

Aidan's cheeks flushed. I saw the pleased smile on his lips.

"Colette, I'm going to walk out with Aidan, and I have a quick errand to run. You'll be safe here. I'll even make sure the doors are locked."

My stomach tightened and I worried at my bottom lip. It wasn't the club that made me feel safe here. It was Surge himself. What if someone came by? Or worse, what if they got into the house and made me leave? I didn't know anything about the men here. I still didn't understand why Jacques and I had been invited in the first place. Something had felt off about it, but Jacques had insisted we come. He'd been right, but still…

Shaking off the doubts, I gave them both a nod and went into the bathroom. Surge had already set out a clean towel for me, so I started the shower and waited for the water temperature to adjust. Once it was warm, but not too hot, I stepped under the spray and wet my hair. I could feel the ache between my legs. I'd gone from being a virgin to having sex multiple times last night. But it was a good kind of hurt.

The best kind.

I didn't have a way to dry my hair, and I didn't want it to soak my new dress. Without hairpins, I didn't have many options. I found a ponytail holder in one of the drawers and tried not to think of why it might be there when Surge and Aidan both had short hair. After quickly braiding my hair, I tied it off. Reaching up, I pulled a few tendrils loose around my face and wound them around my finger to form curls.

I didn't have makeup, but I'd never worn much, anyway. Giving myself one last look in the mirror, I went back into the bedroom and put on my new things. Surge leaned against the dresser, arms folded, as he eyed me with a hungry gaze. Wherever he'd gone, it must not have been far. Or had I taken a longer shower than I'd realized?

I loved the way he watched me as I slowly dressed. It felt sexy and a little naughty. Something told me if we weren't in a hurry, he'd have pinned me to the bed and done wicked things to me again.

And I'd have let him.

"I'll be quick," he said, striding into the bathroom. I heard the shower start up again and hoped I'd left him enough hot water. He came out five minutes later with a towel around his waist and another rubbing his hair. "I didn't think to ask. Would you like me to shave before we go? Sometimes I grow out a short beard and other times I shave every two or three days."

"You're asking me?" My brow furrowed. Was that typical? Wouldn't he have more say over whether he had hair on his face?

"You're about to be my wife, and we're getting married. Do you want me to go as-is, or want me to shave? I'm fine with either," he said.

I eyed the whiskers coming in along his jaw and pressed my thighs together. Why did that bit of scruff make him even sexier? I licked my lips, and he smirked.

"All right. I guess it stays," he said. He dropped the towel and got a pair of boxer briefs out of the drawer. He stepped into them and opened the closet to take out a pair of jeans. And yes, I shamelessly watched him. I wanted to ask about the ink on his body. He had many designs, and I wondered if they had a special meaning to him. "I'll make sure you have room in the closet for some dresses later. We need to buy you more clothes and shoes."

"I don't need much," I said.

"No arguments. I'm going to take care of my wife. Expect Aidan to spoil you too." He hesitated after shrugging on a button-down shirt. "I want to ask him to move in here with us, assuming the club gives the okay. Would you be all right with that?"

"As you told him, he's just as much a part of this relationship as you and I are. It wouldn't be right to exclude him from our home."

Surge came over and kissed me. It was a hard, brief one, but it made my toes curl in my shoes. "You're fucking perfect, Colette. Don't ever change."

His words warmed me and made my cheeks flush. I pressed my palms to the heated skin and grinned at him. "I'm glad you found me last night. I know we're still strangers, but I feel... feel..."

He nodded. "I know. It's not just you."

"What will people say?" I asked. "Your club. Will they think we're moving too fast? What happens if they don't accept Aidan?"

"I don't have the answers to any of those questions. I'm going to piss off a lot of people by marrying you without taking this to Church first. They need to vote for you to be my old lady. By marrying you, I'm taking away that option. Whether they accept you or not, you're here to stay. If they don't like it, we'll live outside the compound."

I tipped my head and studied him. "Can we do that? There are so many homes here. I thought you didn't have a choice but to live inside the gates."

"It's safer, and I'd much rather you be in this house than out there. But if it comes down to it, we'll find a place of our own. You, me, and Aidan." He kissed me again then finished buttoning his shirt before he tucked it into his jeans. "You going to be okay riding to the courthouse on my motorcycle? I didn't think about you wearing a dress and heels."

"I'll be okay." I wasn't going to admit last night had been my only time on a motorcycle. He'd not driven very fast. Would I be able to hold on when we went out into the city? The last thing I wanted to do was embarrass him or cause problems. I didn't like the fact he felt like he had to hide me from his club. And Aidan... he'd mentioned the same. While he'd been seeing Surge, it had felt like he was a dirty secret.

I let him finish getting ready, and I waited by the kitchen door. I could see his motorcycle through the window, parked in the carport. The night before, I didn't get a good look. In the daylight, it looked beautiful, and a bit scary. Had I really been on the back of it last night? It felt like it had happened weeks ago.

Surge came up behind me, placing his hand at my waist. I stared at our reflection in the glass and had to admit we looked good together. He towered over me and made me feel small. Delicate. I'd even go so far as to say beautiful, and I'd always known I was average at best.

"Ready to become Mrs. Price?"

"Is that your last name?" I asked. He'd told me his first name, but nothing else. It felt strange marrying someone I'd just met.

"It is, and while I'm thinking about it, when I created your new documents, I changed your last name. Instead of Fontaine, it's Moreau. Even though I erased every trace of you in France, I wanted to make it even harder for someone to find you."

"What happens if they question the files you made?" I asked.

"They won't. I've gotten good at not only erasing and recreating people, but forging documents as well. Like a birth certificate. I made up a mother for you and put father as unknown. I know that's a shitty thing to do since you had parents who probably loved you, but again, I want to keep you hidden from anyone trying to find you."

I leaned into him. "It's fine, Cam. I think they would understand, and I know they would appreciate the lengths you've gone to in order to keep me safe."

"Then let's get married. I have everything we need."

I took his hand and let him lead me out to the motorcycle. It took a bit of finessing to get on the machine and tuck my skirt under my thighs so it wouldn't blow around in the wind. Once I'd settled against his back, he started the bike and backed it down the driveway. He still drove slowly through the compound, even though he went a bit faster than the previous night. As we approached the gates, someone opened it to let us through. I'd worried they might question him. Would they wonder who I was? Or were they so used to men coming and going with women they didn't even care?

Surge pulled into a parking spot in front of a three-story building. It didn't look like much, but I saw the garden Aidan had mentioned. He stopped the bike and turned it off. I tried to stand, but my legs felt like jelly. Surge grinned at me as he stood and held out his hand.

"You'll get used to it," he said.

I saw Aidan heading our way and smiled at him. He seemed frazzled and still had an uncertain look in his eyes. I hated that he felt like he didn't belong, as if he weren't part of our new family. I'd do whatever I could to change that, but I knew Surge would be the main one to convince Aidan he was right where he should be.

"I didn't think about you having to bring her on the motorcycle. I should have offered to come pick you both up."

"I enjoyed it," I said. "Once I stopped being afraid I'd fall off."

Surge curled his arm around my waist and kissed my temple. "I wouldn't have let that happen."

"Pictures before or after?" Aidan asked.

"Both?" I suggested.

An older couple approached, and I hoped they were trustworthy. I took Surge's phone from him, after getting him to unlock it, and smiled at the older woman.

"I hate to bother you, but we're getting married today and I'd like a picture with all three of us. Would you mind?" I held the phone up.

"Not at all," the woman said. She reminded me of the grandmothers on TV shows. The kind who baked cookies, gave warm hugs, and always had a ready smile. She took the phone from me, and I stood between Aidan and Surge, my arms around their waists.

We smiled and the woman took two pictures. Before she handed the phone back, she hesitated. My gut churned and I wondered if I'd been wrong? Was she about to try to steal Surge's phone? I'd seen such a thing happen more than once since being brought to this country. People would act nice, then take off with your things.

"I'm not sure which one you're marrying, honey, but would you like one with just the two of you?" the woman asked.

Aidan stepped to the side. "I think that would be a great idea. Colette, stand by your husband-to-be. We'll take another one after the two of you are married."

The woman snapped another picture then gave the phone back to us. She and her husband continued down the sidewalk and I took Aidan's hand, giving it a squeeze. I knew it must have hurt, hearing her ask that particular question.

"I want more photos of the three of us," I said. "After we're married. And, Aidan, Surge was right at the house. It's not just me and him. It's all three of us, together. I don't just belong to him, I belong to you too."

Surge folded his arms over his chest. "Technically, you're both mine."

Aidan's cheeks flushed, but I saw the pleasure in his eyes over Surge's words. At least things seem to be on the right track. I knew it would take time to make Aidan feel like he was part of the family, but I hoped we'd get there. Surge had done some damage, even if it had been unintentional, and he'd need to repair their relationship.

"Time to get your license and get married," Aidan said.

We went into the courthouse together, and an hour later, we had our license in hand and were waiting for the judge. A man in his sixties came to greet us, a black robe on his shoulders.

"Cameron Price and Colette Moreau?" he asked.

Surge nodded. "That's us. If possible, we'd like Aidan to join us for the ceremony."

The judge eyed the three of us and nodded, a slight smile on his lips. "Come on in. All of you. Let's get you married and on your way to your honeymoon."

Honeymoon? I didn't think we'd have one of those. Not considering the circumstances. Although, I could only imagine how lovely one would be.

We entered the judge's chambers, and he shut the door behind us. I took Surge's hand on one side and Aidan's on the other. Nerves left me feeling shaky as the man rounded his desk and stood behind it, facing us. He eyed our joined hands and looked at a picture on the wall behind him and slightly to the right.

"That's a picture of my wife... and my husband. But as far as anyone else is concerned, he's our best friend, and that's why he's in the picture. Some people are very closed-minded." He watched us for a reaction. I tried not to give one. Why was he telling us this? "Legally, I can only marry two of you. I'm guess that will be Mr. Price and Miss Moreau. But I can alter the ceremony a little to include all three of you, if that's what you'd like."

"Really?" I asked.

He nodded. "Poly relationships are frowned upon in a small town like this, but you'll find most people turn a blind eye to it. Others will spew hatred your way. Just ignore them and live a happy life."

"I'd like to marry both of them, even if it's just the words and not on paper," Surge said.

The judge nodded. "Very well. And your name?"

I gave Aidan a nudge, who seemed to be frozen in place.

"Um, Aidan. Aidan Styles."

"Very well. Let's proceed." The judge began the ceremony, prompting each of us when it was our turn. It felt like my tongue had stuck to the roof of my mouth and I stumbled over the words.

"Do you have the rings?" the judge asked.

Surge nodded and pulled three boxes out of his pocket. He set them on the desk. The judge reached down and opened each one, and I gasped at how beautiful mine was. The other two were men's bands and were a plain silver color. I didn't know if that was the actual metal, or if they were something else like white gold or platinum. I heard a soft noise from Aidan and glanced his way, seeing tears misting his eyes.

"Cameron, will you be placing the rings on both their fingers?" the judge asked.

"Yes, sir."

He nodded. "Very well. If I might make a suggestion, when it's time for your ring, they should do that part together. It's what we did for my ceremony, and I think it made us all feel like we had an equal part in it."

"That sounds perfect," Surge said.

The rest of the ceremony passed in a blur and then I heard the words, "Husband and wife... and husband. You may kiss your bride and groom."

Surge smiled and tugged me against his chest, tipping my head back. He kissed me soft and slow, his lips lingering on mine. When I felt boneless, he set me aside and did the same to Aidan. I reached up to touch my lips only for Aidan to pull my hand away so he could kiss me too.

"Thank you, Your Honor," Surge said. "It means a lot that we were able to all participate in the ceremony."

"I understand. I wish the three of you many years of happily wedded bliss."

We left the judge's chambers and went back outside, where we took pictures in the garden before going to lunch at a nearby restaurant. It felt like I was floating the entire way there, my feet barely touching the sidewalk.

Yesterday had started as a nightmare. Full of fear and anxious over my next meal. Then I'd met Surge, and it felt like a fairy godmother had blessed me. Whatever brought the three of us together, I hoped we would last. I'd thought I needed Surge and no one else, but I'd been wrong. I needed both of them, and I was starting to think maybe they needed me too.

Chapter Five

Surge

Colette seemed to glow with happiness. I hated not being able to give her a real wedding or marrying her for the right reasons. It felt like I'd cheated her out of something special. Now that she'd tied her life to mine, there was no going back. The men in my club didn't believe in divorce. Once we claimed someone, it was forever. Which meant Aidan was now mine as well.

I'd requested a table on the patio, thinking Colette might enjoy the atmosphere. The restaurant had a small fountain nearby and various plants scattered about. It wasn't the most upscale place in the area, but it was nice enough I didn't feel bad bringing her here for our first meal as husband and wife. Aidan and I had been here a few times before.

Colette fidgeted, her gaze constantly scanning the vicinity. I didn't know how long it would take for her to settle and realize she was safe now. Aidan and I wouldn't let anything happen to her. As for my husband... I rubbed at my chest. Even thinking those words gave me a pang right over my heart. I knew that's what he'd wanted. Eventually. Did he resent the fact I'd legally married Colette instead of him? He had yet to hold my gaze for more than a few seconds.

Being at the compound wasn't going to make things easier. We needed time to bond. To grow closer. Not just Aidan, but Colette too. We'd moved at warp speed, and I worried it would come back to bite us all in the ass later. Unless we slowed down a little.

"If the two of you will excuse me for a moment, I need to make a call," I said, standing and leaving the patio. I left the restaurant and walked far enough away

I wouldn't worry about my voice carrying to Aidan or Colette. I hadn't lied. Not exactly. I would make a call just as soon as I did a little research.

I pulled up the browser on my phone and searched for cabin rentals nearby. Nothing close enough my club would come knocking on the door at any moment, but I didn't want to travel for a day to get there either. I found something about two hours away and booked the cabin. Starting tonight, we'd be on our honeymoon. I had a feeling Fox would be doubly pissed when he found out what I'd done, especially when I disappeared for three days.

I went back to the restaurant and found Colette and Aidan sitting in silence. My brow furrowed as I scrutinized the surrounding area. Had something happened while I was gone? They'd seemed to be getting along before now.

"Everything all right?" I asked as I retook my seat between them.

"I knew she looked familiar. I was right," said a voice behind me. One of our Prospects was at a nearby table.

"What the fuck, Joe?" I stood, ready to take the little shit down if I needed to. I didn't like the look on his face. Had he seen Colette and Jacques last night? I'd thought I'd been the only one to find them. What if I was wrong?

Joe held up his hands. "Easy, Surge. I'm not trying to encroach on your territory."

I growled and advanced on him. Before I could get hold of him, he stood and backed up.

"You don't look at her. Don't speak to her. And sure the fuck treat her with respect if you *have* to talk to her."

"Got it." He licked his lips. "I'm the one who

invited her and that guy."

I froze. I'd wondered who had asked them to come to the clubhouse. It had bothered me. We didn't usually approach people about the parties. Word got around and the girls showed up.

"Listen." He dropped his voice almost to a whisper. "I saw them digging in the dumpsters. I'd caught sight of them around town a few times before. I only meant to offer them a chance for some food and to get out of the elements for a bit. I know I should have told someone, but I didn't know for sure if they'd even show."

His words mollified me. A little. But just because his punk ass claimed to have altruistic reasons, didn't mean it was the truth. Actions spoke louder than words, and I didn't get a good vibe off Joe at times. No one else seemed bothered by him, and I hadn't found anything when I'd dug into his background. Still...

"So you wanted to help them?" I asked.

He nodded. "Where's the guy? He seemed protective of her. I figured they were a couple."

There. Right there. The way he asked about Jacques. It hadn't been Colette he'd invited to the clubhouse, but Jacques, and I didn't know why. Joe had never seemed to be interested in men. So what was his angle?

"Jacques is gay. I offered to let them stay at the house last night. Instead, he tried to sell Colette to me in exchange for some food."

Joe paled and audibly swallowed. His response seemed honest enough. Either way, I knew I'd be keeping an eye on him.

"Shit. I had no idea. Is she okay? That's not what she was wearing last night, so I'm assuming you're helping her out?"

The less Joe knew the better. If I told him I'd married Colette, it would put him in a bad spot. The second Fox, or anyone else, heard he'd known before them, the shit would hit the fan. I didn't want to possibly cost Joe his position in the club. While he was still paying his dues, he hadn't quite reached the point of being patched in.

"I need you to forget you saw me here. Or her," I said. "If someone asks you directly, tell them you thought you saw me in town today, but no details. I hate asking you to do that."

Joe looked from me to Colette and back again. "She's in serious trouble, isn't she?"

I nodded, refusing to say more. I'd meant it. The last thing he needed to do was keep digging. If Fox demanded answers, I wanted Joe to have very little to say.

"I'll keep quiet. If anyone asks, I'll tell them you were in town, but I won't mention the woman or anything else. I'm glad you found her last night, Surge. I tried to keep an eye out, but I must have missed them. What happened to the guy she was with?"

"I told him to meet me at my house and I'd give him some sandwiches. I think he knew I wanted to beat the shit out of him for trying to sell her to me, and he never showed. Colette said he had someone he wanted to meet. She thought she was slowing him down." I leaned in closer. "When it's time for the club to know about her, you can admit you invited her to the party. Leave it at that. You're a good kid, Joe, and I think you have what it takes to be part of the Hades Abyss. Don't fuck it up."

"Is there anything I can do?" he asked. "I mean, to help with her situation?"

"I've got it under control. Mostly. The club is

going to rip me a new one, and it won't be pretty. They don't know about her yet, and I want to keep it that way a little bit longer."

"If anything changes, if you need help, I'll do whatever I can. She seems sweet. Scared. Actually, I think she was terrified of me last night when I approached them in the alley."

"It's going to take her some time to adjust. It's why I'm going to disappear for a few days. I'm sure Fox will call me later tonight or tomorrow, wanting to know where I am. I'll talk to him about everything then." I motioned to his table. "Sit and eat your food."

I rejoined Aidan and Colette. She stared at Joe like she'd seen a ghost. Or maybe something more horrifying. I reached over and took her hand, giving her fingers a squeeze.

"Is the gas tank on your truck full?" I asked Aidan.

"Yeah. Why?"

"I want Colette to ride with you. I'll lead the way when we leave here. Follow me out of town. We're going somewhere special."

Aidan glanced at Joe and back at me. "Is this the type of thing I need to pack for? Or will we be back later?"

"I'll buy whatever we need when we get to our destination. The sooner we're away from this place, the better. It's only a matter of time before the Pres is blowing up my phone. I'd rather have a good hour or two between us when we talk."

"I'm causing problems for you," Colette said so softly I nearly didn't hear her. I saw tears gathered in her eyes and it broke my fucking heart.

"No, angel. None of this is your fault. You understand? We're going on a honeymoon for a few days. The three of us. Aidan will help me keep you safe, even though I feel a little better when you're behind a locked gate. I haven't had time to dig into the people who brought you here."

"A honeymoon?" Aidan asked.

"You heard me. I booked us a cabin. I think it will be good for us to get away for a few days." I noticed Colette watching Joe and leaned in closer to Aidan before lowering my voice. "I think it would be good for her."

He nodded and I knew I'd sold him on the idea by mentioning Colette. Really, I wanted the time with both of them. I'd done some damage to Aidan without realizing it, and I needed to fix what I'd broken. I couldn't do that with my club so close and watching our every move. It would be stressful enough telling them about Colette, and then claiming both her and Aidan. I didn't know what would happen.

"Is it just me, or is it taking entirely too long to order our food and drinks?" Aidan said. "No one came by while you were gone, and they haven't been out here since you got back."

"We can go somewhere else," Colette said. "If you really want to go on a honeymoon, I'm all right waiting a little longer for food. Maybe the next town will have something?"

I studied her. The way she'd asked seemed innocent enough. Except I saw the tension in her body. There was a reason she wanted to leave now. Had seeing Joe upset her that much? Or was something else going on?

"Let's go," I said. "Colette, are you all right riding with Aidan?"

"*Oui*. Be careful." She took a breath and pressed her lips together. "I don't want to lose you."

"I'll be right in front of you the entire way. No one's taking me away from you, okay? Neither of you. We're in this together."

Aidan stood and so did I. I took Colette's hand and led her from the restaurant, flipping off the manager as I went past. The fucker had to have known we were there. I didn't know why Joe had gotten food and we hadn't. For that matter, he hadn't been there when we arrived, so how did we miss a server bringing him something?

I helped Colette into Aidan's truck, kissed her softly, then shut the door. Aidan leaned against the front fender, hands in his pockets.

"I'm obeying the speed limit the entire way. I know she said we'd eat in the next town, but I'd like to go a little farther."

"I agree," he said. "Something feels off. Maybe my imagination is just going nuts. But it's like... there's a heaviness in the air."

"I think she feels it too, or she saw something and isn't speaking up. Watch your rearview. If you think you're being followed, find a way to signal me. I don't see how anyone could have tracked her here, but I guess it's possible. For all I know, this is a high-tech operation, and they used facial recognition in every major town between here and New Orleans. They could be watching and waiting."

"I'll take care of her," Aidan said.

I pressed my forehead to his. "Take care of yourself too. I don't want anything to happen to either of you. The judge called her my wife and you my husband. Don't forget that. Ever."

"I won't." Aidan brushed his lips against mine, then got into the truck. I went over to my bike, keeping an eye on my surroundings.

We rode through town and hit the open highway, but I couldn't shake the feeling something bad was waiting to happen.

* * *

Colette

I couldn't stop my hands from shaking. I should have said something to Surge, but I wasn't certain. Jacques had said he was leaving the area, heading elsewhere to meet someone. Except I'd seen him while we were at the restaurant. Not just him… one of the men who'd kidnapped me had been with him. My stomach had knotted when they leaned in close and seemed to be together voluntarily.

Then Joe came out of nowhere. When the hostess had led us to our table, he hadn't been there. He'd not only taken a seat without us being aware, but he'd had food. Either he'd brought it to the table with him, or we'd been so out of it we hadn't even noticed the server. No, I didn't think all three of us would have missed someone speaking so close to us. Something about Joe set me on edge. I hadn't trusted him in the alley, and I still didn't.

I didn't understand any of it. Jacques had been a captive, just like me. He'd helped me escape. Had kept me safe, fed, and gotten me this far. Then he'd left me with Surge. Why was Jacques still here? And why was he with one of our captors?

And did he have some connection to Joe? He'd readily accepted the offer to the clubhouse, even after I'd been wary and said it didn't feel right. Now that I had time to think about it, the entire thing seemed suspect. I should have asked more questions, or not put so much faith in Jacques. Granted, it led me to Surge and Aidan, and for that I'd always be grateful. I knew others would never understand how I'd accepted the two of them so easily.

From the outside looking in, I should have run. Men had never given me a reason to put my trust in them, and yet, Surge had made me feel safe from the very first. And Aidan... he'd been so sweet to me. I knew why he'd been upset when he'd first entered the room. I understood his pain and felt awful about it.

Aidan reached over and took my hand. I jolted a moment before giving him a strained smile.

"What's wrong, Colette? Something happened at the restaurant, but I'm not sure what it was. Did seeing the Prospect upset you?"

"I'm fine. Really."

He slid his hand up my arm to my shoulder and kneaded the muscles. I closed my eyes and moaned at how incredible it felt. "Yep. Totally fine. You're too tense for nothing to be wrong."

It seemed my racing thoughts weren't just making my brain hurt, but it was affecting the rest of me too. I wasn't ready to tell him about Jacques, or how much I didn't trust Joe. What if it was all in my head? It was possible I was making too much out of the situation.

"Surge is my husband now. And he's your husband too, right?" I asked.

"Yeah." Aidan looked down at the ring on his finger. "Not quite what I had in mind when I went to his house. I'm still processing everything."

He wasn't the only one. My life had changed so much. Not only my abduction, but the past twenty-four hours had been mind-blowing. With Jacques abandoning me, I'd had little choice when it came to accepting Surge's offer. Of course, as kind as he was, only an idiot would have refused him. I didn't know why he'd remained single for so long.

I studied Aidan. I wasn't the only one stressed by everything going on. I could see it in the tension in his jaw, the way he gripped the steering wheel... hear it in the tone of his voice. We'd jumped into this with both feet, and no safety net. For better or worse, we were married to Surge. But what did it mean for us?

"Does that mean you're my husband too? We had sex last night, and all three of us slept in the same bed. I'm not sure how this works, and I don't want to upset someone or do the wrong thing." The words tumbled from me and I winced, hoping I hadn't said too much.

"Easy, Colette. You're getting wound up again. I'm not sure there's a right or wrong way for us to be together. I guess the question is whether you want me to be your husband, or do you want us to be friends?"

"I liked being with you last night," I said softly. How could I possibly like two different men? It felt wrong, and somehow right at the same time. It left me confused.

"You're beautiful, Colette. I've not been attracted to many women, but if you're asking if I want to be intimate with you again, the answer is yes. Surge seems to think this can work between the three of us. I've never tried anything like this before, but I'm willing to put in the effort to make it work. Are you?"

"*Oui*. I like both of you, and I want us to be happy. But I'm also worried that caring about two men will mean losing both of you will be twice as hard. What if those men are still after me? I don't want you or Surge to get hurt trying to keep me safe. I should have never gone with him last night."

Aidan grew quiet. The silence dragged on, and I worried I'd done something wrong already.

"Why did you?" Aidan asked. "If you're so concerned about him, and think he's in danger by marrying you, why did you leave the clubhouse with him? Or maybe I should ask why you stayed? I can understand if you'd hoped for another meal or two, but marrying him? That's a different thing altogether."

I stared out the window, not sure how to put it into words. Any other man would have taken advantage. They'd have joined us.

I didn't know how long Jacques had planned to stay in that room. He'd said it wouldn't take long for someone to come find us. Now that I thought about it, his words had seemed odd. I'd been too scared at the time to think much of it.

His exact phrase had been *it won't take long, someone will be here any minute.* As if he'd known exactly who was coming in the door. But I'd seen the way Surge looked at me. He'd been taken by surprise, and then infuriated on my behalf. He hadn't faked it.

If someone else had come to the room, things could have gone differently. Maybe they'd have even hurt me in the process, and not even cared.

Surge had realized something was off, and instead of continuing to undress, he'd offered help instead. No one had ever done such a thing for me. I knew love at first sight only existed in fairy tales. But I did feel something for him. More than just caring or fondness.

If we were separated, I knew it would feel as if my heart had been ripped from my body.

And none of it made sense.

We were still strangers. Married, perhaps, but we knew little about each other. Hadn't spent nearly enough time together to be in love. So what was this feeling? And why did I want to hold on to Aidan too?

"He made me feel safe," I said, trying to keep it simple.

Aidan grunted. "I guess you haven't had a lot of that in your life. Not recently, at any rate."

"Not since my family died," I said. "I've been alone for so long. And now... I have to wonder why Jacques saved me. At the time, I didn't question it. We'd been on the run, constantly looking out for danger and worrying about what to eat. Now that things are calmer, and I feel safe, I'm realizing there were little things that didn't quite add up."

"Have you talked to Surge about it?"

I shook my head. "What if I'm wrong?"

"Colette, if it's worrying you, you need to tell him. How can he keep you safe if you aren't completely honest with him?" Aidan tucked my hair behind my ear. "He's a good guy. Maybe fate stepped in and put him in your path. The men in his club don't do things halfway. When they claim a woman, it's forever. From what I've seen of them around town, the couples seem happy. I think you can find that same happiness with Surge, if you let yourself."

"And you?" I asked.

"I guess I still feel like I'm dreaming. It hasn't really sunk in yet that all this is for real. And part of me worries about what his club will say. Legally, the two of you are married, so they can't make him leave you. But me? There's nothing tying us together except a few words and a ring."

"It seems like we both need to sit down and talk to Surge," I said.

Aidan nodded. "We do. Probably should clear the air before we start the honeymoon part of the trip. We can talk about a few things when we stop to eat. It looks like he's pulling off the highway, so we'll follow and see where he goes."

At the end of the ramp, Surge took a right and about two miles down the road, a little town came into view. He stopped in front of a café and got off his bike.

Aidan parked a few spots farther down, and by the time he'd shut off the truck, Surge stood outside my door. He opened it and helped me down, then waited for Aidan to join us. Together, we walked into the café.

"Sit anywhere you'd like," a woman called out from behind the counter. "I'm short-staffed but I'll be with you as soon as I can."

"Where do you want to sit?" Surge asked, looking down at me.

I looked around the café and pointed to a table in the back corner. It would give a good view of the rest of the space, but it kept away from the windows. I still couldn't shake the feeling of dread I'd had ever since I saw Joe and Jacques.

Surge pulled out my chair for me, then took the one beside it. Aidan sat across from us. I reached over to take his hand, not wanting him to feel slighted. He winked at me, setting me at ease.

"It's about another hour to the cabin," Surge said. "I'll check my phone for nearby stores in the area so we can get what we need. It's stocked with toilet paper, towels, and cleaning supplies. Anything else we'll have to provide."

"It's just a few days, right?" Aidan asked.

"Three days. Why?" Surge leaned back in his seat and put his arm over the back of my chair.

"Today counts as the first day, right?"

He nodded. "It does."

"So we just need one change of clothes, maybe swimwear if there's a lake or something nearby, and a small bottle of detergent. Assuming the cabin has a washer and dryer."

"And groceries," Surge said.

"So one of those twenty-four-hour stores that carries everything would be our best bet," Aidan said. "That way, we only have to make one stop."

"Works for me."

The woman who'd greeted us hurried over. "What can I get you to drink?"

"Water for me," I said.

The men both ordered a soda, and the woman placed menus on the table. While I could read a little English, I liked the fact this menu had pictures to go with each meal. It made it easier to decide what I wanted. When she came back, we placed our orders.

"I think we need to talk about a few things," Aidan said. "Colette had a bit of a panic attack in the truck, and I guess I have some uncertainties I need to address as well."

"All right. Hit me with it," Surge said.

"What happens if your club doesn't accept me? Do you really think they'll let you move out? Even if they do, we won't all fit in my tiny apartment." Aidan spun his wedding band on his finger. "I'm not sure this honeymoon will do us any good if we still don't have answers before we go back. Are you going to talk to your President anytime soon?"

"I'll call him tomorrow. And, Colette. What's bothering you?" he asked.

"I don't like Joe. There's something about him I don't trust, and there are a few things I didn't put together before now. Jacques seemed to be expecting someone at the clubhouse. He made it seem like a man would be joining us any moment, as if it had been planned."

"And Joe invited you, so you think the two of them set something up?" Surge asked.

"I'm not sure. But when we saw Joe earlier, I also saw Jacques. He was speaking with one of the men who'd kidnapped us." I licked my lips. "They weren't fighting, and Jacques wasn't running away. I don't know what it means."

"Shit. I don't have my laptop with me, so I can't dig into Jacques' past right now. As for Joe, he's not my favorite of the Prospects. If he's up to something, I'll figure it out. I'd rather Fox booted his ass from the club before he's patched in than find out too late that he's a fucking traitor."

"If she saw one of the men in town, it means they know where she is. Or where she was," Aidan pointed out. "The only safe place for her back home is behind your gate. And that's not even safe if Joe is in on it in some way."

"If that fucker is part of a human trafficking ring, I'll personally bury his ass. Although, Fox will be pissed as hell too. That's one thing the club won't tolerate." Surge sighed. "Nothing we can do about any of that right now. I'll talk to Fox tomorrow. Right now, I just want to enjoy a meal with my wife and husband, get the stuff we need, and go to the cabin."

I leaned against Surge and put my head on his shoulder. "I trust you, Cam. You'll keep me safe, I know that. You and Aidan both."

"We will," he agreed. "No matter what it takes."

"You're our girl," Aidan said. "No one's taking you from us, Colette."

I nodded, knowing they were telling the truth. I only hoped they didn't die trying to keep me safe. I didn't know what those other men were capable of. If they could smuggle men, women, and children from other countries, then sell them to the highest bidder, what else could they do?

I'd finally found a family. I didn't think I could handle losing Surge and Aidan. It would destroy me.

Chapter Six

Surge

The cabin was small, but perfect for our needs. Aidan helped me haul in the groceries while Colette brought in the new clothes we'd purchased. I'd insisted everyone buy at least three outfits, lounge clothes, and swimwear. Aidan and Colette also got a pair of casual shoes, and I'd grabbed some flip-flops to wear at the lake. Even though I'd only booked the place for three days, if those men really were searching for Colette, I wasn't sure I wanted to take her home just yet. It fucking sucked that I didn't have my laptop with me, and not just any piece of tech would work.

"I don't want to ask the two of you to put everything away, but I need to check in with Fox. I'd rather call before he starts looking for me," I said.

Aidan nodded. "We've got this. Go handle business."

Colette gave me a smile and shooed me from the cabin. I stepped out onto the porch and pulled up Fox in my contact list. Once I pressed the Call button, my stomach knotted. I'd told Colette and Aidan things would be fine. Except I wasn't entirely sure I hadn't lied.

"Where the fuck are you?" Fox asked, instead of giving a normal greeting when the line connected.

"How busy are you?" I asked.

"Jesus. What the fuck have you gotten yourself into?"

I leaned against the railing and took a breath of the fresh country air. "I've done something you may not like, but I thought it was the only way to handle the situation."

"Goddamnit, Surge," Fox grumbled. "Fine. Hit

me with it. How pissed am I going to be? How much damage control is needed?"

"First, what do you know about Joe?"

"Our Prospect? Seems like a good kid. I haven't had any complaints. Why?"

"He invited a homeless couple to a party at the clubhouse. When I asked him about it, he said he just wanted to give them a chance to eat. Except the woman got bad vibes from him, and things she overheard made it seem like he may have an ulterior motive. I don't have my computer with me, so I can't do shit right now, but I'd like to ask Wire and Lavender to dig deeper into Joe."

Fox sighed. "Just what we fucking need to deal with. All right, go ahead and ask them. I don't even want to know why you left town so fast you didn't take your laptop. I thought that thing was permanently glued to your ass."

He wasn't entirely wrong. Most of the time, it was. I hadn't thought to take it to my wedding ceremony, though. If I'd known we'd be leaving town so fast, without packing, I'd have done things differently.

"The woman's name is Colette. Human traffickers brought her to the country illegally from France. I've already wiped out her existence over there and created a new one for her as a US citizen."

"Sounds like you've been busy," Fox muttered.

"I married her." The line went completely silent. I couldn't even hear Fox breathing on the other end. I glanced at the screen to make sure the call hadn't dropped. "Pres? You still there?"

"I know you'd never hurt a woman, so I'm going to assume she agreed to the marriage. Does she understand it's forever?" Fox asked after a moment.

"Yes. She knows. And there's more."

"Of course, there is. Why not? How big can this pile of shit get?" Fox asked.

"Um. I haven't exactly hidden the fact I'm bisexual. I didn't throw it in your faces or anything, but…"

Fox snorted. "Surge, we've all known for a long time. We even knew you were fooling around with Slider before he got married. We don't care. As long as you don't hit on a straight brother, it's all good."

"In that case… I've been seeing someone in town. An artist. His name is Aidan, and even though we aren't legally married, I gave him a wedding band too. I'm claiming both him and Colette."

Nothing. Not a word. The longer Fox remained silent, the more worried I became. If he tossed me from the club, it would be something brutal. I might not even survive. Or worse, he could tell me I could have Colette but not Aidan. I'd already broken that man's heart once. I refused to do it again. Not even for my club.

"Pres? How pissed are you, exactly?" I asked.

"I don't think anyone will have an issue with you being in a relationship with both of them. However, if you want to claim Colette as your old lady, and want the club to acknowledge Aidan in some way, you'll have to take it to Church. Since this is a first for us, I don't know how to handle it, in all honesty. I know Dagger at the Devil's Fury is in a similar relationship, but the other guy is also a patched member. Guardian."

"I don't think Aidan expects a property vest, if that's what you're wondering. I just want everyone to accept that he's mine, same as Colette. I don't want him to feel left out, or for things to be awkward," I said.

"I think we can manage that. Now, tell me more about the situation with Colette. I thought you said Joe invited a couple to the clubhouse."

I went into everything with Fox, telling what I knew so far. Sadly, it wasn't enough. I also voiced my concerns about returning before I knew if Colette would be safe in town. Fox took it all in, commenting very little, until I'd gotten everything out.

"Talk to Wire and keep me in the loop," Fox said. "But be sure to enjoy your honeymoon too. I have no problem with the three of you staying longer, except for one thing. Can you be traced? If these people have someone with any sort of skill on the computer, could they find a paper trail that would lead them to the cabin?"

"Yeah. I had to use my card to book the cabin, and again at the store. I didn't have time to plan this out and get cash, or ask someone else to get the cabin for me."

"Stay the three days. Be cautious, and then get the fuck out of there. Don't come home. Either go to our Mississippi chapter, or head to the Reckless Kings. Fuck, go to Oklahoma and the Savage Raptors. Just call to tell me where you want to go, and I'll set it up. The fewer people who know, the better. If Joe is a rat, I don't want him getting this information."

"Thanks, Pres. I appreciate it. Aidan has been worried no one would accept him, and Colette is terrified those people will find her. I can see the fear in her eyes every time I look at her, and it fucking guts me."

"So you actually like her?" Fox asked. "Because it sounded more like you married her to keep her safe."

"She's sweet. Delicate. And yet the woman has to

be made of steel to have survived everything she went through and not only be standing, but still be able to care about people. I'm lucky to have her. Yes, I may have married her to keep her safe. But I also want to keep her. I've never lost my head around a woman before."

"Make sure she knows that. Otherwise, she may think she's more of an obligation than someone you could come to love. You don't want to travel down that road," Fox said.

"Understood. Before I head back inside, I will call Wire. I'm going to ask him to look into Jacques, Joe, and whoever else was involved in Colette's kidnapping. I don't think Joe is part of it, but I feel like he's hiding something. I fucking hate that I may have missed something when I checked into him."

"When I know where you're heading, I'll get your laptop to you. Want anything else?" Fox asked.

"I can buy whatever else we need. After my first month as a patched member, I started putting part of each payment into an IRA and stocks. So I have money I can access when I need it, and some for when I'm older. Or worse, for Colette and Aidan when I die. At least they'll be taken care of if one of these jobs gets me killed one day."

"On that cheerful note, I'm going. Keep in touch, but only through my cell. And no texts."

"Got it." I ended the call. Before I pulled up Wire's number, I poked my head into the cabin to check on Aidan and Colette. They'd curled up on the futon and had the TV on. "I'll just be another minute, then I'll get the two of you caught up. One more call and I'm finished."

Aidan waved me off and Colette snuggled against him more. I smiled, enjoying the sight of them so relaxed and comfortable with one another. That woman was one in a million. How the hell she could let anyone touch her, much less throw herself into a relationship with two men was something I'd never understand. But I admired the hell out of her for it.

I shut the door and called Wire.

"Hey, Surge," Lavender said when the call connected. "I've got you on speaker because Wire is in the middle of a game."

"And what is he playing this week?" I asked.

"Don't you fucking tell him," Wire said with a growl to his tone.

Lavender giggled. "Spyro. The kids were playing and got stuck on a level, so now he's trying to figure it out so he can walk them through it, without having to watch YouTube videos."

I bit my lip so I wouldn't laugh. Wire would kick my ass the next time he saw me. "That just means he's a good dad."

"The best," Lavender agreed. "What did you need?"

"I hate the fact I call and you automatically think I need something. I apparently need to make more time for my friends." I ran a hand through my hair. "I got married."

"Oh, my God! Seriously? Tell me about her," Lavender said.

"Actually, it's a them. Legally, Colette is my wife, but I gave Aidan a wedding band too."

"I wondered which way you'd go when the time came," Wire said. "Looks like you get to have both. Fox okay with it?"

"Seems to be. The club doesn't know yet. And there's a reason for that, but I need your full attention. I'm not repeating all this a million times. Already went over it with Fox."

"All right. I paused the game. What the fuck is wrong?" Wire asked.

"Not to feed into your idea that I only call when I need something, but... I need help. Colette came to the country illegally, and not by choice. Someone kidnapped her in France, then brought her to the US with a group of people. She said they had men, women, and children. Some were sold already, she said at least one died, and she doesn't know about the ones she left behind when she ran.

"And here's where it gets fun. A man named Jacques supposedly rescued her and they escaped together. They were on the streets, homeless, and either walked or hitchhiked from New Orleans to Missouri. But something feels off. The guy tried to sell her to me in exchange for food, claiming he needed to meet someone. Then Colette saw him in town today and said he looked like he was having a conversation with one of the human traffickers."

"Wow," Lavender whispered. "Got a last name?"

"I can ask her. I have another problem that may or may not be related. I can't look into it because I left my laptop at the compound. Joe freaked Colette out, big time. He's the one who invited her and Jacques to a club party. It's how I met her. I don't know if Joe really did have good intentions, or if he planned something nefarious. I'm at a cabin a few hours from home and have no way to do a deep dive on him. I vetted him when he asked to prospect, but now I'm worried I missed something."

I heard keys clacking and didn't know if Wire or Lavender had pulled out a laptop. When Wire spoke next, I figured it was him.

"What do you have on Joe?" he asked.

"He started prospecting a little over three years ago. He should have been voted in by now, but no one's brought it up, including Fox. I don't know if they feel something is off with him, or if they just feel he hasn't put in enough effort. I don't remember his exact age, but he's in his twenties. Name is Joe Royce. I remember not finding much in the way of a criminal history, and there weren't red flags at the time."

I heard the sound of a pen scratching on paper and more typing.

"I'm taking some notes," Lavender said. "What else do you have for us?"

"I changed Colette's name. Wiped out her existence in France and created docs for her here. She said Jacques was from... Cah... Kay... Fuck."

"Cahors?" Lavender asked.

"Yeah. I don't want to know how you knew that town's name. But that's it. Let me ask her Jacques' last name." I poked my head back into the cabin. "Colette, I need Jacques' last name."

"Dupon," she said. "Why?"

"I'm having someone look into him for us. I'll be in shortly."

After shutting the door again, I gave Wire and Lavender everything I could think of. By the time I got off the phone with them, I didn't have any new information, but I knew the dynamic duo would dig up everything they could. I only hoped it would help me keep Colette safe.

I took a moment to gather my thoughts and take a few deep breaths to lower my anxiety. Colette and Aidan didn't need me dragging any negativity into the cabin. They'd looked cozy and happy. We were supposed to be on our honeymoon. I'd make it the best three days I could before reality had to intrude again.

The only question was where we'd go when we left here.

* * *

Aidan

Surge might have been smiling when he came back inside, but I could tell something wasn't quite right. He couldn't hide the tension in his jaw or the way his eyes had darkened. They only did that under two circumstances. When he was really turned on, or stressed to the max. While this might be our honeymoon, I didn't think it was option one. Which meant his phone calls hadn't gone according to plan.

"Did you tell your club about us?" I asked.

"I did. Fox doesn't have an issue with it. He said to officially claim the two of you, I need to go to Church. But that's going to wait a little while."

I didn't like the way he'd said that. Even worse, he'd tensed up more. If his President didn't care about our relationship, what the hell else had happened during that call?

"Why?" I asked.

"He doesn't want us to return, since it's possible Joe could be implicated in Colette's situation. Until we know for certain he isn't a traitor, we're to stay away. But I booked this cabin with my credit card, so once our three days are up, we'll have to go somewhere else. To another club."

I wasn't sure how I felt about it. Not all clubs would be accepting of our relationship. What would happen if I reached our destination only to be turned away? Or worse, ridiculed? I knew it would be hard enough on me, but Colette? She'd been through so much already.

"No offense, but is that a good idea?" I asked.

"It's the only one we've got. We can't go home yet. Anywhere we stay, I'd have to use credit cards or my bank card, which means leaving a paper trail. We're fine for right now, but we can't stay here forever. We'd be sitting ducks," Surge said.

I could see his point, and I didn't like the idea of Colette being easy to grab. If he thought our best bet was another club, then I'd go along peacefully. Didn't mean I had to like it.

"You said there was someone with a relationship like ours. Could we go there?" Colette asked.

Surge folded his arms and seemed to tense even more. At this rate, his teeth would crack if he ground them anymore. "That club is in southern Georgia, not too far from Florida. If they got their hands on you down there, it wouldn't be hard for them to get you to a boat and take off. It would be much harder to track, unless we had information on it. Even then, it's hit or miss."

I curled my arm around Colette when I saw the fear in her eyes. "We won't let them get you, but Surge is right. We need to be cautious. We don't have to figure it out tonight. Why don't I make dinner?"

"You sure?" Surge asked. "I didn't much think about who would be cooking. I do okay in the kitchen, but I'm not a gourmet chef or anything."

"I don't mind. I can follow a recipe easily enough, and the stuff we bought is all simple dishes. Plus we grabbed those frozen pizzas for lunch tomorrow and lunch meat with bread and chips. So it's just breakfast and dinner that will take some time."

"By all means," Surge said, motioning toward the kitchen. "Want to sit with me, Colette?"

She nodded and went to him without any hesitation. I wasn't sure who needed this time more.

Him or her. Surge looked rattled after the phone calls he'd made, and I could tell Colette felt like she needed to run. Poor thing probably worried about the trouble chasing her down. She hadn't yet realized Surge lived for that kind of shit. The man was a white knight, even if he didn't want to admit it.

I pulled out some chicken breasts, veggies, and olive oil. Surge had said the cabin would have seasonings, so I'd make do with whatever was here. I found the spices in a cabinet to the right of the stove and pulled out the chili powder, paprika, garlic powder, and black pepper. The cookware was easy to locate, and I began warming some oil in a deep skillet before I started slicing the veggies and chicken.

I tossed zucchini, squash, and eggplant into the skillet on medium, stirring occasionally as I worked on the chicken. By the time the veggies had softened, I moved them to a plate. I coated the chicken in the seasonings and added the strips to the skillet, making sure they were thoroughly cooked. While I stirred the chicken strips, to keep them from sticking or burning, I boiled water for some brown minute rice.

As I cooked, I watched Surge and Colette. He'd placed her on his lap and wrapped his arms around her. Poor thing clung to him. I couldn't blame her. She'd been through hell, from what I'd been told, and Surge had *hero* stamped all over him. I'd do my best to keep her safe too, but I knew Surge would be the better option. I had focused my life on artistic expression. Not weapons and warfare. Although, Surge typically handled things from the cyber end, but I wouldn't doubt the man could handle himself in a fight.

"Dinner's nearly done," I said. "Rice just needs to set a few minutes."

The cabin had a table set up for two, but the bar

separating the kitchen and main area had three stools tucked underneath. Seemed like the best option for where we could eat. I'd noticed the sign on the wall near the door, asking people not to eat on the couch or in the bed.

I divided the veggies onto three plates, then added rice. I placed the strips of chicken over the bed of rice and then set all three plates on the bar. Surge and Colette stood, and while I waited on them, I got out the silverware and grabbed three bottles of water from the fridge.

"I thought you said you weren't a gourmet chef," Surge asked, his eyebrows lifting as he stared at the plates.

"There's not really anything to this particular dish. And it's healthy for us." Colette took the stool next to the wall. I wondered if it made her feel safer. Surge sat beside her and I claimed the spot on the end.

Colette took a bite first, and she hummed in appreciation. "It's so good, Aidan."

"I'm glad you like it. I tend to make rice with a lot of meals. If I cook all the time, you'll get tired of it. But it's filling and a healthier option than pasta or those seasoned rice packs."

Surge's gaze slid over my body and I felt my cheeks warm, and my cock took notice of his attention, getting semi-hard. He placed his hand on my thigh and gave it a slight squeeze. *And now I'm hard as a fucking rock.*

"I always knew you took care of your body," Surge said. He leaned in and nipped my ear. "I plan to enjoy it again soon."

I nearly dropped my fork. Colette eyed us with curiosity, and no lack of heat in her eyes. It made me wonder...

"Colette, you said Jacques would often sleep with the men who offered you food on your journey. Did you ever watch them?"

She licked her lips. "Sometimes they asked me to. Especially when they made Jacques suck them off. The men would stare at me the entire time they fucked his mouth."

"Did it turn you on? Seeing them together?" I asked. Her cheeks turned crimson, and she gave a slight nod. "I know you've been with each of us separately. Would you want to be with us at the same time?"

"Easy, Aidan," Surge said. "She was a virgin. The fact she welcomed both of us into the bed, even if it wasn't together, was a huge step. Let's not push her too hard, too fast."

"It's all right," Colette said. "I know the two of you won't hurt me."

Surge glanced at her. "Are you sure?"

She nodded. "Maybe... after dinner, we could watch a movie in bed? Just see what happens?"

"All right. We'll let you set the pace," Surge said.

Eating dinner wasn't easy, not without choking, since Surge hadn't removed his hand from my thigh. If anything, it seemed to inch higher every few minutes. Before long, he'd be grabbing my cock.

"Colette was right. This dinner is great," Surge said. "Keep cooking this way and I may forget I know my way around the kitchen."

Colette gaped at him. "That was an awful thing to say! What if he doesn't like cooking?"

"I like it," I mumbled. And honestly, his comment didn't bother me. Maybe it should have. Colette had seemed offended on my behalf. And it occurred to me that we came from such different backgrounds and families. Maybe what seemed bad to her wasn't a big deal to me, and vice versa. "I don't mind doing most of the cooking for us. I only ask someone takes over when I have a project due to a client."

Surge squeezed my thigh. "We'll pitch in when and where we're needed, and if it's something we aren't comfortable with, we can speak up."

I nodded and pushed my plate away. I noticed Surge and Colette were finished as well. Standing, I reached for the plates and carried them to the sink. The cabin had a dishwasher, but for now, I rinsed the plates and left them in the sink.

"Since I rode my bike here, I'm going to shower," Surge said. "Get the road dust off me. Go ahead and find a movie or show to watch. I won't be long."

I watched him grab the sack of new things he'd purchased and disappear into the bathroom. Colette came closer, placing her hand on my back.

"You should go to him," she said.

"He didn't say he wanted company," I pointed out.

"I may not know him very well, since we just met, but even I could tell he seemed to have something weighing on him. The two of you have been together for a while. I think he needs you right now."

I nodded. "All right. You sure you're okay out here on your own?"

"I'll make sure the doors are locked, and I'll be fine. If anything happens, I'll scream."

"Deal."

I carried my things into the bathroom and quietly shut the door. Surge already had the shower going, and he'd stepped inside. The curtain was plain navy and blocked him from my view. Which meant he couldn't see me either. Stripping out of my clothes, I decided to just go for it. Before I got in, I saw something sticking out of his sack of clothes. Lube. I remembered he'd picked some up, and condoms, at the store. Although, the condoms had been at my request.

I picked up the lube and set it close to the tub, just in case. Then decided to put the condoms nearby too. Surge might consider us married, but I didn't want to presume anything.

I pulled the curtain back and stepped into the shower. I'd expected a tub, but instead, there was a small lip along the floor to keep the water from coming out. The stall was large enough for four men. I placed my hand on his back and slid it up to his shoulders, kneading the muscles.

Surge groaned. "That feels incredible."

"You're going to give yourself a stroke or heart attack before you're forty." I placed my other hand on the opposite shoulder and gave him a massage. Using my thumbs, I worked on the tense muscles in his neck. "I can tell you're worried. You're going to do whatever you can to take care of us, except let us help."

He grunted. "Neither of you are equipped to deal with those assholes."

"Maybe not, but we aren't useless either. I can admit I don't know anything about weapons. But if someone comes for Colette, I'll do my best to stab them, or break their noses. Something to give her time to get away."

He huffed and turned to face me. "You don't get it, do you?"

No, I apparently didn't. "What?"

"Aidan, do you have any idea how pretty you are? And I don't mean that in an insulting way. You're gorgeous, and those human traffickers would love to get their hands on someone like you. It's not just Colette I'm worried about. I don't think I can hold them off on my own. If they find us before we get somewhere safe, I wouldn't be able to keep them from taking the two of you. It would destroy me."

I cupped his cheeks between my palms. "Surge."

He pressed his forehead to mine. "Call me Cam, Aidan. We're married. Only use Surge around my club, or any other clubs we visit."

"All right. Cam," I said softly. "If the worst case happens, Colette and I will do whatever it takes to survive. Because I know you'll come for us, and you'll bring hell with you. Those fuckers won't know what hit them. If you're that concerned, we can leave in the morning and go to one of the clubs. I won't put up a fuss, even if they give me dirty looks or say shit about us being together."

"I don't want to ruin these few days for us. We need time to bond. I think Colette needs it most of all. I don't think she's had a nice life."

"Would your President, or another club, send a few men to stand guard? I'm not too keen on the idea of them hearing us having sex, but I don't want you to worry the next few days either." I wrapped my arms around him. "You feel like it's your job to watch over us. Who's going to keep an eye on you?"

He smiled and kissed me softly. "You were always too good for me. I think that's part of why I kept you at a distance. I knew you wanted more. Part of me didn't feel like I deserved someone like you."

I ran my hand down his chest and wrapped it around his cock. It twitched in my grasp. "I'm the one who was aiming too high when I went after you. You walked in, this big, tough biker, and I almost didn't approach you. It wasn't until I saw you checking out a man on the dance floor I found the courage to go say hi."

Surge thrust into my hand, and I began stroking him. He groaned, and his lips parted. I heard him panting for breath as I tightened my grip.

"Fuck, Aidan. I've missed this. Missed *you.*"

"I put the lube and condoms within reach, just in case," I said.

He drew back. "You said you're clean."

"I am. I wasn't sure... I mean, with Colette..." I bit my lip.

"Aidan, she accepts you and so do I. We don't need condoms, unless it's what *you* want. Since Jacques did use her, even though he wrapped his dick, if you want to be cautious, I understand."

"We've never done it bare," I murmured.

"Do you want to?" he asked.

I only hesitated a moment before nodding. Surge gave me a wicked grin, then turned me to face the wall. I braced my hands and stuck out my ass. He kicked my legs farther apart, and fuck if it didn't make me even harder. I liked this side of him. The bossiness. The... alphaness.

I heard the bottle of lube open, then Surge's fingers were sliding between my ass cheeks. He spread me open and teased me with light touches. When I started pushing back, he worked a finger inside me. It burned a little, but in the most amazing way. I already knew how incredible it felt to have him inside me, and I couldn't wait to experience it again. It had been far too long.

He added a second finger, and I felt my limbs trembling. I couldn't remember ever wanting him this badly. It felt like I'd lose my mind if he didn't get inside me soon.

"Cam, please…"

He held me open wide, and I felt the head of his cock press against me. I winced a little as he popped through the ring of muscle. And then… pure bliss. He rubbed against my prostate, and it took every bit of control I had not to plead and beg for him to fuck me.

He pressed his chest against my back, braced his hand beside mine on the wall, and put his lips near my ear.

"Do you know what I've been thinking about?" he asked, his voice husky. It sent a shiver down my spine.

"What?" I asked.

He pulled back, then slid into me again. "Fucking you. Except while I'm balls-deep in your ass, our pretty Colette is splayed on the bed, her pussy wet and pink. And I get the perfect view of you eating her out while I fuck your ass."

"Oh, God." I shut my eyes, picturing that very thing all too clearly.

"My other favorite is me fucking Colette from behind while you watch. Her pretty tits bouncing with every thrust. Her cries of passion filling the air. And when you can't take it another moment, you press your cock to her lips, and she sucks you off while I fill her with my cum."

"Jesus, Cam. I'm going to… to…"

He reached down and stroked my cock. It only took three pumps before I cried out and came, splattering the tiled wall. He kissed my shoulder before gripping my hips. Surge was nearly savage in the way he fucked me, his cock driving deep, as he took what he wanted. If I hadn't already blown my load, I certainly would have then. He growled and his cock jerked. I felt the heat of his release filling my ass.

He pulled out and turned me to face him, pressing me back against the wall. "You'll have me leaking out of you for at least the next hour or two. It makes me want to bend you over, watch the cum slip from your tight hole, then fuck even more of it into you."

"You're... that's..." I swallowed hard. It was hot. Really fucking hot. And fierce. I felt my cock twitch and knew it wouldn't take much to get me hard again.

He gripped the back of my neck. "Get out of the shower, Aidan. No washing me off your body. Every time you squirm, I'll know why. I can promise before the night is over, I'll be fucking you again."

I got out, my legs shaking, and dried myself off. I reached for my clothes and decided against it. The way Surge talked, we'd be doing far more than watching TV tonight. I walked out naked, feeling a bit dazed.

Colette smiled when she saw me. "I take it things went well?"

"Um, yeah." I ran a hand through my hair. "Does this bother you? Me not having clothes on?"

She shook her head. "*Non.* Come cuddle, Aidan."

I saw she'd changed into a nightgown when she drew the covers back. I slid in next to her, and she immediately curled against me. Putting my arm around her shoulders, I held her close and wondered if she had any idea what sort of beast would be joining us soon. Whatever had taken over Surge in the shower, I'd liked it. A lot. But I worried he would be too much for Colette in that state.

Chapter Seven

Surge

What the fuck was that? I'd never been so rough with Aidan. I scrubbed myself clean, then shut off the water. I needed to get control of myself before I freaked out Colette. If I took her like that, I could hurt her. Or worse, make her think of all the men who'd wanted to use her in exchange for a meal.

I pulled on a pair of boxers I'd picked up at the store and went to find my wife and husband. They'd snuggled in bed and were watching reruns of *Supernatural*. Figured they'd pick something with one of my Hollywood crushes. I'd be hard again in no time at this rate.

"I just want to be clear, Colette. Nothing has to happen tonight unless you want it to. I won't be angry," I said as I slipped in next to her, sandwiching her between me and Aidan. "I don't want you to ever feel pressured to have sex with either of us. All right?"

"I know." She reached up to caress my cheek. "My handsome hero. So kind and caring. Always worried about everyone."

I cleared my throat. "The other side of what I said is that if you do want something, speak up. We want to make sure your needs are met, and not just ours. If there's something you want to try, we're probably up for it. And if it's a hard no from either of us, then we'll try something else."

"The men from before... I liked watching them with Jacques. Do the two of you like watching other people?" she asked.

"Depends, I guess," I said. "At the clubhouse, women get naked all the time. It doesn't really do anything for me to watch them having sex. If you're asking if I'd like to watch *you* have sex, only if it's with Aidan. Another man touches you, and I'll rip his fucking hand off."

"You're going to scare her, Caveman," Aidan muttered.

"Sorry." I sighed. "What is it specifically that you want, Colette?"

"Everything?" she asked softly. "Not all at once, but I want to try new things. I trust you, Cam. And I trust Aidan. I know neither of you will hurt me. I don't want to be scared of sex or men."

I smiled and shook my head. "Little angel, *everything* would encompass things neither Aidan nor I would be willing to try, and I'm not sure you'd be into a lot of that stuff, either. But we can explore, at your pace, and figure out what you like or don't like."

Her cheeks turned pink. "It's our honeymoon. I want to be with you both at the same time."

"There's several ways to do that," Aidan said. He lifted Colette and placed her between his legs, her back flush to his chest. "I could hold you while Cam fucks you. We could put you on your hands and knees with a cock in your pussy and one in your mouth. Or we could fill both holes at the same time."

She panted. "I... I want... to try the first one, but... what about you, Aidan?"

"After Cam makes you boneless from coming so hard you see stars, you can either get me off, or he can. What do you want, Colette?" Aidan asked.

I smiled at him, thankful he was letting her call the shots this time. I tossed the covers to the foot of the bed and settled myself in front of Colette and Aidan. Reaching out slowly, to give her time to pull away, I lowered the straps on her nightgown. Her breasts popped free of the material, her nipples already hard.

Leaning forward, I captured one between my lips and flicked the tip with my tongue.

Colette moaned and her eyes half-closed. "Cam, that feels…"

Aidan reached down to slide her nightgown up her thighs. He slid his palm over her panties and cupped her pussy. The pink in her cheeks traveled down her neck and into her chest. I sucked and nipped at her breasts and nipples, lavishing attention on them, while Aidan ground the heel of his palm against her.

"Oh! Oh, I…" She whimpered and bit her lip, her back arching. I bit down harder on one of her nipples, and she cried out, her body trembling as she came.

"So fucking pretty," I murmured.

I tugged at her panties, pulling them down her legs. Then I discarded my boxers. Aidan spread her pussy open and rubbed her clit. I got so hard watching them, I started to drip pre-cum onto the sheets.

"Make her come, Aidan."

He kept working her clit until she came a second time. She was so damn wet I couldn't wait to be inside her. Aidan adjusted their position, so they were nearly lying down. I braced myself over the two of them and lined my cock up with her pussy. Aidan wrapped his hand around my shaft, and I damn near came. He guided me into her, and fuck if it wasn't pure heaven.

I held his gaze over her head as I stroked in and out of her. Aidan's eyes had darkened, and I knew he was enjoying this as much as we were. Soon, it would be his turn. I drove into her harder, deeper. When her pussy clenched down on me, I couldn't hold back another moment. I fucked her like a man possessed until I came inside her.

Colette panted and grabbed at me, holding me to her. I kissed her, soft and slow. Pulling out, I gripped her hips and lifted her. "Ride him, Colette. I want to watch you and Aidan."

Aidan shook his head. "Condom. They're in the bathroom."

My brow furrowed. "What the fuck, Aidan? Why do you need one with her, but you didn't want one with me?"

Colette licked her lips. "He wants us to know the first baby is yours. So he refuses to come inside me until I'm pregnant."

I wasn't sure if I should be pissed, or humbled. They wanted the first kid to be mine? I didn't care. It didn't matter to me if the baby looked like me or Aidan. Hell, it could look like neither of us. A pretty girl who looked just like her mom wouldn't be so bad. Until she got old enough to date.

"Please, Cam," Aidan said. "I want to give you this one thing. I don't have much to offer this relationship."

"I don't care who our baby's sperm donor is," I said.

"Let us do this?" Colette asked. "After this one, it doesn't matter to either of us who the father is, but we want the first baby to be yours without any doubts."

I sighed and got out of the bed. I grabbed the condom box out of the bathroom and opened it, ripping one off the strip. Aidan tore the package open and rolled the latex down his cock. Colette sank onto him, taking him deep.

I settled back on my heels and watched her ride him. Her tits bounced, and she spread her thighs as wide as she could. Seeing the two of them like this made my chest feel funny. I wanted to rub at the spot but stopped myself. Instead, I leaned in closer and pressed my thumb to her clit and stroked it.

Colette went wild, and I wished I had a way to record us. It would be hot as fuck to watch it another time with the two of them. Maybe try to re-enact tonight.

"That's it. Come for us." I rubbed her clit faster. "Milk every drop of cum from Aidan. Squeeze his cock like you did mine."

Aidan gripped her hips and thrust up into her. It only took a few strokes before he came, and Colette followed right after. I helped her lift up while Aidan held the condom. Then he disappeared into the bathroom to clean up.

"Want a shower?" I asked Colette.

"*Oui*. I'm sticky."

I kissed her temple. "Come on. I'll get the water going. We should probably all clean up, then I think we need some sleep."

She nodded and let me lift her into my arms. I carried her to the bathroom and set her on her feet before starting the water. Aidan pulled my phone from my discarded jeans on the floor and handed it to me.

"Call your President and ask him about guards or extra protection," Aidan said.

"After our shower."

He shook his head. "You won't rest all night and you damn well know it. You're in protector mode. Get something set up so you'll actually sleep tonight."

I hated that he was right. I took the phone and stepped out of the bathroom to make my call. Fox answered right away, and I heard the tension in his voice.

"Bad time?" I asked after his terse *hello*.

"Something like that. Did you need something?" he asked.

"We want to stay the three days, but none of us

feel safe sitting in the open like this. Would it be possible to have a guard or two watch over the cabin? At least at night while we're sleeping?" I asked.

"You spoke to Wire earlier. Do you really think he'd leave you out there without some sort of security?" I heard Fox shut a door, then another. I had no idea where he was or what he was doing. "There's a Dixie Reaper heading your way. Two actually. They're bringing a laptop to you, and they'll stand guard until you decide where you're heading."

"Colette thought we might be more comfortable with the club who has another poly relationship, but that's too close to Florida for my liking."

"Don't blame you. However, I'm going to suggest you stay at the Reapers' compound. I know it's still near the water, but Wire and Lavender are your best bet at getting through this. The Devil's Fury is close enough they can send some help. I can ask if Dagger and Guardian would be willing to go. Maybe take their entire family so Colette can see what she's getting into."

"Thanks, Pres. I appreciate it."

"They're coming in a truck. One of them will drive Aidan's vehicle down to Alabama. If someone has been watching you, they'll recognize whatever you're driving right now. Not much I can do about your bike or the truck. I know you won't leave them behind. At least you'll have more protection on the road than just the three of you."

He wasn't wrong. No way I'd leave my baby here at the cabin, or let someone else drive her back to the Hades Abyss compound. And I knew Aidan didn't want his truck being left at the cabin. Even though he didn't always show it, he took pride in his truck.

"When will they be here?"

"Any minute," Fox said. "Wire and Lavender are sending one of their backup systems to you. After your call earlier, they prepped one and had it ready to go. They've included everything you need to access it, as well as a secure hot spot. Whatever the fuck that is. Call me once at a day, at the very least. I don't care if the call lasts thirty seconds. I just need proof the three of you are safe."

He hung up before I could say anything else. I stared at the phone and shook my head. Looked like I had people watching out for us, whether I wanted them to or not. It felt... nice.

I joined Aidan and Colette in the shower, cleaned up, then put on my boxers and tee. When someone knocked on the door a short while later, I finally breathed a little easier. One glance through the window and I'd known the Dixie Reapers were here. Tank was hard to miss, even in the pitch-black. The man's silhouette stood out because of his sheer size.

I opened the door, and Viking handed me a laptop and a small zipper bag. I found the hot spot inside, as well as a small notebook.

"Wire said to call if you need anything. We'll escort you to the compound whenever you're ready," he said.

"Thanks. And tell Tank I said thank you too. I know he hates being away from his family."

Viking grinned. "Sounds like you have one of your own now. Congratulations."

He stepped off the porch and walked into the night. I shut the door, making sure it locked, and carried the computer and bag over to the small table. As much as I wanted to use the laptop to work on finding who was responsible for Colette being kidnapped and brought to the US, Viking had a good point. I had a family now, and what they needed was my support and affection. There would be enough time to dig into things later.

"She's asleep," Aidan said as I slipped into bed. We cuddled Colette between us, and he was right. She'd already passed out for the night.

"Looks like we wore her out."

He smiled. "Yeah, but I didn't hear her complaining. Everything all right?"

"Yep. The Dixie Reapers are waiting outside. They'll watch over us until we're ready to head south. Wire and Lavender are two of the best hackers I know. They've offered their help."

"And where are they from?" he asked.

"Alabama. Just a few hours from both Georgia and the Florida panhandle. A little too close to the water for my liking, but Fox said they were our best option. He's right, even if I don't like it."

"Looks like I get to see more of the country," Aidan said. "Never been to Alabama. Sure they're okay with... us?"

"Wire and Lavender know about you, and Colette. Viking said congratulations, so I think it will be fine. Only one way to find out, and that's heading down there and meeting everyone. Fox was going to see if some of the Devil's Fury would come lend a hand. You may get to meet Dagger and his family."

"He's the one who..."

I nodded. "Yeah. He's in a relationship with Guardian and their woman. Although, Guardian was just a Prospect when they got together."

Aidan sighed, and the tension drained from him. I hoped Fox could convince them to come. The last thing I wanted was for Aidan to feel uncomfortable, or Colette for that matter. My world was different from theirs, and it would be an adjustment. We had enough shit on our plates already.

* * *

Colette

The three days passed too quickly, and soon we were going to Alabama. The fact no one had made a move to grab me, had me more than a little antsy. The guys didn't seem to know why things had remained quiet either. It was unsettling. I kept shifting in the seat, trying to alleviate the pressure on certain sensitive areas. Aidan only winked at me, and I hoped the Dixie Reaper didn't notice. Tank. He'd said that was his name. The other one followed behind us in Aidan's truck. As much as I didn't like being in the vehicle with a stranger, I appreciated the caution. These men didn't know me, but they were trying to keep me safe.

My men had been very enthusiastic during our honeymoon, and it hurt to sit. Or stand. Or walk. I needed to soak in a hot bath, but since the cabin hadn't had a tub, I'd been out of luck.

Surge had smirked at my predicament and asked if I wanted an ice pack. Aidan had smacked him in the back of the head for me. I winced as I tried to get comfortable, and Aidan took pity on me. He reached over and unbuckled my seat belt, then tugged me over so my head lay in his lap. It took the pressure off my poor, overused pussy and gave me a reprieve.

"Anyone need to stop? Bathroom break? Food? Drinks?" Tank asked.

My stomach rumbled. "All of those? But it's not a rush."

Aidan ran his hand up and down my arm in a soothing gesture, and I shut my eyes, letting the rhythm of the truck lull me to sleep. I dozed lightly, aware of everything around me. I heard Tank and the other man speaking to one another, and the roar of Surge's motorcycle in front of us.

"I'll signal Surge to pull over the next time I see a sign advertising food. Any preference?"

I'd been eating out of garbage cans before Surge took me to his house. I'd learned not to be picky about what I ate. I heard Aidan tell him anything was fine, and I burrowed closer to him. Aidan ran his fingers through my hair and lightly stroked my back. I hummed in appreciation and tried to relax. To be honest, I'd been tense ever since Surge had said we would leave this morning.

He'd introduced us to Tank and Viking, and both seemed nice. However, I still had a problem trusting men. Especially big ones like the two who'd come to help us. They seemed nice, and Tank had mentioned his daughters, so he clearly had a family. But the men who'd intended to sell me could very well have families too.

"We're pulling off for a break," Tank said. "Might want to sit up and put your seat belt back on in case the local cops are around. Small towns tend to get excited about giving tickets to people from out of state."

I did as he said and looked out the window. The area looked like so many others I'd passed through since coming to this country. We went down the ramp and followed Surge as he turned and headed down a two-lane road. A small town came into view and we stopped in front of a breakfast place that advertised being open twenty-four hours.

"Don't let the sign fool you," Tank said. "They have sandwiches, burgers, and other shit. So if you don't want pancakes or waffles, there's plenty to choose from."

Aidan got out of the truck and stretched before helping me down. The truck sat up so high, I nearly had to jump. He put his hand on my waist and led me up to the sidewalk, where we waited for Surge and the other Dixie Reaper.

My sexy biker came closer and leaned in to press his lips to mine. "I'm going to clean up while everyone gets a table. Order me a sweet tea?"

"Of course," I said.

I went inside with the other men, and we waited for the staff to put a few tables together. By the time we sat down, Surge had joined us, and none of us had drinks yet. Or menus. I glanced around the space and saw more than a few people staring at us, and murmuring to each other. Tank, Viking, and Surge all wore their leather vests. No. A cut. Surge had said that's what it was called, after I'd called it a vest yesterday. Only Aidan and I didn't have one.

"Is it just me..." I leaned into Aidan. "Or is everyone watching us?"

"They are," he said.

Tank leaned back in his chair and folded his arms. The man might be getting older, but he still scared the hell out of me. He looked like he could snap me in two without any effort at all. The display made his muscles bulge, and more than half the gawkers suddenly found something better to do.

"Is it like this everywhere you go?" I asked.

"Not usually, but I try not to leave town that much these days. I prefer being home with my family," Tank said.

"It's not like this in larger towns," Viking said. "Small places like this are another matter. Ever heard the saying small towns breed small minds? It's sadly true. They see us and automatically think we're thugs, or that we're going to rape and murder everyone."

My brow furrowed. "But… Surge saved me from that fate."

"And what did you think of his club before then?" Viking asked.

My cheeks flushed. "I was scared of them. To be fair, with the exception of Jacques, all men scared me. Being kidnapped and dragged to another country changes the way you view people."

"I can see that," Viking said. "Are you scared to go to the Dixie Reapers compound? Because you don't need to be. Saint is with a woman who was badly abused by her own family. Her father sold her and her sisters to Surge's club. In fact, Spider is married to one of the sisters, and Rocket claimed another. It's not our first time helping someone out in your situation."

"The men I met along the way weren't very nice. They smiled, offered help, but only if I gave them something in return. Jacques protected me from the worst of it." My hands fidgeted in my lap. "And now I'm not even sure why he did it. I'd thought he cared and wanted to save me."

"So the one person you trusted broke your faith in men all over again," Viking said. "But you're married to Surge and Aidan, right? You wouldn't be with them if they scared you."

I smiled at Surge. "He proved he was different when he didn't take advantage. Then Jacques offered me to him in exchange for some food. You should have seen how angry Surge became."

"I'd have been pissed too," Viking said.

A server came over, menus tucked under her arm, and pinched expression on her face. Her nametag said *Marge*. She slapped the menus onto the table with a loud *thwack*. "What will you have to drink?"

The men each gave their drink order, and I softly requested water. She sneered at me. "Can't hear you. Speak up if you want anything."

Aidan reached for my hand and gave it a gentle squeeze. "She said she wanted water."

"Fine. I'll be back with your drinks." She stormed off, and I couldn't help but feel like she hated us. Or maybe she only disliked me.

Tank stood and yelled after her, "Don't worry about the drinks. We'll go somewhere more friendly."

The rest of the men stood, and so did I. We hadn't made it to the door before a man rushed toward us.

"I'm the manager. Is there a problem?" he asked.

"Yeah. Your waitress is rude as fuck, after making us wait to even get a damn menu. We're going somewhere else to eat," Tank said.

"She scared my wife," Surge said.

"I'm so sorry. Please, I'll get someone else to wait on your table. Your drinks and dessert are on the house!"

Tank shook his head. "I don't trust that woman not to spit in our food, or have someone else do it."

"I will personally oversee your meals preparation and bring it to the table for you," the manager said.

Aidan tipped his head and watched the man. "Why are you working so hard to keep us here? Your patrons don't want us in the same restaurant with them. Your waitress was downright hateful. What do you care if we eat here or not?"

Surge straightened to his full height. "Son of a bitch. You know who she is, who *we* are. You're stalling."

"How the fuck did those bastards know we were here?" Viking asked.

"Move it. Now!" Tank shouted and started shoving us toward the door. Surge ran to his bike and started it up while Aidan helped me into the truck. Tank slid behind the wheel while Viking jumped into the other vehicle, and everyone burned rubber, getting away from the restaurant.

Aidan gripped the bar over the door as the truck fishtailed around a corner. Tank pressed the accelerator harder, and we rocketed toward the highway. I didn't like Surge being out in the open and exposed. But I knew he wouldn't leave his bike behind either. He'd said as much already.

"Not to sound like I watch too many movies, but could they have put some sort of tracking device on her?" Aidan asked.

"It's possible." Tank glanced at me in the rearview mirror. "Noticed anything different. A small bump that wasn't there before? A tender spot?"

"They drugged me the entire trip to this country. They could have done anything to me." I worried at my bottom lip. "Aidan, did you notice anything?"

"No, but I was otherwise occupied."

"Running won't do us any good if they can find her." Tank sped up and passed Surge. After several more exits, he pulled off and went to the first motel we came across. "I'm going to get a room in my name. Aidan, you and Surge need to check her thoroughly. Viking and I will wait outside."

He got out of the truck and went into the lobby. Surge pulled up and shut off the bike. He approached Aidan's window, his brow creased.

"Why are we at a motel?" he asked.

"He thinks there's a tracking device on me," I

said.

"Motherfuckers," Surge muttered. "All right. If we find one, it's going to hurt taking it out. I don't have the equipment we'd need, and I'm not sure who to trust around here. Doctors will ask too many questions."

"I can take it," I said, lifting my chin.

"I'm not sure I can," Surge said. "Last thing I want to do is hurt you."

"It's better than letting those men find me, isn't it?" I asked.

"I know, angel. I just wish there was another way."

Tank came back and handed a room key to Surge. "It's number three, so we don't have to move our vehicles. I told Colette that I'll wait outside with Viking."

"Let's get this over with." Surge opened the truck door and Aidan slid out, then they both helped me down. We went to the room and Surge led me straight to the bathroom. "Strip and get into the tub. If I have to dig something out of you, it's best to keep the blood in a place that's easy to clean."

I kicked off my shoes and removed my clothes, handing them to Aidan. He set everything on the counter outside the small room. Stepping into the tub, I tried to calm my nerves. Surge ran his hands over my head, down my neck, onto my shoulders... he explored every inch of me, and if it hadn't been for such a scary reason, it would have turned me on. Instead, I wanted to cry.

"Wait." Surge ran his hand down my right arm again, pausing between my shoulder and elbow. "Found something."

Aidan rubbed the spot too. "It feels almost flat.

Like a chip. I always thought they'd be big, fat things like you see in the movies."

"They use RFID technology, which means it's not 100% accurate when trying to locate someone. But it's also small enough to go undetected. Colette, I'm going to have to make an incision and cut it out of you. I'm so fucking sorry." Surge pulled a knife from his pocket, then turned on the sink. "Not the best way to sterilize it for something like this, but I'm hoping the hot water will do the trick."

When he'd decided it was clean enough, Aidan got into the tub behind me and braced me. Surge gripped my arm and let out a breath before slicing into my skin. I ground my teeth together so I wouldn't scream and draw attention to us. He removed the chip. Then stomped on it several times before flushing the pieces down the toilet.

"Shit. None of us thought about bandages," Surge said. A fist pounded on the door, making me jolt. "Colette, put on your bra and panties. Don't put on anything else yet. I don't want you to get blood on everything."

He went to answer the door, and I heard Tank's voice. Surge came back with a sack in his hand.

"What's that?" Aidan asked.

"Viking saw a pharmacy on the corner. He ran to get some supplies. On the off chance we had to cut into Colette to get the tracker out. Good thing he was thinking ahead. I'm going to disinfect the wound, then put some ointment on it and wrap it up, all right?"

I nodded. The alcohol stung, and I nearly bit my tongue in two, trying to be quiet and brave. Surge smeared the cream over the cut, then placed a cotton pad over it. He wrapped something around my arm.

"Best I can do until we get to the Dixie Reapers.

Tank said he'd call their doctor and have him on standby. You may need stitches. Unless the wound manages to close by then. We have about five more hours on the road." Surge kissed my forehead. "We still need to get some food too, but I don't want to stick around this place. Think you can hang on for another few exits?"

"Yes. I just want this to be over. I don't want to run anymore."

He hugged me tight and kissed me again. "We'll put all this behind us and go somewhere amazing for a real honeymoon, all right? I think the three of us will have earned it. You've already been through hell, and poor Aidan is about to be baptized in fire. He's not been around this part of my life before."

"I can handle it," Aidan said. "I think. If it means keeping Colette safe, and having your back, I'll do whatever is necessary."

"I know." Surge smiled. "I'm one lucky bastard. The two of you are beyond amazing, and I know I don't deserve either of you. I'll probably fuck up from time to time, but I hope you both know I'll do what it takes to make you both happy."

I tried not to cry, but his words touched me. No one had ever cared what happened to me, not since my parents died. He hadn't given me a declaration of love, and I didn't expect one. Still, the words he'd said meant so much to me, and I could tell it was the same for Aidan.

"Get dressed," Surge said. "We need to get out of here."

I put on my clothes and shoes, and we drove farther down the highway. Tank refused to pull over again until we'd put another forty miles between us and the motel. And I couldn't blame him. Knowing those men were after us, that they'd had a way to follow us from the cabin? Worse. That they'd likely been tracking us since we'd left the Hades Abyss... It terrified me.

Chapter Eight

Surge

The trip from the cabin to the Dixie Reapers compound left me feeling like I'd been backed over by a truck. Twice. Finding out Colette had a tracker in her had sent me spiraling, even if I hadn't outwardly shown it. She and Aidan needed me to be strong. For them, I'd keep my shit together and focus on making my family safe. Whatever it took.

I hadn't been to this place in a while, and it had changed a lot. It proved how different their club was these days. It looked like a massive gated neighborhood... on steroids. We'd passed a playground, a community pool and barbeque area, and so many houses. It also looked like they'd either expanded and purchased more land, or they'd cleared enough trees it just appeared to be bigger.

Tank led the way toward the back of the compound. If I didn't trust him, and the others, I might be concerned we were being led to our doom. Then I saw why we'd come so far into their sanctuary. A community of what appeared to be tiny homes were clustered in a group of ten.

Tank stopped in front of the one on the far end. I parked my bike on the parking pad out front and noticed a covered area on the other end of the tiny homes. Two other motorcycles were parked underneath.

"If the weather gets bad, take your bike over there. Otherwise, you're fine to park it here. You'll be staying in this house during your... visit." Tank grimaced. "Let me show you the inside while Colette and Aidan stretch their legs."

Which told me he wanted to say something to

me without an audience. My gaze clashed with Aidan's and he gave me a slight nod, letting me know he understood. He took Colette's hand, and they walked a short way off, admiring the landscape.

Inside the house, it seemed more spacious. Certainly bigger than the cabin we'd been using for our honeymoon.

"Fridge should be somewhat stocked," Tank said. He opened the appliance and grunted.

I peered inside and saw a case of beer, a half-gallon of milk, some eggs, butter, and the usual condiments. When he opened the freezer, I bit my lip so I wouldn't say anything. Two empty ice trays were the only thing inside.

"Motherfuckers," Tank muttered. "Fucking Prospects didn't do their damn jobs. I'm going to kick their asses."

"It's fine. I didn't expect your club to feed us. I can give someone a list with some cash." I paused. Except I didn't have any cash.

Tank snorted. "Remembering a few more details now? Like not being able to use your bank card or credit cards? Or the fact you told Wire you didn't have much cash?"

"Shit. I'll pay you back, or whoever gets the groceries."

Tank waved me off. "No need. But if you want to make a list, I'll see someone gets everything you need and drops it off. I'll tell them to leave it on the porch. Your woman seems a bit skittish, and your man looks jumpy as a cat on a hot tin roof."

"Aidan isn't used to any of this," I said, rubbing the back of my neck. "I tried to keep him away from the club life. Didn't work out so well."

"No one here will judge you. The house next

door is empty. Dagger is arriving tomorrow with his family. They'll be staying there. Thought it might give Colette and Aidan some comfort, being so close to another couple in a relationship like yours."

"I appreciate it," I said.

"There's something I need to show you." Tank moved farther into the house. We passed a bedroom with a queen-size bed, five-drawer chest, and nothing else. Another door stood open and showed the bathroom with a shower/tub combo, sink, and toilet. But the last door..." Stackable washer and dryer. And if you pull back the rug, you'll find a trap door. That's the reason you have this house."

"Where does it go?" I asked.

"Tunnel. Originally, we built a bunker underground that only the officers knew about. Things blew up in our faces before we were ready to disclose exactly what we'd been working on. Now it's larger and has a tunnel system that connects various homes to the bunker. Each officer has an entrance, this house has one, and three others in the compound. Things go to shit, send your woman into the tunnels."

I nodded. "Thank you for sharing this with me. I'm sure it's top secret to ensure your families are safe when necessary."

Tank grunted. "Torch wanted you to have this place and know about the bunker. It has a fuck ton of beds, a bathroom, kitchen, and even a living area with a TV, movies, and a game system for the kids."

It sounded... familiar. Where had I heard about something similar? "Did you talk to someone from our Mississippi chapter?"

He grinned. "Might have. As well as a few other clubs. You'd be surprised how many have something like this set up. Not to this extent, though. The others

I've heard about only have one or two entrances."

"And the doors to get into the actual bunker? Secure? Because there's no point sending her down there if she's just going to be a sitting duck," I said.

"Reinforced steel. No offense, but I'm not telling you how to unlock the doors. Besides, it's not something you could do anyway. Just trust me when I say your woman is going to be fine down there."

"Guess I should bring her and Aidan inside, get our bags, and start on that list of groceries."

"I'm going home to my family. There's a list of phone numbers on the fridge, and a landline. Just give one of us a shout if you need something. I already told you Dagger is coming with his family. Charming said he'd send one or two men from Devil's Boneyard as well."

I walked out with Tank and waved over Aidan and Colette. While they went into the house, I retrieved our bags from the truck, and carried everything inside. I found a pad of paper and a pen in one of the kitchen drawers. It looked like the house had kitchenware, towels, and laundry detergent. The bathroom had a drawer full of sample sized shampoo, soap, and even some packages of toothbrushes and disposable razors.

"This place is pretty great," Aidan said.

"It's nice. I didn't ask why they had them. Since there were two bikes parked at the end of the row, I'm assuming some of the Reapers live in them. This one and the one next door seems to be for guests. He said Dagger would arrive tomorrow with his family."

"What are you doing?" Colette asked, coming to stand beside me.

"We need to make a grocery list. Tank thought the place already had food stocked, but it doesn't."

"Since I'm most likely cooking, maybe I should

make the list." Aidan nudged me out of the way. I lifted my eyebrows at him, but the bastard only winked at me. "Any food allergies we didn't cover yet?"

"Not for me," I said.

"*Non.*"

"All right. How about shrimp pasta, meatloaf with mashed potatoes, baked chicken with glazed baby carrots and steamed broccoli, and…"

I placed my hand over the paper, where he'd already started on the list. "We need some quick things too. Not to mention lunch and breakfast."

"We should have brought some of the stuff we'd purchased for the cabin," Aidan said. "I was so flustered I just ended up tossing everything out. I'm not typically the wasteful sort."

"Good to hear since the price of things keeps climbing. At this rate, we'll be paying ten dollars for a gallon of milk." I nudged his shoulder with mine. "Make whatever you want for dinner, just don't get carried away. We have no idea how long we'll be here. Could be a few days, or a week. Any longer than that, and we're all doing something wrong. With three hackers present, there's no way we shouldn't be able to find these guys and destroy them."

"Do you need to go meet with them?" Aidan asked. "Because Colette and I will be fine. We'll just hang out here in the house, put our things in the bedroom, and find a movie to watch."

"Are you sure?" I asked.

Colette nodded. "*Oui.* You should go. Who do we give the list to?"

"Tank said his number was on the fridge. Just let him know you're ready for someone to get the list, and they'll pick up the groceries and bring them back here.

You can ask to have them left on the porch." Colette kissed my cheek, then Aidan pressed his lips to mine. "Aidan, you know my number. Call if you need me."

Colette shooed me from the house and I left, shaking my head. Only married a short while and those two were already teaming up on me. I liked the fact they were comfortable enough for me to leave them alone in a strange place with people they'd never met before. Sure, they knew Tank and Viking, but only barely.

I couldn't remember where to find Wire and Lavender, so I gave them a quick call. Lavender answered immediately, sounding out of breath.

"He-hello."

"Um. Is this a bad time?" I asked.

She laughed. "Yes and no. But I know where your mind went and that's not what I'm doing. What's up?"

"I was going to head to your place, except I don't know where it is."

She gave me directions and I ended the call. After I started my bike, I pulled onto the road that snaked through the compound and found Wire's house easily enough. Two bicycles were in the front yard. One blue and one purple. I figured they belonged to Atlas and Livvy. A jump rope and chalk lay abandoned on their driveway. I stepped over everything on my way to their door. I didn't even get a chance to knock before it opened.

"Welcome!" Lavender lunged at me, hugging me tight. "I'm so glad you're here, even if it's under horrible circumstances. You didn't bring Aidan and Colette?"

"They wanted to stay at the house. When I left, they were working on a grocery list and said they'd probably watch a movie." I lifted the laptop in my hand. "Brought this and thought we could brainstorm and try to track down the assholes who are after Colette. Did Tank tell you they'd chipped her like a damn dog? They were using GPS to keep tabs on her."

I stepped into the house and Lavender shut the door, motioning for me to follow her to the kitchen. I saw Wire already had his laptop out, and a giant mug of coffee was within reach. I sat across from him, waiting until he'd finished typing before I said anything.

His gaze lifted to mine and he smiled, though it looked strained. "Glad you made it safely."

"I just told Lavender those assholes had a GPS tracker inside Colette's arm. They were keeping tabs on her."

"Combined with what you've told us so far, I think her rescuer, Jacques, is in on it. I have no idea what game he was playing. Frankly, none of this makes a damn bit of sense, but what else is new?"

Lavender poured me some coffee and slid the mug over to me. I took a few swallows, letting the hot liquid soothe me. "Just hook me up to an IV of this stuff and I'll be good to go."

She smiled. "That's what Wire always says too. I looked into your Prospect, Joe. He has some gambling debts. Really big ones. I don't think he's a bad guy, however, he's in over his head and when men get desperate..."

I nodded. "All right. We need to let Fox know. Can you send the info to him? He'll probably want to check it out himself and have proof if he confronts Joe. I find it odd Joe invited Colette and Jacques to the clubhouse. Sought them out specifically. And Colette said it seemed like Jacques knew for certain someone would come down the hall."

"So you think when you found the two of them, you ruined whatever plan had been set in motion?" Wire asked.

"Best guess I've got so far. But if Joe was that deeply in debt, I doubt he was making a play for Colette. The question is how does Jacques know Joe, and where do the two fit into the human trafficking ring?"

Lavender sat down and yanked her hair up in a messy knot before shoving chopsticks through it. "Fox is going to have a fit if Joe turns out to be dirty."

"He's probably going to chew my ass out for not catching on sooner," I said.

She shook her head. "No. None of this is your fault, Surge. Joe has been covering his tracks, living his life as normally as possible. I doubt he's done anything, before now, to tip you off that something wasn't quite right."

"The guy always set me on edge a bit," I admitted. "But when I looked into him the first time, nothing came up. No red flags at all. I figured it was just me since no one else seemed to have an issue with him."

"Let's divide and conquer," Lavender said. "I'll take Joe."

"I'm already working on the human traffickers," Wire said.

"Then I guess I have Jacques." I cracked my fingers before I opened the laptop and got to it. I probably should have called Colette and Aidan first. Experience told me we could be at this for a while. I started with the few things I knew about the man.

Lavender stopped a few times to refill our coffees, and she put pretzels and popcorn in the middle of the table for us to snack on. The more I dug into Jacques, the more confused I got, until I finally hit pay dirt. The motherfucker wasn't really Jacques Dupon. He wasn't even French!

"Son of a bitch," I muttered.

"What?" Lavender glanced my way but kept typing, her fingers flying over the keys.

"Jacques Dupon is really Jack Carson from Pennsylvania." I looked up and saw Wire's brow furrow. I could tell what I'd said triggered something. He worked like a possessed man until he grunted and leaned back in his chair. "Find something?"

"Once you said his real name, things started falling into place. He has a brother. Thomas Carson."

"And I'm going to take a guess and say Thomas has something to do with Colette being kidnapped and brought here?" I asked.

"Definitely. I hacked into his financial records. The man has multiple offshore accounts, as well as various domestic ones, all under aliases. To the average person, he owns a chain of car dealerships specializing in foreign imports. From what I can tell, he brings those cars over on ships, and he's smuggling people onto the same boats." Wire folded his arms over his chest. "If Jack was being treated like another captive, and was stashed with the others on the ship, then he's in on it to some extent. Anything pop in his records?"

I shook my head. "No. I mean, he has a healthy bank account, but it's not the sort you'd expect to see for that kind of work. And I didn't find any offshore accounts. He does have a few aliases. Not only Jacques Dupon, but also Karl Schmidt from Germany, Oliver Taylor from England, and Lorenzo Ricci from Italy."

"If he can pull off all those accents, I wonder if he pretends to be a captive from each place. They must hit a different country each time to make it harder for the police to catch them." Wire frowned. "That's a lot of trouble to go to. Which means they must have a special client list. Men seeking foreign women, specifically."

"Colette said some children and a man were sold before she and Jacques ran. So it's not just women. If I had to guess, the men are being sold for labor. I'm trying not to dwell on where those kids ended up. I think I'd puke if I did." I ran my hand over my chin, feeling my beard starting to grow in. I needed to shave in the worst way. "Jacques told Colette he was heading north to meet with someone he knew. I wonder if he'd planned to go home to Pennsylvania?"

"Found the connection with Joe," Lavender said. "You're not going to like it."

"Of course not," I mumbled. "Hit me with it. What's this fucker into? How badly will I want to kill him?"

"Joe's debts were purchased by the Carsons. I found some encrypted emails. Looks like they offered him a deal. He'd take possession of a special package and see it safely delivered to the new owner. It's worded carefully, but I'd bet money on it being Colette." Lavender grabbed a handful of pretzels and munched on them. "You said she mentioned it seemed like a setup? That Jacques had said something about a man joining them. Do you think the show he was putting on wasn't for anyone coming into the room, but for Colette? He'd have to make it believable, make her really fall for all his lies."

"But why travel on foot and go to all the trouble to give sexual favors in exchange for food? Something seems off about the entire situation," I said.

"Not really." Wire grimaced. "Think about it. If Joe offered Colette safety, then managed to get her to the man who'd purchased her, he could make it seem like he was helping her into a better life. She'd go willingly to the rich guy, thinking she'd lucked out. Do you think she'd have given in and had sex with the man without being forced?"

As much as I wanted to say no, I couldn't. Part of me had wondered if she'd given in to me so easily because she felt like she owed me. I'd been a bastard and married her, so now she had no choice in the matter. Not that I'd ever force myself on her, but I knew a woman like Colette would feel it was an obligation to sleep with the man she married. Or in this case, men.

"She may have," I admitted. "So you think the guy wanted to buy a woman, but still wanted her to be willing?"

Lavender growled. "I think the asshole didn't just want someone to spread their legs without complaint. He wanted to be her hero. Every time she thanked him for saving her, or stared at him like he hung the moon, it would make the entire thing even sweeter for him. He'd be the sleazy dipshit who bought her, caused her all that pain and suffering, and she'd never know."

"Write down those names," Wire said, sliding a pad and pen toward me. "I may be able to connect the aliases to other missing women. Or anyone else on Thomas Carson's list of sales."

"List?" I asked.

"Fucker thought he had everything hidden, but he doesn't. Not if the right person is looking. He has the women's names, where he snatched them, and who bought them. Your wife sold to Hugh Marsh of Marsh Enterprises for half a million dollars. Not sure I should tell you the rest."

"There's more?" I narrowed my gaze. "Just spit it out, Wire."

"There was a promised bonus of another half million if she arrived with her innocence intact, but…" He glanced at Lavender and pressed his lips together before he finally finished. "He wanted her ass broken in and said it was fine to teach her the finer points of oral sex. He just didn't want anyone to finish inside her unless they wore a condom."

I stood and went outside. The door slammed behind me, and I stared up at the sky, my chest heaving, as I fought back the rage building inside me. I tipped my head back farther and screamed out all the anger and pain. I was sick as fuck of entitled assholes with so much money they thought they could have anything they wanted. They didn't give a shit who they destroyed in the process.

I felt Lavender's hand on my back and glanced down at her. "Sorry. I probably scared every kid around here just now."

She smiled. "Not hardly. You think no one vents their rage around here?"

She had me there. "The buyer. He has to know by now he isn't getting Colette, or that she's no longer a virgin. Is he still looking for her? Are the Carson brothers after her?"

"Wire and I are going to keep working on this. Someone will watch the kids until tomorrow. As to your questions, unless they communicate and we find the emails or texts, there's no way to know what the buyer wants now. You need to go back to your wife and husband. They need you more than we do. I'd imagine they're scared being in a strange place full of people they don't know, and having monsters chase your wife down is a nightmare all its own."

I nodded. "You're right. I just wanted to be the one to save her, I guess. Maybe I'm no better than Hugh Marsh."

Lavender smacked me so hard I worried she'd left a handprint on my cheek. "Don't you *ever* say something so stupid ever again! You are *nothing* like those men. You hear me? You want to save her because she's your wife and you care about her. Even if you hadn't married her, I know you, Surge. You'd never leave a defenseless woman or child in a bad situation. You want to be her hero because that's who you are."

"I'm no hero, Lavender."

"Really?" She put her hands on her hips. "Shall we go talk to all the women you've helped save over the years? The children your hacking skills helped rescue? Because I don't think they'd agree with you. To them, you're their savior. So if I ever hear you compare yourself to someone like Hugh Marsh ever again, that slap will seem like I hit you with a feather."

I smiled faintly. "Fine. I get it. But if my wife asks about the handprint on my face, I'm going to tell her you hit me."

She rolled her eyes. "Whatever. Get out of here."

"Just let me grab the laptop. I know it's technically yours, but if I can't sleep, I'd like to have it handy."

"Just reach out to Wire and see where we are before you go digging into anything else. I'm hoping we'll have all the answers by morning. Or at least close to it."

I kissed her cheek. "Thank you. Both of you."

Chapter Nine

Aidan

I didn't miss the way Colette would look over at the front door every fifteen minutes or so. Surge had told us why he was leaving, and I knew if he wasn't back, then it meant he still had work to do. But our wife was worried.

I'd found some first aid supplies under the bathroom sink, and I'd already doctored her arm. It didn't seem to need stitches, but I couldn't promise her it wouldn't scar. She hadn't seemed concerned. Then again, she had heavier things to worry about. Like men wanting to sell her to the highest bidder.

Her gaze wandered to the front door again.

"He's coming back," I assured her for what felt like the tenth time. Or more.

"I know." She cuddled against me and started watching the movie again. We'd gone through three so far. If Surge didn't return soon, I'd go ahead and start dinner without him.

"Is it Surge you're checking for, or are you concerned someone will come through the door to hurt us, or take you away?" I asked.

She shook her head. "He wouldn't have left us if he didn't think it was safe. But did you see how tense he looked?"

Yeah, I'd noticed. He tried to hide it but failed miserably. The fact our wife was in trouble bothered him. A lot. Same for me, except I knew there wasn't a damn thing I could do to fix this mess. Surge, on the other hand, had the skills to keep her safe.

"He wants to be able to tell you everything's fine," I said. "I promise that's all it is. A guy like him won't rest until his family is safe. We just need to give him the time and space he needs when he asks for it and support him the best we can."

"You love him," she murmured.

My cheeks warmed. "I do. I'm not sure he feels the same way."

"There are people in this world who can't say the L word. Did you ever wonder if he's one of them? He might not say the words, but he could still feel love for you. I've seen the way he watches you when you aren't paying attention. He cares for you deeply, Aidan." Her shoulders sagged and she seemed to deflate. "If he's going to love anyone, it will be you."

It hit me right then. The one thing Colette wanted, what she needed, was someone to love her. She'd said her parents died when she was younger. For so long, she'd been alone. Then snatched from her country and brought here.

I tipped her chin up, forcing her to hold my gaze. "Colette, you're a sweet, beautiful woman. Anyone would be lucky to have your love and love you in return. That man you're waiting for? He would die for you. If that's not love, I'm not sure what is."

She gave me a soft smile. "You think so?"

I pressed my forehead to hers. "I love you, Colette. It may not be the deep sort of love people have after they've been together a while, but I do feel that emotion for you. We have all the time in the world to grow closer. All three of us. It's not a race to the finish line."

She nodded. "All right. I'll be patient. But, Aidan… I love you too. And I love Cam. So very much. No one's ever treated me as nice as the two of you, and what he's done for me…"

"I know. He's pretty amazing, but so are you."

She pressed her lips to mine, and I kissed her

back. I hated the way she doubted her place in our lives. Yes, we were virtual strangers to her, but we were going through hell together. She'd been through the brunt of it alone, but there was still a rough road ahead. By the time we made it to the other side of this fiasco, we'd be stronger for it.

"Think of our relationship like a clay pot," I said. "When it starts out, it's messy and doesn't look very pretty. But with patience and care, it's shaped into something more eye-catching. Then it's baked. The fire hardens the pot."

"I'm... not sure I understand."

"We're like the pot. The fire is everything we're going through right now. When we make it out of this, we'll be stronger. Not just individually, but as a family."

"That's rather beautiful," she said.

My cheeks warmed again. "Guess it comes from being an artist. Surge is the tough one. He can fight, will defend those who are weaker than him, and is just all around amazing. I'm not very useful in this situation."

"Yes, you are," she said, lacing our fingers together. "I like your softer side. You see things differently than he does, and your touch is gentler. The two of you complement one another, and together, you give me everything I could ever need. Two halves of a whole."

I smiled and kissed her again. "Maybe I'm not the only artistic one. You should write that down. It's rather poetic."

The door opened and we both jolted. Surge came inside, pausing to stare at us.

"I feel like I missed something," he said. "Sorry I was gone so long."

"We've just been talking and watching movies," I said. "Think our wife has been worried."

Colette looked away and Surge came closer. He forced her to look at him.

"You were worried about me?" he asked.

"*Oui.*"

"I'm fine, sweetheart. Found out some unsettling things about Jacques and your situation. You said he was from France, but he's not. He's American."

I blinked. I hadn't expected that.

"He has aliases in multiple countries. His accent fooled me, and probably everyone he came into contact with. He's a chameleon, seamlessly blending no matter what country he's in. I'd be willing to bet you weren't the first he'd tricked." Surge sighed and hugged her tight. "I'm sorry, Colette. I wish I had better news. Jacques is actually Jack Carson. And he was part of it from the beginning."

She turned her face into me and clung to my shirt. "Why? Why do this?"

I saw the hesitation on Surge's face. "Tell her. No secrets, Cam."

"Someone purchased you, Colette. We found encrypted emails. Jack was supposed to hand you off to Joe, who would transport you to your new owner. The idea was for you to be so thankful for all the nice things he could give you, that you'd basically be a willing slave."

"That's fucked up," I said. "So he preys on those women? Lures them in, acting like he's saving them, when in reality he's one of the men responsible?"

"I'll deal with Jack if I can catch him," Surge said. "Neither of you want to know the details. What I do won't be pretty, and I don't want either of you to be scared of me. I've typically let the club handle the more violent side of things, but that guy is mine. He's hurt my family, and I'll be the one to make him pay."

"That doesn't scare me," Colette said.

"Or me." I placed a hand on his shoulder. "I know you'll do whatever it takes to protect those you love. And even if you haven't admitted it to yourself, or anyone else, I can see you love Colette."

He swallowed hard and held my gaze. "I do. I love Colette, and… I love you too, Aidan."

"Why don't you and Colette spend some time together while I make dinner?" I suggested.

"What's the gourmet chef making tonight?" Surge asked with a smirk.

I rolled my eyes at him. "I'm not *that* great a cook. I was thinking chicken breasts with bacon strips over them, topped with barbeque sauce, and mashed potatoes on the side."

His brow furrowed. "While that sounds amazing, do we have everything here for you to make that? I didn't check the kitchen well enough to know what cookware is in there."

"I already looked. I have what I need."

"All right. Then I guess our sweet wife and I will watch a movie. Although, she may be tired of them by now."

Colette tipped her head back. "Could we go for a walk? Is it safe?"

Surge nodded. "As long as we keep to the more populated sections and away from the fence line and gates. I don't see any harm in going outside. Aidan, are you sure you don't mind staying here to cook? You could join us, and we could just ask someone to grab a pizza for us."

I wrinkled my nose. "Pizza is fine every now and then. But I'm cooking. Go have some fun. Maybe she can meet some of the Dixie Reaper ladies. Depending on how long we're here, it wouldn't be bad for her to make some friends."

"True enough," Surge said. "All right. We'll be back in... twenty minutes?"

"The chicken will take closer to an hour. They picked up really thick breasts, and I don't want to chance them not being cooked all the way through."

"Okay. We still won't be gone the entire time. You know my number if something comes up. I've got my cell phone in my pocket."

I waved them off and went to the kitchen to get to work. First, I wiped all the surfaces down with an antibacterial wipe. Then I got out the cookware and ingredients I'd need and preheated the oven. I really did enjoy cooking, and as much as I wanted to spend time with Surge and Colette, I was used to being on my own. Knowing I had the house to myself relieved some of the pressure building inside me. I didn't know how I'd handle living with two people when we went back home. At least I'd have my studio when I needed an escape.

Or rather, I'd thought I would have it. What if Surge didn't want me to keep the place in town?

I shook my head. There was so much we needed to discuss, but I knew there were more important things to tackle right now. I didn't fool myself into thinking it would be easy to live with Surge and Colette. We each had different personalities, and I knew we'd eventually butt heads over stuff. It was all part of being in a relationship. I only hoped we figured out how to solve any issues that arose and could live together somewhat harmoniously.

While I waited on the oven to reach the right temperature, I checked my voicemails. I'd missed quite a few calls since I'd met Surge and Colette at the courthouse several days ago. Since I didn't like the idea of being dependent on Surge, even if he did claim me as his husband, I couldn't afford to lose out on projects that came my way.

I made a few notes from the messages and called back one of my favorite clients as I cooked. Not having any idea when I'd be back at my studio, I told them I'd had a family emergency and was away for a short while. They promised to call again in a week and see if I was back. I could only hope the others would be as understanding.

A fist pounded on the door, and I wiped my hands on a kitchen towel. I cracked the door open and peered outside, seeing two large men, a woman, a boy, and a girl. Since the men wore cuts, I could see their names easily enough.

"Surge here?" Dagger asked.

"He went on a walk with Colette. I think he wanted to introduce her to a few people. I'm Aidan."

Guardian reached out his hand and I shook, then Dagger offered his.

"We're from the Devil's Fury. This is our wife, Zoe. Our son, Luis, and our daughter, Avelina. We'll be settling in next door until your situation is resolved." Guardian smiled. "Nice to know we aren't the only family with two dads. Assuming the three of you want children."

I relaxed even more and stepped back. "Yes, we do. Would you like to come in? I'm cooking dinner but haven't put anything in the oven yet. We have enough if you'd like to join us?"

Guardian waved me off. "Thanks, but the kids are going to be a handful tonight. But if you'd like to stop by after dinner for a cup of coffee, it would give

Zoe a chance to meet your wife. Then the two will be acquainted if the rest of us get called into Church."

"Sounds great. We'd heard you were coming, but they said it would be tomorrow."

Dagger shrugged. "Why put it off? Didn't have to pack up much, so we decided to make the trip today."

"It was nice to meet you, Aidan," Zoe said, a soft smile on her lips. "I can't wait to meet Colette. I only wish it was under better circumstances."

I nodded. "Me too."

Dagger and Guardian gave me one of those chin lifts I'd seen Surge give people a time or two and then led their family to the little house next door. I noticed there were two motorcycles and an SUV parked out front. Dagger opened the rear hatch and set three duffle bags on the ground, before reaching in for a box that seemed to hold quite a few toys. At least the kids wouldn't be bored.

I shut the door and went back to the kitchen to finish dinner.

If the two men had been surprised I didn't have a cut, they hadn't shown it. I wondered if someone had already told them I wasn't part of the Hades Abyss. Smiling, I realized I was looking forward to getting to know them better. It would be nice to talk to a couple with a pairing like ours. And hopefully Zoe would answer any questions Colette might have. Not only about a poly relationship, but also about life with a motorcycle club.

Hell, I needed that crash course myself.

* * *

Colette

Surge had taken my hand after we'd left the

house, and we'd walked the curving road closer to the front of the compound. He kept me away from the fence at all times. In fact, he walked on the outside, using his body as a shield to protect me.

"Are we going anywhere in particular?" I asked.

"I'd like you to meet Wire and Lavender. They're hackers like me and are working hard to make sure you'll be safe. I think they can take a short timeout to say hi. You'll like Lavender. She's sweet and easygoing. Well, to most of us she is. Wire may say differently when she does something that irritates him."

"Are there other women here?" I asked.

"A lot. The Dixie Reapers have families with full-grown children. Venom, their VP, has two daughters who were claimed by men in the Devil's Fury. Torch, their President, has a daughter who's claimed by the President of the Reckless Kings. Another of the Dixie Reapers' patched members, Cowboy, has a daughter who's also with the Reckless Kings. Now that I think about it, Preacher's oldest daughter, Leigha, just settled down with someone at the Reckless Kings too."

"So there are wives and daughters." I looked around. "I haven't seen any."

"In the event the human traffickers are able to find you here, they've probably warned their families to stick close to their homes. Hell, they may have told them not to leave at all. I wouldn't blame them. I can't imagine the terror of those assholes taking you again. And if we had kids and they took them too? I'd lose my fucking mind."

We stopped in front of a home that clearly belonged to a family with children. "Is this where they live?"

He nodded. He led me up to the front door and

knocked. A moment later, a pretty woman answered the door. She smiled widely when she saw Surge, and I felt a spark of possessiveness. I knew it was ridiculous. He'd said she was married to another man. So why I did want to hold onto him a little tighter?

"Surge! You're back awfully soon." Her gaze slid to me, and her eyes widened a little. "Oh my. You must be Colette! It's so nice to meet you."

Before I could process what was happening, she wrapped her arms around me and hugged me tight. I awkwardly patted her back, not sure how to react. Other than Surge and Aidan -- and Jacques, whom I'd just as soon forget -- it had been a long time since I'd been hugged.

Surge chuckled. "Lavender, I think you're scaring her. Let my wife go, you crazy woman."

She gave him a mock glare after releasing me. "I'm going to tell Wire you were mean to me."

"No, he wasn't," a man yelled from somewhere inside the house. "Stop making them stand outside."

She huffed and motioned for us to follow her inside. When we got to the kitchen, I saw they had two computers set up at a long table with six chairs. Coffee cups and snack bowls littered the space, as well as pages with notes.

"You must be Colette," the ginger-haired man said. He gave me a smile and slowly stood, holding out his hand. I shook it, not sure what to make of him. "I'm Wire. You already met my woman, Lavender. I'm afraid our kids are off playing elsewhere or you could meet them too."

"C..." I glanced at my husband. "I mean, Surge, said you were helping him keep me safe. Thank you."

"This is what we live for," Lavender said. "When I met my husband, someone snatched me and another biker. Outlaw. They mistook him for Wire. I know they didn't have a pleasant fate in store for me, and I've met so many women who've been abused by men. If I could take down every asshole who thought a woman could be bought or sold, I'd do it."

"We try," Wire said. "But they're like cockroaches. Take down one, and there's ten more."

"And you help people like me and don't expect anything in return?" I asked softly.

Wire and Lavender shared a look. "We don't do this for monetary gain, if that's what you're asking. And certainly not for sexual favors. That woman right there is enough to keep me on my toes. I'd go insane if I had another one to deal with."

Lavender gave him a playful nudge. "Wire may drive me crazy sometimes, but I love him. There's no one else in the world for me. If I had to guess, I'd say it's the same for Surge. The only people he wants are you and Aidan. Since we consider him family, that makes you our family as well."

My lip trembled and I held back tears. When Surge said he'd marry me, it seemed like a dream come true. I'd belong again. Have a chance to have children of my own. Have people to love, who would grow to love me in return. Now he'd given me an even larger family?

"Shit. You made her cry," Wire said, tossing his wife an accusing glare.

"No. I'm sorry. I'm just very emotional lately. Thank you. For everything. It's very nice to meet you both." I smiled at them. Surge curved his arm around my waist and kissed the top of my head. "I didn't know what to expect when he said we were coming here, but now I'm glad I get to meet so many nice people."

"You should introduce her to Ryker and Laken," Lavender said. She glanced at me. "I don't know if you've met Spider? He was the President of your husband's club, until he stepped down. Now Fox is in charge. But Spider's son, Ryker, lives here with Laken."

"I thought the clubs stuck together?" I asked.

"They do. Laken is the sister of a Dixie Reaper," Lavender said. "And Ryker has since joined our club. He used to be Diablo with the Hades Abyss. Now he's…"

Wire snickered before Lavender could finish.

"I didn't realize Ryker officially patched in. I knew Spider told him to do what he needed and dissolved his membership with our club. Although, he's still welcome anytime he wants to come up there. Why are you laughing at his name?" Surge asked.

"It's Dice." Lavender burst out laughing. "Because he rolled the dice when he slept with Flicker's sister and ended up getting her pregnant."

I could tell Surge tried to keep a straight face, but then he joined Lavender and Wire in their laughter. I didn't quite get it. But I smiled and hoped this new crazy world would make sense to me some day.

"That's fucking priceless," Surge said after he got himself under control once more. "I'm giving him shit about it at some point. So be warned."

Wire snorted. "You'd have to get in line. He takes the ribbing good naturedly so far, but sooner or later, he'll have had enough and come out swinging."

"Surge said a lot of the daughters here end up marrying into other clubs. Is that normal?" I asked, wondering about any children we may have in the future. Would they grow up and move far from home?

"I don't know if I'd call it normal." Wire rubbed

at his beard. "But it does seem to happen a lot. I guess most of them grow up with the other kids in the compound and look at them as more like brothers or sisters. But if the Devil's Fury and Reckless Kings could stop stealing all our daughters, that would be awesome."

"Maybe it's time your sons started taking the daughters from other clubs. Even the playing field," Surge said.

Wire smiled. "One day, maybe. The boys tend to be a bit wilder. I doubt any will settle down before they're thirty or close to it. The girls on the other hand, seem content to start their own families before they're twenty-one."

I noticed the age difference between Lavender and Wire, and I'd realized immediately Surge had to be older than me. I wondered how many others had paired off with men older than them.

"I can see you have questions," Lavender said. "I'd be happy to answer, but I want to get back to solving your problem first. If the three of you want to stay after this mess is handled, I'd be delighted to spend the afternoon with you, Colette."

I smiled. "I'd like that."

"If you two decide you need help..." Surge let his sentence trail off.

I wondered if he'd come home because he'd been worried about us. I knew how badly he wanted to catch the men who were after me.

"We should head back and see if Aidan needs help with dinner," I said. "I know he likes to cook, but it wouldn't hurt to at least offer to help prepare one of the dishes."

Surge reached up to cup my cheek. "You're right. We'll go back to the house and see what he needs."

"You're welcome to stop by again," Lavender said. "I'm not trying to shove you out the door."

Wire chuckled. "Yes, you are. It's for a good reason, though, and they know it, baby. Sit your ass down and get to work. Surge knows the way out."

My husband led the way back to the home we'd be staying at until it was safe to return to our own house. The smell that hit me when we walked in the door had my mouth watering. I'd have been happy with a frozen dinner, but Aidan seemed to go all out for every meal he made. I didn't know if he genuinely liked cooking, or if he was trying to fatten me up.

I knew it bothered both him and Surge that I'd gone so long without regular meals, had to eat out of trash cans, and been treated like I was less than human. Living on the streets had been hard. Not only had I been easy prey for men, but people often gave us dirty looks or spat at us. A few had yelled at us, saying we were making their city filthy.

We'd met other homeless people who'd chosen that way of life, and many who hadn't. Some had fallen on such hard times, they didn't know how to crawl their way back up. My heart went out to all of them.

"You've said money isn't an issue," I said, choosing my words carefully. "I don't know what you do for a living, or how well Aidan's art pays. I'll need a way to contribute to our family and have money for things I want to do."

Surge stopped in his tracks. "What is it you need money for? Because we'll handle any household expenses, your clothes and shoes... pretty much everything. You don't have to work, Colette. Not to mention, if you want a baby right now, I'd prefer you be at home with our children. Maybe it makes me a caveman, but --"

I squeezed his hand to stop him. "I do want to be with our children, but there are other things I want that aren't for our family. I've seen so much ugliness since coming to your country. I've experienced, firsthand, how people treat the homeless. It doesn't seem fair that I get this amazing life while people still struggle and lose themselves more each day."

He smiled and tugged me against him, holding me close. "Colette, you're fucking amazing. If you want to do something to help the homeless, I'll help you. Since you were going through trash to find food, I'm going to assume our town doesn't have a soup kitchen."

"No, but I also didn't see many homeless in your town. There's a small handful near an old railway overpass."

"Tell you what. When we get back home, you tell me what would help those people, and we'll gather the stuff and carry it down there. All three of us can go. Hell, the entire club might pitch in."

"Most of them didn't choose to be homeless," I said. "There's a family. A man with two children. He lost his job, and when he couldn't find employment, they had to leave their home and everything else behind. Another was replaced at his job with someone younger. He's an elderly man. A few prefer to live on the streets."

"Then we'll try to help them get back on their feet." He kissed me softly. "I love you, Colette. You have a big heart. After all you've been through, you're worrying about other people. Not many women like you in the world. At least, I haven't met but a few."

I hugged him, not knowing what else to do. The emotions flooding me kept me from speaking. If I tried,

I might start crying. I attempted to pull myself together before asking Aidan if he needed help. These men were beyond wonderful, and I knew I'd been lucky to find them.

Chapter Ten
Surge

Dinner had been amazing, as always. Aidan didn't seem to like compliments when he cooked, always brushing us off. I didn't know a lot about his past. He'd once confided about his family and how they'd kicked him out when he'd been caught with a boy. I admired how far he'd come since then, the life he'd created for himself. It seemed he didn't realize how remarkable he was.

"There's something I need to show you," I said. "In case someone does come for Colette, and somehow manages to get into the compound, there's a secret door that leads to a bunker. Only the Dixie Reapers can access it, so you'll be safe once you're inside and the doors are shut."

"You want us to hide while you fight the monsters?" Aidan asked.

I saw the uncertainty in his eyes, and knew he was once again thinking he wasn't enough. I put my hand around the back of his neck and tugged him closer, kissing him fiercely.

"Get the fuck out of your head," I said, making my voice hard and demanding to get his attention. "I want you with Colette so she won't be as scared and knowing you're with her will allow me to focus on kicking some ass. It has nothing to do with me thinking you aren't capable of fighting alongside me."

The tension in Aidan's body relaxed and he sighed. "All right. I get it."

Colette squeezed herself between us, and I smiled. She managed to cuddle us both at the same time. If I hadn't known it already, her reaction would have cemented my belief she was perfect for us. Her sweet nature was different for me. I hadn't had someone so good, so pure in my life for a long while now.

"Come on." I led them into the laundry area and pulled back the rug. "I was told you go down to the tunnels and take a right. I'm sure there will be other women and children down there, so try to find someone and go with them. You'll be locked into the bunker, which has multiple beds, a living room area, kitchen, and bathroom. I'd imagine with everything going on, they've already stocked it in case you're down there long enough to eat a meal or two."

"I'm scared, Cam," Colette whispered.

"I know, angel. This will all be over soon. Wire and Lavender are putting the final pieces together, and then we'll come up with a plan." I hugged her then Aidan. "I love you both. We'll get this handled, then we'll go home, where you can meet the rest of the Hades Abyss."

"On the plus side," Aidan said, "after running from people willing to sell other humans, meeting your club doesn't sound quite as scary as it did before."

My phone chimed with an incoming message. *Church. NOW.*

"Looks like I'm needed elsewhere. Aidan, keep your phone on you at all times. Listen for a text or call. I need the two of you to be safe while I'm gone."

Aidan audibly swallowed. "You're going to miss dessert. Apple pie."

"It will be worth it if we're all safe again and a few more bad guys are six feet under, or wishing they were."

I gave them each one last lingering look, then made my way out to my bike. I rode over to the clubhouse and went inside, following the Dixie

Reapers into Church. Since this wasn't my club, I didn't have a seat at the table. I leaned against the wall by Dagger and Guardian. I hadn't even realized they were here yet.

"Met Aidan earlier," Dagger said. "Told Zoe to head over there with the kids after we left. They'll help take Colette's mind off everything."

"I appreciate it."

Torch came in and took his seat. The last of the Reapers filed in, and the doors were shut. Torch cleared his throat. "We're going less formal today. Not enough time. I'm turning everything over to Wire, Lavender, and Surge. For those who aren't caught up, Surge came here with his family because someone has sold his wife. Thankfully, she's safe behind our gates for now, but the men responsible are still after her."

He motioned toward Wire. The hacker stood and took his wife's hand. I hadn't even realized she was here until Torch had mentioned her name. I knew it was odd for women to be in Church, but since she'd been helping me solve this disaster, it made sense she'd be permitted to join us tonight.

"This actually affects more than just Surge. The ring we discovered is big as fuck, and they're bringing people over from multiple countries, as well as snatching them off our streets here in the US. The organization is headed up by the Carson family. No mafia connections that I can find. Just assholes in general."

A few chuckles went up around the table at his assessment. Wire gave them a tired smile. I pushed off the wall and went toward them, standing on the other side of Lavender.

"Jack Carson is the one who tricked my wife. He can mimic accents and has multiple aliases. He was using Jacques Dupon when he told Colette he would help her escape, pretending to be a captive as well. Sadly, there was someone in my club, a Prospect, who was going to help him get Colette to her owner. Fox will be dealing with Joe." I glanced at Wire, giving him a nod to take over again.

"From what we've found, most of their buyers are powerful men, including some politicians. I did find one that was more interesting than the rest. A man in the Bratva purchased a young woman. The handoff hasn't happened yet, but it's coming soon. Within days. Since we're helping Surge and his family, it's my hope the Hades Abyss might be willing to send two or three members to intercept the girl before she makes it to her buyer." Wire held my gaze. "Think Fox would go for it?"

I nodded. "Probably. I can give him a call when we wrap things up. If you have a secure file, I can email it to him so he'll have all the facts."

"We can do that," Lavender said, speaking up for the first time. "Jack Carson doesn't seem to have left Missouri, unless he's using cash and not leaving a paper trail. Or has an alias we didn't find. His brother, however, has three men tracking Colette. It seems to have slowed them down when the tracker was removed from her arm. Or maybe they needed to regroup. If our information is correct, they're here in town."

"Which means they know she's here," Tank said. "I'm going to text my wife and have her reach out to everyone. Women and kids are going in the bunker immediately."

I pulled out my phone and texted Aidan, letting him know it was time to go into hiding. I reminded them to take some clothes, just in case this wasn't over quick and easy.

"I've used the cameras around town and found the men holed up in the roach motel on the outskirts of town," Wire said. "The fact they haven't made a move makes me wonder if they're not certain Colette is here, or if they're waiting on reinforcements. The organization is rather large. They have over fifty men working for them. Most are in the US, but they do have a handful in four other countries."

"Do they know we're onto them?" Torch asked.

"Not yet." Wire smirked. "But I'd like to make my presence known."

"What did you have in mind?" Venom asked. "Because knowing you, it's going to hit them where it hurts."

"I want to drain their accounts. All of them. Bounce the funds around until they can't track them." Wire put his arm around Lavender. "Then we want to give a nest egg to Colette for the pain and suffering she endured at their hands. Anyone rescued will also get part of the funds. Anything left over will be donated to foundations set up to spread awareness of human trafficking."

Venom nodded. "Sounds good to me. You okay with it, Torch?"

"I'm all in," the President said. "Do your worst to those fuckers."

Lavender pulled away from Wire and headed for the door. "In that case, I'm going to start on that while you gentlemen wrap things up. Once I've got everything set up, and the funds are withdrawn and hidden, I'll go down to the bunker with everyone else."

"I want to take a few men over to the motel and flush out those assholes," Tank said. "Maybe we can cut them off at the pass and stop them before they ever come to the compound looking for Colette."

"I want in on that," I said. "I owe those bastards some pain."

Tank nodded.

"Grimm, Hammer, Gears... I want the three of you to go with Tank and Surge," Torch said. "The rest of us will make sure our families are safe and no one makes it into the compound. If they do slip inside, they'll be leaving in pieces."

I grinned. It was nice to see Torch still had it. The man was getting up there in years, but he still held the reins with an iron fist. Anyone who underestimated him would end up dead. I fucking loved it, and I hoped I was just as badass when I was his age.

"Wire, keep everyone updated via text," Venom said. "Anything changes, those fuckers look ready to make a move or something else goes sideways, we need to know."

"On it," Wire said.

"Anyone staying with the women?" Saint asked. "We herded our old ladies and children down to the bunker. Some can hold their own, but others..."

"Like your delicate flower?" Venom asked, eyebrows raised.

Saint flipped him off. "Not everyone can kick ass like Ridley. I'm pretty sure if the enemy got their hands on her, they'd offer us a fortune to take her back."

Venom smirked. "Yes, they would, but she'd cause some chaos first. God, I love that fucking woman."

"We know," Torch said. "The two of you still fuck like rabbits and aren't bothered by the fact anyone within three houses of yours can hear the two of you going at it. I'm surprised your children aren't scarred for life."

"You're one to talk," Flicker muttered.

"Bats and Cowboy, stay with the women and children," Torch said.

"Aidan went with Colette," I said. "From what little I know of his past, he's never won a fight. But he can help keep everyone calm."

"Not a fighter?" Guardian asked. "He seemed a little…"

"Soft," Dagger said.

I sighed. "He's an artist. Sculptures mostly. It's why I tried to keep him separate from the club. Didn't work out so well."

Dagger and Guardian grinned at me. I had a feeling I'd get shit about the fact Aidan didn't ride a motorcycle or know how to shoot a gun. I had to wonder if the Devil's Fury had accepted Dagger's relationship with Guardian because the other man had been a Prospect. But part of what I liked about Aidan was his softer side.

"Everyone get the fuck out. Tank, gather your crew and hit the motel. Go in fast and quiet. But I don't want those men brought here. No telling if they have GPS hidden on them somewhere. No sense leading the rest of their men right to us." Torch stood. "Let's try not to lose anyone."

Tank lingered while most of the men filed out. Gears, Grimm, and Hammer remained, and so did I. It only took a moment to realize Dagger wasn't leaving either.

"I know Torch didn't assign me to this crew, but I want in," Dagger said. "My sweet Zoe suffered at the hands of men like this. No one should endure that fate."

"All right." Tank stood and cracked his back, groaning. "Getting old fucking sucks. I'm assuming everyone is armed or can be in a short amount of time?"

"I didn't exactly take a firearm to my wedding, and we didn't make it back home before we left town. Something felt off with Joe, so we hightailed it out of there. Haven't been back since," I said.

"We can loan you something," Grimm said. "Not sure what your preference is."

"Knife. Gun. Whatever." I shrugged. "Personally, I want to fuck them up with my bare hands."

"I can get you a set of throwing knives," Grimm said. "Assuming you can use them."

"I can," I said.

"And I can loan you a 9mm." Tank held my gaze. "It has an extra clip. Make sure both are loaded just in case."

"We meeting at the gate?" Hammer asked.

"Yeah. Everyone at the gate in fifteen minutes," Tank said. "We'll go in two of the trucks. The bikes would be too noticeable."

We split up and I went with Grimm. With some luck, we'd pull some information from the dickheads at the motel before we fucked them up. Either way, they were dying today.

* * *

Aidan

Everything seemed quiet up top. Then again, I wasn't sure if we'd be able to hear anything down here or not. Two of the Dixie Reapers had joined us, as well as one of their Prospects. The others were working hard to keep everyone safe. I wished I were stronger. Tougher. I should be up there fighting alongside Surge instead of hiding with the women.

"Whatever you just thought, you're wrong," Bats

said. "Your man clearly adores the two of you. Can't say I understand being attracted to another man, but as long as the three of you are happy, what other people think doesn't matter."

"I'm useless to him," I said.

"No, you aren't." Bats moved closer and leaned his elbows on his knees. His gaze held mine. "You're down here with Colette, and that's going to give him peace of mind. You'd do anything for her, right?"

"Of course. I love her."

"Right. And Surge knows that. Out of everyone at this compound, you're the one who will protect her the most, aside from him. So you being here is exactly the sort of help you can give him right now."

"He said something similar," I muttered. "I can't help feeling like I'm going to be a disappointment in the long run, or that his club won't accept me. I know Guardian and Dagger are together, but they're part of the Devil's Fury. I'm just an artist."

Bats snorted. "*Just* an artist? Dude, I'd give my left nut to be able to paint, draw, write… anything creative like that."

His words warmed my heart. No one had ever thought of my job as being something amazing. Except Surge. Typically, when I told people what I did for a living, I'd get the usual comments of, "You can make money doing that?"

I scanned the area and found Colette with a small group of women. I recognized Zoe but hadn't been introduced to the others yet. The women had boiled some water and made hot tea. Colette had wrinkled her nose at the tea bags, which I'd found cute as hell, but she was happily drinking it.

"She's going to make friends easily," Bats said. "She still has an innocence to her that will lure everyone in. Same as you."

I snorted. "I'm far from innocent."

"Since you're both married to Surge, I figured none of you were virgins." Bats grinned. "But you haven't lived a life full of blood and violence either. That's a good thing, by the way. I think the light inside the two of you is exactly what a guy like Surge needs in his life."

I opened my mouth to respond when I felt a vibration under my feet. Bats' eyes widened and he yanked his phone from his pocket. Right about the time he unlocked the screen, his phone and all the other Reapers' phones went off.

"Motherfucker," he whispered. "They breached the compound. The men at the motel were a decoy."

"What's going on?" I asked, my stomach knotting. "What the hell was that I felt?"

"They have to be tracking her a different way," Bats said. "They know where we are. There's no fucking way they found the bunker, but those fuckers set off a grenade above us. Directly on top of the bunker."

I paled and glanced at Colette. Her new friends gathered closer to her, and Zoe put an arm around her shoulders. I went to Colette and knelt beside her chair.

"Angel, the bad men are here. They duped the club. Bats thinks there's another tracker on you somewhere."

Her eyes filled with tears. "You saw Surge check me. The only place he found one was in my arm. Where else could they have put one?"

"I don't know. No way for us to check until we get out of here, but you'll need to see a doctor. Maybe they can find it."

Another vibration shook us, this one stronger.

The top of the bunker began to crack. The women bolted for the other end of the structure, their kids being tugged along with them. I stood and held Colette as I backed away from the falling pieces of concrete.

"Can they get through?" I asked Bats.

"Looks like it. Fuck. Get Colette back with the others."

"*Non.*" Colette took a deep breath and let it out. "They want me, no one else. If I hide with the others, it will put a target on them. I won't be responsible for your women and children being killed or hurt."

"Damnit, Colette. Surge is going to kill me if anything happens to you," I mumbled. My heart hammered against my ribs, and my palms were slick with sweat. I'd never been so damn scared in my life.

A hole opened in the ceiling and a rope came through. Men slid down, landing mere feet away from us. They grinned maniacally and brandished guns, pointing them at Colette. I stepped in front of her, shielding her as best I could.

"You can't have her," I said.

One of them laughed. "Who's going to stop us? You?"

"How about me?" Bats asked, shooting the man in the chest.

He fell to the ground, his mouth slack, his eyes bulging in shock.

"Boss said to prepare for anything," one of the men said. "Looks like he knew what we'd be walking into."

Another grinned. "If you wanted this place to remain a secret, you should have lined the walls better. All the gadgets in here still leave a signature."

What the fuck? These men had found the bunker because of what? The TV? The appliances? I didn't know what was going on, or how we'd make it out of this alive.

"Someone wants you real bad, little girl." The man, who seemed to be their group leader, smiled at Colette. "Too bad you spread your legs for filthy bikers. Your life won't be so pleasant now."

Motherfucker! No way I'd let these men take Colette. Surge would never forgive me, if we even survived. I saw two of the men distancing themselves from the others, their guns raised. Before I could say or do anything, all hell broke loose. I heard the kids behind us screaming, the women slamming doors as they hustled their families into the various bedrooms. I kept Colette behind me, knowing they wouldn't hesitate to kill me if it meant they'd walk out of here with her. The Reapers were shooting back, and I felt a hot pain sear my side.

I looked down and watched red blossom across my shirt. I'd been shot. I tried to calm my racing heart and tried to think of a way to get Colette out of here. We were trapped. When the Reapers built the bunker, they must not have considered someone bombing the top of it.

"Aidan, get out of here," Bats yelled.

I couldn't. My legs wouldn't move, and it felt like I'd piss myself at any moment. Surge had entrusted Colette to me, and I was failing him. More pain hit my shoulder and I saw blood again. I swayed but refused to fall. I was the only thing keeping Colette alive. Those monsters would have to go through me to reach her. And I'd die to keep her safe.

"I love you, Colette," I murmured just loud enough that she could hear me. "Remember that, okay?"

"Aidan?" I could hear the fear and worry in her

voice, but it couldn't be helped. One of the fallen men lay within two feet of us. His gun still rested in his hand. I moved as fast as I could, yanked up the weapon and pointed it at the remaining guys who'd come for Colette. I squeezed the trigger multiple times, just hoping I'd hit them.

The world turned fuzzy, and my body felt wracked with pain. I heard Colette scream as I slowly tumbled to the floor. And then everything went dark.

Chapter Eleven

Colette

"Aidan!" I fell to my knees beside him, tears streaking my cheeks. "Don't you dare die! I need you."

The deafening sound died down, leaving my ears ringing. Bats staggered over to me, blood trailing down his leg. I noticed he dragged it along and couldn't put weight on it. The one they'd called a Prospect lay on the ground staring sightlessly up at the ceiling. I sobbed, knowing I'd brought this tragedy on these people. Surge would lose Aidan because of me.

The other Dixie Reaper came over and knelt beside Aidan. *Cowboy*. I stared at him hopelessly, not knowing what to do. Was Aidan already gone? Had he died trying to protect me?

Cowboy placed his fingers against Aidan's neck. "He's alive, but his pulse feels weak. Needs a doctor."

"You hurt?" Bats asked the two of us.

"I'm okay," I whispered. "He saved me."

"Just a crease in my arm. I'll be fine," Cowboy said.

"I'm going up top to check out the damage and see if I can get some help down here. Keep the women and kids in the bedrooms. They don't need to see all this."

"How?" I asked, eying the bloody pants.

He smirked. "Up the rope. Legs help but aren't required."

My jaw dropped as I saw Bats grab the rope, and hand over fist he moved up and out of the hole at a faster pace than I would have thought possible.

"Where's Surge?" I asked. "He'll want to see Aidan."

"He went to the motel, thinking the men hiding

out there were the only ones in town. I'm sure Tank and the others have been notified. They're probably on their way back, if they aren't here already." Cowboy reached over to squeeze my shoulder. "Everything will be okay, Colette."

Tears slipped down my cheeks. "How can you say that? Aidan might die! That man over there already lost his life. How many others are gone because of me?"

"No," he said harshly. "Not because of you. Those men were monsters. All they do is take what they want, sell people like they're cattle. They rape, murder, steal. If you'd not stayed with Surge, if you'd gone to your buyer, how long do you think you'd have lived? Or would even want to? He would have broken you mentally and emotionally, before your body finally gave up. None of us are sorry for protecting you. Understand?"

I nodded. "Thank you."

I heard voices and several men came through the door, all wearing the Dixie Reapers cuts. Two started removing the dead bodies while three others headed our way. I heard my name being screamed from somewhere down the tunnels, and when Surge burst into the room, I couldn't stop sobbing and blubbering nonsense at him.

His arms closed around me, and I collapsed against his chest.

"I'm sorry. So sorry," I said, over and over.

He petted my hair, but when he whispered sweet words to me, I heard how broken he sounded. He'd seen Aidan, and my guess was that we might very well lose him. Would Surge ever look at me the same way? Could he forgive me? I already knew I'd live with regret the rest of my life.

* * *

Surge

I'd been in the middle of cutting out a tongue when the Reapers' phones went off. I only caught bits and pieces of what Tank was saying, as I focused on torturing the shit out of the man in front of me. I'd already killed the other two, their blood staining my hands.

Tank yanked me back. "We need to go. The rest are at the compound. They got into the bunker."

Everything went still and it felt like the world stopped for a moment. I sucked in a breath and ran for the trucks, not giving a shit about the bodies I'd just left behind. Let someone try to pin their murders on me. I wouldn't go to jail, not when Aidan and Colette needed me. I'd die to protect them and kill anyone who tried to keep us apart.

We raced through town, the truck fishtailing around corners. When we entered the compound, Tank put on the brakes and the truck slid to a stop. Bodies lay around the compound, and my throat tightened when I saw more than one had on a cut.

"Where?" I asked. "How do I get to them?"

"My house. I can't go with you," Tank said. "I'm needed here."

Flicker came over, looking like he'd been to hell and back. "I'll go with him."

I got on my bike and followed Flicker to Tank's house, and we entered the tunnels through what looked like a storm shelter in the backyard. When I entered the bunker, I saw Colette and Aidan. So much blood. My eyes burned as I saw the multiple wounds on my husband, and the way my wife screamed and cried over him.

I took Colette into my arms and let her sob until she had nothing left. Drained, she sagged in my arms, and I realized she'd passed out.

"How is he?" I asked Bats.

"Alive, but barely. Doc is on his way. Need to get him back to the house."

"I'll help carry him," Flicker said.

I followed the men carrying Aidan, Colette clutched in my arms. How had it all gone so wrong so fast? If we lost Aidan, I didn't think Colette would ever be the same. Hell, I wouldn't either.

"Who did your club lose?" I asked once we reached the top.

Torch heard me and gave me a sad smile. "Prospect named Spencer. He was a good kid. Had a lot of potential. Coyote and Acid are gone too. Neither had a chance to find their women or start a family. I still remember Coyote being a Prospect. Same for Acid. Sometimes seems like yesterday, and other times I feel so damn old I wonder if I have one foot in the grave."

"What were their names?" I asked.

"Pete and Diego." Torch's voice was so soft I nearly didn't hear him. I could tell losing his men hurt him deeply, and I felt like an asshole for coming here. If we'd gone somewhere else, those men would be alive.

We made it to the house we'd been assigned, and Flicker paused in the living room.

"Probably better to pull out the sofa bed. Not sure the bedroom has enough space for Doc to move around and treat him."

"Let me lay Colette in the bed and I'll get it," I said, walking past him. Her hair spread out on the pillow as I eased her onto the mattress, and I leaned down to kiss her forehead. "I love you, angel."

I went back to the living room and pulled out the sofa bed. It already had sheets on it, so Flicker and Merlin set Aidan down gently. I pulled out one of the knives Grimm had loaned me and I cut Aidan's shirt and pants off.

"Probably shouldn't move him any more than we have," Flicker said.

"I'm here," a voice said, sounding winded. I turned and saw a man in a white lab coat with a black bag in his hand.

"Thank you for coming, Dr. Franz," Merlin said.

"I was told this was the most critical patient. I'll treat the others once I have this man stabilized."

I took a step back, as did the others, and we gave Dr. Franz room to work. He examined Aidan, listened to his heart, checked his pupils, and got to work cleaning and stitching the wounds.

"He has two through and through shots," Dr. Franz said. "One in his shoulder, another in his thigh. Somehow he lucked out and nothing major was hit. The wound on his side looks worse than it is. The bullet only grazed him."

I looked at the furrow of missing skin on Aidan and wanted to ask the doctor his definition of a graze. It looked like the bullet had dug a trench through my husband's side right above his hip. Aidan was going to be in pain for a while, and I had no idea what this would mean for his business. I didn't think he'd be working anytime soon.

"I'm going to leave instructions for you," Dr. Franz said. "Before I move to the next patient, I'll run an IV and give him fluids. You'll need a way to hang the bag."

"I think there's an old-fashioned coat rack in one of the houses over here. I'll go find it," Flicker said.

"Doc, my wife is in the bedroom. It doesn't look like she's been physically hurt, but... she saw Aidan get shot. When I found her, she was inconsolable. She passed out in my arms. Is there something you can give her for when she wakes up?"

He nodded. "Yes. I'll get that for you in a moment."

He finished with Aidan, left the medication for Colette, and a list of instructions, then left to help the next person. I sank to my knees beside the sofa bed and reached for Aidan's hand, stopping partway when I saw the blood still coating me.

Everyone had left with the doctor, and I was left alone with my husband and wife. I got a change of clothes and went into the bathroom, where I scrubbed the hell out of my skin. After the water ran clear, I got out and dried off, pulling on my underwear and a pair of jeans.

My phone chirped and I checked it, not really feeling much like having a conversation with anyone. It was Tank. *Sending a clean-up crew for those bodies.*

Thank fuck! One less thing I needed to worry about. But I did need to make a call. I pulled up Fox in my contacts and pressed the button.

"Surge? Everything all right?" Fox asked when the line connected.

"No. It's not," I said, my throat feeling raw as I held back my tears. Tough men didn't cry. Or at least, not when their President was on the phone. I'd fall apart later.

I told him what happened, from me leaving to go to the motel, to Aidan being shot and Colette being so upset she passed out. When I finished, he told me what he'd been doing on his end.

"Joe has been evicted from the club and told to

leave the entire fucking state. I spoke with Torch earlier. He said you were going to call, but I guess you got caught up in the moment. I have Patch and Breaker going after the girl purchased by the Bratva. We'll see how that turns out. Now I'm wishing I'd sent more men."

"Sorry for this clusterfuck, Pres. I screwed up so damn much," I said.

"Surge, you're human. And seriously, you haven't fucked up nearly as much as some of your brothers. Just come home when Aidan is able to travel. Want me to send someone to drive him and Colette home?"

"His truck is here." Except… I stood and went to the front door, pulling it open. Yeah, his vehicle was still on the parking pad. And it was shot to hell and back. It looked like someone took an AR-15 to it. "Damnit. Aidan is going to be pissed when he wakes up. I think he was still paying it off."

"Not sure he can file an insurance claim for gunfire," Fox said. "The club will pay off the loan, scrap the truck, and get your family a new vehicle."

"Thanks, Pres."

"Take care of your family, Surge. I'll have Bear come get you in one of the trucks. Aidan and Colette can ride with him while you head back on your bike."

"It might be a while. Aidan's pretty fucked up," I said.

"No rush. You get back when it's time and not a moment sooner."

He ended the call and I set my phone aside. As much as I wanted to keep holding Aidan's hand, I knew Colette needed me too. I stood, but before I could go to the bedroom, someone knocked on the door. I opened it and saw Venom and Torch waiting for me.

"I'm sorry about the losses your club suffered," I said. "But I appreciate everything y'all did for us."

"Don't get too relaxed," Torch said. "Heard your girl has another tracker somewhere. Since Dr. Franz is busy, I called Dr. Myron. He wants you to take your woman to the hospital immediately. He said he'll meet you there, and they're going to do everything they can to find the device that's still inside her."

I put my hand over my face and wondered how much more shit life was going to pile on me today. "Aidan... I don't want to leave him."

"We'll both sit with him," Torch said. "Take care of your wife."

I nodded and went to the bedroom. I pulled on a shirt, my socks, and boots, then shrugged on my cut. Thankfully, I'd removed it before torturing those men earlier. I'd learned the hard way blood didn't come out of leather. Not completely. Lifting Colette into my arms, I carried her to the living room.

"I'll have to borrow a vehicle. Aidan's truck is totaled."

"We already anticipated that. There's an SUV out front. Keys are in the ignition," Torch said.

"Thank you." I took my woman to the car and buckled her into the front seat. Her head slumped, and I felt awful. She hadn't woken yet. Had this been too traumatic for her? What if she never fully recovered emotionally or mentally? I'd take care of her, no matter what it took.

At the hospital, I found Dr. Myron easily enough. It took about two hours to run a complete battery of tests. The device had been inside her all right. They'd implanted it in her like a Goddamn IUD. I didn't know how she hadn't felt it, since it wasn't quite as flexible, according to Dr. Myron. They managed to extract it, then destroyed the device so it couldn't be used anymore.

"It would be best for her to stay overnight for observation," Dr. Myron said.

"I can't be in two places at once, and Aidan hasn't woken yet either."

The doctor paused. "I know you don't want to hear this, but I can tell you're already at the end of your rope. You need to rest as much as they do. Stay here with Colette. I'll give you a sedative to help you sleep. If you're worried about Aidan, I can have my partner go stay with him."

"Why would you do that for us?" I asked.

"Because Torch asked for my help." He smiled. "I've seen the Dixie Reapers do some incredible things. They save people, and I'm happy to help when I can."

"All right. We'll both stay the night."

"Good. I'll get the paperwork going."

He hurried off and I wondered if I'd just made a mistake. What if Aidan woke up and I wasn't there? But if Colette stayed and I went back to the compound, she'd be terrified if she came to and found herself in a strange place.

"Fuck," I mumbled. Like it or not, we were staying the night.

Epilogue

Fox had called Church and asked me to bring Aidan and Colette with me. We were finally home and trying to figure out our new normal. Aidan still couldn't go to his studio since he needed physical therapy for his shoulder and leg. The last thing we wanted was for him to do more damage trying to work on the big sculptures he created. He walked with a limp and possibly would for the rest of his life. Turned out the bullet had done more damage than the doctor had first thought, and he'd had to go back in and remove fragments. By then, an infection had set in.

My wife had handled everything like a champ. She'd had her moments, where I caught her looking over her shoulder. All in all, she seemed to be doing all right physically and mentally. I'd known she was strong, even if she looked small enough a strong wind would knock her over.

"You look beautiful," I told Colette.

She smiled, but I noticed it didn't quite reach her eyes. She was worried. Aidan didn't look too thrilled either. I led them into Church and saw everyone else had already arrived and taken their seats.

Fox stood. "As everyone knows, Surge married Colette after saving her from being trafficked. You all know the part Joe played and that he's no longer here. We did get the information we needed before he left. And it helped us track down Jack Carson, as well as a few others. We still don't know the entire story, but we filled enough gaps it doesn't matter. Surge has requested to officially make Colette his old lady. I know we normally would vote on this, but I don't think a single man at this table would deny his request. Not after the hell those three have been through."

He lifted a box from the center of the table and took off the lid. He held up a cut that said *Property of Surge* on the back. I took it from him and helped Colette into it. She ran her hands over the leather and smiled at me. "It's like yours."

I nodded. "It means you're mine in the eyes of the club."

"Aidan, we didn't want you to feel left out, but since Surge can't make you an old lady, and you don't ride a motorcycle, we had to get a little creative." Fox picked up the smaller box. He handed it to me, and I lifted the lid smiling when I saw the contents. I took out the silver cuff with *Property of Surge* stamped into it and put it on Aidan's wrist. "Now they're both yours. They have been all along, but now everyone will know."

"Thanks, Pres. This means a lot to me. To us," I said.

"Aidan, I know you haven't been able to work, but your art is more than just a job to you. So, we're going to have a contractor come by next week to speak with you. We'd like to set up an art studio for you here at the compound. If you want a storefront in town, that's doable, or you can work from here and only take custom orders. You'd have to meet your clients outside the compound, but I would imagine you could manage that."

Aidan's jaw dropped. "Are you serious?"

Fox nodded. "Very. You're part of Surge's family, which makes you *our* family. Welcome home."

I put my arm around him and hugged Aidan tight. "Told you not to worry."

Fox cleared his throat. "Not quite done. Colette,

Surge told me how you want to help the homeless, especially here in our town. While the three of you were in Alabama, I sent a few guys down to the overpass you mentioned. They found jobs for anyone who wanted the chance to improve their lives, and the club paid for a month's rent for each of them. The old ladies managed to get clothing and essentials together for them, and I'm happy to say all but one has managed to stay off the streets."

I saw Colette swipe a tear off her cheek. I hadn't known the club was going to do all this. My heart felt like it might burst. I loved everyone in this room, and knowing my club had my back like this? There were no words to describe how it made me feel.

"Surge, I know you wanted to take care of Jack Carson yourself. I couldn't make that happen, but..." He grinned and slid some photos over. I stepped to the table and peered down. "He went to prison for his crimes. Then he had a little accident in the showers a week later. When the inmates found out he'd been the cause of children being raped and abused, they didn't take it well."

I smiled, knowing exactly how much he'd suffered. I hoped the fucker was rotting in hell.

"As for the others in the Carson organization, several clubs went after them. Most were killed or sent to prison. A few buyers are still on the loose. Not Colette's. The man who wanted her has been taught the error of his ways. Trust me when I say no one wants to see *those* photos. I may never be able to remove the images from my brain."

"So Colette is completely free from all this?" I asked.

Fox nodded. "Wire sent over the account information for Colette. He also set funds into an account for Aidan, and any others we were able to rescue off the list of women and children sold. Each one will be taken care of and helped to transition into a new life."

"*Merci*," Colette said.

"The Mafia connection is a bit more tenuous. I've been informed by Charming there may be more to it than we realized, so I'm backing off. He's going to have his Bratva connections look into it and handle it accordingly. I'm going to trust him with this since he knows more about them than we do." Fox looked around the room. "I think that about covers everything."

One by one, my brothers stood and came to hug Colette and Aidan, welcoming them to the club. Even though they'd already met everyone, this made it official. The old ladies had set up a party in the main room, and everyone migrated that direction. Music blasted from the speakers, as my club let loose. Just not in the same way they would at a club party. The old ladies and children were present, and everyone looked like they were having fun. Even Aidan and Colette, who couldn't stop smiling.

I scanned the room again, taking note of the little ones. It wasn't our turn yet. Colette had her period late both months since we'd gone down to the Dixie Reapers, and each time she'd take a test, only to be disappointed. I'd asked Dr. Myron to check her over once more, and he'd assured us everything was fine, but said the stress on her body was probably the culprit.

It would happen when it was time. Until then, I'd shower my wife and husband with affection, and create lots of memories with them. Nearly losing Aidan had scared the fuck out of me, and I no longer took any day for granted.

When I'd found Colette and Jacques at the clubhouse, I'd only thought I'd have some fun. Instead, I'd gotten the sweetest angel as my wife, made Aidan my husband, and for the first time I could remember, I looked forward to what tomorrow would bring.

Harley Wylde

Harley Wylde is the International Bestselling Author of the Dixie Reapers MC, Devil's Boneyard MC, and Hades Abyss MC series. When Harley's writing, her motto is the hotter the better -- off-the-charts sex, commanding men, and the women who can't deny them. If you want men who talk dirty, are sexy as hell, and take what they want, then you've come to the right place. She doesn't shy away from the dangers and nastiness in the world, bringing those realities to the pages of her books, but always gives her characters a happily-ever-after and makes sure the bad guys get what they deserve.

The times Harley isn't writing, she's thinking up naughty things to do to her husband, drinking copious amounts of Starbucks, and reading. She loves to read and devours a book a day, sometimes more. She's also fond of TV shows and movies from the 1980s, as well as paranormal shows from the 1990s to today, even though she'd much rather be reading or writing. You can find out more about Harley or enter her monthly giveaway on her website. Be sure to join her newsletter while you're there to learn more about discounts, signing events, and other goodies!

Harley at Changeling: changelingpress.com/harley-wylde-a-196

Changeling Press E-Books

More Sci-Fi, Fantasy, Paranormal, and BDSM adventures available in e-book format for immediate download at ChangelingPress.com -- Werewolves, Vampires, Dragons, Shapeshifters and more -- Erotic Tales from the edge of your imagination.

What are E-Books?

E-books, or electronic books, are books designed to be read in digital format -- on your desktop or laptop computer, notebook, tablet, Smart Phone, or any electronic e-book reader.

Where can I get Changeling Press E-Books?

Changeling Press e-books are available at ChangelingPress.com, Amazon, Apple Books, Barnes & Noble, and Kobo/Walmart.

Changeling Press, LLC

ChangelingPress.com

Printed in Great Britain
by Amazon